TO CATCH A THIEF

MOLLY KERR

Copyright © 2026 by Molly Kerr. All rights reserved. Printed in the United States of America. No part of this book may be used or reproduced in any manner whatsoever without written permission except in the case of brief quotations embodied in critical articles or reviews.

This book is a work of fiction. Names, characters, businesses, organizations, places, events and incidents described herein are the product of the author's imagination or are used fictitiously. Any resemblance to actual persons, living or dead, events, or locales is entirely coincidental.

For information contact:
http://www.mollykerrauthor.com

Cover design by Aisling, Pretty Indie Book Cover Design

ISBN: 979-8-9903402-1-3

First Edition: January 2026

"Light is to darkness what love is to fear;
In the presence of one the other disappears."
— Marianne Williamson

For all of those who have navigated the darkness,
and found light on the other side.

This novel contains elements of trauma and mental health stemming from past domestic abuse. Please read at your own discretion.

Prologue

It wouldn't stop...
A buzzing drowned out her footsteps as she approached yet another identical, featureless door. Her fingers reflexively wrapped around the tarnished knob and turned, easing the door open a crack to reveal a glimpse of a dimly lit space, and refused to go further.

She lowered her shoulder to the cracked paint and pushed, or tried to. A snarl ripped free when her feet skidded in the dirt and debris littering the floor, but inch by inch, the door retreated into the room, and then, without warning, flung wide open.

She stumbled, nearly sprawling into dust coating the wide plank floor in a layer thick enough to be snow. The buzzing was magnified in the small space, so much that when the door hit the wall, the impact vibrated through her bones but didn't quite reach her ears.

Before she could react, the door swung back the other

way. It collided with her shoulder, shoving her a step further in before closing her inside. Pain shot down her arm, but she forced it away as she scrambled for the knob, but no amount of twisting or pulling would make it open. She pivoted and pressed her back against the door with a whimper, clutching her shoulder.

Across the room, the buzzing concentrated in the deep shadows a spear of light from the lone uncovered window couldn't quite reach. She blinked hard, forcing her eyes to adjust to the gloom, a stark contrast to the brightly lit hallway, and took a hesitant step, and then another into the room.

Small specks drifted through the light like dust motes, becoming more and more agitated the closer she got, the buzzing increasing in volume with each step. She froze, her hammering heart making it difficult to get a deep breath. The specks swarmed together, twisting and turning in a cloud that circled the perimeter of the light, gaining in speed and volume until, as one, the specks all turned and flew straight at her.

She staggered back from the swarm, clapping her hands to her ears as the buzzing rose to a crescendo. Small bodies bounced off her arms and tangled in her hair. She swatted them away as she retreated until her back collided with the door, turning then to scrabble once again for the handle, twisting and pulling as more little bodies landed on her.

With one last desperate yank, the door gave way. A cry of relief rose up her throat as she dashed for the hallway and pulled the door shut behind her, trapping most of what she now recognized as bees inside while trying to keep a single, angry one from alighting on her nose.

Dull thuds sounded as little bodies collided with the door

like bullets from an automatic weapon. The buzzing continued to grow louder though only a fraction of the bees had escaped. She beat frantically as they swarmed around her, landing in her hair, on her bare shoulders with a stinging force like standing outside in a hailstorm. They crept along her skin, their tiny legs leaving a trail of ice in their wake that sank in deep as they moved to encircle her neck forming a macabre necklace. Her breaths came in gasping sobs as their combined weight pressed in like a hand squeezing around her throat.

As one, the bees sank their stingers into her flesh and with her last remaining breath, she screamed.

ONE

Her eyes flew open, and she gasped for air, gulping it down like she'd never get enough. A pale, early morning light filtered in through threadbare curtains, bright enough to spark prisms off the glass cat on the dresser across the room.

She put a hand to her throat and found only smooth, warm skin. There was no pain, none of the cold that chilled her bones in her dream. She closed her eyes again only to crack one open again, her head cocked to one side.

She pushed against the weight of the blankets piled on the bed and levered into a sitting position, blinking hard to dispel the last of the nightmare. She shook her head to try to clear the noise, but it continued. With a growl, she threw back the covers and shivered as she stuffed her feet into a pair of slippers and shuffled to the door, digging a sweater out of the basket of clean clothes beside it.

The buzzing continued, an off-key mechanical sound that wobbled and spluttered as if it too had been awakened from a deep sleep and hadn't quite figured out how to work yet. It seemed to be coming from the far side of the living room, from the door. She narrowed her eyes and wrapped the sweater around her as she scuffed her feet across the concrete floor.

Since when has this place had a doorbell? She glanced at the clock in the kitchen and whimpered. *It's only 7:30?*

"I'm coming..." she grumbled as she swept a curtain of disheveled black curls out of her face and peered through the foggy scope in the door.

Who could have the gall to ring the doorbell at 7:30 in the morning? No one knew where she lived, and she'd bet that even her neighbors would have trouble picking her out of a crowd. Just how she liked it.

A man stood in the hallway, his face stretched and distorted as if it was a carnival mirror. The hallway wasn't as bright as the room behind her, but she could make out that his hair, which was just long enough to tuck behind his ears, was a medium shade of brown, and his eyes were dark. They were also trained on the scope as if he knew she was watching him.

For a moment, she just looked back. There was something familiar about him that tugged at the fringes of a memory that was still foggy with sleep. Though she was awake enough to appreciate that he had a face that made getting out of bed worthwhile.

Then she remembered that he had been ringing her doorbell for at least the last five minutes, and still had his finger pressed firmly to the cracked plastic.

"Hello?" she called through the door while still pressing one eye to the scope.

The buzzing cut off abruptly, though it continued to echo

in her ears for a few more moments. "Jal?" he asked, his voice, though muffled, was smooth as silk. "Jal Morrow?"

"How do you know that name?" she demanded. Of the few people who knew her face, even fewer knew her name.

He dug in his pocket and held something up. For a moment, panic gripped her that it would be a badge, but there was no metal shield attached to the leather wallet he held up, just a New York State driver's license— with her picture on it?

Her eyes flew to the cloth satchel on the kitchen counter a heartbeat before she dove for it and dumped it out, swallowing hard when only an empty water bottle, lip gloss, and a handful of receipts tumbled to the counter. Nope, no wallet. Shit.

She threw the bag back onto the counter. The empty bottle clattered to the floor, but she ignored it as she dashed back to the door and furiously flipped the locks. She yanked the door open a foot, the cracked paint digging into her palm as she studied his face.

Without the foggy lens of the peephole, his hair was like a rich milk chocolate, and his eyes, which had seemed almost black in the hallway, were much lighter, reminding her of a glass of whisky held up to the light.

Those eyes...

Her own narrowed as recognition finally hit her. She pulled the door open a little further and braced her arms out wide between door and frame. "You!" she exclaimed. "You picked my pocket!"

One corner of his mouth turned up. "You picked mine first." He reached down and pulled a pocket of his dress pants inside out in illustration.

Jal held out her hand. "Give it back."

The other side of his mouth lifted and stretched into a grin, showing lots of straight, white teeth. "Only if you return the favor."

She was too annoyed to try to identify the strange cadence of his voice. She lunged for the wallet he tapped idly against his leg, but he dodged her hand and held it up by two fingers overhead and made a tsking sound with his tongue.

He easily had six inches of height on her, so it didn't take much to put it out of reach, even if she were inclined to make an undignified jump for it. Which she wasn't. Instead, she blew her hair out of her eyes with an irritated puff of air and quelled the impulse to kick him where it mattered and take it while his balls were still in his throat.

Is it really worth it? She wondered for a heartbeat. The cards were fake anyway, just to make it seem like she had more assets than she really did. The driver's license was real but easily replaced. Probably should anyway, since she'd obviously been out of her mind giving the DMV her real address in the first place.

He braced a forearm on the door frame, bringing those whisky eyes closer. Their gazes locked, and her breath hitched. He just stared right back, and for a moment, the amusement went out of his eyes, but it quickly returned. He raised an expectant eyebrow.

"You know what? It's just a wallet," she told him, with a casual tone to her voice that belied how much she wanted to grind her teeth. "I don't need it back."

She took a quick step back and pushed the door closed, but he stuck his foot in at the last second and used one hand to push it open, brushing past her easily, despite using all her strength to close it on him. He stopped a few feet inside and looked around.

"What the hell do you think you're doing?" she demanded. Her nerves crackled with energy, but she locked it down. Like hell was she going to let him see how much her hands wanted to shake. Instead, she clenched her fists tight enough for her nails to bite into her palms, and used the pain to clear her head, though her traitorous heart still raced.

When he'd been in the hallway, there had been the door between them, but now that he was inside? Their difference in size was stark, and terrifying. He could easily overpower her, rape her, and dump her body. And there wasn't anything that she could do about it.

A scream started to crawl up her throat, but it froze in place when he turned those whisky eyes on her and winked. Actually, *winked* at her. She watched wide-eyed as he pulled a kitchen drawer open, and then another.

Finding nothing but utensils and aluminum foil, he scanned the room and drifted toward the dining table, its worn surface the dumping ground for anything and everything that hadn't been put in its proper place. His eyes sparkled as he crossed the room, but instead of sifting through the clutter, he set her wallet down on the top of the pile and bent his knees.

Jal watched in horror as the stranger wrapped his hand around the top of one leg, his fingers finding and pressing the hidden catch as if he knew exactly where to look. A ten-inch-wide section of the table skirt popped free, and he drew open the hidden drawer.

"For such a talented thief, I expected you'd have a better

hiding place." He mused in that hypnotizingly melodious voice of his as he sifted idly through the pile of coins and jewelry in front.

"You have no right!"

He chuckled. "This from a thief?" he tsked at her and pulled the drawer out a little further. Sorting through with one finger, he grunted in satisfaction as he plucked his wallet from underneath a few others at the back. "You really need a better hiding spot."

She bristled. "I thought it was pretty good," she snapped. "The fireplace and the freezer were too obvious. I'd never expect someone to check the table." She snapped her mouth closed, and narrowed her eyes again. "Wait, what am I saying?"

She blamed the lock of hair that had fallen in his eyes when he bent over the drawer, and the smooth velvet of his voice. Was he Scottish? Irish? She shook her head, trying to break free from his charm, and demanded again that he return her property.

He slid the drawer in with deliberate slowness until it closed with a quiet click that practically echoed in the silent space, perched a hip on the edge of the table and generally made himself at home. He plucked her wallet from the table and made a show of rifling through it, lifting each card up and examining both sides before moving to the next.

Just as she took a step forward to take the wallet back, he snapped it shut and tossed it at her. His eyes danced with amusement as she leafed through it herself.

"Wait, there was a hundred bucks in here!"

"Call it a finder's fee, lass."

Jal growled low in her throat and got a little satisfaction when the twitch of his mouth was more unnerved than amused.

He regained his feet and flipped his own wallet open, barking a laugh when he pulled apart the sides of the main pocket to find it empty. "I'm the one who should be complaining," he told her. "There was four times as much in here."

"Five hundred bucks is better than four," she pointed out, glad that she had stowed the cash elsewhere in the apartment. It was becoming clear that this guy was no idiotic tourist.

"Fair enough," he said ruefully and tucked the wallet into the pocket of his black felted jacket. But he made no move to leave.

Jal clutched the neck of her sweater closed and fought the urge to shift nervously on her feet. "You have your damned wallet back now, so get out!"

He glanced around the apartment one more time with interest, taking in the cracked drywall, the worn carpets, the kitchen appliances that had been around far longer than she'd been alive. "Aye, I'll go," he said, eyes sparkling. "But I'll be seeing you around."

"Oh, I don't think so."

He winked again and strolled unhurriedly to the door, stopping at the threshold.

She grabbed the door in one hand and started pushing it closed, but he held the door open easily. "We'll see each other again quite soon, I think."

"Well, whoever you are — "

"It's Ciaran," he told her. "Ciaran Gray."

"Well, Ciaran Gray, now that we've met, I wouldn't object

to never seeing you again." She replied and added a second hand to the effort.

He craned his neck around the door and locked eyes with her and a dimple flashed as his mouth turned up again in a knowing smirk. "About that fireplace..."

Her hands dropped away, her face blank with shock. The smirk became a grin as he took hold of the doorknob and closed the door behind him.

Jal leaned against the door until his footsteps reached the stairs. The elevator was broken again, had been broken more often than it was functional lately. It was a pity, though, as the mental image of the door opening with no car and the smug Ciaran Gray stepping in and plunging five floors to his death was all too appealing.

Then his parting words sunk in and she ran to the fireplace along the back wall. Behind the loose brick two rows below the mantel was a lot of nothing. In place of the cash and jewelry was a scrap of paper. Jal pulled it out with trembling fingers and unfolded it. In a slanted but clear hand was an invitation to dinner the next night at a trendy, and expensive restaurant in Midtown.

Dress elegantly, he'd written below.

Jal struggled to put the brick back with shaking hands and crushed the note in a fist. Her brain felt like it was going to explode. The only way he could know where to look was if he had been here before. Her empty stomach twisted on itself at the thought. And showing up a second time under the guise of exchanging the wallets back? Just a means to taunt her.

She rushed around the apartment, checking the rest of her stashes, becoming more and more frantic, her vision more red as she found hiding place after hiding place stripped bare, the same mocking invitation to dinner placed on top of the few token pieces, if any, that he had deigned to leave behind.

As she jumped down from the counter after replacing the cover over a vent over the kitchen cabinets, she growled again and damned him to hell.

She was going to have to see him again after all.

Two

The hangers screeched against the bare metal rod that served as a closet as Jal searched for something, anything, that would be considered elegant. Jal dismissed hanger after hanger of cozy sweaters, brightly colored long skirts, and cotton sundresses, occasionally tossing a possibility behind her onto the bed.

At the end of the rack, she sighed and did a quick check back the other way before turning to her bed and the small, brightly colored pile on top of the cream comforter.

As she bent to smooth out a black knee-length dress, her phone began to ring from somewhere in the pile. Jal tossed dresses and blankets aside until she unearthed it, answering just in time. "Hey, girl."

Elena returned the greeting with a smile that creased the corners of her dark eyes. Despite the early-evening hour and the fact that Elena had been running around a hot kitchen all afternoon, her makeup was perfect, her eyes expertly lined and with immaculate mascara. A thick brown braid draped over one shoulder of her gray hoodie and white wireless headphones partially obscured the gold hoops hanging from her ears.

After the morning's stressful start, Elena's call couldn't have been better timed. She was Jal's oldest friend in the city, and when she wasn't making her money using a five-finger discount, Jal sometimes worked in the little restaurant in Hell's Kitchen that Elena's father owned.

Elena had practically lived in that kitchen from the time she was a teenager, though her desire to pursue a career in a certain performing art her father hadn't agreed with caused a rift that had only recently started to mend.

Tall buildings and streetlights bounced in the background as Elena expertly navigated a busy sidewalk while holding her cell phone at arms-length as only a native could. "I was just heading to grab a drink at Darcy's, if you want to join me."

"Don't I wish." Jal replied as she propped up the phone on the table beside her bed and returned to laying the dresses out. "I'd much rather hit the pub than this dinner I have to go to."

"Dinner?"

"Long story..." Jal said dismissively. "Short version is that some random guy took something of mine and I have to meet him for dinner to get it back."

Elena snorted. "*Ay, Dios,* he doesn't know who he's messing with, does he?"

Jal grinned and winked at her friend. "Dinner's in an hour," she said, picking up a green dress and laying it down flat on the bed. "Help me pick something out."

From the phone came a sudden stream of grunts and

muffled cursing. On the screen, Elena elbowed a well-dressed businessman out of the way so she could settle into a bench with a contented sigh. She shrugged her shoulders as if making herself comfortable and then nodded her head. "What've we got for choices?"

Jal rolled her eyes but couldn't hold in her smile as she held the black dress up in front of her where Elena could see. "We're going to Amicetto."

Elena scrunched her nose. "That dress screams garden tea party at best." she said and flicked her hand dismissively at the camera. "You want sultry minx."

She swapped the black dress for a green wrap that tied at one hip. It formed a deep vee between her breasts and parted at one leg when she walked. "How about this?"

Elena considered for a moment as Jal held the hanger under her chin and fanned out the long skirt, swaying to show how the buttery-soft yet heavy fabric moved.

"Better," she replied. "We've gone from tea party to wedding reception. What else do you have?"

Jal turned back to the bed and retrieved the final possibility. "Just this one," she replied. "I got it at that place in the Garment District after a particularly good day. People should really pay closer attention to their wallets, especially ones with several grand in cash in them."

Elena snorted and gave Jal a closer look at her expert hand with the eyeliner as she leaned in to study the ice blue dress Jal now held. It was silk, with a layer of beaded embroidery that started at one shoulder and cascaded down the length of the dress catching the light like the sun on a rippling stream. The asymmetrical hem started just above the knee on one side and reached nearly to the floor on the other.

"Forget 'just,'" she purred. "Style those curls over one shoulder, add your strappy black stilettos, and that thieving asshole won't know what hit him."

Jal looked down at the dress and smoothed it over one hip. "Yeah, I think so too."

"So, who is this guy?" Elena asked. She pushed up off the bench and resumed her walk. Jal turned away when the movement made her stomach turn. Or maybe it was the thought of dressing up for a guy she didn't even know. One who had stolen from her.

"I'll tell you tomorrow."

"Come on, *nena*," she whined. "You gotta give me something."

"Bye Elena." Jal sang cheerfully and hung up. She tossed the phone on the bed and turned to the full-length mirror propped in the corner.

She studied her reflection and almost laughed at the stark contrast between the dress and her hair, which was half-falling out of a messy bun on the top of her head, and the rainbow felt slippers on her feet. After a moment, she tossed the dress down on the bed and headed for the shower.

Ciaran checked his watch for the fifth time in as many minutes and took a sip of his drink. He propped his elbow on the table and tipped his head to study the way the light bounced around the crystal glass when he swirled the deep amber liquid.

She was twenty minutes late and he was already on his

second scotch.

The tables around him were full of the usual suspects for a high-end restaurant in Midtown. It was just far enough from the theater district that the well-heeled locals outnumbered the tourists playing dress up for dinner after their once-every-few-years stroll down Broadway.

Here the light glittered off diamonds bought from Harry Winston, not any store with a jingle. The men wore cufflinks and tailored suits, and the air was redolent with a pleasant blend of Italian spices and expensive French perfume.

Just as he was starting to debate between leaving and ordering a third scotch, the maître d' appeared from the front of the restaurant. A sparkling vision in pale blue followed on his heels, close enough that it wasn't until he rose to his feet and the maître d' bent to pull out the chair across from him that he was able to really take her all in.

The dress fit her like a glove, the sheath beneath the beading and embroidery clinging to her curves in all the right places. Her thick mane of black hair was draped over one shoulder in a cascade of curls, and at her ears glittered a pair of earrings made from a blend of diamonds and a bright teal stone he couldn't put a name to.

Ciaran forced himself to look her in the eye as she slowly sank into her chair while the maître d' slid it in for her. Once she was settled, he sat back down himself with much less grace and picked up his glass. The waiter came over and he ordered another drink then raised an eyebrow at her.

Jal picked up the drinks menu and her eyes went at once to the bottom of the list and ordered the most expensive red wine sold by the glass.

Inwardly, he winced. He could get two full bottles at the local store for what that one glass cost, but then he wouldn't have gotten to see her in this dress. Worth it, he decided.

Jal set the menu off to the side and shifted in her seat as if crossing her legs under the table.

He knew he was staring, but his jaw didn't seem to want to do anything other than hang slightly open. The waiter's return snapped him out of it and he was able to move again, at least to gulp down the remaining whisky in his glass and hand it over. It burned down his throat and stoked the heat already burning in his belly.

"What are you trying to do to me, lass?"

She wrapped those delicate pick-pocket fingers one by one around the stem of her wine glass and lifted it to the light to give it a swirl, just as he had done with the whisky. Satisfied, she took a demure sip before regarding him over the rim of the glass, her dark emerald eyes flickered with heat. What kind, he wasn't quite sure.

He swallowed hard as that look punched him straight in the gut, leaving him even more confused. He should be feeling at least a little satisfaction that his plan had worked. That she was here meant she had found most of her stash gone and the dinner invitation left in its place. But even before he'd left, she seemed more to be contemplating how many ways she could hide his body just for stealing her wallet.

Pot, meet kettle on that one.

The corners of her lips curled up just a little. "Kick your ass."

Her voice curled around him like smoke and he swallowed again. "Mission accomplished then, lass."

Jal chuckled and took pity on him by scooping up her menu, the large white card obscuring most of her face as she examined the options.

Ciaran did the same, and his eyes went again to a pasta dish with langoustine. He had the thing half-memorized, having read over it so many times while waiting for her.

"So, tell me," she said casually, eyes still on the menu, "how did you get into my apartment?"

Ciaran leaned back in his chair and decided there was no use lying. "It was a simple matter, really," he replied. "Your building is old. I climbed up the fire escape and jimmied open one of your bedroom windows."

Jal pursed her lips, though she gave an appreciative nod as she set the menu aside. "I guess the important question then is why?"

"Why?"

Only one corner of her mouth lifted this time and there was the barest flicker of something dark in her eyes. "Yes, why?"

"Well, now, a thief never reveals his motives." He admonished her with the same taunting tone he had used before. And if he wasn't mistaken, she was yet again struggling against the urge to grind her teeth.

"I see," she replied and shifted again in her seat. Her movements were smooth, a gentle sway of her shoulders as she adjusted the position of her legs under the table.

The brush of her foot against his ankle sent a shock of electricity up his leg.

Ciaran's knee hit the underside of the table, rattling the silverware. He glanced around the surrounding tables, but no one even glanced their way. He leaned back in his chair as, slowly, the arch of her foot slid up the inside of his leg to his knee, back down, then up again.

All the while, she continued to casually sip her wine and study his reaction. Whatever she saw in his face, or in his eyes, brought a sparkle to hers.

His trousers were suddenly a little too tight and there was a prickle of sweat at one temple. *What game is she playing?*

She set her glass aside and put her elbow on the table and a finger to her chin. "Then I have another question..." Her voice was a sultry purr.

He couldn't help himself from leaning forward. "And what would that be?"

Quick as lightning, her foot left his calf to spear between his legs and give him a firm tap where it counted.

The pleasant haze of good whisky and attractive company immediately vanished. He jumped and pressed back as far as he could in his seat, but the vixen didn't give him any space.

"When am I going to get my money back so I can get the hell out of here?" she asked him, the smoke in her voice, and her eyes, replaced with ice.

"Seeing the position you have me in," he replied, "I doubt I have much of a choice in the matter, do I?"

Jal shook her head and pressed harder nearly crushing his balls into the chair. "Christ, woman!" he exclaimed. "I have your money. Can you please give my bollocks a wee breather?"

There was a breath of laughter from the table next to theirs and Ciaran glanced over as he reached into his jacket. The couple next to them was trying to act like they weren't paying any attention, but not at all succeeding. Before he looked away, the man glanced up and gave him a look that said, "better you than me, mate."

Ciaran set a white envelope on the table and slid it in her direction as best he could without leaning into the pressure that threatened to emasculate him.

Jal lifted the flap with a fingernail and studied the pile of bills inside, then cocked an eyebrow at him. "And the jewelry?"

Ciaran started to reach a hand under the table to push her away but she tapped him again. Stifling a groan, he replaced his hand beside the bread plate, his back rigid against the high back of the chair.

"Fenced it," he replied, voice tight, and tried not to squirm like a worm on a hook.

Ridding himself of the better part of a dozen pieces of fine jewelry at a fair price hadn't been easy by any means. He didn't nearly have the network in the States that he had back in Scotland, but he'd had a favor or two owed to old associates who thankfully had connections on this side of the pond that could be trusted not to rip him off or turn him in to the police.

"It's a shame you got rid of that sapphire ring," she mused, running a thumb along the stack of bills as if counting them. After a moment, she slid the envelope off the table and into her purse. "But this will do nicely."

When she took another sip of her wine and made no move to release him, Ciaran cleared his throat gently and jerked his head down to the goings-on under the table.

She gave him another one of her half-smiles and slowly slid her foot away.

All of the tension in his body fell away with it, and if

they hadn't been in the middle of a busy restaurant, he would have put his head down on the table and eased his wounded... dignity.

"I'm much obliged to you, lass."

Jal took her last sip and slid the chair back to secure the strap of her shoe. "Thank you for the wine, and for," she made an illustrative noise and raised her clutch, "and if you don't mind, I'll be going now." She rose to her feet but didn't make it more than a step before Ciaran wrapped his hand around her wrist and pulled her to a stop.

"Please Jal," he said, all too aware of the crowded restaurant, and especially the couple next to them who had given up on trying to be discrete.

Dinner and a show, fabulous.

"I can't believe that you got all fancied up for ten minutes. Come, have dinner with me."

Jal looked down at his hand and though his grip was gentle, her pulse skittered under his fingertips. It would have taken very little for her to pull free, but instead she stood rigid, her chest rising and falling nearly as rapidly as her heartbeat.

He let his hand slide away, and they stood for a moment before he took hold of the back of her chair and gestured to the empty seat.

She took a deep, steadying breath, briefly met his gaze, and walked away.

Jal pushed open the door to the ladies' room and headed for the sink. She braced her hands on the black marble counter and studied herself in the mirror. Her cheeks were flushed, her pupils wide enough that she was nearly blinded by the light fixture above the mirrors. She grabbed for a hand towel from the neat pile at the edge of the sink and knocked most of them to the floor.

With a whimper, she bent and gathered them up and tried to rearrange them, but her hands were trembling, and the pile came out rumpled and crooked.

Get a freaking grip, Jal...

He'd barely touched her, but even that slight pressure of his fingers wrapped around her wrist had sent her heartrate skyrocketing and not in a good way.

She flicked on the tap to wet one of the hand towels and pressed it to her neck, her temples, her cheeks, until she felt less like she was going to vomit, or pass out, or both. Yet even then, her body still vibrated with adrenaline, her neck merely a string holding her head to her shoulders to keep it from floating away.

She opened her clutch and dug a small, light orange pill from inside the lining pocket and swallowed it with a handful of water from the tap. She chased it with another handful of water and drew in a shaky breath.

It would take a few minutes for the medicine to kick in, so she picked a swirl on the textured wall to stare at and concentrated on her breathing. In and out. Again. And another.

The door opened and a woman in a black dress hesitated a step inside. She was probably in her fifties, with wine red hair twisted tightly up. Jal sighed in relief as the tingling faded from her fingers. Talk about fast acting.

"Are you all right, dear?"

Jal smoothed her hair back over one shoulder and nodded at her reflection, managing a weak smile.

The woman nodded back and continued into a stall.

After one more peek in the mirror, Jal tucked her purse back under her arm. The envelope crackled inside. The transaction was complete, there was no reason to even think about Ciaran Gray again. The thought repeated over and over in her head as she reached for the door handle.

The cacophony of instrumental music, clinking silverware, and overlapping conversations hit her like a wave as she emerged back into the restaurant. She hesitated in the short breezeway, eyes fixed on the front door to the restaurant directly ahead on the other side of the bar, no more than twenty feet away. *It might as well be a mile.*

The woman in the black dress emerged from the bathroom and collided with her back.

Jal stumbled forward out of the breezeway and the woman skirted around her with a glance over her shoulder that was equal parts confusion, annoyance, and oddly enough, sympathy.

Her mouth twitched in what was meant to be a smile and the woman continued on her way. Jal's eyes followed her across the room and widened as she passed their table. Ciaran sat frozen, his glass of amber whisky half-way to his mouth, his lips slightly parted.

His eyes, which were almost the same color in the flickering candlelight, were curious. He had rolled up his sleeves while she'd been away, and even from across the room, the grooves of muscle in his arms were clear.

She took a step towards the table and paused again.

Ciaran slowly set the glass down on the table, but didn't otherwise move for a long moment. When he finally did, it was only to make a subtle sweep of his hand in the direction of her empty chair in invitation.

Jal swallowed, then squared her shoulders and fled out the front door.

Three

"Hey Scotty!"

Ciaran shook his head ruefully and turned to watch his friend Cliff use his not inconsiderable bulk to push his way through the crowd to the bar where Ciaran perched on a stool in front of one of the TVs dotting the wall.

Cliff put the Jamison in Dougherty, Jamison & Russo Architects and was for all intents and purposes, Ciaran's boss. But he was also one of his closest friends. Although he was in his early forties with a wife and young son, Cliff still kept his brown hair high and tight out of habit though gray was starting to appear at his temples. He was built like a linebacker and smoked like a freight train.

"Hey, Cliff, you alright?"

His friend smiled at that, then scrunched up his face and spoke carefully. "I'm fine, you?"

Ciaran chuckled as he removed his jacket from the stool and hung it on a hook under the bar. He appreciated Cliff's effort. For most Americans, the first response to that particularly Scottish way to say, "how are you?" was simply, "yes."

Cliff settled into the saved seat, then pulled a pack of Marlboros out of his pocket, turning the open end Ciaran's way. It was a token gesture, since Ciaran always refused. Besides, Cliff knew full well that he couldn't light it indoors anyway, but the man couldn't go more than an hour without one in his hand, lit or not, and probably thought he could get some kind of a contact hit just by holding it.

"The usual?"

At Cliff's nod, Ciaran ordered another round of Scotches, his neat and Cliff's on the rocks. They sipped in silence and watched the ice hockey game on the TV. The team in blue and gold had just scored on the team wearing orange and white, but Ciaran had no idea which team was which.

Half a period went by with each team scoring a goal with only token celebrations from the patrons in the bar. *Guess neither one is the home team.*

Cliff said something to him, but his words didn't register.

Ciaran looked up from the drink cradled in his hands. "Hmm?" he asked and looked over at Cliff. "What were you saying?"

His friend's fidgeting with the cigarette had moved on to tapping the filter end on the bar. Give it a few minutes, and he'd either be spinning it around his fingers or elbowing his way back outside. Ciaran's money was on the latter.

"I said you're being quiet," he repeated. "And it's not just tonight either. The past few days you've huddled over the Johnson project without saying a word. What gives?"

"It's nothin'," Ciaran said and took a sip of his Scotch. It slid down his throat in a most pleasing way and kindled a fire in his stomach.

"It's not nothin'." Cliff said, in a horrific attempt at his accent. The man would forever be a New Yorker, linguistically speaking. He studied Ciaran for another few moments, then snapped his fingers and pointed a finger in Ciaran's face. "It's a woman, isn't it?"

He batted Cliff's hand away and tossed back his drink, suppressing a cough as it burned the whole way down. "Of course not." It was always a woman with Cliff.

"Bullshit, Scotty." Cliff said, calling his bluff. "Who is she? A stunning blond? A spunky brunette?"

"She's not any of those." he snapped, then lifted his glass to hide his wince, only to find it empty. He set it back on the bar with a thump.

"So, it *is* a girl!" Cliff crowed, elbowing Ciaran in the ribs. "Come on Scotty, fess up."

Ciaran pushed him away, an act that only seemed to amuse Cliff more. "Shut it, Cliff."

"Just one hint."

"Give it a rest, Cliff." Each word was punched through clenched teeth.

His friend continued to badger him, and Ciaran ignored it for as long as he could. Before he gave into the urge to wrap his hands around Cliff's thick throat, as if it would really have any effect, Ciaran planted his hands on the bar and pivoted to face his friend. "Look, if I tell you that her hair is dark like ebony will you shut the hell up already?"

Cliff let out a hearty laugh and smacked his hand on the bar. "I knew it!" he cried. "She really got into your shorts to have you so worked up." When Ciaran remained silent, he hit the bar again. "Or maybe it's that she hasn't yet?"

"I shouldn't have said anything."

Cliff's eyes sparkled with amusement. "You need to find yourself a girl, man." He took a sip of his whisky and bit down hard on a piece of ice he'd slurped in with it, chewing contentedly for a moment. "You've been here what, six years? I bet you can count the number of dates you've had in that time on one hand."

Ciaran smiled tightly. "It would take both hands, fuck you very much." he replied and turned to the screen when a few cheers went up from behind him.

Cliff guffawed and clapped him on the back. "You should give it another go, as you Scots would say." He reached in his pocket and pulled out a pair of tickets. "Look, I've got the company seats to the game tomorrow night. It'll take your mind off this goddess with the ebony hair that shot you down."

"She didn't—" Ciaran started, then clenched his teeth together hard enough to make his molars groan. What else was there to call what she had done?

"Sure, fine, whatever," he said finally. "You can explain the game to me."

Cliff's jaw dropped. "Are you serious? You've never been to a hockey game?"

"Most hockey in Scotland is played on a field with a much shorter stick." he answered with a shrug. "I'm more of a rugby or football man."

Cliff laughed. "Then you should have no problem. Hockey is rugby on ice. All the hitting, checking, fighting... you'll love it."

Ciaran sighed and tossed back the last of his whisky. "Sure, fine," he replied as he stood and retrieve his jacket. "It's late, Cliff, and I'm off to my bed."

It was only nine o'clock, but his friend didn't argue as Ciaran patted his shoulder and started weaving through the crowd.

Instead of going directly home, Ciaran drove by Jal's apartment, noting as he pulled into an empty spot across the street that many of the windows were lit, but not hers. He considered waiting until she got home, but then she'd probably think he was stalking her or something.

He still had so many questions after their encounter at the restaurant, not least of all what had driven her from the table. Questions he hadn't been able to ask that night since she'd emerged from the bathroom, took one step in his direction, her eyes only slightly less alarmed, and without warning, bolted for the exit. It was that expression that had pinned him to his seat at the table, rather than run after her.

Hell, it still did.

Regardless, she didn't owe him any kind of explanation. She had her money back and the transaction was complete. What more did he want from her?

What more, indeed?

Ciaran gripped the steering wheel until the leather groaned under his fingers.

She intrigued him. There, he admitted it. More than any woman had since coming to America, since Annie had left him for a Cambridge man with a Bentley. Sure, he'd dated, but hadn't met anyone that he'd consider more than a few dates with, only a couple stretching out a month or two of casual dating.

Even in the few encounters they had, he knew she was different. Jal didn't fawn over his accent, or that he stayed fit enough to run right out onto the pitch if his hometown team ever came calling.

She had a fire in her that drew him as if he were a moth. At least when she was in control, anyway. The speed with which that fire had fizzled out still gave him whiplash. And it had only taken the slightest pressure on her wrist.

He shoved both hands through his hair and glanced once more at the string of darkened windows. He yawned wide enough that his jaw cracked. The honest truth was, even if she was home and deigned to let him inside, the only thing that he would probably do was fall asleep on the couch. Too many late nights this week working on that godforsaken design proposal. So, Ciaran drove home.

He made himself a cup of tea and grabbed a slice of cold pizza from the fridge then flopped down on the couch, remote control in hand. A few minutes later, he switched it off. American late-night television was worse than the British variety, if that was even possible.

Before he could drift off on the couch, he took a quick shower to rinse away the stale smoke clinging to his skin. It had been decades since New York instituted an indoor smoking ban, yet the walls of the bar still seemed to exhale an invisible cloud over its patrons. As he dressed for bed, he found that the fatigue that had him nearly crawling away from the TV had buggered off to somewhere he wasn't likely to find it any time soon.

He ground his teeth. Knowing that laying down in bed and waiting for sleep was the last thing that would actually invite sleep, Ciaran returned to the living room and grabbed his briefcase from the couch where he had thrown it. He set it on the coffee table and pulled out the folder for a new downtown office building that he was supposed to design and began to study photographs of the current location and the written prospectus for the dozenth time.

He let his mind wander, imagining himself standing in front of a shadowy outline of a skyscraper. Should the building be a modern tower of glass, or should it reflect the style of the surrounding buildings?

Much of that part of Manhattan was dominated by gently-aging office buildings no more than fifteen or twenty stories high. It reminded him a bit of the city center in Glasgow, and no wonder, since so many Scottish architects had contributed to rebuilding the city of New York after it was ravaged by the British in the early nineteenth century.

The pencil in his hand began to move, transferring the building as it sharpened in his mind's eye almost without any conscious thought. Drawing was something that had come to him almost as easy as breathing. It was something that had stayed with him throughout his life no matter how challenging everything else became.

When he finally looked up from the page and glanced at the clock, he winced. Lost in his work, which always happened once the ideas began to flow, whole hours had passed. Even though there was more to do, Ciaran forced himself to put the pencil down, and pack everything away.

There was no way that he could pull an all-nighter and be completely conscious for Cliff's hockey game. Hopefully, the handful of hours left in the night would be enough. As he crawled under the covers and set the alarm on his phone, he had a feeling that tomorrow was going to be a long day.

Four

From out in the bedroom, her phone started to ring. Jal quickly finished drying her legs and dropped the towel, scrambling into the robe she'd draped over the vanity. She secured the belt and dashed for the doorway only to have the hem snag on a drawer handle and bring her staggering to a halt with enough force that her wet hair slapped her in the face.

"Really?" she complained to the empty room as she cleared her eyes and back-pedaled far enough to free herself. The phone continued to ring as she lurched forward and tripped over the towel.

Jal snarled. She kicked the offending heap of cloth aside and dove for the phone, putting it on speakerphone while she retrieved the towel and wrapped it around her hair. "Shouldn't you still be asleep?"

The deep, throaty laugh in response told Jal everything she needed to know about how Elena's night had gone. "Why would I still be asleep after working until two and then dancing my ass off at Fuego?"

"Those would be two," Jal replied with a jaw cracking yawn.

There was a time when Jal would have been right there with her. After the last of the dough had been prepped for tomorrow's bread, and the last dish had been washed, they'd raised hell up and down the Upper East Side, usually financed by a few tourists with unguarded pockets, only to stumble into Bob's for breakfast the second they unlocked the doors. Instead, it had been nearly a week of dreams filled with endless hallways with endless doors leading nowhere while she searched for God-knew-what unable to even find the way out. Actually, getting up and taking a shower was an accomplishment given the lack of restful sleep.

Jal rubbed a finger over one eyebrow. "You haven't been to bed yet, have you?"

"Not to sleep, anyway." The saucy wink she would have given in person was implied.

Jal rolled her eyes as she shimmied into a pair of leggings, and almost cracked a smile. "You're incorrigible."

Elena's laugh was like a seductive curl of smoke and Jal understood how her friend always seemed to have at least three men circling her at all times. "You know that's your favorite part about me." she replied. "Come meet me for coffee and I'll tell you all about it. I know you're dying to know."

Jal pulled the towel off and tossed it toward the hamper, nearly overflowing with clothes that needed to be lugged down five floors to the laundromat to be washed. Not to mention, brought back up. She scooped up the phone and took it off speaker. The floor of the living room was cold beneath her feet, sucking away the residual warmth from her shower as she went to the kitchen and opened the fridge. A week's worth of takeout containers stared back at her.

Deciding that she didn't have the energy to play a round of "is this edible" roulette, Jal grabbed a bottle of water and closed the door again. She plopped down on the sofa and tucked her knees under her. "Not this time."

"Thought so."

Three knocks sounded on the door. Jal jumped; her heart started to claw its way up her throat. She might have also let out a squeak before swallowing it down.

Elena said something that sounded much like a curse as the line went dead. Sure enough, when she pulled the phone from her ear, the screen was full of the usual collage of brightly colored icons.

"Are you going to let us in?"

Jal threw the phone onto the cushion beside her and hurried to flip the column of locks, then flung the door open to find Elena lounging against the half-wall beside it. She was smiling like the cat who'd gotten the cream with her arms crossed under her ample chest, a white satin top barely visible under a black cardigan, not that there was much of one to begin with. The hip resting on the wall was covered by a blue skirt that barely contained her curves. A pair of strappy heels dangled from one hand.

Beside Elena, their friend Lexi, dressed far more seasonably in leggings and a denim jacket, carefully balanced a tray of coffee cups and a carry bag that looked fit to burst. The heady scent of fresh baked bread mixed with the tang of cream cheese wafted through the doorway, making her mouth water.

Elena pushed off the wall and strode into the apartment, pausing only to peck Jal on the cheek in greeting. Her heels clattered to the floor beside the door, and she disappeared into Jal's bedroom.

Jal looked at Lexi, who simply shrugged. With the barest smile, Jal shook her head and took the bag from her. Lexi took advantage and wrapped her free arm around her shoulders.

Lexi's straight, blonde hair tickled her nose with the scent of lilies from the boutique salon shampoo that she used. "Hey, chick." It was her nickname for everyone.

"Hey, yourself." Jal closed the door, and followed Lexi into the kitchen. They deposited the food and drinks on the counter and Jal started unpacking foil wrapped bagels from the bag while Lexi shed her coat and draped it over a chair at the table.

Elena emerged from the bedroom tying the string on a pair of Jal's sweatpants that were only slightly too short. Her sable hair was now in a ponytail, the scraps of white and blue tucked under one arm.

"By all means..." Jal murmured with a sarcastic wave of her hand as if it wasn't normal for them to share clothes, but Elena's answering smirk had a smile curling her lips for the first time in a while.

Lexi pushed one of the foil-wrapped bundles in her direction and turned to toss another at Elena, who caught it mid-flop into a chair and held it aloft triumphantly. Jal grabbed the roll of paper towels off the holder and carried her food to the sofa with Lexi following in her wake with the drinks. Elena reached over and tore off a sheet for each of them while Lexi passed them each a cup.

Jal took a sniff through the small hole in the lid as Lexi sat down beside her and a familiar homey scent filled her head. Matcha green tea with honey and cinnamon, her favorite. She took a cautious sip and hissed set it aside on the coffee table with the lid off to cool. Her stomach growled from the fragrant steam that wafted up as she peeled the foil back from her bagel.

"Pumpernickel, toasted, with garlic and herb cream cheese and bacon, just how you like it." Elena informed her around a mouthful of blueberry bagel, and licked away a trickle of butter from the side of her hand. "Good thing you don't have to kiss anyone after you eat that."

Jal bit into her bagel and sighed with contentment. It was the perfect combination of crunchy bacon, cool cream cheese, and toasty rye. She raised an eyebrow at her friend. "Speaking of kissing..."

Beside her, Lexi sat up a little straighter. Elena's mouth spread into a wide grin as she chewed. "His name is Eric," she replied. "He was at the bar ahead of me at Fuego and we got to chatting. And let me tell you, he's some of the *finest* Dominican chocolate to ever come in a six-two package. And then there's his package..." She swiped a thumb across her bottom lip leaving a gloss on her skin.

Lexi looked scandalized. "Elena!"

Elena's grin only widened, and she winked. "What? They used a lot of butter this time."

"That's not what I meant, and you know it," Lexi protested, then turned to Jal. "Though I can attest to how hot he was. Enough for her to ditch me to shake it on the dance floor for *two hours*."

"As if that was a hardship?" Elena popped the last bite of bagel in her mouth. "It's not like I left you alone. You had a certain Legion defenseman in the VIP area to keep you company."

"We're just friends, you know that." Lexi sipped her coffee, though there was the faintest hint of pink high on her cheeks.

Elena laughed and crossed her legs over the arm of the chair.

Jal's heart clenched. Her two closest friends had gone clubbing without her. Again.

Turn down enough invitations, she supposed, and people stopped asking. Not that she'd been in any mood the last few days anyway. She also never really begrudged her friends of their romantic exploits.

But it *had* been a while, mostly by design. Mostly.

Out of nowhere, the memory of Ciaran strutting through her apartment like he owned the place drifted through her mind. She reached for her tea, now cool enough to drink, and swallowed half of it in a few gulps. She realized her mistake when she sat back to find both her friends looking at her.

Elena's eyebrows drew down over her dark chocolate eyes, then they rose. Shit, Jal knew that look.

"You know, you never told us about that dinner you went to last week."

Lexi looked at her. "Dinner?" she asked. "What dinner?"

"Some mystery man."

Jal got to her feet and started clearing trash just to escape their crosshairs.

"Oh, I like a good mystery man." There was a creak as Lexi

adjusted her position on the couch. Their eyes burned holes in Jal's back as she stuffed the trash bin back under the sink.

Jal turned back to her friends and leaned on the counter. "There's nothing to tell," she replied. "Like I told Elena, he took something of mine, and I had to go to dinner with him to get it back."

"You didn't tell me what he took though."

Jal sighed and went back to the sofa. "He took my stash, or most of it anyway."

"Your stash?" Elena asked, she looked around the room, though nothing was visibly out of place. "You mean he broke into your apartment and somehow found all of your little hidey holes?"

Jal nodded. "I still have no idea how he did it." she said. "I picked his pocket, he picked mine, and somehow he managed to get in here and clean me out before I got home. The next morning, he showed up here pretending to return my wallet, and to get his back, but it was all a trick."

"He took her to Amicetto." Elena told Lexi in a sing-song voice prompting their friend to respond with a low whistle.

"Don't get too excited," Jal growled. "We didn't even get to the food."

Lexi frowned. "What happened?"

"I got my money back and, when I got up to leave, he grabbed my wrist, and..."

"You panicked?" Elena asked.

Jal stared straight ahead as she mentally tried to keep the lid over a box best left unopened from wriggling loose, a box that had been tightly sealed for two years, except in her dreams. She nodded, gripping her knees to keep her hands from trembling.

Elena got to her feet and sat on the wide arm of the sofa. Lexi scooted over and placed her arm across the back behind her head.

"I got what I wanted." Jal pried her hands away and flexed her fingers in her lap. "It wasn't a date. The transaction was finished. There isn't anything else to say."

For a long moment, they sat together in silence, her friends encircling her. Jal understood then that *this* was what she had been missing.

Jal's eyes burned as they fixed on the table across the room, the shaft of sunlight spilling across the surface seemed to point at the hidden drawer. Sitting between them, the tightness in her chest released and she took her first truly deep breath in months. Slowly, she reached out a hand to each of her friends and wove her fingers with theirs. Only then, did they both shift closer and tip their heads to hers.

FIVE

After a long morning of meetings, Ciaran was going to lose his mind if he didn't get outside at lunch. He stretched his legs on the short walk to Washington Square Park, its magnificent white marble arch a shining beacon drawing him in. He stepped under the white and red striped awning of his favorite café and sat down at a table near the railing that bordered the sidewalk where he'd done some of his best people watching.

When the server came around, he ordered a coffee and a sandwich and returned to scanning the crowd for a familiar tan hat and tried not to be disappointed when the server returned and he hadn't spotted her yet. He had, however, managed to spot a half dozen people she would have targeted had she been there. Some people really were oblivious.

His fingers tingled as he wrapped them around the coffee cup as a woman passed by in a blue NYU hoodie and a white backpack slung over one shoulder, its main pocket gaping open to reveal a glimpse of textbooks and a bright yellow clutch purse shining at him like a beacon.

"Excuse me!" he called, setting his cup down with a clatter and half-rising from his seat.

The woman stopped a few feet away and half-turned looking around for who had called. If the hoodie wasn't already an indication, the fact that she stopped pegged her as a non-native.

Ciaran waved to draw her attention then pointed at her back. "Just wanted to let you know your bag is open."

She glanced over her shoulder and her jaw dropped. "Oh, my goodness, thank you so much." she replied, her voice thick with a Southern drawl as she zipped it up. "That could have been bad."

Ciaran smiled and nodded, flexing his fingers reflexively. If only she knew.

"Thanks again!" she called with a wave and walked away.

He settled back in his seat with a satisfied sigh as his good deed for the day disappeared around a corner.

The cafe had been his favorite place to people-watch, ever since he'd moved into his apartment nearby. It had also been a place to test himself. At first, it was making it through a day without dipping his hand in to an unguarded pocket, like an addict avoiding a hit. Then, it was a week since he'd picked a lock, even his own, just to make sure he still could. A month. Until one day, he had sat at this very table and watched Jal pick three pockets and a purse in the time it took him to drink his coffee, and for the first time in two and a half years, the hairs on his arms lifted, adrenaline buzzed in his blood, and seared her face into his memory.

It wasn't just her appearance that drew him in. Even from a distance, the quick, practiced movements of those talented hands mesmerized him. From that day on he watched for her, and when she did appear, he studied her, marveled at her choice of targets, and the cunning mind it took to plan out steals that he never would have attempted had he had her delicate hands.

Weeks, and sometimes months, passed between sightings, but she always reappeared. This last time, it had been the latter, long enough that he was starting to wonder if he would ever see her again. But part of him refused to believe that, even though he didn't even know her name. Yet.

But then he'd spotted that tan slouchy hat, near bursting with the dark hair she sometimes tucked inside, and he had shot up out of his chair. His next conscious thought was her plowing into him, sending them both sprawling to the pavement. He'd swiped her ID as he helped her to her feet, fully aware that she had taken his wallet too. He knew better than to have anything more than a little cash in it, something he found she hadn't learned at thief school when he opened hers to find cash, cards, and... a driver's license.

Jal Morrow.

Ciaran had tasted the name on his tongue dozens of times since then, and there was something melodic about it that made him want to say it over and over again. It only took a little searching in the right corner of the internet to confirm that the address was genuine. She should have known better than that.

He ignored the cold glare and snapped words she flung his way for she was even more beautiful up close. Now, he could see the slender, muscular build that was mostly hidden under a baggy jacket. The hair that had fallen from under her hat was long, curly, and black as night. If he thought he hadn't been intrigued before, he certainly was now.

Three days ago

The small black zippered wallet stared at him from its place propped against his monitor and Ciaran just stared right back at it as if willing that zipper to open and tell him what to do next.

No more stealing. It was a promise he'd made to himself as soon as he'd stepped foot on the plane at Glasgow Airport bound for New York. His past would stay in Scotland, and that included his former profession. Yet there in front of him was glaring evidence that, after six years, he'd relapsed. All over a woman who had absolutely no qualms about stealing from *him*.

Heaving a sigh, he picked up the wallet and opened it, reading again the name and address on the ID. Hers was an unusual name and he wondered where it came from even as he admitted that it suited her. The address, which he had already memorized, was somewhere on the outskirts of East Harlem, halfway across the borough from his converted townhouse apartment.

He tossed the wallet back down on his desk and a few of the cards slipped free to fan across the wooden surface. Ciaran gathered them up and zipped the wallet shut, replacing it carefully where it had been against the monitor and forced himself to raise his attention to the screen and get back to fleshing out the wire-frame skyscraper taking shape on his computer.

Yet, his mind kept drifting uptown. He should just go and knock on her door. He'd practiced over and over what he would say if she answered. She'd dropped her wallet, and he was just being neighborly. It was the right thing to do. It was what the new Ciaran would do.

But that part of him that had reawakened just a little had a different idea. One that the rational part of his brain should have dismissed immediately. But the bastard had buggered off arm-in-arm with his common sense and most of his sanity. What was the saying? In for a penny...

Within an hour, he had the impulse control and concentration of a toddler, squirming in his chair, bouncing his leg, jumping from task to task. His coworkers probably thought he had lost his mind, or had enjoyed something much more illegal at lunch than coffee and the almost forgotten rush of adrenaline at the prospect of getting caught. At the stroke of five, he sprung out of his chair as if shot out of a cannon.

He meant to go home, he really did, but the soot-stained eight-story building he found himself staring at twenty minutes later was not it. He didn't even remember making a conscious decision to take the 6 Train uptown instead of walking home.

The entrance, a wide wooden door with opaque glass fortified with chicken wire, was tucked between a laundromat and a fried chicken restaurant. The door was unsurprisingly locked, so he leaned against the building and scrolled through his phone. It was an unseasonably warm day, and with his tie loosened and sleeves rolled up, he looked like he could be someone catching some fresh air while waiting for their laundry.

When a food delivery driver was buzzed inside, Ciaran followed him in. The elevator had an "out of order" sign on it, but the driver didn't even try to use it, pivoting instead to an open doorway and the stairs inside as if he'd done it a hundred times. He also didn't spare Ciaran a glance as he disappeared through the second-floor door, leaving Ciaran to continue to climb the dingy, cracked stairs. Three stories later, his heart pounded from nerves as much as from exertion. God help the people who lived on the top floor.

Apartment 516 had three dead bolts installed over the original skeleton lock. He had to give her credit there, no thief, not even him, could pick all three quickly and quietly enough to evade the Busy-Body Neighbor. Every building in this city had one, their only job was to make noise complaints and keep one eye firmly pressed to the peep hole into the hallway, the police ready on speed dial.

Ciaran retraced his steps and ducked into the alley next to the laundromat, skirting trash and puddles best left unidentified. He waited until a man at the mouth of the alley finished his cigarette and disappeared back out onto the street before scrambling onto a dumpster with far less grace than he'd once had and pulling down the ladder. His heart inched into his throat as he crept up the creaking flights of stairs back to the fifth floor, glad for the cover of approaching darkness.

He took a moment to get his bearings, and realized that hers was the last apartment on this side, so the first few windows had to be hers. He stopped at the first window, its paint worn and flaking and pressed an ear to the single-paned glass. When the only sound was the rush of blood through his own ears, he moved on to the next set to find them uncovered, revealing a large living area, and no sign of Jal.

Returning to the first set of windows, through which he could just make out a bed and dresser through a small gap in the curtains, he pushed against the wooden frame, but the window was firmly locked. His lips twitched as he reached into the pocket of his coat and removed a small bundle of lock picks. They'd long ago become a reminder of the past, and more practically, insurance in case he ever lost or forgot his own keys. But now his fingers tingled as he pulled a long, slender pick free and used it to flip the lock on one of the ancient casement windows. So much for those points he'd given her for security in the hallway.

You're probably the only one mad enough to try, he told himself as he took a deep breath and slid the window up. Either she wasn't home, or she was about to get one hell of a surprise. He prayed it was the former.

Her bedroom, like the rest of the building, had a feeling of age not yet going to seed, but also not too far off. It was decorated in blues and golds, but full of contradictions. The bed was neatly made but the floor was strewn with clothes. The room did not have a closet, but the clothing rod made from tarnished metal pipe held a dizzying array of color interspersed with an equally boring selection of threadbare cozy sweaters and hoodies.

She had a flare for decorating for sure, but what really stood out to him was the lack of anything personal, anything that just screamed out "Jal." Sure, the room smelled faintly of vanilla from a bottle of perfume on her dresser, but there were no mementos, no sports memorabilia or pop culture anything to tell him a little something about *her*. Only a lone strip of photo booth pictures tucked into the mirror of her dresser gave him even a hint.

Jal and two other women were crowded into the cramped off-white space making silly faces for the camera. Jal sat with one arm wrapped around the shoulders of a blonde beauty, while a no-less-stunning Latina sprawled over both their laps. They were all dressed for a night out and looked thick as, well, thieves.

Jal was beaming, her whole face aglow, so different from any expression he had seen on her before. It drove the air from his lungs, and for one irrational moment, no longer than a few heartbeats, he wondered what it would take for her to look at him with an expression like that. He drove that thought down and forced himself to walk away before she came home and caught him staring.

He moved to the door and briefly put an ear to the wood. Hearing nothing, Ciaran eased it open and stepped through into a single room that was living room, kitchen, and dining room all in one. It had the same high ceiling as the bedroom, but his architect's brain marveled at how it seemed to soar even higher out here with the larger, taller windows that let in much more light.

A brick fireplace with a large granite mantle dominated the space on the wall to his left, its exposed chimney climbing until it disappeared into the ceiling between two massive beams supporting the floor above. In the middle of the dining area stood a huge antique table made of some light-colored wood.

Figuring the kitchen to be the best place to start, Ciaran sifted through the drawers and cupboards, but came up empty.

She had to have some, if not all, of her takings in the apartment. Banks tended to ask too many questions... So, where would she have put them?

He turned a slow circle, his eyes searching for shadowy spaces, odd scratches on the floor, any possible clue. Back in Scotland, he'd kept most of his stash under a loose floorboard in the back of his bedroom closet, but there were plenty of other possibilities in a place like this, so he just started poking into every possible nook.

His first success was a roll of bills inside a pizza box in the freezer. He chuckled at the obviousness of that one, but left the money alone. It only helped to convince him that she had far, far, more clever places.

He found the next one in the desk under a window dividing the living and dining areas. A false bottom in a middle drawer concealed an impressive hoard of foreign coins and a few jewels. He pocketed a few of the smaller baubles before replacing the cover and the small stack of files and a battered notebook that sat on top.

He moved on to the fireplace. There had to be something there, but the flue was empty and none of the bricks moved when he pushed on them. He tapped a finger on his chin as he studied row after row of identical bricks. Just as he was thinking of giving up, his eyes fell on a brick just under the granite mantle that stuck out just a fraction of an inch farther than its companions. The mortar was very slightly chipped, and gone completely in one corner. A new rush of adrenaline went through him as he gripped the brick and gently gave it a tug. At first, it didn't budge, but with a bit more pressure, it started to move.

This must be it, he thought.

With the closest thing to a pop that masonry could manage, the brick came free, and inside the small depression was likely her biggest stash, a couple grand in cash, a stunning blue sapphire bracelet, and a large diamond pendant. He'd pocketed most of it before he even realized what he was doing. He froze, staring down at the sapphire in his hand.

What are you doing, lad?

He flipped the bracelet around in his hand, running his thumb over the facets of a stone the size of his thumbnail. The band was a wide braid of dozens of thin silver strands, each with different textures. This too was headed for his overloaded pocket before he stopped himself. His hand trembled as he returned the bracelet to the hiding place, the old Ciaran battling, but ultimately losing, to the new.

He slid the brick back into place and resumed his search, locating another in the bedroom, in the floor next to her dresser. But still no wallet.

He had already lingered too long; she would be home soon. Dejected, he headed for the open window but stopped halfway when an idea struck him. A slow smile spread across his face as he withdrew his leg and ran for the desk to tear a couple of pages from the notebook and scribble a message on each. He raced around the apartment and placed the same note in each hiding place, draining a little more of the treasures in each until his pockets were fit to burst.

He turned away from the fireplace to study the room,

slowly spinning an emerald tennis bracelet around his hand as if it were a rosary. He spotted a heating vent on the wall just outside the kitchen that he'd missed the first time and strode toward it. His toe caught the edge of the living room throw rug and he tried to catch his balance, only to stagger awkwardly into the back of the sofa and crash to the floor with a jarring thud. The bracelet flew out of his hand and slid under the table.

By some miracle, he hadn't hit his head, but his brain still sloshed around in his skull as if he had. With a groan, Ciaran dragged his knees underneath him and took deep breaths until his stomach settled and his vision cleared enough to crawl across the rug to retrieve the bracelet. As he did, he studied the underside of the table though nothing seemed out of place, even to his practiced eye. But something told him to keep looking so he stayed on his back, studying the skirting and the scrollwork on the legs until, wait, what was that?

He wormed on his back over to one of the legs and slid his hand up, his fingers finding the edges of a small wooden catch almost completely hidden at the top of one leg. Curious, Ciaran pushed it and heard a soft click. Scrambling back to his feet, he swayed as the room spun. When it settled, he gaped at a section of the table skirting that had popped loose and pulled open the drawer and sifted through its contents, some cash, and a few wallets, including his own.

He flipped through it and found nothing missing besides a few hundred dollars in cash. His ID and all his cards, most of which didn't even work, were still there. Halfway into his pocket, he paused, his mouth splitting into a wide grin. He put the wallet back where it had been, added a note on top, and slid it closed.

He had just placed the last note in her dresser when he heard the clatter of keys against the front door and froze. Silently, he hurried into her bedroom and eased an eye around the frame. She entered the apartment, flipped all the locks, and went immediately to the stove. Putting the kettle on, she slumped into one of the couches, unaware that there was anything amiss. A moment later, an ear-numbing blast of synthesized keyboards and electric guitar of some decades-old alternative song filled the air.

Under cover of the deep voice that boomed out the lyrics somewhere between singing and growling, Ciaran crept to the window. He froze when a floorboard creaked, then took a chance and scrambled through the window, sliding it shut as quietly as he could. From where he crouched on the fire escape, he could just make out Jal's dark curls bobbing in time to the music, and he heaved a sigh, bracing a hand on the wall when his knees went suddenly weak.

So much for the nerves of steel he'd prided himself on back home.

He pushed off the wall and found his legs unsteady enough on the descent that he had to rely heavily on the railings. He made it down two floors before a woman noticed him outside her window and threw a flowerpot at his head. He ducked and half-ran, half-stumbled the rest of the way, not caring who heard.

A new surge of adrenaline gave him the boost he needed to sprint for the subway station, his heavy pockets swinging with enough force, he was surprised they didn't burst. By pure luck, he caught a train pulling up to the platform and picked up the pace, his feet a blur on the stairs, dashing aboard just as the doors began to close only to crash into a disheveled man in a fraying coat who was standing in the doorway. The stench of body odor and urine radiating off the man had Ciaran swallowing back bile as he leapt away, apologizing as he went when the man swung a fist and cursed at him.

Ciaran moved through the crowd as politely as he could to the other set of doors to get some distance, and though the man didn't come any closer, he continued to yell the whole way downtown. By the time Ciaran emerged back at street level a few blocks from home, his legs were shaking so hard, the treasure in his pocket like so much lead weight, putting one foot in front of the other had him staggering like one of those television zombies. He gave serious thought to crawling up the last stairs into his apartment and collapsed hard on a kitchen chair, dragging in one raggedy breath after another until his heart finally slowed to normal.

He emptied his pockets onto the table and marveled at the piles of money, coins, and jewels that covered its surface. But this time, there was none of the heady exhilaration that he'd felt dozens of times back in Glasgow. This time, there was only a cold emptiness.

After a hot shower and a gallon of scalding hot tea, he spent the evening putting the pieces of his plan in place. The dinner reservation. Calling in the favors he needed to turn almost everything into cash at rates that even criminals would deem fair. But afterwards, he found himself restless, pacing the runner between kitchen and bedroom.

The sun was just starting to color the sky when he left his house, but instead of heading downtown to the office, he went uptown. A young brunette dressed in a business suit blinked blearily at him as she sipped from her travel mug and held open the door to Jal's building as she was coming out. Her heavily-lashed blue eyes widened, and spots of pink appeared on her cheeks, when he flashed her a wide, grateful smile.

His smile faded as he climbed the stairs and stopped in front of her door. For a long moment, he stared at the peephole, as if it would let him look inside if he stared at it long enough.

Just knock, he ordered himself.

His heart pounded once, twice, the sound too loud even for his own ears and he shook his head and shoulders, like a dog shedding water, to clear it. He smoothed his hands over his hair, straightened his coat and let a little of the cocky, over-confidence of Ciaran the thief rise to the surface, then lifted his hand and pressed it firmly to the doorbell.

Present Day

Ciaran glanced at his watch and swore. He tucked a twenty under his coffee cup, more than enough to pay for his lunch and a tip, and headed back to the office, his long legs chewing up the distance at a clip he usually saved for the football pitch.

Cliff wouldn't mind him coming back from lunch a little late, or a lot late in this case, but Lional Dougherty, who most referred to not-so-affectionately as Old Man Dougherty, had it in for him, despite Ciaran never having done anything to antagonize him. Something rubbed the man the wrong way. He never approved of Ciaran's work, though to be fair, OMD never gave him any decent projects in the first place. But Ciaran had made the best of everything he had been given and Cliff and Julia Russo, the firm's other senior partner, were highly impressed by his work ethic and his results. Just not Lionel.

He needn't have worried. No one, not even his desk mate Catherine, even noticed his late return. Ciaran put in a few more hours sculpting the new high-rise on the computer before Cliff poked his head out of his office. "Ready for the game?" He asked, waving the tickets.

Ciaran looked up and nodded. "I totally forgot about that."

"Let's go then."

SIX

Her footsteps echoed down a corridor so white it was almost blinding. The floor, the walls, all seemed to emit a pearlescent glow that blurred any detail. She reached out both arms, searching for the doorways that were always there, but this corridor was wider, and both hands touched nothing but air.

She shuffled a few feet in each direction, but the walls moved with her and no matter how much she reached, she could never quite touch them. The brightness stung her eyes, and even closed, the light seemed to burn through her eyelids leaving her stumbling along, unable to see where she was putting her feet.

From somewhere in the distance, a whimpering started. She froze, head tilted to hear better. As quickly as the sound started, it stopped, only to begin again but from a new direction. The mewling keen of an animal in pain, the terrified shriek of an infant, each new sound was different. Soon, they stopped fading away, instead building and overlapping until the din was as overwhelming as the light.

"Is anyone there?"

Her voice was distorted, both too loud and too soft at the same time, the words disappearing into the brightness as if it were mist, yet also booming through it.

She clapped her hands to her ears, but it was as effective as closing her eyes. Determined, she continued to lurch forward, but the floor seemed to ripple under her feet, one step landing on thin air, the next stubbing her bare toes.

"Answer me!"

In response, the cries rose to a deafening roar, and it was her turn to whimper. But still she continued staggering drunkenly forward. There was no way out but forward.

The light began to pulse, and her whimpers turned into moans. It penetrated her head and threatened to burst her skull to escape again. But still she put one foot in front of the other.

Until there was no more floor.

Her foot met nothing but air and she pitched forward, arms pinwheeling, her fingers scrabbling for something, anything to break her fall as she plunged down, down, down into the light.

Jal slammed back into consciousness, and for a moment, she couldn't breathe. Something soft was plastered around her, bright sunlight glowing through as if she was inside a cocoon. Her arms and legs thrashed, as she gasped for breath in the cloyingly warm space, unable to fully voice the screams lodged in her throat.

The whole right side of her body throbbed, punctuated with sharper pains as her limbs connected with solid objects that had her hemmed in. But then a kick straight back broke free of whatever was smothering her and a rush of cooler air flooded in, and with it, a familiar floral scent that made most of the panic dissipate. Laundry detergent. Coming from the fleece throw she'd fallen asleep under. A fleece that had become wrapped around her body when she'd rolled off the couch. Because that's where she was, on the floor, pinned between couch and coffee table.

Now that she could think straight, Jal wiggled until the blanket loosened enough to get to her knees and then sit back on her heels as she finally tossed it back onto the couch. Static crackled as she brushed a curtain of tangled curls from her face and looked around. The lingering scent of pancakes replaced the cloying floral scent.

The sky had been full of thick, black clouds when she'd curled up with a book after breakfast and promptly fallen asleep, but now shafts of sunlight streamed in through the multi-paned windows, one directly aimed at the cushion she'd used as a pillow. No wonder the hallway this time had been full of blinding light.

She rubbed the grit from her eyes as she climbed back onto the sofa and sat, taking in the room around her while her fingers massaged a lingering ache in her shoulder that must have taken the brunt of the fall. Her cheeks blazed with shame even though the room itself was on the cool side.

You're being ridiculous, she told herself, scrubbing chilled hands over her face. *How can you be embarrassed when no one saw anything?* She reached for the full mug of tea, long since gone cold, on the coffee table and gulped down its contents. She'd left the bag in, and the tea was bitter, and did very little to soothe a throat as raspy as sandpaper.

She reached for her phone and set the mug back on the table at the same time, but misjudged the distance. The mug teetered on the edge but her fingers only brushed the handle before it shattered on the floor. Cursing, she gathered the pieces up in a fold of her sweater and dumped them in the kitchen trash.

The cabinet door slammed shut as she turned and surveyed the room, taking in the nest of blankets on the sofa and the clothes spilling out of the bedroom doorway from the overflowing basket just inside. It had been the better part of a week since her friends had visited, and she'd barely left the apartment except to visit the bodega on the corner for essentials that couldn't be delivered. The nightmares were not easing up and all she had to show for it was a string of sleepless nights and a laundry situation that had gone from desperate to nothing left.

Hiding away until the dreams passed had been a good plan, it had worked before. This time though, they seemed to be sticking around, and if that was the case, no good was going to come from caging herself inside these four walls.

After she showered and dressed, Jal shrugged into the baggy jacket she usually wore when she was out to make a score or two. She started twisting her hair up to tuck under the slouchy knit cap and let out a jaw-cracking yawn.

She dropped her arms to her sides, her hair cascading

down over her face and shoulders, and sighed. This was not the day to go out and do any stealing, not if she didn't want to get caught. Her reflexes with the teacup should have been enough to prove that.

It didn't mean that she was going to stay inside and continue to wallow, so she swapped the jacket for a hip-length black coat and scooped up her purse and keys.

The day outside had become as beautiful as it looked through the window. The light breeze had a bit of spring to it even though most of the trees that lined the street had barely begun to bud. Jal breathed deeply anyway, the air so crisp it immediately clearing some of the fogginess away.

She walked a half dozen blocks and entered the park at 101st Street into the shade of a wide canopy of trees. The breeze rustled the branches overhead, as if the trees were whispering to each other, sharing secrets only they knew or understood.

Maybe they were whispering compliments and encouragement to the mother picnicking with her two young children who seemed more interested in using the checkerboard pattern of the blanket as a game of Twister than the food she was serving up on paper plates. Or maybe they were gossiping behind their buds about the couple cuddling together under a tree lost in the haze of young love.

There was a time when she and Andy had been like that, so caught up in each other that the outside world could have been blown to pieces and they wouldn't have noticed.

Jal cut that thought off as she crossed the ring road and turned onto the path that circled the baseball diamonds. Not even half an hour out of her apartment and already she was thinking about Andy. *Glutton for punishment today, aren't you?*

Most of the baseball fields were empty, but a father and son had taken the opportunity to fly a kite over one of the outfields, and from a little further ahead, there were shouts and the rhythmic thumping of a ball being kicked around.

She crested a rise in the path and saw a group of men playing soccer on a chalked-in field wedged between two baseball diamonds. They were all down to at least their t-shirts and a few were bare-chested despite the slight chill to the air. Jal leaned against a tree and watched as they ran back and forth across the field passing to each other, dodging good natured checks and trips.

One of the shirtless men, a young redhead who looked like he spent more time playing soccer with a video game controller than the actual game, laughed as a slender black-haired man tripped over his leg, and ran off with the ball in the other direction.

Another dark-haired guy, dressed in soccer shorts and a form-fitting jersey, stole it back and headed in her direction, leaving his friends in the dust. His muscles rippled as he did one trick after another, twisting, and turning, and flipping the ball up in the air to avoid the few players who made half-hearted attempts at stopping him.

Her lips drew up and she let out an appreciative low whistle as he completed a neat spin around the last remaining defender, tapping his feet in quick succession, two, three, four times, then kicking it through the goal marked out by their jackets.

A burly man cursed and dropped his hands to his knees as the victor pumped his fist in the air and shouted like he had just scored the winning goal in the World Cup. His friends, not nearly as impressed, stood yelling at him to stop showing off and bring the ball back.

He gestured to them with two fingers in the air, and went to retrieve the ball, which had crossed the path and rebounded off the tree at her feet.

As he drew closer, the wide grin on his face froze, then disappeared. He stopped a few feet away, paying no heed to the ball. Sweat streamed down his face and plastered a blue jersey already stretched tight across his chest to every rigid muscle in his torso, and there were a lot of them. He was breathing hard through his mouth, that chest rising and falling with each one.

Jal's heart stumbled over a beat or two before his face, and those wide whisky-gold eyes registered. Of course, it was him... the cocky son of a bitch that had stolen her wallet, and broken into her place. What was his name again? Oh, right. Ciaran. *And who am I?*

They stood staring at each other for a long moment until the breeze picked up and blew her hair across her eyes. Jal batted it away with an annoyed growl that could have been for him as much as the wind, or with herself even.

Before she'd realized who he was, she had been impressed with his skill with the soccer ball and with his obvious love for the sport. Before she could truly identify his features, the bright, white smile and the gleam in his eyes as he danced around his friends as if they were standing still had entranced her. Until she had seen his face, she had been attracted to him. Hell, she was still attracted to him.

Ciaran blinked quickly as if the wind breaking their eye

contact had also broken some kind of trance. "Jal?" he asked and took a cautious step toward her. *Oh right, that's me. I'm Jal.*

It was reflex that had her taking a step back, and another, until her back collided with the tree. "What are you doing here?"

He was close but he hadn't touched her. Yet. She didn't know what would happen if he did. "I would think that was somewhat obvious, lass."

That voice poured over her like the honeyed whisky his eyes reminded her of, but she put up a hand before he could get any closer. Suddenly, it wasn't the rough bark of a tree at her back, but a cold, smooth plaster wall.

He collided with her hand like it was a magnet that had drawn him in. Beneath the sweaty shirt, his heart beat a furious rhythm against her fingers.

That alone should have been enough to keep herself from spiraling; Andy had always been cool and collected. But it didn't help at all. Her vision narrowed until the park disappeared and even Ciaran was fuzzy. A roaring filled her ears, distorting his words. The pancakes threatened to make a reappearance.

When her head cleared a moment later, she was facing a different direction, and he had a hand under her elbow to steady her. A tingling warmth seemed to radiate from that touch, and some small part of her did feel anchored by it.

Two lines were etched deeply between lowered eyebrows, and he was close enough to see sparks of pure gold in his eyes. "Jal, are you alright?"

"Fine," she snapped, and snatched her arm away. The warmth from his touch both lingered and faded away far too quickly.

Ciaran took a step back and put his hands in his pockets. His shoulders crept up towards his ears. "Look, Jal," he said, "I don't know what I've done t—"

She cut him off. "You stole from me, that's enough."

"You stole from *me* first, you know." Ciaran replied evenly. The lines had smoothed out on his forehead and one corner of his mouth twitched as he was trying not to smile. "We're even."

"Not even close, you broke into my home." she said, that same rush of anger and humiliation came back at the mere mention of it. "Now, leave me alone."

He followed as she tried to storm off between the trees, but stayed a few steps back. "You can't stay mad forever."

"Watch me." She pivoted in a different direction and he cut her off.

This time he didn't touch her, and he didn't hold his arms out to the side like he was the defender, and she was the one driving forward with the ball. He just stood casually with his hands in his pockets, his body filling the gap between two trees, though the tight muscles of his forearms told her he wasn't truly at ease. How could he when she was acting the way she was?

"Look, I'm sorry," he said. "For everything."

She stared at him. Gone was the cocky guy who strode into her apartment like he owned the place. Instead, his eyes were filled with warm compassion, which was almost worse.

As the silence drew out for a moment, he rocked back on his heels, then his head tilted slightly to one side. "Is there some way I can make it up to you?"

The earnestness suddenly filling the tawny depths of his eyes made her look away. "I—"

Whatever she was going to say was cut off by the scuff of footsteps on the path behind her heading their way.

Ciaran looked up over her shoulder and then stalked past to where the ball lay. He passed close enough that she could smell him, salty sweat and a smoky, sweet scent that she remembered from her apartment. It filled her nose and somehow cleared her head.

"Hey, Scotty, you could have at least thrown the ball back first." One of his friends, the burly one with gray at his temples, said as he stepped onto the grass a few feet away.

Ciaran scooped up the ball with both hands and tucked it behind his head, his muscles flexed into a position she was sure he'd held a thousand times from the sidelines of a soccer game.

"I mean this in the best way possible," he said, the last word ended on a grunt as he sent the ball flying through the air back onto the chalk-outlined field, "but piss off, Cliff."

Jal used the distraction to slip away. She was halfway back to the park entrance before Ciaran caught up with her, stepping directly into her path, but kept his hands to himself. There was a fine tremor to his shoulders and arms that said it was taking all his restraint not to reach for her.

A small part of her wanted to feel his touch on her skin again, to soak in that warmth that seemed to radiate from him. A fresh breeze set off a whole-body shiver that wasn't entirely from the cold. "Please, just tell me what you want, so I can go home."

The thin smile that appeared on his lips was hesitant,

almost sheepish. "Can we just start over?" His tone was not quite a plea. "Let me take you to dinner, for real this time."

"You should get back to your game."

The smile grew. "Answer me, and I will."

Jal sighed and clamped her lips together to keep from mirroring his expression. "Why do I get the impression that I will only get rid of you if I say yes?"

He put his hands in his pockets again and rocked back on his heels. There was a flash of white teeth as the smile grew a bit more. "That's a distinct possibility," he replied, and that accent wrapped around the words like a caress down her spine.

She rubbed her forehead and huffed a laugh through her nose. He just crooked an eyebrow and rocked again, bouncing slightly when his feet landed flat.

For a long moment, she bit the inside of her cheek and tried to keep the smile at bay. But it was a losing battle. Finally, she shook her head and waved a hand at him in surrender. "Fine," she replied, "if it will make you go away, then yes. I'll have dinner with you."

Now he was grinning. "That's great, let me just get your number." Just as quickly, his face fell. He withdrew his hands from his pockets and then patted them as if his phone could magically have appeared. He felt for back pockets that didn't exist in soccer shorts and one hand briefly slapped at the white lion and shield emblem on his chest where the pocket in a coat or dress shirt would be.

He rolled his eyes and sighed. "Bollocks, it's back at the pitch."

Her laugh was triumphant with just a subtle hint of sultry

smoke. "Oh? Now, that's too bad," she replied, and with a wink, she walked away.

Ciaran watched her disappear up the path with her head high and a swagger that would have been at home on the runways of Fashion Week. The breeze sent tendrils of that raven-black hair swirling around her head and made the tails of her black coat billow out around her, revealing a backside that her jeans hugged in all the right ways.

She didn't look back, but he got the impression that she knew he was still watching and checking out her ass. Which he certainly was not doing. Nope, not at all.

A voice from behind him said, "Well, she sure is pleased with herself."

Ciaran turned as Cliff walked up beside him with a broad grin on his flushed face, the ball tucked under his arm and patted Ciaran on the shoulder. "What did you say to her?"

One of his hands curled slowly into a fist, but he resisted the urge to drive it into Cliff's stomach. "Get stuffed, Cliff." Ciaran growled and snatched the ball away. He turned back to where their friends were waiting, taking the opportunity for a water break.

Cliff laughed, falling into step beside him. "She's a looker, I'll give you that." he said wryly, looking in the direction that Jal had gone.

Ciaran refused to agree with him out loud because his friend would never let him live it down. But still his eyes drifted back to where she had been but was now far out of sight.

With a sigh, he stepped back over the chalked line and dropped the ball, catching it with the top of his foot so it bounced back up. He continued to juggle it across the field between his feet and knees.

Mike squirted a stream of water into his mouth and brushed sweaty red hair out of his eyes. "Are you gonna play all day, or can we get back to the game?"

Ciaran bounced the ball off one knee, then the other, and let it drop to the grass. He placed his foot on the top of the ball to stop it and regarded his friend with a raised eyebrow. A corner of his mouth twitched up as Mike took a step in his direction. Before he could take another, Ciaran slipped his toe underneath it and sent the ball flying straight into Mike's groin.

Mike's face turned the same shade of red as his hair as he dropped to his knees with his hands clasping the offended area. The others groaned in unison.

Ciaran passed the ball to Kurt with a grin and they went back to their game, leaving Mike where he was on his knees.

SEVEN

The next morning, there was a knock on the door. Jal set her tea down on the counter and pressed her eye to the peephole expecting to see one of her friends, or at worse, Ciaran, but the hallway outside the door was empty. She waited a full minute before she flipped the locks and eased it open until the security chain stretched tight.

Outside, the hallway all the way to the stairs was nothing but scuffed drywall and dusty tile. Her eyebrows furrowed in confusion. She turned to close the door and caught a flash of white out of the corner of her eye. On the doormat was a white envelope and a long, narrow box.

She tried reaching through the gap, but the box was just out of reach. With a sigh, she stood and pushed the door closed to release the chain, opening it only far enough to retrieve the items before securing the door again. She deposited the box on the counter next to her cup and dug in the drawer beside her for a sharp knife to slit open the heavy, off-white paper. Inside, was a single thick sheet folded in half. At the top of the page was a logo with interlocking initials DJ&R and a swanky Fifth Avenue address, and in the middle were a few lines of script written in a neat, masculine hand.

> Jal,
> Since I didn't get your phone number, I figured this would have to do. I made a reservation at Amicetto at seven tonight. Hopefully you can make it.
> If not, I understand.
> Ciaran

Jal slowly set the note aside and tried to ignore the butterfly that had started to flutter its wings in her stomach. The white box was about two feet long and four inches square. She turned it right side up. On the lid, was an embossed sticker with the name of a flower shop a few blocks away.

She retrieved the knife to slit the tape and pried the box open. Beneath a layer of tissue paper was a half-dozen dark pink flowers, each one a foot long, carefully packed head to tail inside. The buds were half as wide as the box, each covered by a white foam mesh to compress the blooms and protect them in transit.

Jal lifted one flower free and removed the covering, allowing the delicate ruffled petals of a peony to spring open. Jal pressed the flower to her nose and inhaled the heady sweet scent. Oh look, the butterfly has friends.

After taking another deep sniff, she reluctantly set the flower back in the box to find something to put them in, eventually settling on a wide-mouth mason jar, the largest container she had. She filled the jar and returned to the table to trim the stems then placed it in the middle of the dining room table, where she could see them from almost anywhere in the apartment.

She went back to the kitchen and looked down at the note, ran her fingers over Ciaran's words, the paper smooth and cool to the touch. A weight settled on her shoulders as she thought back to the last time they had been to the same restaurant, how her earlier confidence had so easily come crashing down.

Sure, she'd gotten her money back, but the look on his face, somewhere between confusion and hopefulness, before she'd fled—yes, fled—for the exit, was an expression she wouldn't soon forget, and didn't want to see ever again. For some odd reason, she wanted to find a way to make it up to him.

This meeting should have ended a half-hour ago, Ciaran grumbled to himself as he slipped his hand under the desk to check his watch. The dozen or so people sitting around the wide, oval table had been there for over an hour and still, there was no end in sight. If he didn't leave soon, there was no way he was going to get home in time to get changed and make it to the restaurant.

From his left, Cliff leaned over the armrest of his chair and murmured, "got somewhere to be?" His voice was too low for Old Man Dougherty to hear, but he was too busy holding court to notice anyway. A quick glance around the table told him that most had already tuned out his running commentary on recently completed projects, describing what went well, with a heavy emphasis on what didn't.

Some, like Ciaran were already getting antsy about the time, with trains to catch, kids to get home to, dinner to get on the table. Or at least ordered.

His throat suddenly felt a little warm and his collar too tight, but he resisted the urge to loosen his tie in front of the whole office. "Sort of."

Cliff smirked but sat back.

Inwardly, Ciaran sighed. Cliff wouldn't say anything else now or risk drawing attention, but he'd have something to say for sure the next time they were alone.

The tone of Dougherty's voice changed. "Oh, and Gray?"

Ciaran sat up a little straighter, "Sir?"

"I heard from the people over at Johnson & Weicott this morning. They're pleased with the plan for their new building." The corner of his mouth quirked up briefly, the closest Dougherty ever got to a smile. "Well done."

"T-Thank you, sir." he replied, but Dougherty had already moved on to another associate down the table.

Cliff turned his head, eyes wide and flashed him a thumbs up.

Ciaran nodded his head and suppressed a smile. Old Man Dougherty was impressed... Little did anyone in the room know, but that was the biggest compliment of his career, short as it was. He tapped his fist on the armrest once, the only outward sign of celebration, and checked his watch again.

He was less successful in suppressing the wince this time, but just as he started to think of a good enough excuse to duck out of the meeting early, Dougherty made his last comment and thanked the room for their "willingness to stay behind a few extra minutes."

"Try thirty-five," Cliff muttered out of the corner of his mouth as he piled up his laptop and note pad and tucked them into the crook of his arm.

Ciaran did smile then, partly at Cliff being as annoyed as everyone else, and partly in relief. He gathered his belongings, made his goodbyes, and tried not to run as he left the conference room.

He was none too gentle as he stuffed his laptop and other essentials into his backpack and made for the elevator. He wasn't the only one waiting impatiently for the elevator to arrive. A half dozen of his fellow coworkers, most of which were married with young children, looked about as harried as his sister and brother-in-law had the few times he'd visited them and their then-newborn twins.

Once outside, he ran for the uptown train two blocks down and forced his way into a car already crowded with a couple hundred fellow commuters. The air inside was fetid. Sticky with too many smells that he'd rather not think about identifying. Thankfully, he only had to go a few stops before he was elbowing his way out onto the platform and racing up the stairs.

He made it to his apartment in record time, but he still only had about forty minutes to make it to the restaurant. He dumped everything onto the small table in the kitchen, and headed for the shower, leaving a trail of discarded clothes in his wake. Within ten minutes, he was showered, dressed, and heading back down the stairs.

His heart was beating a mile a minute and it didn't start to slow until he was seated in a yellow cab heading back uptown toward the restaurant.

"Hot date?" The cabbie asked wryly.

Ciaran looked up from fixing his hair in the reflection of the security glass and caught the driver's eye. He was a middle-aged man wearing a white baseball cap with a blue pin stripe and an interlocking NY logo. Ciaran hadn't yet learned which baseball team went with which logo.

"Something like that,"

The cabbie chuckled. "Amicetto is a nice place," he said, his accent an odd mix of Italian and New Yorker. "Took the missus there for dinner for our thirtieth wedding anniversary last year. The vongole with the lemon risotto is—" he kissed his fingertips and pulled his hand back, splaying his fingers, a classic Italian gesture.

"I have no idea what that is, mate, but I'll keep an eye out for it."

It was the cabbie's turn to be confused, though many people did when he spoke. He just scrunched up his nose and nodded in agreement, though it was clear the guy had no idea what Ciaran had just said. The last few blocks were spent in silence and, soon enough, the cab rolled to a stop in front of the restaurant and the valet pulled open the door. He paid quickly with a tap of his phone and tipped generously.

"Good evening, sir," the valet said as he closed the door of the cab and tapped twice on its roof.

Ciaran smiled and gave him a nod as he strode up the black mats to the front door, his long legs eating up the distance in seconds. Inside, Ciaran felt, as he always did, like he had stepped back in time. Little had changed inside since the days of Sinatra, but it was well preserved, with a few modern tweaks that made it even more upscale. A heavy red curtain, tied back to one side with a thick gold cord, served as a divider between the bar area just inside the front door and the dining room. In the colder months, the curtain could be closed to keep the restaurant warm and cozy, safe from the cold air being let in every time the door opened.

He wove through the crowd of people clustered around the small tables near the bar and stopped at the host stand perched in the shadow of the curtain. The woman behind the gleaming white podium looked up at his approach and smiled, her teeth very white in the dim lighting. She tossed her long brown curls behind one shoulder and stood up a little straighter. She was very pretty, and the movement made her not-inconsiderable breasts more prominent, but he didn't feel even a flicker of interest and kept his attention on her face as she asked, "Can I help you, sir?"

"Gray, party of 2. I think I'm a few minutes late." He informed her, leaning forward to be heard over the din at the bar. "Is my companion here yet?"

"Gray..." She looked down at her reservation book, and made a mark next to an entry. "No, it looks like you're the first one here, but I can take you to the table if you would like."

His stomach sank. "Aye, that's fine."

She gathered up menus and ducked past the curtain.

Ciaran couldn't help a sigh of relief as she led him past the table they'd been given last time, toward the back where the din from the bar didn't quite reach. She placed the menus on the table and didn't wait for him to sit down before returning to her station. He took the seat facing the doorway and took out his phone, making sure that it was on silent, even though it was unlikely to go off given that pesky little problem of her not having his number.

He'd thought of sharing his when he sent the flowers, but held off, wanting to stretch their game out a little longer by waiting to see if she'd come. *It might already be Game Over*, he thought as he checked his watch. It was already quarter past seven, and Jal hadn't arrived yet. He wouldn't blame her if she stood him up, it had been short notice after all, but he couldn't help feeling a little flicker of hope that she would come.

The waiter approached and he ordered a Macallan 15 neat. He felt like celebrating the win at work at least a little bit. And if Jal didn't end up showing? Well, then he'd at least have a first-class glass of Scotch to wash away the disappointment.

Eight

"I think he's here."

Jal continued to study the bubbles that clung to the sides of her vodka soda before rising to the surface to burst. She idly ran her finger up and down through the condensation on the glass. "You've said that the last five times the door opened."

Lexi flapped a hand at her almost-bored sounding tone that was taking all of her willpower to employ. If only Lexi knew how much she wanted to gulp down her drink, but the butterfly mosh pit in her stomach wouldn't allow it.

"This time, I really think it's him." There was amusement in her voice, and something else that brought Jal's head up high enough to look in the mirror behind the bar, but there was no one walking the carpet along the back wall. Her gaze moved to her own reflection and she pushed the glass away.

She didn't feel like herself with her hair all twisted up and her makeup done. The weight of all that hair on the back of her head made her neck work overtime. And her makeup, which shaped and sculpted every contour of her face, was pure perfection, more than ready for a night on the town. Or a date.

Lexi turned back to her and waggled her eyebrows. "Tall, brown hair kind of falling in his eyes, and man, he's got some shoulders filling out that trench coat. If that's not your guy, Jal, then I swear to God, I'm going to go talk to him myself."

"He's not 'my guy,'" Jal protested following Lexi's line of sight as she turned back. Sure enough, over by the host station, a man was shrugging out of a tan trench coat. He had an athletic build with a narrow waist that widened to shoulders that were barely contained by a dark suit. She couldn't see his face, and it was hard enough keeping her eyes on him through the milling crowd around the bar, but there was something familiar about the cock of his head. "But yeah, that could be him."

Jal turned her chair back to the bar and scooped up her drink. Bubbles tickled her throat as she swallowed half of the glass in one go.

"Oh my God, the hostess just stuck her chest out at him!"

She choked, the vodka burning into her sinuses. She nearly dropped the glass in her haste to set it aside, then curled over the bar, coughing.

Lexi reached across the bar and took a cocktail napkin from the pile and handed it over while patting her sharply on the back until Jal shook her off. Jal dabbed carefully around her mouth and cleared the moisture from the corner of her eyes, careful not to ruin Lexi's handiwork that had taken most of the afternoon to complete.

Jal was almost ashamed how excited Lexi had gotten when

she'd finally managed to tear her attention away from the peonies, and the ruffled shadows they cast on the table, to pick up the phone and ask to meet her for a drink.

Lexi had come barreling through the door half an hour later, arms laden with clothes, a travel case full of makeup the size of her head balanced precariously on top. She'd practically shoved Jal in the shower and then fussed over her for the rest of the afternoon, teasing and tweezing and crafting the perfect winged eyeline all the while peppering her with questions.

Jal had just squirmed in the chair and dodged every one of them with a quiet smile or a sarcastic comment until she'd finally just poked her friend playfully in the side and said, "Can't we just go out for once and have a nice time?"

Lexi had stopped with the questions, but she'd studied every muscle twitch and fidget as they finished getting ready, and on the ride over to the restaurant.

It wasn't until they'd settled into the two remaining seats at the bar and ordered their second round of drinks that Jal had told her the real reason she had fresh flowers on the table and why she'd chosen this particular restaurant. Only a stern warning look and a threat to go home right then and there had kept Lexi from making a scene, but still she'd bounced in her chair with excitement.

Her friend had a date with the hot Scottish guy.

The same friend whose blue eyes were suddenly wide and full of mischief. "Your guy didn't even look at her boobs." she assured her, nudging Jal in the side with her elbow. "He just handed over his coat and followed her into the restaurant. Gotta give him points for that at least."

Jal just huffed a soft laugh through her nose and took a

cautious sip of her drink. It still burned as it went down, but it kindled a little fire in her stomach, which was suddenly much too empty.

Lexi picked up her phone from the bar and glanced at the time. "You better get in there. It's already a quarter past."

The last sip of her drink sent the heat up to her cheeks and summoned the butterflies back into place. She reached into her purse for cash, but Lexi was already placing a black credit card on the bar. "I got this."

Normally, Jal would have protested, even when she knew Lexi could afford it with her cushy PR job, but she had bigger things to worry about tonight.

"Can I help you?"

Jal suppressed the urge to roll her eyes when the hostess didn't even look up from her reservation list. She certainly wasn't puffing out her chest.

"I think the reservation is under Gray," Jal replied and cursed inwardly at the nerves in her voice. "Party of two."

The brunette finally looked up and though her dark eyes were aloof, the quick flare of her nostrils betrayed her surprise. She coldly studied Jal, from the elegant twist of her hair, to the tips of her simple maroon heels. The black dress in between hugged her curves, the draped neckline pooling between her breasts. Lexi had loaned her a gold necklace with a large emerald-cut diamond that sat perfectly in the hollow of her throat. Matching diamonds swung gently from her ears throwing sparks of light into the shadows where the hostess stood.

Who the hell does she think she *is?* Jal shook off the weight of her scrutiny, and stood up to her full height, which even in three-inch heels wasn't all that impressive, and leveled her with an impassive gaze instead of the sneer that was waiting just beneath the surface.

When the woman didn't move, she raised one perfectly sculpted black eyebrow and held out her coat with both arms. She could have left it with Lexi, who promised to wait at the bar until Elena got out of work and could join her, but the look on the hostess's face was priceless.

The woman exhaled loudly through her nose and took the coat, draping it over her arm with a deliberate care that said she'd rather stuff it into a ball as she stalked silently into the restaurant.

They quickly passed the table from last week, now occupied by an elderly couple sharing a plate of tiramisu between them. The woman's back faced Jal, but the warmth in the man's eyes as he looked at his wife made Jal's heart ache. She hadn't had a man look at her like that in a very long time. Hell, she'd *never* had a man look at her like that.

Then the hostess rounded a large table full of businessmen with loosened ties who were one drink away from a scene and turned for a cluster of tables in a small alcove and Ciaran came into view. They were most of the way to the table before he looked up from the menu to see her approach. The lines between his eyebrows immediately disappeared, and his eyes locked with hers, a flame flickering to life in those whisky-colored depths.

A heartbeat stretched into an eternity as he rose to his

feet. He was dressed in a smart waistcoat and tie in shades of blue; his jacket draped over the back of the chair. He'd tidied his hair, but a thick lock had escaped to fall across his forehead almost into his eyes. She doubted that any change to his clothing or hair could ever completely erase the air of mystery about him, laced with just a hint of scoundrel.

Jal stopped a few steps from the table. Her heart pounded in her rib cage so hard it practically bounced the necklace away from her skin.

The hostess cleared her throat with more force than was necessary, but it was enough to break their eye contact. Jal looked over at her, wondering just how long they had been staring at each other. Long enough, she decided, when the woman gestured stiffly to the empty seat across from Ciaran and walked away.

They reached for the chair at the same time, but Ciaran got there first. Jal let out a nervous laugh and stepped to the side so he could pull it smoothly back from the table. Having never experienced such chivalrous behavior, she copied what she had seen in the movies and stepped into the space he'd created, then slowly sat, praying that Ciaran pushed the chair in so she didn't sprawl out in a heap on the floor. Not that she wouldn't have blamed him if he did.

But the chair caught her perfectly, and she could see why women in the movies had always been so impressed. The backs of his fingers left goosebumps behind as they trailed across her skin when he released the chair.

"Should I be worried about my coat?" Jal asked, eyes on the retreating hostess.

Ciaran chuckled as he settled back in his chair, the sound

wrapped around her neck as if it were his hand reaching to cup the back of her head. She leaned into the sensation without realizing that she was doing it, but his eyes tracked her every motion as he placed his napkin back in his lap and wrapped his hand around a glass, obscuring the finger of honey-amber liquid.

A waiter in a white button-down shirt and a long red apron approached and asked for her drink order.

Jal's fingers toyed with the diamond around her neck while she examined the drinks menu and selected a mid-price Italian red that sounded good, something about dark cherries and sweet herbs. The waiter nodded and walked away with assurances he'd be back momentarily to take their orders.

But still Ciaran didn't move. "What?" she asked cautiously, resisting the urge to shift in her seat under his gaze, and not from the anger she'd expected to feel. She picked up the menu hoping that a physical barrier would help. It didn't.

"You're quite the mystery, Jal Morrow."

She lowered the menu and glowered at him as he took a sip from the glass that had been poised at his lips and slowly set it back on the table.

"Look who's talking," she quipped, the indignation flooding back in a rush. "You haven't told me anything about yourself either. All I know is that you broke into my apartment, robbed me of most of my stash, then traipsed in a few hours later under the guise of exchanging wallets to hide the fact that you'd been there in the first place."

There was a flash of white teeth. "Was that all in one breath?"

She huffed. "I've got to hand it to you. It took balls to do what you did."

"Thank you," he said, then his lips twisted. "I think."

"It wasn't a compliment, merely an observation." She told him. "I still want to know why."

He studied her for another moment and said nothing. Before he could speak, the waiter returned with her wine and took their orders. She ordered a shrimp pasta with a lemon-garlic sauce praying she didn't ruin Lexi's dress. Ciaran studied the offerings closely, his eyes searching carefully until he finally requested something unintelligibly Italian that started with a "V" and handed the menus over.

He waited until the waiter was out of earshot before he began. "I don't want you to take this the wrong way, but after I moved to town, I started going to this one coffee shop on the edge of Washington Square Park and people-watched from the terrace. One day, I saw this person bundled up in a loose jacket with a floppy knitted cap on their head slowly weaving through the crowd. They'd walk just close enough to an unguarded jacket pocket, a bag left that bit too open under an arm, and then, continue on their way." He swirled the small amount of what she presumed was whisky around in the glass. "To the untrained eye, nothing suspicious was even happening."

To her horror, she felt her cheeks warm and tried to cover it with a sip of wine. Not the best idea given her head was already feeling a little too light from the earlier drinks on an empty stomach. As if sensing her need, the waiter appeared with a basket of sliced focaccia and a small plate of olive oil, grated cheese, and ground herbs. Jal reached for it eagerly. The bread was still warm, and the dip had a crunchy sweetness of dried roasted garlic that burst on her tongue.

"Imagine my surprise when I was crossing the park on my way back to work and felt those talented fingers slip into *my* pocket."

Jal's voice was strained when she said, "and then, you suddenly changed direction and down we went."

Ciaran nodded. "I knew you had my wallet, but didn't say anything as we righted ourselves." He scratched at the back of his neck and the light flashed off his silver watchband. "I don't know what came over me, but I think a part of me just wanted to see if I could still pull it off, see whether you'd catch me if I tried to pick your pocket in return." He reached for a slice of bread and tore off a piece to dunk in the oil mixture. In response to her raised eyebrow he added, "I used to be a thief."

"Used to be?"

"Aye, back in Scotland," he replied, speaking carefully as he chewed. "And I was pretty good at it, too. Broke into pretty much any building anyone ever asked me to, and quite a few that no one expected me to. Private houses, offices. I did a museum once and cannily too I might add."

The soft smile that played on his lips as he reminisced brought the butterflies back full force. She didn't know what "cannily" meant but she also didn't doubt that he was capable of it.

"I hid in a storage closet, waited for the middle of the night when the museum was empty and stole about a thousand Pound worth of Jacobite-era coins. I still have a few."

He seemed genuinely impressed with himself. She didn't know what had prompted this sudden reminiscence, but she found herself leaning forward to listen. Curious as she was of what he might say, she couldn't help a little doubt showing on her face.

Seeing it, he added, "granted, the security wasnae too tight, but I had to chase off a guard dog or two before I made it out."

"Congratulations." She replied dryly, and raised her wine in salute. "Why did you stop?"

He sighed and, for a moment, she didn't think that he was going to answer. But then he shrugged. "I got caught."

NINE

Her eyebrows rose, and his shoulders started to creep toward his ears when she opened her mouth. Before she could ask any questions that would dredge those memories back up, their waiter chose that moment to appear with their meals stacked up one arm. That impeccable timing alone had earned him a big tip.

Ciaran thought for sure that Jal could see the heat working up his neck and resisted the urge to run a finger under his collar. But she just accepted her plate with a smile and went straight for her silverware and dug in. Though maybe dug in was too strong a term. She used her knife and fork properly, unlike most Americans, taking small bites, using her knife to push the food firmly onto her fork and lifting each bite carefully to her ruby red lips as if afraid that she'd ruin her dress.

By Christ, that dress.

If she'd meant for the blue dress she'd worn the first time

to "kick his ass," as she had so delightfully put it, the sight of her sweeping in like shadow and smoke , her hair tamed into an elegant twist revealing a long neck encircled by a glittering diamond, had punched him in the gut, hit him over the head, and almost brought him to his knees. Last time, she had dressed up only because he'd told her to, and she had ultimately used it to her own advantage.

Part of him couldn't help wondering what she intended this time. Could he be crazy enough to think that she'd dressed up because she'd wanted to look nice for him? The twinge in his balls gave him that answer. At least they remembered how she had treated him, the rest of him better follow suit soon.

Ciaran looked down at his own plate and his eyebrows rose. He had only given the menu a quick glance to confirm the cabbie's recommendation was still on the menu, and his rudimentary Italian telling him it was some kind of seafood. Sure enough, a dozen small clams were scattered across a plate of light-yellow risotto, A white wine sauce heavy on the parsley and chopped garlic pooled around each tasty pearl in their shell.

He plucked a clam from its shell and popped it in his mouth where it seemed to melt away, leaving a hint of garlic behind. The first bite of risotto left a burst of lemon on his tongue in an almost effervescent way. That cabbie had been spot on with the recommendation.

The waiter returned halfway through dinner to check on them and refresh their drinks. The silence stretched endlessly between them, punctuated only by the clink of silverware on plates, a bubble of quiet in an otherwise noisy dining room. It wasn't very long before their plates held only a smear of sauce and empty shells.

Just as the waiter started clearing their plates, there was a buzz of a phone. He reached for his jacket draped over the chairback as Jal reached into the clutch purse in her lap. She raised her phone to signal that it was hers and started typing furiously, one corner of her mouth quirked up in amusement at whatever she was reading.

"Do you need to be somewhere?"

Jal glanced up and smiled. "My friends are waiting on me to join them." But she didn't make any move to leave.

Ciaran leaned back in his chair and covered an irrational wave of relief with a sip of whisky.

Her phone buzzed again, and she laughed out loud at whatever was on screen.

The sound went straight to his gut.

She covered her mouth with her hand, an adorable flush coming to her cheeks when the party at the table beside them glanced their way. She typed out a rapid response and tucked the phone away again. "Sorry about that," she said as she reached for her half-empty glass of wine. She caught his eye over the rim of the glass, her eyes still twinkling.

He made an inquiring noise in his throat and raised an eyebrow.

Her smile turned coy. "Woman of mystery, remember?"

"Fair enough," Ciaran replied with a chuckle. "You'll have to tell me about whatever it was sometime."

The noise she made in response could have been an agreement or non-committal. Their eyes met and held, and it was like an electric current passed through his body, stealing his words.

"Do you want dessert or another drink?" The waiter appeared just as his hand started inching across the table towards hers. He jerked it back and the sensation fizzled out. This man was either a savior or the worst wingman ever.

She picked up her glass, looked down at the sip remaining and cocked an eyebrow at him. For a moment, he couldn't move or think. Their first time here, she couldn't get out of there fast enough, and now she was leaving it up to him?

He glanced at his watch, though the fact that it was almost ten p.m. had about as much influence on him as two a.m. or noon would. "Fancy the tiramisu?"

Jal tipped her head slightly as she considered, the movement landed a second punch low in the gut, and then nodded.

"Two tiramisu, please." Ciaran said, suppressing the urge to shift in his chair.

"One is fine," Jal responded quickly. "Two spoons."

The waiter glanced at Ciaran for confirmation, and he nodded woodenly.

The waiter tucked his little handheld machine back in the pocket of his apron and went to check on other tables. Jal pushed her seat back and tucked her purse under her arm. "While we're waiting, I'm just going to go to the restroom." They rose together and the corners of her mouth tightened, but it was gone so quickly he wasn't sure if it was a cautious grimace or a small smile. "I'll be right back."

A cool breeze from an air vent in the hallway landed on her heated skin and made her shiver as she pushed open the heavy restroom door. The room inside was also cool, a welcome reprieve from the fugue of the dining room and its occupants. She used the facilities and studied her reflection as she washed her hands. Her hair and makeup were still in very good shape, and there was a bit of color in her cheeks.

She dried her hands on a towel and then ran it under the water and had just pressed it to the side of her neck when the bathroom door opened, and Elena and Lexi clattered in, clutching each other and giggling.

Elena had clearly gone home after work because she was wearing a cobalt blue top that bared a narrow strip of tan skin above a fitted white skirt. Her hair was down in a cascade of cinnamon streaked ringlets and her makeup highlighted her already stunning features. The clothes were modest by her usual clubbing standards, but her sky-high heels were plenty scandalous for an upscale restaurant like Amicetto.

She released Lexi when she caught sight of Jal and let out an appreciative whistle. "My, my, my... I haven't seen you this dolled up in *years*." She perched a hip on the countertop next to Jal and threw a wink over her shoulder. "Nice work, Lex."

Lexi ducked her chin, pink coloring her cheeks.

She turned back to Jal and waggled her eyebrows. "And how's your date going with the 'thieving asshole?'" she asked. "That *is* what you called him, right?"

"I never called him that." Jal protested half-heartedly, though the name had certainly crossed her mind a time or two.

"Oh yeah, you're right," she waved a hand in the air between them, then pointed to herself. "That was me."

Lexi chuckled as she stepped up to the mirror and smoothed the line of her bottom lip.

"Well?" Elena asked, impatiently.

Jal dabbed at her neck but the towel wasn't as cool as it had been. Or her skin was suddenly warmer. "It's going just fine," Jal replied. She didn't bother correcting her friends that this dinner was more of an apology than anything. Probably because she would be lying if she did.

"If you need an SOS call, just let me know."

Jal laughed. "Lexi tried that already," she replied and nudged her with a hip. "Fluffy McFluffpants is wandering the hall? Really? I don't even have a cat let alone one with such a ridiculous name."

Elena threw back her head and howled with laughter. "You didn't tell me that's what you said!"

Lexi made eye contact with Jal in the mirror and grinned as she continued to adjust the pins in her hair.

Jal tossed the towel in the basket and headed for the door. "I need to get back before Ciaran thinks I've run off again." Her tone had been light but, inside, there was a part of her that regretted letting panic take over the first time. Despite the reason they had come together, she found that she was eager to get back to the table.

"We'll be at the bar if you need us."

Jal took a step out into the small hallway and froze. She put a hand to her lips and realized why her cheeks felt so tight. There was a broad smile on her face.

The door closed behind her and almost immediately opened again. Elena drew up short so she didn't crash into her, but Lexi was not paying as close attention and sent Elena stumbling into her after all. They clutched at each other, wobbling on their heels until Jal caught her balance with a hand on the wall, and Elena was able to steady herself. The smile still plastered on her face, if anything, was even bigger.

Elena released her and glanced meaningfully over her shoulder at Lexi. The two women exchanged a quick, pleased look before Elena shooed Jal back into the restaurant. Clutching each other and laughing, her friends headed back to the bar area.

Jal laughed with them, even as the sound of theirs faded into the din clustered around the bar. She quickly checked her hair and dress before returning to their table. Ciaran rose to his feet as she approached and helped her back into her chair.

She hoped he didn't notice her descent into the chair was a little less graceful this time. There was no mistaking that the trail of his fingers across the back of her shoulders was a little more deliberate, and the heat they left in their wake radiated up her neck and made her head spin more than it already was. Just how many drinks had she had?

In the middle of the table sat a beautiful stack of lady fingers covered in coffee and cream and dusted with cocoa powder. Her wine had been refilled, as had his whisky, but beside both was now also a glass of water. There was a small dessert plate and a spoon in front of each of them.

Ciaran caught her examining the table. He picked up his spoon and waved it at the dessert perfection between them. "I wasn't sure how you wanted to share, so I had him bring plates too."

His thoughtfulness was putting deep pits in the wall of ice she'd tried to construct between them. The warmth in his eyes had rivulets of water dripping down the sides. For a long moment, it was too much and she debated putting the spoon down and saying goodnight.

Ciaran lifted an eyebrow and indicated with his spoon that she should go first.

Her cheeks warmed as she moved the empty plate to the side and dug in. She put a hand under the spoon until the dessert was safely in her mouth and her eyes fluttered closed. The explosion of vanilla, coffee, and chocolate on her tongue was like nothing she'd ever tasted. She opened her eyes to find Ciaran's fixed on her mouth, his own slightly open.

"What?" she asked, and self-consciously brushed a finger along her lips. "Do I have something on my face?"

Ciaran blinked and cleared his throat. "No, lass." he replied. He took a bite himself and nodded. "But I do understand your reaction. This really is very good. Rivals any I've ever had in Italy."

That got her attention. "You've been to Italy?"

He nodded and took another bite. "Aye, a few times," he replied around a mouthful of cream. "My family went every few summers as a child. It's a bit like someone going from here to say, the Caribbean on your summer hols. I mean, holidays." He waved the spoon in the air as he swallowed. "I mean, vacation."

Jal chuckled. "I've only ever lived in two states, and never set foot outside either of them." She replied and took a moment to savor another mouthful of bliss on a plate. "Italy is more than just a plane ride away, for someone like me."

Her throat tightened and her eyes threatened to grow wide as soon as the words left her mouth.

He froze, his hand hovering halfway back to his mouth. "What do you mean for someone like you?"

Her heart started to race, and she thought for a long moment on what to say when clearly her sub-conscious wanted to say anything. Everything. And that was not entirely a good thing. Answering his question could invite more questions about her upbringing that were, at minimum, embarrassing. "Just that I've never really had much money or opportunity. I didn't become what I am because I was bored."

Ciaran studied her face for a moment and must have been satisfied enough with her response to resume eating. But still, his eyebrows drew down thoughtfully as he chewed.

Needing to change the subject, she set her fork down and took a small sip of her wine. "Tell me more about Italy."

He smiled and launched into a recounting of summers spent with his parents, siblings, and their extended family who all rented a Tuscan villa or a townhouse in Venice. The antics he and his cousins would get up to, especially once they hit their teenage years.

Jal just sat back and listened, and tried not to look relieved that he didn't press the subject of her upbringing.

Soon, the dessert was gone, and so were their drinks, and the waiter returned one more time, his ordering device in hand. He turned to Ciaran and showed him the screen which must have had a summary of their bill. Ciaran reached for his pocket as she opened her purse and flicked through the cash she had brought.

"What do I owe—"

"No worries, lass. I have it." Ciaran pulled a credit card from his wallet and tapped it to the reader.

Jal sat back, her hand still in her purse. "No, really."

"Yes, really." Ciaran replied as he signed the bill. "It's the least I can do."

The waiter glanced at the screen and his eyes widened briefly before he smiled. He thanked them profusely, bid them a good evening, and walked away.

Jal stared at Ciaran for a long moment as he rose and shrugged into his jacket. "Wait here a moment. I'll go get our coats."

She nodded and watched over her shoulder as he walked to the host stand. He passed out of view, but in her mind, she saw the woman who had clearly been flirting with him earlier—and who even more clearly blamed Jal for his lack of interest in return—look up from her precious guest list and greet him again with her ample cleavage. The thought was almost enough to bring her out of her chair and stalk over there. But that was something a jealous person would do. And she wasn't jealous. Not at all.

She swallowed and glanced over her shoulder again to find him turning the corner, her coat draped over his arm. He stepped up to the table and held down a hand to her. "You'll be happy to know that your coat is unharmed."

Jal snapped her clutch closed with an audible click and pushed back her chair. She looked at his hand for a moment before placing her hand in his. The room swayed only slightly when she stood, or maybe that was her.

Ciaran tightened his grip and the room settled.

"Should I be checking the pockets for death threats? Or maybe her phone number to pass on to you?"

Ciaran winced slightly and then chuckled. "She tried it with my coat."

"Oh, she did, did she?"

"I declined." He replied and flashed a wide smile as he held out her coat for her to slide her arms into the sleeves. He settled it onto her shoulders and smoothed the lapel at her neck. A tingle went down her spine as his fingers brushed across her skin.

Jal turned and he held out an arm to her. She hesitated for only a second before tucking her hand in the crook of his elbow. Who knew such a gentleman could live under that veneer of scoundrel?

They walked together toward the bar area. Jal couldn't help glancing at the hostess as they passed, and one corner of her mouth turned up at the stony expression she received in return. She suppressed the urge to flutter her fingers in a farewell wave.

As they passed through the bar area, Jal caught sight of her friends sitting where she and Lexi had started their night. Lexi was talking to someone whose back was to her, but going by the dark blond hair brushing his collar and the broad shoulders, not to mention the small crowd of women vying for his attention, it was her friend Maks. New York City's newest Most Eligible Bachelor.

Elena, on the other hand, was sitting facing the restaurant with her legs crossed at the knee, one arm draped over the back of the chair, the other holding a martini glass. Her eyes locked on them immediately, studying Ciaran, and her hand tucked into his arm. She nodded approvingly and subtly raised her glass.

Jal was smiling at her apparent approval as Ciaran pushed open the door.

He made a curious noise in his throat as she brushed by

him and out into the cool night, the din of a hundred people packed into a small space was replaced with the quieter but ever-present drone of traffic that was the soundtrack to New York City.

"Do you need a ride?"

She shook her head. "I'll get a cab."

For a moment, they stood at the curb, still arm-in-arm, and just looked at each other. A charge seemed to build up in the air between them the longer it went on, but she found herself unable to look away even to look up at the sky to see if that charge could be blamed on weather moving in. She knew it wasn't that at all.

"Would I be asking too much if I asked to see you again?" His question was hesitant, and it pulled at something deep in her chest. Despite her better judgement, she was attracted to him, and more than a little tipsy, a dangerous combination.

She steeled herself and tried to harden her gaze, to dredge up any of the bravado she'd so easily turned on him before. "It was a lovely dinner, Ciaran, but I came here as a way to make up for you having stolen from me. But now that it's over, I don't think we have a reason to."

He smiled, a wicked gleam dawning in his eyes as if her words were a challenge. Before she could react, he gently slid his arm along her back and bent down at a careful, deliberate pace that even in her state, she knew was meant to allow her the chance to pull away. There was nothing she could do about her heart kicking into a gallop and the muscles under his hand tensing up. She also didn't pull away.

He paused an inch away, his eyes still locked on hers. Her lips parted with an almost inaudible gasp for breath, but before their lips could touch, he drifted past and pressed a kiss high on her cheekbone. Still, her eyes drifted closed at the softness of his lips, but they were already drifting to the shell of her ear.

His breath tickled the sensitive skin there and she couldn't help clenching her thighs against the rush of heat that shot to her core. "Now, now. We both ken that is a lie."

Her eyes flew open as he eased back so their faces were only inches apart again. Gently, he slid his arm away and finally took a step back.

The cool air of the spring night flooded the space between them. She swallowed, and drew her coat tightly around her.

He signaled the valet who walked up to the curb and raised a hand. As if he had some magic most ordinary citizens of Manhattan lacked, a yellow cab immediately turned off its light and came to a stop perfectly centered on the rubber carpet. The valet opened the door and waited.

Ciaran drifted over to it and stopped with one leg halfway into the car, one hand braced on the doorframe. "You should go back inside, Jal. " He winked then climbed inside. "I'm sure your friends will want to hear all about it."

Ten

A few days later, Jal woke up feeling almost… rested. The dreams were still there, but they weren't nearly as bad. The hallway still stretched endlessly into the distance, but it had been just an endless corridor of locked rooms. There had still been an element of frantic searching, going from one door to the next with her heart beating almost out of her chest.

But, there had been none of the usual sounds, no bright light or total darkness, no obstacles or attacks, just urgent wandering that hadn't nearly been as jarring to wake up from as other dreams.

After a cup of tea, and a few pages of a novel Lexi had given her, she'd fallen right back to sleep and awoken with more energy and focus than she'd had in a long while, enough so that she got dressed and bundled up in her loose tan jacket almost on auto pilot.

She was halfway to the stairs before she remembered her hat and had to double back but, once it was safely in her pocket, she emerged onto the street and hoped that luck was with her.

It struck her as she descended the stairs to the subway that it had been weeks since she had last hit the streets, not since her first run-in with Ciaran. She didn't *need* to steal, not really, between the money Ciaran had given her, which she suspected was overly generous, and the occasional nights bussing tables and washing dishes at Lima y Sazón, the restaurant Elena's father owned, she had more than enough.

But nothing beat the rush of adrenaline, and the boost of confidence that came with it. As she rode the subway downtown, her fingers tingled as she surveyed her fellow passengers, looking for any easy marks. Most were clutching cups of coffee and were far too alert, but there...

The train stopped at 8th Street and the doors rattled open. Jal stepped out onto the platform close on the heels of a woman in a smart business suit who had so many bags stacked up on one shoulder that her purse was practically sideways.

It took little more than a gentle tap for her wallet to fall out into her hands. Jal slid it into her pocket and made a show of straightening the stack. The woman turned her head at the more substantial contact and edged away.

Jal gave her a reassuring smile as she passed, murmuring, "I'm sorry, just wanted to adjust your purse so nothing fell out." The woman's expression became thankful, though Jal didn't wait around to see if the woman stopped to check her belongings.

She was two blocks away before she took the wallet out of her pocket and examined it. From her ID, Ms. Sally Benevento was well into her fifth decade of life, lived in the East Village, and going by her credit cards, she liked her shopping, and not at the stores Jal could afford.

Thankfully, she was also a fan of cash. It was one of the reasons that Jal tended to target those of a certain age, especially those that dressed like they had money to flaunt, even if they did take the subway.

The wad of cash, easily several hundred dollars' worth, disappeared into one pocket, while she dug out a soft cloth from the other to carefully wipe away any fingerprints she might have left on the pricy, designer leather.

Up ahead, near the corner of Washington Square Park stood a big, blue mailbox waiting to gobble up letters and packages to send on their way. Jal gave the wallet a last once-over inside and out with the cloth and tossed the wallet inside. It hit the bottom with a soft thump. The post office would help the wallet make its way home, just a little lighter.

Jal dusted off her hands and walked into the park, stopping in the shadow of the white marble archway to get her bearings. There was a good mix of commuters using the park as a cut through, along with a steady stream of teachers and hoodie-wearing students making their way to different parts of the university that nearly surrounded the green space.

On her left through the trees was a playground full of shrieking children and crying toddlers. A handful of untended strollers dotted the area around the fence, but there was no more vigilant a group than moms of young children at a public park.

No, she was better off with the college professors and the tourists, who were already out and about with their phones glued to their hands, and their attention on everything but their purses or back pockets.

Within minutes, she had her first target, and a minute later, the man's wallet was in her pocket instead. She moved on, matching pace with a tourist with a large, unzipped tote bag. Her heart was already pounding in her ears as she casually scratched an eyebrow and reached for the wallet she could just see poking out behind the woman's elbow.

"Hiya, Jal."

Her heart stuttered in her chest at the cheerful, slightly too loud greeting from behind her. She yanked her hand back and whirled, her coat billowing around her like a cape, so the weight of the professor's wallet whacked into her thigh.

Ciaran stood by the fountain, a few yards away. He had on the same tan overcoat, one side drawn behind the hand casually tucked in the pocket of his tailored dress pants, the other balanced a cardboard tray of takeout cups. His hair was neatly styled but that lock in the front still lifted in the breeze. "What brings you to this side of the city?"

As if he didn't already know.

She stormed over to him, stopping a few feet away. He rocked back on his heels slightly, but she couldn't tell if he was forcing himself not to take a step back or if he was bringing his cocky self to work today. If it was the latter, he had chosen the wrong place to stand, especially this time of year.

"If you are following me, Ciaran, I hope you're ready to get wet."

Ciaran glanced over his shoulder at the rippling water, which looked cold despite the sunlight throwing rainbows in the mist. He turned back to her with a raised eyebrow. "Going to throw me in, are you?"

Not a bad idea... Jal took another step forward, close enough for the tails of their coats to brush together and raised her hands toward his chest, tensing her legs. He merely looked down at her and grinned.

She instantly regretted taking that step. With him this close, her bravado began to falter, and he just stood there and watched it crumble. Her heart stuttered at the memory of his breath caressing the shell of her ear, the slide of his hand along her back. And then, he'd called her bluff.

She blinked and the park came back into focus. Her hands were still poised to push him, all she had to do was lean forward and put a little weight into it and he'd tumble into the frigid water. She raised her eyes to find him still smiling, but it had shifted to something a little more curious, which meant she'd zoned out longer than she thought.

One side of his mouth quirked up even further and she balled up her fists and shoved them into her pockets to keep from touching him. Her moment of surprise was gone, and she refused to give him the satisfaction.

Besides, there wasn't any other reason for her to touch him. Nope, nothing else. And certainly not something insane like wrapping her hand around his tie and pulling him closer.

He looked away and pointed with the tray of cups. "Now, if I remember right, we met just over there."

Her nose filled with an odd, but not unpleasant, blend of fragrant steam as she turned her head toward the heavily wooded path that led to the north-west corner of the park. She turned back and found he had drawn close enough that she wouldn't be able to get her hands up between them let alone push him in.

Jal took a step back before she could catch herself. At this angle, his shoulders seemed to blot out the mid-morning sunshine that filtered through the trees and cast his face with dramatic shadows. The corner of his mouth twitched at something in her expression.

"What are you doing here, anyway?" she demanded.

"I volunteered to go on a morning coffee run." He removed his hand from his pocket and pointed at the name on the coffee cups then threw a thumb over his shoulder to the matching logo on a striped awning across the park. "No better coffee in the city, I've found."

"Ah yes, your favorite stalking spot."

"People watching, lass. People watching." He corrected, as he wiggled a cup out of the tray and held it out to her.

She looked down at the cup like it was a grenade and removing it from the tray had pulled the pin. All she had to do was take it and bam!

The other corner of his mouth turned up. "Call it a consolation prize," he moved the cup closer to her. "I *am* sorry for interrupting you just now."

"No, you're not," she protested.

He grinned and offered a third time. She tried to hold on to her stony expression, but the smirk, and that damn twinkle in his eye, like the glimmer of light on ice in whisky... What was he doing to her?

She yanked a hand out of her pocket and took the cup. "Happy?" She asked, then wrapped both hands around the warm paper sleeve, only then realizing how chilled her fingers really were. "Now, tell me what you want."

"So hostile," he teased.

Jal growled but it sounded half-hearted even to her ears. She tried to move past him, but he stepped into her path. She took another step, and he matched it. Another step and he followed, and again, dancing around each other. Finally, she stamped her foot and glared at him.

He met her gaze, and there was an energy vibrating through him so strongly she could feel it pressing on her skin. "You know, I'm actually glad I ran into you," he said. "Given that I *still* don't have your phone number..."

He gave her a pointed look, but she refused to take the bait. Better he got to whatever he needed to say, and then she could decide if she wanted to give it to him.

"So... I have a match coming up and I was hoping that maybe you would want to come and watch."

"Match?"

"Football."

It took a second for her mind to supply the translation. In a flash, she was back in a different park, leaning against a tree, watching him turn tricks with a soccer ball that no normal human could manage. A rush of heat went through her at the memory, and though he'd been fully clothed, the speed and agility he'd demonstrated hinted at a high level of body awareness and muscle cont—

She cleared her throat and cut that thought off, though the flash in Ciaran's eyes was evidence enough that her thoughts had been clear on her face. That, or he'd caught her eyes boring into him like she could see the muscles, and other things, through his clothes.

"My firm is in the finals of some Corporate Challenge tournament. It's this Saturday back at the pitch you saw us playing on in Central Park."

Jal tried to cross her arms, but she made a mess of it with the cup in her hand. After a moment twisting her arms this way and that, she managed the pose with the cup balanced on her elbow, but the struggle had only served to lighten the mood rather than convey the annoyance she had intended.

She made every effort to keep the daggers shooting from her eyes, but the half-smile she couldn't completely suppress ruined the effect. "Tell me, why exactly should I attend this game?"

He blinked at her for a moment, then said as if it should be obvious, "To bring me luck."

She wanted to laugh, she really did, but the earnestness in his voice seemed to tug at a string he'd somehow wrapped around her heart. "I don't know, Ciaran..."

Some of that wicked gleam that had come into his eyes outside the restaurant returned and Jal's heart kicked up a notch. The distance between them seemed to melt away.

It took a moment for her to realize that she had been the one to move. It was as if that string had drawn her to him simply through the intoxicating color of his eyes. When she did stop, it would take only a deep breath, one she found herself too breathless to take, and their bodies would touch.

"I tell ye what, lass," he said, his voice descending into that deep burr, "I'll stay on my side of the pitch and you can stay on the other. I won't come over unless you give me the all clear." The long column of his throat seemed to ripple as he swallowed. His face moved an inch closer to her. "I would like you there, though."

"Again, why?" To her dismay, her voice was disconcertingly breathless.

"Just having you there will give me more confidence, knowing that someone's supporting me," Ciaran murmured, and claimed another inch.

Jal's chuckle cut off when his chest brushed her arm. His eyes flared and he closed the distance until she could feel his breath on her lips. "I'd rather 'support' the other team to see if you get pounded."

There was an amused puff of air on her lips. "Ouch," he murmured. "That stings, Jal."

"You deserve it." Why was he so close? More importantly, why wasn't she moving away?

His hand slid inside her jacket and onto her waist, but his touch was light, only the barest bit of pressure to suggest she should move closer.

"Be that as it may," he said and his lips brushed across hers, the contact so brief she wasn't entirely sure if she had imagined it or not. "Please... don't make me beg."

She could just picture it... him down on his knees, his hands reaching for her, sliding around her thighs, her bare thighs—wait, why were her thighs bare?—his mouth moving clos— "I can't, Ciaran." she insisted against his lips. "I'm.... busy."

His breath left her skin as he pulled back enough to look at her.

Her eyes lifted to his, and it was like she was poured back into her body all at once. Her arms were still crossed, the cup still balanced on her arm, and he was everywhere. His hand on her waist, his face inches from hers, the tails of his coat wrapping around her legs in the breeze.

She took a step back and for the second time, the cold air rushed into the gap between them with a fury that made her shiver.

"You're busy?" he asked curiously, and for a moment she was sure that he would keep pressing, but he didn't. He released a breath that ended on a bemused chuckle. "Aye, that's fine, but if you change your mind, it's this Saturday, four o'clock."

She uncrossed her arms, the one not holding the untouched cup falling almost limply to her side. "I'm sorry that I can't be there." She found herself saying.

"Me, too." he replied and his tone made her wonder which rejection had affected him more. But then he straightened his shoulders and winked. Gesturing to the cup he said, "better drink up, I bet you'll like it."

His sleeve brushed hers as he walked away, and though she whirled around to watch him go, he didn't look back.

Once he was gone, heading in the direction of his offices at the foot of Fifth Avenue, she gently pried back the cover over the drinking hole and took a cautious sip though the liquid was fully drinkable by this point.

The sweetened tea slid down her throat and rekindled some of the warmth that had left her when she'd broken contact with him. Her eyes popped wide, and she stared again in the direction he'd taken as if she could see through trees and buildings to find him.

She took another sip and checked the cup for a label. Matcha green tea with honey and cinnamon. How could he know? She wondered, even as she greedily drank down the rest of the cup. The man was full of surprises.

Eleven

Ciaran was glad to have a few blocks' walk to get back to the office. He was also glad for the loose coat that, when buttoned securely, did a lot to cover the fact that his tailored dress pants had become unconscionably tight.

He was half-hard, and it had only taken the barest brush of his lips over hers. And now that he had a taste of her, he found that it wasn't nearly enough. He'd expected as much, but the force with which it had hit him in the—well, it was a surprise even so.

While waiting with the crowd for the light to change, he resisted the urge to adjust his pants, though it took almost all his restraint not to. He hadn't looked back as he walked away from her, but now he did, only to find that the trees obscured his view.

Yet somehow, he knew that she was still somewhere in the park, perhaps still looking this way. Was he really selfish enough to hope that she was?

He hadn't been following her, not exactly. But if volunteering to do the morning coffee run meant he crossed the park to his favorite place not once, but twice each day, possibly putting her in his path, then so be it. The fact that he had gotten to Thursday, with her not yet having made an appearance, hadn't exactly been concerning, but it had been disappointing.

But then, there she was, leaning against the arch in that baggy coat, and his heart had beat faster than any drum at the summer tattoo in Edinburgh.

He still couldn't put a finger on what it was that drew him in. She was a feisty wee thing to be sure, but much as he enjoyed their verbal sparring, it was more than that.

She challenged him, and the fire that came into her eyes when she tossed his teasing right back hinted at a passion she might have in other activities.

His cock twitched at the images *that* thought conjured and he suppressed a groan. Unsuccessfully, if the look, and the cautious step to the side the woman next to him took, said anything.

He rolled his eyes, and finally gave in, using the cover afforded by the press of bodies around him to adjust the situation. Christ, it was going to be a long day.

The light changed and Ciaran was swept out into the crosswalk, leaving the park, and Jal behind. For now.

By the time he walked through the glass doors of Doherty, Jameson & Russo, Ciaran had done his best to put the encounter behind him until he was away from prying eyes. Starting with the pair belonging to his boss slash friend, who was making a beeline from his office.

"It's about time," Cliff groused.

Ciaran turned the tray so Cliff could wiggle his drink free. He remained bent over the tray, turning the other two cups to study the labels, noting the slot that hadn't been empty before today. "Did you get the green tea today? Julia asked me to grab it for her."

Ciaran fought the urge to wince. He'd guessed at Jal's favorite drink going by the tight cluster of mostly-empty ingredients in her kitchen cabinet and until today, it had apparently made its way onto his other boss's desk. "Em, no, sorry. I forgot today."

But Cliff only shrugged and followed Ciaran to his desk. He perched a hip on the corner as Ciaran placed the remaining coffee on a far corner of his neighbor's desk.

Catherine thanked him with a wave of her hand, her attention focused on the building plan she was carefully stenciling with a fine-tipped pen and a complicated-looking sliding contraption.

Ciaran shrugged off his coat and threw it over the back of his desk chair, sending it spinning. He wrangled it into position, before dropping down heavily, while telling the chair to do something highly improbable with itself in Gaelic.

"What did you just say?" Cliff took a sip of his coffee and scrunched up his face. "Damn it, Ciaran, it's cold."

Ciaran took a sip of his own Americano. It was colder than he'd like, but still drinkable. Worth it.

"You don't want me to translate." he replied, tapping keys to wake his computer up for the day. "My Nan, God rest her soul, is probably spinning in her grave just because I thought that. She'd say that she didn't teach me the Gaelic just so I could curse like a sailor on the Minch."

"Was *that* even English?"

Ciaran scowled, not in the mood for their usual back and forth.

Cliff, to his credit, paid attention to the look on his face for once. "Say, what happened that's got you so upset? Could it be the reason that green tea went missing?"

Or maybe not... The way he waggled his eyebrows set Ciaran's teeth on edge and he gave his boss a look that would have melted glass, or gotten him fired if he'd turned it on anyone other than Cliff.

Cliff got to his feet and held up his hands. "Sorry I asked."

Ciaran didn't respond as he opened his email app and picked up a pencil, idly spinning it between his fingers as he waited.

"She shoot you down again?"

The pencil snapped and Ciaran dropped the pieces onto the desk. There was no use denying it. "What would you have me do, Cliff? Cosh her over the head and drag her back to my cave?"

"Whatever works," Cliff said with an exaggerated wink.

"Honestly, I don't understand how Tricia puts up with you." Ciaran replied. He fell silent while he ordered his thoughts, but before he could speak, Cliff's voice barged in.

"I wouldn't make the effort if I were you." He sipped his coffee, winced, and dropped the cup in the trash at the side of Ciaran's desk.

It was Ciaran's turn to grimace, thanking whatever gods there were that the lid hadn't come loose and ruined hours of Catherine's hard work.

Still, she'd jumped, looked at the trash, and then accusingly up at Cliff. But their boss was oblivious as he continued leering at Ciaran. "I saw you guys in the park the other day, remember? She left you hanging and sashayed away."

He rose to his feet and did what Ciaran supposed was his best impression of Jal's "stroll down the catwalk," as he'd called it. Behind him, Catherine almost managed to suppress a snort of laughter.

"I repeat again, how are you still married?" He asked with a wry smile and turned to his computer. "Was there any other reason you came over here other than to bust my b—" he glanced at Catherine's profile and the smirk she had going around the pencil clamped between her teeth. "Uh, chops."

"What?"

"You didn't just come over here for fun."

Cliff thought for a moment, it looked like it hurt. "Oh yeah, now I remember. We ran your sketches for the country club upstate by the board this morning." He leaned in closer. "Good job, you're two for two with Old Man Dougherty. He likes all the glass looking out over the course. Though you didn't hear that from me, if you know that I mean."

"Aye Cliff, I know what ye mean." He said with a smile. "Cheers."

Cliff left without another word, and Ciaran tucked in to his desk and started organizing his emails.

There was a clatter over by Catherine's desk and he looked up to see that she had tossed down her pen and was looking right at him. He lifted an eyebrow.

"Cliff is an idiot." She leaned forward and braced her forearms on her knees. Her almond eyes blinked soulfully at him. "All the best women are the ones you have to work hard for. If you think she's worth the effort, don't give up. She'll come around."

"Aye, Cath, you're right." Ciaran said with a smile. "The best ones are."

Saturday came and Ciaran met his co-workers at the pitch. They were facing an accounting firm called Morrison, Inc. in the final. There had been several weeks of preliminary matches leading up to today, and despite it not truly being a proper match on a proper pitch, just a bunch of corporate execs thinking themselves football players, Ciaran was just happy to be playing.

Cliche as it was, he had lived and breathed football when he was younger, an interest that his father greatly encouraged. At fourteen, he had been assistant captain on a traveling team that went to international tournaments and won repeatedly.

At fifteen, he was scouted by one of the largest teams in Glasgow and would have played for them as soon as he left school. Unfortunately for Ciaran, they wore the wrong colors for his father's liking. His son would wear green and white and call Paradise his home, or he wouldn't play. The day Ciaran played for the enemy was the day Adrian Gray saluted the cross of St. George and called himself English.

Ciaran himself didn't much care who he played for as long as he got to play, but his father made enough of a fuss that the scouts moved on, and when the ones from Ibrox his father swore would come calling next never did, Ciaran ignored his mother's pleas to go to university and left home after graduation. It was then that he had turned to stealing to keep a shabby apartment in one of Glasgow's worst neighborhoods, though he hadn't really been a stranger to it before.

As his skills, and by extension, his reputation grew, he started to get bigger jobs stealing important documents from offices, personal possessions from private residences, and antiques from low-security museums like the coins that he had told Jal about. Annie went away to Edinburgh University, but Ciaran would hop a train and visit her, never the other way around.

He should have seen the signs by the end of her second year that they wouldn't last. As long as his "work" stayed in Glasgow, she was happy, but he couldn't bring it to Edinburgh with him, or even talk about it.

Then there was that last job, where he'd gotten careless and tripped a silent alarm in an antique store and the police had been outside waiting for him. It was then, while sitting in a holding cell, that he sat down and really considered his life and its direction, or lack thereof.

Miraculously, he got off with a generous amount of community service, thanks to Annie's family solicitor, but he was done with that life. And Annie was done with him. Turned out that she had met some Eton boy at a party, and she'd rather ride around in his Bentley than take the bus with an unemployed scoundrel like Ciaran.

It was the wake-up call that he needed. So, once his community service was completed, Ciaran took out a portfolio of student loans, secretly cosigned by his mother with whom he had stayed in contact, and moved to America.

He graduated with degrees in Architectural Design and

Engineering four years later. He stayed away from anything that would remind him of his former life, and that included football. It had been six years since he had last set foot in Scotland and, after only the occasional kick-around by himself, the past few weeks playing for some semblance of a team felt pretty good.

"Earth to Scotty."

Cliff's voice snapped him back to the present.

"Hmm?" He asked, realizing that he had been frozen bent over his foot with the laces of his half-tied boot—cleat, as the Americans said— in his hand.

His boss clapped him on the shoulder with enough force to nearly topple him off the folding chair. "You want to beam the rest of us up to whatever world you were just on or are you going to join us here?"

Ciaran groaned inwardly. "Not a good idea." He tied a knot with more force than needed and stood. "What time is it?"

Cliff glanced at his Rolex. "Three-thirty." He replied, and dramatically scanned the crowd ringing the chalked sideline. "Your girl here yet?"

Ciaran's eyes scanned the crowd. "No, but if its only half-three, she still has time." *Fuck, he got me again.* He snatched the captain's armband from Cliff's hand. "And she's not 'my girl.'"

Cliff snickered and gestured to where most of the other players were joking around the Gatorade cooler. All but Mike, who was on the sidelines hitting on his girlfriend, and Cameron, currently lying on his back on a bench, one arm draped over his eyes against the sun. "All yours, Cap."

Ciaran walked over and gave the underside of the bench a swift kick.

Cameron bolted upright and rubbed his eyes.

Ciaran turned his attention to the ginger with his arm around the curvaceous hips of his girl. "Oi, Mike, get your ragged arse over here."

Mike got a good luck kiss and reluctantly joined the group. He brushed his red hair from his eyes and glowered at Ciaran who had to remind himself that Mike had been voluntold to play anyway.

"Okay, lads, we need to do some warming up." He told his team as he fit the armband in place. He hadn't worn one in a long time, and its grip around his bicep was oddly uplifting, even if it was just a beer-fest Corporate Challenge. "I don't want anyone getting a stitch in the middle of the first half."

The others grumbled, but Ciaran returned their glares with only icy authority, and they got to stretching. As he jogged in place, Ciaran scanned the crowd for Jal without seeing her, and even after the match had started, there was no tell-tale flag of black curls on the sidelines or in the stands that had been wheeled over from the baseball fields for the event.

He forced himself to keep his mind on the game, Morrison's guys were better than he had expected. The score stayed close at five goals to three in favor of Dougherty, Jamison & Russo at the halftime whistle.

Mike and Cameron were panting and sat down gratefully on the bench. Kurt passed around the water bottles, which they drained almost immediately. The day had turned sunny, and unseasonably warm.

"Good first half, lads," he told them. The goals had been

scored by four different players, with Ciaran himself netting two. Kurt was the odd one out, but there was still time. "Just another twenty minutes. Then you can hit the pub."

Mike whooped, anxious to get back to his girlfriend and get a drink in his hand. Ciaran was supposed to join them, and a good dram of Glenfiddich wouldn't go to waste if it was put in front of him, but that all depended on whether or not Jal showed her face.

Halftime ended and still she wasn't there. It started out in their favor as he buried the ball in the net five minutes in off a surprisingly nimble steal from Cliff, but then the ball was quickly taken back the other way and put past Jake, the goalkeeper. Another goal a few moments later gave DJ&R only a slight 6-5 lead.

Steaming back the other way, Ciaran had just accepted Kurt's pass to shoot it into the open side of the net when a slide tackle caught him at a bad angle and sent him tumbling to the ground.

He rolled a few times and clutched his lower leg, pain radiating from where the spikes from his opponent's boot had connected.

The bastard who'd tripped him blocked out the sun as he loomed over him with a smug smile peeking through his long Viking beard. He'd been hounding Ciaran all afternoon and had four of Morrison's goals. "Not so flashy now, are you?"

"Get tae fuck away from me, mate." Ciaran snarled and grabbed the hand Cameron held down, leaning into his support as he hobbled to the bench.

As he sat to examine his leg, he glanced one more time at the crowd and caught sight of a familiar curtain of black hair flying out as she pivoted away from the field. In the barest glimpse he got of her face, he could have sworn that her pale skin had gone bone white.

So, she came after all.

TWELVE

Jal hadn't been planning on going to the game at all, but their encounter in the park lingered on her mind. After he left, she only managed another wallet and a fancy portable cell phone charger before calling it a day.

Elena called the next morning looking for help at the restaurant, but there was no way she could be around her friend without the subject of Ciaran coming up. In true Elena fashion, she'd be full of questions that Jal didn't have answers to yet. Questions like what, if anything, Jal wanted from him, or whether she was ready for another relationship after Andy. So, even though the guilt tore at her, she'd told her friend no, and hit up Times Square instead, returning home after a few hours with a sizeable addition to the envelope full of cash in her bedroom ductwork.

Saturday morning dawned dark and dreary with rain lashing the windows at the head of her bed. She rolled over and lifted a corner of the curtain. *Mother Nature to the rescue!* she thought and snuggled back under the covers. Sure, the pros played in the rain, but a bunch of corporate wannabes? The rain would certainly wash them away, right?

She spent the morning at the laundromat downstairs, with her nose buried in a tattered old romance novel from the shelf near the vending machines so her stuff didn't get tossed in some random place when she didn't move it the second the machine stopped. Every time she looked up, her mood soured, as the view through the fogged-up glass showed the weather improving. By the time she stepped back outside, the bag of folded clothes perched on her shoulder, the sun was playing hide and seek with the thinning clouds and the city street sparkled, the way it only did after a good rain.

She went back upstairs and tried to busy herself cleaning, but her attention kept drifting to the clock, to the sunny skies outside. Three o'clock came and she found herself bouncing all over the apartment, never really finishing a task. There had been a necklace on the coffee table when she'd cleaned it off, which had led to rearranging her jewelry box and the cluttered dresser. Moving the accumulated makeup on her dresser back to the bathroom turned into reorganizing the linen closet for an hour.

All along, her stomach churned as her mind continually ran through the list of tasks still to be done, never truly forgetting the one thing she was avoiding. Running out of cleaner had led to her going back to the kitchen for more only to start scrubbing the kitchen counter instead, pausing half-way through when she realized that she'd already cleaned the counter, at least three times.

"This is asinine," she grumbled and pitched the scrub into

the sink. She blew a lock of hair out of her eyes and checked the clock again. Three-thirty. Her anxiety spiked wondering what Ciaran could be thinking right now. Why did she care so much about what he thought, anyway?

She retrieved the scrubber from the sink with a hand that trembled slightly and went to scrub the stove only to find it too had already been cleaned. Her chest grew tight, making her heart flutter and each breath feel like it was through a straw. She braced her hands on the edge of the stove and tried to stop thinking. When her thoughts continued to spiral, she stumbled to the cabinet next to the sink. Her shaking fingers sent several bottles clattering down before she managed to grasp the right yellow bottle and start in on the cap.

It finally popped loose and a handful of small orange pills spilled out over the counter. They scattered further as she made a grab for one, any one, but they either skittered away into the sink or onto the floor until she finally managed to trap one and raise it to her mouth. Something stopped her hand, and she looked down at the pill clutched between her fingers.

"Get... a grip," she wheezed and dropped the pill back to the counter with a clatter, she folded her arms over the countertop, concentrated on a single drop of splattered sauce that she had missed on the wall, and focused on just breathing. In for a count of four, hold for four, out for four, repeat.

A dozen cycles later, the straw was gone and her chest was no longer crushing her heart. She took one more deep breath for good measure, blew it out on a sigh and scooped the pills that hadn't fallen into the sink back into their bottle and went to grab her coat.

The game was nearly over by the time Jal got there, but she found an open space in a corner of the field and hadn't been there for more than a minute when some burly blond meathead with a Viking fetish swept Ciaran's feet out from under him. As if in slow motion, he sprawled to the grass and rolled to a stop clutching his calf. His shirt and face were streaked with mud and grass, and her heart may have skipped a beat or two, or ten.

She turned away, unable to watch him writhing on the ground, his yelp of pain seeming to echo in her ears. She lifted her hand to her mouth as she pivoted back. When his friends helped him to his feet and supported him over to the bench, she was surprised when her eyes prickled with tears.

Maybe she should have taken that pill after all if her emotions were this close to the surface. She had to remind herself that there had been a time not that long ago when she would have gotten pleasure from him being literally knocked down a peg. What changed?

The crowd around her started to shift during the break in play. She soon lost her line of sight, just as a petite female paramedic was staggering over from the medical tent under the weight of a gigantic black duffle full of supplies.

Jal found herself drawn through the crowd until she was able to tuck into the shadows beside a set of bleachers near the bench where she could observe him but not be easily seen. The paramedic handed him a cloth for his face and hands, and got him to put his leg on the bench so she could clean a wound on his calf and wind a bandage around it.

Once she finished, Ciaran stood and bounced on his leg. He flashed a wide smile in response to the paramedic's question and raised his hand, signaling to the referee that he wanted to return to the field. The wave of relief nearly buckled her knees. She scrabbled for a grip on the bleacher railing to keep her feet.

The redheaded player came off and sank gratefully down onto the bench, even though he'd only been out on the field for a few minutes. Ciaran didn't miss a beat, intercepting a pass and was off like a shot and Jal found her knees going weak for a completely different reason.

Ciaran passed the ball, looped around the Viking wannabe, who cursed and lost his footing trying to catch up, and accepted the return pass almost without looking. Jal marveled at the awareness he had on the field, at his relaxed focus as if playing was as natural to him as walking down the street.

The dreamy smile playing on his lips had her transfixed. He played with the same intention to his movements that she was sure he did with everything else, dodging another defender and sending the ball soaring into the net. Moments later, the referee blew the whistle three times and judging by the celebrations, Ciaran's team had won.

The teams formed two lines for the end of game handshake, then the deputy mayor strode across the field and presented Ciaran with a trophy, a surprisingly fancy one for such an event. It had a cup on top of all things and years of names etched around the side. The crowd began to disperse, and she held her ground against the bleachers, letting the crowd pass by. She fiddled with the cuff of her sleeve as people brushed by her, momentarily obscuring her view of Ciaran and the rest of the players milling around the benches.

The sea of sweatshirts and light jackets eventually parted and, as it did, Ciaran looked up from tying his sneakers and met her eyes as if he had known exactly where she was. He smiled and she found herself giving him a wobbly smile in return. He gathered up his belongings and went to take a step in her direction, but paused with his foot comically in mid-air, one side of his mouth twitching at the warning tilt of her head. He lifted his eyebrow byway of asking her permission to cross.

She tapped her chin thoughtfully, and somehow managed to keep her face neutral while he stood there still as a stork, waiting. For a moment, she thought about seeing how long he could hold it up without falling, but she dismissed it, and nodded with all the grace of a queen granting a boon.

The smile that spread across his face had just enough of a wicked gleam that Jal's fingers started tingling from the adrenaline. The air between them crackled with energy the closer he got, as if the morning's thunderstorm was returning.

He stopped a few feet away, his duffel bag looped over one shoulder. "I didnae think you were comin'." His Scottish accent, usually so tightly controlled, came out in full force. She had a feeling that he forced his voice into a pattern more understandable to American ears. But she also wasn't complaining as the sound of it sent a shiver down her spine.

"My plans changed last minute." she replied, though the lie tasted bitter on her tongue.

"Glad I am, that they did."

Jal ducked her head to hide the heat that burned on her cheeks at the sincerity in his words. Her eyes fell on the bandage wrapped around his calf. "How does your leg feel?"

She felt, more than saw, him shrug. "It was touch-and-go there at first. I half expected the paramedic to pull a saw out of her bag and try to take it off."

Jal swatted his shoulder.

Ciaran laughed and adjusted the strap. "It doesn't pain me much now," he amended. "But it probably will do tomorrow."

"That's good." She winced. "Not that it'll hurt tomorrow, but that it doesn't hurt now."

He chuckled, and the rumble of it filled the air between them.

She mentally thumped her forehead with a fist, repeatedly, as if it would help unwind her tongue. On the outside, all she did was tug her sleeves down over her hands and twist the cuffs around and around her fingers. His gaze drifted down to her hands and she froze, then dropped them to her sides. *Don't start stubbing your toe in the dirt next,* she told herself. All the snarky words she normally had around him had dried up. "It looked like a bad fall."

"Aye, it was a cheap shot." Ciaran's voice was suddenly soft. "Jal, I—" He moved closer, and put a finger under her chin to bring her gaze to his.

His fingers were gentle as they slid across her skin to cup her cheek. A warmth seeped into her from his touch, and she leaned into it as if she could draw in more, though she was far from cold. It would only take a step, maybe two, and she would be in his arms, but her feet wouldn't move. She could only look up at him and watch what she could only describe as wonder flicker across his face.

"I'm a patient man, Jal," he said softly. "But even I have

limits. There's something here I think, between us, and I think we should see where it could go."

She opened her mouth to deny it, but that would be an even more bitter lie. Much as she hated to admit it, that thread between them had been growing stronger. Enough that the air almost crackled with energy any time he was near.

He closed some of the distance between them. "If you'll let me in."

Standing half in the shadows with her back to the bleachers, and him crowding her front, she should have felt caged in and maybe she did, but not in the way she'd expected. Instead of trying to get away before the lid on the bad memories started to lift, she forced her feet to remain rooted in place, and took a deep breath to keep her heart from racing too much. The brush of his thumb across her lips brought the butterflies back in her belly, each wingbeat sending a pulse of heat between her legs.

Slowly, she placed a hand on his chest, his heart beat a furious rhythm under her fingers. His skin was warm, his jersey still damp from the exertion of the game, but she didn't care. All the while, her eyes remained locked on his, the amber depths dark and curious.

He bent closer, but stopped a few inches away, waiting. For what? For her to give him a signal? For her to close the gap and take what she wanted from him?

The tip of her tongue darted out, wetting lips suddenly gone dry, and brushed against the pad of his thumb still poised at the corner of her mouth. His eyes darkened at the contact and that was all she needed. Her hand curled, taking a fistful of his shirt, and pulled. His hands burrowed into her hair, tipping her head back further as his lips captured hers.

A soft growl escaped as he opened his mouth to slide his tongue along the seam of her lips, begging her to open to him. She did, and he swept in, his tongue exploring hers, seeking to taste every part of her mouth.

He pulled back to change the angle of the kiss, but before he could capture her lips again, a voice called from across the field. "Hey Scotty, you forgot your— oops, sorry."

"Ignore him," Ciaran muttered against her lips, the words tickling her sensitive skin.

But the bubble that they had been existing in had popped. Jal settled back on her heels, giving them just enough distance, though she didn't ease her grip on his shirt, nor did he drop his arms. "This better be worth it," Ciaran grumbled.

Her answering chuckle had a good dose of self-consciousness mixed in. As his friend drew closer, she removed her hand and rubbed a knuckle over her lips, which still tingled from his kiss, and the stubble that covered his jaw.

His hands slid away, though the one in her hair only went as far as her shoulder. He turned her gently to face the man who approached wearing an open zippered sweatshirt over a matching red jersey stretched tight across his broad, burly chest. His graying brown hair was plastered to his temples with sweat.

"Aye, Cliff, what is it?" Ciaran demanded as the man drew even with them.

"You forgot your phone." Cliff held up the item in question. It had a navy-blue case and a cracked screen.

Ciaran frowned and pulled a phone from his shorts pocket, its intact screen lighting up with the movement to show a photo of two toddlers, lying head-to-head in a grassy field. He caught the direction of her gaze, and he gave her a look that said explanations would come later.

But the photo remained seared in her mind. Did he have kids?

He squinted at the phone in Cliff's hand. "That's Mike's phone, you numpty." Ciaran chastised. "Remember? The screen broke last autumn when you knocked it off the bar at Darcy's during that World Series game?"

Cliff looked down at the phone in his hand and huffed a not-entirely-believable laugh of surprise. "You know what? You're right."

Jal resisted the urge to hide her grin in the folds of Ciaran's sleeve and covered her mouth with her hand instead. Her movement seemed to draw his attention finally to her.

Cliff smiled then lifted an eyebrow at Ciaran. "Going to introduce us, Scotty?" There was a twinkle in his slate blue eyes that said he knew who she was, or at least suspected. She wondered what Ciaran might have said to the other man.

Beside her, Ciaran stiffened slightly, and she glanced up to see his jaw was tight enough that Jal was afraid his molars would crack. "Cliff, this is Jal," he replied gesturing between them. "Jal, this is Cliff, my boss."

Cliff's meaty hand engulfed hers as they shook briefly in greeting. "That's such a unique name, Jal," he said, pronouncing her name with an odd emphasis. "Short for anything?"

She shook her head. "Nope, just Jal."

Cliff smiled and stood there looking at them, at Ciaran's arm around her shoulders, while he twirled an unlit cigar around his fingers.

Ciaran cleared his throat, which seemed to jolt Cliff out of whatever thoughts he'd been lost in. "Well, I'll leave you to—" He snapped his fingers. "Wait, I remember what else I came over here for. The corporate challenge folks need you to sign out the trophy before it can leave the event."

"Can't you do it?" Ciaran asked, his eyes narrowed at his friend, likely smelling the same rat she was. His expression was telling his friend to "bugger off" if that was the right phrase. She was pretty sure she'd heard it in a movie somewhere.

The sparkle in his eyes as Cliff shook his head was the only confirmation that he saw the daggers being shot his way. Beyond his eyes, the man had one hell of a poker face. "Nope, they said only the captain could, or the person who filled out the initial registration paperwork, who is also you."

Ciaran dropped his head and sighed. He turned his chin to look at Jal through his eyelashes. "Can you wait a minute?"

"I should really get going," she replied. Not that she had anything else to do, but the weight of Ciaran's boss's scrutiny made her feel like little needles were pricking her everywhere at once.

Ciaran nodded as if he understood and his grip on her shoulder tightened slightly, but only for a moment, before he stepped back. He hitched the strap of his bag a little higher on his shoulder and pivoted toward his friend so the bag swung and hit Cliff squarely between the shoulders, forcing him to stumble.

"Oh sorry, Cliff." Ciaran said, but there was no remorse in his voice. Jal hid a chuckle behind her hand.

Ciaran clapped a hand on his boss's shoulder, further

disrupting the man's balance and steered him back toward the field, and the small group milling around a folding table, the sunlight glinting off the small bowl at the top of the trophy. He glanced back at Jal with an apologetic twist to his mouth, though his eyes held a wicked promise in their amber depths.

A shiver went through her that had nothing to do with the temperature and she smirked, lifting a hand to shoo them away with a flick of her wrist.

Ciaran grinned and turned away, wrapping a hand around the back of his friend's neck to direct him forward, though Jal was sure he was suppressing the urge to squeeze. Hard.

Jal didn't blame them as she watched them step up to the table. Ciaran glanced back, and when he noticed that she was still there, the smile that spread on his face was wide, showing lots of straight, white teeth.

She lifted her hand in a wave, then headed up the path that led in the direction of her apartment. She turned her head to glance back over her shoulder. Ciaran was still watching her, a pen in his hand, as she winked and strode away.

Thirteen

Jal slipped inside her apartment and leaned against the door. Her head fell back with a thump, the events in the park replaying on the inside of her eyelids. How Ciaran's eyes had gone from sunlit whisky to deepest amber just before his lips had captured hers. How the hand he'd woven into her hair had gently cupped the back of her head and kept her close, without gripping or restraining. And then, his boss had shown up.

A laugh bubbled out of her at the memory of Ciaran's face as he drew back from their kiss. She never thought that she would be amused when faced with someone who had murder in their eyes, but here she was laughing, truly laughing, at Ciaran's boss—or was it friend?—manufacturing an excuse to cock block him. No wonder Ciaran looked like he was ready to kill him.

She laughed again and her eyes sprung open. Her fingers flew to her mouth where a smile tugged at the corners. Her fingers slid down her chin to rest over a heart that was still beating a little too fast for how slowly she'd walked back to her apartment.

Part of her had hoped that Ciaran would catch up after he was done with his post-game duties. With each passing block, the hope had grown. *This* would be the corner where she would stop and turn, and there he'd be, coming toward her with that damned trophy clutched in one hand, the breeze carrying the sound of that voice of his calling her name.

But she'd made it all the way home, alone. Again.

The smile slid away, like she had slipped away from him. It had only been a few weeks since that first meeting in the Washington Square Park. It hit her then just how much had changed in such a short time. She had gone from nearly crushing his balls with her foot in a crowded restaurant over money to getting caught up in the earnestness in his eyes and dragging his mouth to hers by a handful of his shirt. She'd kissed him, and he'd taken it from there.

And boy, had he *kissed* her. The brief brush of their mouths, with her arms, and a paper cup pinned between them in the park had done nothing to prepare her for the rush that had gone through her when he'd really put some effort into it. Better than any spike of caffeine. Better than any pump of adrenaline after a successfully picked pocket.

And what had she done? At the first interruption, she'd proven that so little really had changed. She'd. Walked. Away.

Again.

Who in their right mind would walk away from someone like him, who could kiss like *that*?

You are some kind of idiot, she berated herself, tapping the back of her head on the door in frustration. She looked around then, taking in the size of the apartment, and it had never felt emptier.

Regret wrapped a fist around her heart when the vow he'd made, for that was what it was, came back to her, and she clapped her hands over her face with a groan. A patient man, he'd called himself, but a patient man with limits. Limits, she'd already begun to stretch, had perhaps even broken.

She dug her phone out of the pocket of her hoodie. The screen lit up as she raised it, revealing the strip of photobooth pictures taken shortly before her life had fallen apart. Back then, instead of avoiding their company, spending time with her friends had been a different kind of escape. She remembered that day, crammed on top of each other in that little photo booth, making faces and laughing like they hadn't a care in the world. But even in those pictures, the wide, brilliant smile on her face didn't truly brighten the shadows under her eyes.

Little had her friends known that Lexi's weight, made the bruises on her thighs ache, that Elena's arms were wrapped around ribs that screamed in protest, churning her stomach until she'd almost run for the bathroom. She hadn't told them about any of it, not until that last night, until it had almost been too late.

Jal shook off that thought before it could smash through her defenses and opened the contacts on her phone, and then laughed, bitterly this time, and shoved the phone back in her pocket.

She still didn't have his number.

She whirled around and wrestled with the door. Maybe,

if she left now, she could catch him at—shit, she didn't have his address either. Her mind whirled over options as one of the deadbolts stuck. Maybe he was still at the park? Maybe he lived somewhere near work or the park where they'd met? She didn't allow herself to think about where else he could be if he'd gone out with the team after the game as the door popped loose and she rushed through, only to collide with something solid.

Panic rose up at the big body that filled the doorway, standing still as a statue, hand poised to knock. Jal studied him, from a worn pair of black sneakers, up to the pair of tall socks that had been pushed down to his ankles. Up to the loose pair of black shorts, the red jersey stretched tight across a muscular chest and up further, her gaze locking with a pair of whisky eyes.

One corner of his perfect lips quirked high at the sight of her. "Sorry about Cliff, sometimes he likes to—"

Something far stronger overwhelmed the panic and she reached across the threshold, took a handful of his shirt, and pulled him inside. She had to be nearly half his weight, but Ciaran staggered inside, only to be pushed against the door where she'd been standing a moment before. His duffle ended up pinned awkwardly behind him, but she didn't care as she wound her arms around his neck and stood on her tiptoes to fuse her lips to his.

He grunted in surprise, but recovered quicky, wrapping his free arm around her waist and holding her firmly to his chest while his tongue speared into her mouth to slide along hers, and took his time exploring every inch.

She chased his tongue with hers, tasting mint, the kind

from a breath mint or chewing gum. The smell of him filled her nose. There was sweat, sure, but it wasn't unpleasant. It was mixed with something that was spice, citrus, and smoke all blended together to set her head spinning.

Then, it wasn't just her head that was spinning as he smoothly pivoted so it was her back that was against the door. The press of his body forced her thighs to split around his hips, the toes of her sneakers barely brushing the floor. He lifted his head, and Jal opened her eyes to find his only a few inches away, dark and intent on her.

"—Torture me." he finished, breathless. His chest rose and fell quickly as he tried to regain his breath.

Jal chuckled deep in her throat, then hissed a breath through her teeth as his hips bucked against her at the sound. Ciaran's eyes flared as if the motion had been involuntary but not unappreciated. She curled her lower lip in between her teeth and brushed a lock of hair off his forehead and out of his eyes.

Ciaran moved to wrap his other arm around her, but the trophy bounced off the door with a clang. They both looked down at the ridiculous thing that he was still holding and Ciaran scowled. Jal's chuckle was cut off when he leaned over to put the trophy down, which only brought his hips closer, an obvious hardness pressed into her inner thigh.

The trophy hit the floor with a thump and then a clatter. He tensed at the sound, muttered something that sounded like a curse, though it wasn't in English. His duffle hit the ground next, and then, his eyes came back to hers. She only had a second to draw in a breath before he was kissing her again. His now-free hand slid up her arm and brushed her hair behind her shoulder, then slid up to tangle in the strands.

He kissed her until she could hardly breathe, and then moved on, blazing a trail across her jaw and down her neck, the stubble on his cheek left her skin tingling in his wake. She moaned when he found a sensitive spot just behind her ear. Against her skin, his lips curled up before he latched on, nibbling and sucking in a way that sent a flood of heat straight to her core.

Despite the hard press of his body against her, his hands were gentle. The one pinned behind her was splayed across her lower back and inching lower, while the other buried in her hair, cupping the back of her head. His body vibrated beneath her fingers and at any other time she would have wondered why he was holding himself back, since no other man had bothered with the same restraint, but her mind had gone blessedly silent, and her body was on fire.

She tilted her head so she could gently drag his earlobe between her teeth. "You *can* touch me, you know."

He pulled back to stare into her eyes for a moment, as if considering. Then he smirked, and his hands slid down to palm the backs of her thighs, scooping her feet off the floor, encouraging her to wrap her legs around his hips. She did, and locked her ankles together on his lower back.

Jal let out a yelp and clutched his neck as he spun away from the door and carried her into the apartment. She half-expected him to set her down on the counter or the table, but he continued to the living room as if her weight was no concern. He bypassed the sofa under the windows, heading instead for the overstuffed chair that was Elena's favorite place to lounge when she visited. She uncrossed her ankles as he sat down in the chair, ending with her straddling his hips.

They both let out a soft groan as her core pressed fully against the hardness straining his shorts. He stroked one hand up her back into her hair and brought her mouth crashing back to his. This kiss wasn't as gentle. Lips, and tongue, and teeth sparred until both were breathing heavily. Of their own accord, Jal's hips started rocking against him, his cock sliding along her core through the thin layers of clothing between them.

His hands slipped beneath the waistband of her hoodie, and swept up her sides, bunching the fabric up in their wake. The brush of his thumbs across her peaked nipples where they pressed against the lace of her bra was enough to make her core throb. He broke the kiss only long enough to remove the garments and toss them aside, before returning to plunder her mouth again.

Her hands slid into his hair as she kissed him back with equal enthusiasm. A few moments, or hours later, she pushed his head down, urging him to shift his attention elsewhere. He obliged with hunger in his eyes and he leaned her back over his arm, trailing kisses down her collarbone, her chest, finally wrapping his mouth around one taught nipple. She gasped at the contact, but the lace of her bra was in the way of what she really wanted, his mouth on her bare flesh.

She reached behind her back for the clasp, but his hand was already there, releasing it with a flick. Jal shrugged the straps down her arms and tossed it aside.

Ciaran studied her for a moment, his breathing ragged, and she found that she wanted him to look. The feral gleam in his eyes made her feel as if she was something he wanted to devour completely. And she would happily let him.

"Christ, Jal," he said breathlessly. His hands lifted to cup her breasts, gently, reverently, before sweeping his thumbs across her nipples. With nothing between them, the contact was more electric, each flick sending another spark of heat down her spine. "You're beautiful."

Her heart was racing, and she felt every beat deep in her core. His mouth soon replaced one of his hands, his tongue circling the sensitive flesh for a moment before taking the tight nub between his teeth and nibbling gently.

Jal rocked her hips against him, seeking more friction, anything to ease the throbbing that was building as he used every part of his mouth to pay homage to her breasts. One of his hands slid down inside her leggings to grip her ass and press her even tighter against him as his hips pressed up to meet hers. He kissed his way over to her other breast and sucked her nipple into his mouth hard enough to make her cry out.

He let out a satisfied chuckle and did it again.

Jal dragged his mouth back to hers and made him pay for that little stunt with her tongue and teeth. His hand slid even lower on her ass, practically to her entrance, and held her to him for a particularly forceful thrust of his hips. Through her leggings and his shorts, she could clearly feel every hard, torturous inch of him sliding along her core, certain that the hand on her ass could feel just how turned on she was. But neither of them made a move to relocate or remove any other clothing, and she could feel a release already building.

Ciaran must have sensed it as well in the subtle tensing of her muscles, in her thighs gripping his hips just a little tighter, in the frantic thrusting against his cock. His hand left her ass and slid between them, his fingers easily finding and pressing firmly against her clit through the fabric of her leggings.

She whimpered against Ciaran's mouth at the first tingling flutters of impending release. The direct pressure of his fingers stroking her through the cloth, giving her just what she needed. Their tongues continued to war for another stroke, then two, three and her orgasm ripped through her hard and fast.

Jal pressed her forehead to Ciaran's as she shuddered over him, continuing to ride his hand through the waves of sensation coursing through every nerve. She threw back her head and cried out as a second, more powerful orgasm followed immediately behind, crashed into her from nowhere, barreling through her like a freight train charging up her spine shedding explosives that detonated in every blood vessel and nerve ending, leaving her shuddering uncontrollably in his lap.

He continued to stroke her until she stilled. When she finally opened her eyes, Ciaran stared at her, transfixed.

His throat bobbed as he swallowed. "Absolutely beautiful."

Fourteen

The second release caught them both off guard. One moment, she was shuddering over him, her forehead pressing hard to his and in the space of a heartbeat, a single flick, then two, of his fingers, she erupted.

She threw her head back with a cry that filled the room and nearly tipped him over the edge with her. Yet somehow, he managed to keep it together, despite her knees clenching around his hips. With her back bowed and head thrown back, her breasts thrust out, and that riot of heavy black curls lit by the sunlight streaming through the windows that dominated the opposite wall, she looked like an enraptured, fallen angel.

He continued to stroke her through the waves of her orgasm, until she slumped in his arms, and the frantic thrusting of her hips slowed to a gentle rock, then came to a stop. He swallowed hard, and though his mouth had gone dry, he murmured, "Absolutely beautiful."

At first, he wasn't sure if she'd heard him, but then, she

lowered her chin. Her cheeks were flushed, her eyes smoldering embers, all that remained of the fire that had erupted through her. Banked now, he guessed that it would take the slightest touch to send it blazing back to life.

His hands rested on the curve of her hips, and he found that he was content to watch her, though the weight of her, slight as it was, pressed on his still-hard cock. Yet his thoughts were not on his own pleasure. Not with that satisfaction glowing in her heavy-lidded eyes.

His thumbs stroked the soft skin of her abdomen as his breathing slowed. Her hands, which had been buried in his hair, started to move, stroking along the curve of his skull as if she enjoyed the feel of the strands sliding between her fingers.

No one had ever just played with his hair before, and the sensation of her fingers gliding along his scalp, massaging gently as she went was equal parts soothing and arousing. He drew in a deep breath and released it. He shifted beneath her to ease some of the pressure.

A corner of her mouth tipped up. She brushed the hair off his brow and bent to kiss him, slow and deep, her tongue stroking almost lazily along his. Breaking the kiss a moment later, she rolled her hips, the movement sinewy as a snake, bringing those beautiful breasts back within reach of his mouth.

He eased her back on his lap a bit, just enough so he didn't embarrass himself, not with her. He didn't want to stop, but his first time with her was not going to happen here on this chair.

"Take a moment, lass," he murmured against the skin of her breast. The nipple before him tightened from his breath, but he only just kept himself from taking the rosy nub into his mouth.

Her hands slid from his hair to rest on his shoulders. For a moment, she was still taking one long breath after another, and then she moved.

Ciaran glanced up just as her hands slid down his chest, and then she crawled off of his lap and sunk to the floor between his knees. Her hands darted under the hem of his shirt and slid up his abdomen like two firebrands, the muscles tightening under her touch. Without warning, she curled her fingers and raked her nails down across the ridge of muscle, surely leaving thin red lines in their wake. He hissed and his softening cock was instantly at full attention again.

Then her hand slid over the slick fabric of his shorts and the length that strained beneath. "*A dhia,*" he muttered as his head kicked back against the top of the chair, staring sightlessly at the ceiling as she stroked him until his breath grew ragged.

She let out a satisfied hum. "That's right," she cooed.

He tipped his head, his eyes focusing on her just as her fingertips dipped beneath the hem of his shorts and started easing them down.

"Is this what you want?" Her breath was warm on the skin of his abdomen as she eased the material away and his cock sprang free.

"Jal—" His voice choked off on a groan when she wrapped her fingers around him.

Her voice was a sultry purr as she said, "You know how much I like how hard you get."

Ciaran's eyes narrowed and he lifted his head. Something

about her words didn't sound quite right. He couldn't see much, just a curtain of black curls covering his stomach and hips, though he was all too aware of where her hand was and what it was doing.

She swept that curtain over one shoulder and looked up at him as her lips closed around the tip of his cock, a quiet moan vibrated down his length. His balls tightened even as warning bells started going off in his head, for though her expression said she was enjoying what she was doing to him, her eyes were distant and vacant. Gone was the satisfaction and fire he'd expected to see blazing there.

"Jal, what are you doing?"

She released him with a pop and smiled, but like the expression in her eyes, it was wrong. "Taking care of you, baby, like always."

Her words were like a bucket of ice water being poured over his head. Ciaran sat bolt upright, and pushed her hands away.

Jal followed, climbing half into his lap to reach for him again. He wrapped his hands around her slim shoulders and pressed her back. For another moment, her hands continued to grasp for his cock until he trapped them between his own. "Lass!" he cried, "lass... Jal, stop!"

"You don't want me to take care of you?" she asked. A deep crease formed in the middle of her forehead and though her body was coiled to spring at him, her expression eager, her eyes were still hollow.

He'd never seen anything like it before. Ciaran adjusted his grip on her hands, pinning her wrists to the arms of the chair. Then, like a gentle breeze on an ember, the light returned to her eyes. It was faint at first, as if there was some great weight that she had to push aside first. But once she did, awareness flared to life with enough force to yank her out of his grip and she landed on her ass on the floor.

She drew her knees up to her bare chest and wrapped her arms around them. Those emerald eyes, which had started to look on him as more than a persistent annoyance, were wide, but still unfocused.

After a few endless moments, she blinked and shook herself as if to shed the last of whatever hallucination she'd fallen into. It was the only explanation he could come up with.

Jal looked around the room as if trying to remember where she was until, finally, she turned her attention to him.

He'd righted the situation with his clothing by that point, but remained sitting back in the chair to keep from looming over her.

Her hair spread around her like a cloak, doing its best to cover her nakedness, though the points of her shoulders peeked through. She shivered once and he searched around for her sweatshirt, finding that it had only fallen to the floor at their feet when he'd cast it aside.

"Ciaran?" His name was a broken whisper.

He gave her what he hoped was a reassuring smile, though his heart was still beating a mile a minute, his brain frantically trying to figure out what had just happened. "Aye, lass. It's me."

She closed her eyes and dropped her forehead to her knees. Another tremor shook her shoulders.

Ciaran shifted to the front of the seat as quietly as he could, though she seemed to make herself smaller with every sound he made. Every twitch of her shoulders was a dagger to his heart. "Are you alright?"

Her chest heaved as if she had been running, each exhale ending in something like a whimper. Of shock, or surprise, or pain, he didn't know.

Whatever it was, his heart broke at the sound. He retrieved the sweatshirt from the floor and gently wrapped it around her, draping the sleeves over her shoulders. His fingers cupped her upper arms, sliding to her elbows, then back up, and down again.

Under his hands, the muscles of her arms were as rigid as steel. For a moment he thought about sliding off the chair and joining her on the floor, but thought better of it and instead, gave her the space to sort out whatever it was on her own.

Before he could decide what to do next, she was scrambling up off the floor and into his lap, sitting across it rather than straddling him. She threw her arms around his neck and curled up against his chest, her head fitting snuggly under his chin.

He couldn't help a small grunt of surprise, but his arms came automatically around her shoulders and knees and he held her close, settling back into the depths of the chair. Her shoulders began to shake in earnest, the cloth of his shirt directly over his heart grew damp with her tears.

Ciaran stroked her back in long, slow sweeps, over and over, murmuring quiet reassurances, the kind his Gran would murmur in his ear when he was little. It didn't matter what language he spoke them in, Jal was like a skittish horse, needing only calm, comforting words and a gentle hand.

Bit by bit, the tension left her body until she at last lay still in his arms. Hers had loosened their death grip on his neck, now only looped loosely around it.

"You don't have to say anything, lass." he said into the shell of her ear, his hand keeping up the rhythm of slow, soothing strokes. "Your truth is your own, and yours to tell or not. When you are ready, whenever that is, just know that your truth is safe with me."

She didn't speak or even move, though he heard her breath catch. She nodded, just once, and released a long sigh of what he hoped was relief.

Content to just hold her while she was receptive to it, Ciaran adjusted her on his lap and continued stroking her back. After a few moments, the weight on his chest had become even more boneless, her breathing had smoothed into a deep and even rhythm, and he knew she had fallen asleep. He dropped his head back against the cushion and closed his eyes.

Since they'd met, it had only ever been about the present or the future, never the past. But something had set her off, and he didn't know what it was, or how to help her. So, he just sat there, holding her as she slept until his legs began to go numb.

As gently and slowly as he could, he adjusted his grip and stood and headed for her bedroom, carefully skirting the coffee table and nudged the bedroom door open with one shoulder. Her room was as it had been when he'd climbed in through the window, the bed neatly made, but clothes strewn around on the floor each threatening to trip him up on his way to the bed.

He set her down, placing her head on the simple jade green pillow. The sweatshirt had fallen away when he'd stood, so he gently removed her shoes and drew the cream comforter up to her chin. He tucked the blankets in around her and smoothed the hair on her head one more time before pressing a kiss to her temple.

She burrowed a little deeper into the covers and murmured something unintelligible that he took as a thank you. He left her to sleep and went back to the living room. Its sunny cheerfulness was not at all dimmed by either the debauchery on that living room chair, or a reminder of whatever horror was lurking in her past that had followed.

He scrubbed a hand over his scalp as his eyes swept across the room, landing on his duffel bag near the door, the gold trophy fallen over beside it. He winced at the dent in the cup, visible even from a good distance away. Who knew how much *that* was going to cost to fix...

His eyes fell on the dining table, its hidden drawer invisible from this angle, and spotted her cell phone lying on the scarred wood. He crossed the room and picked it up. It was an older model, the casing scratched and a long crack stretched diagonally almost from corner to corner.

Ciaran pressed the button on the side and was greeted by the same strip of photos that was tucked into the frame of her dresser mirror. There was a small stack of notifications from a group chat, but he could only make out the name of one person. Elena. Only the first few words were visible, but it looked like an invitation of some kind. He tried tapping the top tile, but the phone first tried scanning his face, then when he looked nothing like the phone's owner, demanded a code.

Having no idea what it could possibly be, Ciaran set the phone aside with a sigh, and spotted a notepad and pen tucked under a vase of wilting peonies. He smiled, seeing the florist's card propped up at its base.

He picked up the pen and left her a note, repeating the words he'd murmured in her ear as she was drifting off to sleep. Her truth was indeed her own to tell, he just hoped that one day soon she would let someone, anyone, in. Preferably him.

He signed his name with his usual flourish and left the note on the table.

As he picked up the trophy and swung the duffel bag onto his shoulder, Ciaran put a hand on the doorknob and surveyed the apartment once more from dated kitchen to closed bedroom door. When his eyes fell on his note, he hurried back to the table and added his phone number to the bottom of the page.

With a small, hopeful smile on his lips, he set the pen down neatly beside the notepad and headed home.

Fifteen

The corridor stretched before her, disappearing into shadows in the distance. The space was devoid of color, the walls and floor a dull, lifeless beige. Long stretches of cracked and crumbling plaster on both sides were interrupted by closed doors, each set with a large pane of frosted glass. Harsh, cold light filtered down from above as if from an equally endless number of fluorescent fixtures, but the corridor didn't look like a place that would have active electricity.

In some places, chunks of plaster the size of a grown man had fallen away in piles that spread across the floor. The only furniture, a small table sitting outside each door. She ran a hand across the nearest one as she passed and dust coated her hand in a sticky film.

She made a noise of disgust and brushed her hands together. The sound boomed through the space as dust flew up into the air, choking her. She waved the cloud away and reached for the knob. The metal was cold under her fingers and refused to budge. Locked or rusted in place, she didn't know.

She continued down the corridor, weaving from one sealed door to the next. After a half dozen doors, she stopped and looked back, mentally tallying up her steps. The doors were getting closer together, she was sure of it. She took deliberate, measured steps to the next one across the hall, eight steps. And to reach the next, seven. Yep, they were definitely closer together, and all firmly closed.

She looked to her left to where the end of the hall had always disappeared into the distance and her heart started hammering. The end had never been visible before, but there it was, and the narrowing of the corridor? Definitely, not an optical illusion.

She abandoned the doors and broke into a run. Within moments, the crumbled plaster had thickened until it was coating the whole floor like windblown sand dunes and just as treacherous. There was no noise, but the walls pressed in, the tables toppled over without warning, forcing her to weave and jump every few steps to avoid them. Soon, she was shuffling sideways to be as narrow as possible.

She grunted as her hip collided with a table, the force of it nearly sending her flying over the top. She shoved it aside and pressed her hand to the offended spot, her frantic pulse throbbing under her fingers and continued on, half-limping, half-slithering in the dust that now covered her feet nearly to the ankle.

The end was growing tantalizingly closer, but sweat prickled at her scalp as the air grew thicker and warmer, as if the walls were compressing it too. Her weaving had become unbalanced, her shoulders and hips throbbing now as she ricocheted from one wall to the next, grunting with each impact as if the hallway had turned into the floor of a pinball machine.

A chunk of plaster skidded out under her foot, and sent her crashing to the ground. The room spun and her forehead collided hard with a fallen table. Choking dust flooded her nose and mouth, and coated her from head to toe.

With no time to lose, she shook her head to clear the bells that now rang in time with the drumming of her heart and half-crawled, half-stumbled forward. There were only a pair of doors left, but the space between them had continued to shrink. She tripped over the last fallen table and nearly fell again. The end a tantalizing brightness just ahead.

With only a few feet to go, the walls started to crush her shoulders with a frigid unyielding pressure that was a stark contrast to the fetid air. She grunted, pushing back against the walls that threatened to freeze any exposed skin. Somehow she forged forward, gaining inch after precious inch though the space continued to contract, the air so hot her lungs felt charred on the inside.

Ahead, the last foot of wall seemed to curl around her, becoming a seemingly impenetrable wall of cracked beige. But still, she continued to push against them, her feet struggling to find purchase to help drive her forward. A whimper of desperation escaped her throat, her arms strained against the wall, her thighs and calves screaming.

It wasn't fair that she was this close to the end, only to be crushed by the collapsing walls. She gasped for oxygen as if the heat had burned it up, her skin thickly coated in white, but she couldn't stop. She didn't dare look behind her, but there was something about the weight to the air that told her there was no going back.

The walls contracted further, bracketing her shoulders in a shroud of solid ice. It was now or never.

Her whimper turned into a scream of rage as she rallied her strength for one last hard press. Her feet slid, then found traction, while her hands pushed against the two ends of the wall, winning a fraction of an inch, the faintest crack of light appearing between them.

"Let me out!" she screamed at the wall. Still, she pressed forward, the gap widened to the width of a finger, then her arm. One hand slipped off and she thrust her shoulder forward into the gap instead. Her legs continuing to drive, until suddenly with a pop, she was free.

Her momentum should have launched her into the wall a half-dozen feet away, but instead, she staggered only a single step forward. She looked down at herself and found all of the plaster dust that had coated her skin and clothes had disappeared.

No longer choking on dust, she gratefully filled her lungs with air that, while musty, was at least clean and significantly cooler. A resounding boom filled the air, the first sound other than her own voice. She scrambled away, arms covering her head, and whirled to find only a blank wall, its plaster, while still aging and cracked, was at least still intact. There was no sign of the corridor that had haunted her dreams for weeks.

She panted, her chest heaving, as she looked up and down the dimly lit corridor. It was the opposite of the one she'd just escaped. No doors or windows, just identical, endless stretches of beige extending into the distance in both directions.

Find a way out, her mind screamed, and she stood for a moment, debating her next move. There was something in the air, a crackling tension as if energy was building up the longer she stood still. Building to what, she didn't know, but she also didn't want to wait around to find out. But which way? Right or left? They both looked the same.

Her heart raced, her feet shifting uneasily under her until she was almost jogging in place. She drifted slightly right, then left, then back. Each time to the right, there was a subtle increase in the charge that prickled along her skin, to the left, it eased.

She did it again, on purpose this time, and sure enough, the air grew more charged to the right, enough to lift the hair on her arms. The sensation wasn't unpleasant, but it also got stronger with each step, like a static charge built with each shuffling step on a carpet. And she didn't know what might happen if she let it build up too much, and then, like static, it somehow released.

She back-pedaled to the left again and the charge dissipated. A few steps further and the temperature eased a little as the barest whisp of a breeze brought a loose strand of hair brushing against her cheek. Soft and gentle like a caress that said yes, left was the right direction.

"I'm on my way!" she called into the gloom and headed off at a slow jog down the hallway.

Jal woke with a start, as she always did from one of her nightmares, but this was different, not nearly as violent an awakening as before. She opened her eyes and, for a moment, she didn't know where she was.

Light coming in through the window forced her to squint while she got her bearings. The pillowcase under her cheek was soft, the sheets and duvet covering her warm, but tucked around her so tightly she could barely move. Her nose filled with the familiar floral scent from the fancy laundry soap that she'd splurged a little over a month ago.

Her room. She was in her room, and the light coming in the window above her was tinged with orange. She sat up, the covers pooling at her hips and gasped as the cool air of the room hit the bare skin of her breasts and back. Jal snatched up the covers and clutched them to her chest, her mind reeling.

She glanced beside her and found only an empty bed. "Ciaran?" she called out and received silence in answer.

How had she gotten into bed? Had they... she lifted the covers and glanced beneath. No, she still wore the same black leggings and slouchy socks as before. He must have carried her to bed after...

The memories hit her like a freight train, and she collapsed back on the bed with a groan, one hand clapped over her eyes. The afternoon's events replayed in her mind, Ciaran appearing at her door, her pulling him inside and kissing the ever-loving shit out of him. She felt an echo of the swoop in her stomach when he'd scooped her feet off the floor and carried her to the chair in the living room where he'd made her come with his hands not once, but twice.

Her face heated and her thighs clenched around a throbbing that began at the memory of his touch. Good Lord, had he known just what she needed from him. And then some. And when he'd set her back to take a breather, she'd... The rosy haze of memory shattered and her whole body went cold.

"Oh no..." She bolted upright again. "Oh, no, no, no, no, no."

At first, she'd wanted to reciprocate by kneeling at his feet, rubbing his considerable length through his shorts. She'd *wanted* to touch him. But then, something had come over her like a haze, and it was a very different pair of feet she'd been kneeling between, a different cock, attached to a body that had very different expectations of her.

She had stroked him, and taken him into her mouth... "Oh, Ciaran..."

Jal flung back the covers and dove into the sweatshirt laying on the floor. A different one, she noted from the one Ciaran had removed however many hours ago, the one he'd draped over her shoulders after he'd shaken her free of the daze she'd fallen into before she'd cried herself to sleep in his arms.

She dashed out into the living room, to find it empty. Her stomach twisted in knots, as did her fingers, knotting together under her chin. They dropped to her side a moment later when the spear of hope that maybe, just maybe, he'd fallen asleep out here, pricked her heart instead. Why would he have stuck around? She asked herself. Especially after everything she'd done, and said while doing it?

She glanced out the window, expecting the light to be coming from the right, from the west, meaning she had only been asleep for an hour or two. But instead, the sun's rays, still tinged with orange, were slanting in from the left, from the east. She had slept through the whole night.

"Phone, phone..." she murmured as she headed for the kitchen. Where the hell was her phone?

She found it on the dining room table beside a notepad. His voice echoed in her ears as she read the words, the same as the ones he'd murmured as she'd fallen asleep against his chest, his heartbeat strong and steady under her ear.

Your truth is safe with me.

His voice curled over and through her even in memory. No harsh words, no condemnation, just patience. Beneath his note, as if an afterthought, he'd scribbled his phone number. A shaky laugh escaped her.

It had been a little game between them, that they hadn't exchanged phone numbers, or emails, or anything really of any importance. Yet, even in a city of millions of people, their paths had continued to cross.

Jal snatched up her phone to find a stack of notifications. She winced and unlocked it, noticing the missed calls but going first to her texts, the dozen or so from Elena that got increasingly more worried when she didn't answer. There were a few from Lexi, too, Elena must have looped her in. Sure enough, she had missed calls from both of them.

Jal pulled up their group chat.

> Jal: Hey, guys, sorry I missed you. It has been a DAY...

Elena's response was almost immediate. Lexi's hot on her heels.

> Elena: She's alive!

> Lexi: OMG Jal! Is everything okay?

Jal sighed, though her lips twitched at her friends' obvious relief.

> Jal: Yeah, sorry, crazy afternoon. I fell asleep and only just woke up. I'll tell you about it later.

> Jal: Still need help at the restaurant?

> Elena: You better believe it. Eduardo quit yesterday and there is so much that needs to get done.

> Lexi: Ugh, my morning is slammed with meetings. Don't go discussing anything juicy when I'm not there.

> Elena: lol, no promises.

> Jal: I'll be there as soon as I can.

Jal dismissed the messages and added Ciaran's phone number to her contacts. For a long moment, her finger hovered over the buttons to text or call him, but there was so much she needed to talk out first, so she locked the screen and headed for the shower.

Sixteen

The lock to the back door of Lima y Sazón stuck, so much so that the racket Jal made just from trying to turn the key, echoed down the alley that ran the length of the block packed with shops and restaurants. Inside, any small noise sounded like someone was trying to bust down the door, which was why Elena's father hadn't bothered to fix it.

"A little WD-40 would be nice," she muttered as the battered steel door finally squealed open. It took a few more moments standing in the doorway doing some creative wiggling until the key popped free with a force that sent her staggering back a step.

She yanked the door closed and locked it firmly, wiping away the bead of sweat at her temple. It had been five years since the last robbery attempt, largely thanks to that door, but it didn't have to be *that* hard to open. From deep inside the cavernous kitchen came a sigh of relief. Jal blinked to adjust to the fluorescent lighting reflecting off spotless stainless steel like the sun beaming onto the windows of a Manhattan skyscraper.

Elena stood alone at one of the prep stations dressed in her usual uniform of a black apron over a sleeveless top, surrounded by an array of small crates and bags of vegetables. Her caramel-streaked brown hair was tied tightly back in a bun under a backwards black baseball cap. There was a brilliant smile on her face and a wicked-looking boning knife in her hand, poised over a pork shoulder the size of a breadbox. "Hey, *nena.*"

Elena called nearly every woman she knew "*nena,*" which just meant "girl" in the Spanish of her mother's native Puerto Rico. At this point, Jal was used to it, but the word still threw Lexi off, something that amused Elena to the point where it had almost fully replaced their friend's name.

"Hey, yourself," Jal replied with a warm smile on her face as she crossed the room. Her head filled with the scents of roasted meat, garlic, citrus, and so many other spices that were a permanent fixture in the room, even when nothing was actively being cooked. Jal's stomach growled despite having just eaten breakfast, and she thought, as she had so many times, *Lime and Spice, indeed.*

She watched in fascination as Elena's skilled fingers pinched and pulled at the meat, the blade flashing in the light as it sliced through skin and sinew, followed by long sweeps that pared away fat until only a thin layer remained and none of the meat was wasted.

Finally, with a flourish that almost made Jal applaud, Elena deposited the meat into the last remaining spot in a large plastic tub nearly briming with her family's secret marinade. It was a concoction of deliciousness that Jal only knew included lime and orange juices, garlic, blended peppers and onions, and a dizzying variety of spices, because she had helped prepare it a time or two.

Elena wiped her hands on a towel and held out an arm for a much-shorter Jal to duck under and give her a brief, tight hug. She picked up the knife and cutting board and gestured with her elbow to the bags of vegetables spread out on one side of the station. "Why don't you start with the onions?"

Jal dropped her backpack with alacrity on an empty station behind her and followed to the sink to wash her hands. Beside her, Elena rinsed the cutting board and started in on the knife. "Remember how I showed you to chop them all the same size?"

Jal nodded and accepted the towel and cutting board Elena passed to her.

They worked in companiable silence for a while. The plastic container at Jal's elbow filling with neat squares of onion. Jal clutched the knife as Elena had taught her as she first sliced most of the way horizontally through half of the bulb, then cut vertically into strips before finally slicing the other direction. The knife still felt foreign in her hand, and the movements required almost all of her concentration just to keep from cutting herself with the sharp blade, but there was still something soothing in the repetition.

Before Elena had invited her a few months ago to pick up a knife and help, she'd never really known more than the basics-- if the "basics" could be considered boiling water or punching buttons on a microwave. Orphaned at seven when her parents died in a car accident, she'd gone to live with her last remaining grandparent in a worn-out trailer in Eastern Pennsylvania who'd lived mostly on frozen dinners and cigarettes. Spaghetti sauce came from a jar. Macaroni and cheese came from a box, if they were lucky enough to have milk, usually only at the beginning of the month when the food assistance card was reloaded. Even salad was a delicacy for people far richer than them as far as her grandma was concerned.

When the bag of onions was empty, Elena had her start in on the peppers, stopping her work on more delicate herbs to give Jal another lesson in removing the seeds and trimming the ribs of the peppers to get uniform pieces.

Satisfied, Elena returned to her side of the table and brushed a bead of sweat off her forehead with her forearm. She picked up her knife, pinched the pile of herbs between her fingers and went back to work. "So, you fell asleep, huh?" She asked after they'd worked for a few minutes. "Did that guy have anything to do with that? What's his name again? Keegan? Kevin?"

"Ciaran," Jal corrected. "And not exactly."

Elena set down her knife. "What do you mean 'not exactly?'" Her dark eyes were full of mischief.

Jal told her everything. From the soccer match to him appearing at the door, to carrying her to the chair, what he had done to her on that chair.

"Remind me never to sit there again." Elena groused, jumping in before Jal could say anything about what *she* had done. "That was my favorite chair."

Jal chuckled, her cheeks warming.

"But good for you, nena!" she exclaimed. "It's about time."

Jal ducked her head to hide the blush that darkened her cheeks, not from pleased embarrassment, but from shame, and concentrated on the pepper in front of her.

"What is it?"

Jal kept chopping, even as Elena set her knife aside and circled around to her side of the table.

"Jal?" Elena prompted. Her fingers gently wrapped around Jal's hand and brought the knife to a stop. "Talk to me."

Jal let her take the knife and wiped her hands with a towel. "When Andy and I were together, it didn't matter what we had done, or how many times either of us had... you know." She swallowed hard against the bile rising up her throat at the memories. "He always had to finish last, and in my mouth. It didn't matter if I was tired, or didn't want to do it, if I refused or tried to go to sleep, there would be problems."

She didn't elaborate on what those problems were, Elena knew all too well. "It got to the point where I would go on a kind of autopilot. I could say all the right things, do what he wanted and make him think that I enjoyed it, but I'd go somewhere in my head to wait until it was over."

"Oh Jal," Elena whispered. "Did that just happen with Ciaran?"

Jal looked up at her friend, and her eyes filled with tears as she nodded.

Elena wrapped her arms around her and held on tight as Jal sobbed into the scratchy apron. The tears didn't last long, though, and soon Jal eased back and dabbed her eyes with the towel.

"I can't imagine what Ciaran is thinking right now," Jal sniffled, and dashed to the office, coming back with a handful of tissues, one of which she used to blow her nose. "He was gone when I woke up. He left his number, but I haven't worked up the nerve to reach out yet."

Elena chuckled. "Well, you finally have a phone number, at least." She perched a hip on the edge of the table, shaking her head wryly. "That has to be a good sign."

A corner of Jal's mouth twitched, and needing to do something with her hands, she took up the knife again while she finished the story, reciting Ciaran's words that he could be trusted with anything she wanted to tell him.

Jal chopped the rest of the pepper before Elena's hand covered hers on the knife. "He's out, you know."

Jal jerked, releasing the blade on the cutting board. Had Elena's hand not been there, it probably would have hit the floor. Jal's head whipped around. Only one "he" would put *that* look on her friend's face. The one that said, "say the word and I'll grab the car keys and a shovel."

Jal's heart missed a beat, two, as Elena's words sunk in. Her legs gave out and she crashed to her knees. Pain radiated up and down her arm when her elbow hit the counter with an echoing boom, but it was the one thing that kept her from sprawling on the floor. Elena let out a cry and scrambled to pull her to her feet and deposited her on a stool.

Elena released her, but kept her hands close for a moment, prepared to step in if Jal started to tip over. When it became clear it wasn't going to happen, she dashed to the sink to fill a glass of water, which she pressed into Jal's hands.

The cool water sliding down her throat helped to steady her nerves a little, but it did nothing to calm the roaring in her ears.

"What?" she croaked, and took another gulp of water, the glass clenched between both hands, so it didn't go crashing to the red tile floor. "Why wouldn't they tell me he was being released?"

Elena crouched in front of her and set the glass aside so she could take both of her hands. Jal looked down, at those strong, capable hands, a few shades darker than her ivory complexion, and gripped them like a lifeline. For a long moment, she held on and concentrated on her breathing, the same as she had done in the courtroom two years ago when they'd read out the verdict.

Find three scents: cilantro, and lime, and chili pepper...

Now, three sights: the bank of ovens stacked neatly on top of each other, the chipped paint of the restaurant logo Elena's mother had painted over the serving window nearly a decade ago, the warm brown of Elena's eyes as she waited patiently...

Lastly, three things she could feel: the calluses of Elena's hands, the hard steel of the stool beneath her, the tickle of a lock of hair falling across her cheek...

Slowly, the sensation of breathing through a straw eased and the panic receded enough for her to process what Elena was saying. "They probably couldn't find you," she explained. "You moved, and you've changed your phone number a half-dozen times in the last two years." She came around the workstation and took one of her hands. "Not to mention, you changed—"

Jal squeezed her hands tighter, and a wince of pain flashed

across Elena's features. With a grimace, Jal loosened her grip. "How did you find out?"

"He came in yesterday asking for you," Elena replied, her voice deep and gritty. "That's why I was calling you yesterday." There was a flush high in her cheeks that wasn't embarrassment. Jal was certain that had she been able to hear her friend's thoughts, they would be in Spanish, full of inventive curses, and none of it complimentary.

"He said he went by the old place and was surprised to find you gone."

Jal scoffed. "He actually thought I would just be sitting there for two years, waiting for him?" Though she shouldn't have been surprised. She met Elena's hard brown eyes. "What *did* you tell him?"

She dropped Jal's hands and paced a few feet away to lean on the counter with her hands braced on either side of her generous hips. "I told him that you'd left town after it all happened and I hadn't heard from you since."

Jal released a breath and the tightness in her chest eased a little. "Good," she took another deep breath. "That's really good. How did he take it?"

"About as well as you could imagine." Elena said. "Red face, clenched fists, the usual. Thankfully, we were open, so he couldn't make too much of a show. You know, I don't know what you ever saw in that guy, Jal."

Jal chuckled, though there was no humor in the sound, and wrapped her arms around her stomach. "Neither do I."

"You know, if you want to come stay with me for a little while, you're welcome." Elena's apartment was in the Kitchen, a few blocks from the restaurant. It was also small enough that the whole thing would fit in Jal's living area with plenty of room to spare, but the generosity of the offer meant more than she could possibly know.

Jal shook her head. "Like you said, he doesn't know where I live now, and it might as well be half-way around the world from the Bronx. I just might want to keep my distance from here for a little while in case he comes back."

Elena nodded. "Yeah, might be a good idea." She clicked her tongue. "Though I *was* going to ask if you could come in more often." She winked and a sly smile spread across her lips. "Papá and I will make do somehow."

Jal managed a weak smile at that, considering she'd only worked maybe a grand total of fifteen hours over the last two months. Elena and her father Roberto had been part of her life from the moment she'd stepped off the bus at seventeen and staggered up to the first food cart she came across, tired, alone, and clueless on where to start a new life in the big city. Roberto had taken pity on her and given her a hot meal and a lead on a room for rent from a family friend. It was a kindness that he didn't need to make, she knew, and she'd never been able to really feel like she'd repaid him. Even working in his restaurant, which he and Elena's mother had opened a few years later, didn't put much of a dent in that debt.

"Did Andy say anything else?"

Elena shook her head. "Only that he had found a job at an auto shop in Hunts Point and he's rooming with a buddy near your old place." she said. "He left his number, but I burned that the second he left. So as long as you stay in Manhattan, you should be good. He'll give up eventually."

Jal nodded. "Thanks, *nena*," she said, and eased off the

stool. Elena took a step toward her, but Jal's legs were surprisingly steady. She set the glass in the sink. "I should probably get going."

Elena smiled, though it was brittle. "I'll call you. Maybe get the gang together for a night out, all the fancy places that Andy would never think to go."

Jal nodded and gave Elena a quick hug, then headed for the door. Just as she wrestled the thing open, Elena's voice called out.

"Ciaran sounds like he's a good guy," she said.

Jal's cheeks flushed and her heart expanded a little, as if just the mention of his name was enough to clear away some of the grime talk of Andy had left on her skin. "Yeah, I think so too." she replied. "I just have to hope that I haven't screwed everything up."

Seventeen

A few days later, Jal was curled up on the sofa, a book propped on her knees, reading the same paragraph for the tenth, or maybe fiftieth time, she wasn't sure. Every time she tried, her attention drifted to the coffee table and her phone, screen innocently dark, beside a cooling cup of tea. Every time, she unlocked the screen to stare at the contact with Ciaran's name at the top, the buttons for call and text side by side beneath it. Every time, she stared at the options until her adrenaline spiked high enough that she tossed the phone back down with a sigh and returned to her book. Lather, rinse, repeat.

It wasn't because the book wasn't any good. She'd devoured the first half of it, a romance novel currently climbing the best seller list set in a fictional medieval world, but that was before she and Ciaran had... before *she* had...

She closed the book with a snap and tossed it down on the cushion at her feet. It bounced off and thumped onto the rug. Her temples began to throb as Jal swung her feet to the floor and scrubbed her face with her hands. Her eyes were gritty and dry, her body ached as if she were training for a marathon. It was as if her body was feeling the exertion in her dreams, which had only become a new kind of torture ever since she'd escaped the hall of many doors. Now, every time she closed her eyes, she'd found herself in an endless labyrinth of colorless, featureless walls filled with a silence so deafening, the pressure on her ears and on her mind quickly drove her into a full-on sprint around one corner after another just to find a way to escape it.

A few nights ago, she ran on, and on, and on, until she smashed into a wall, that then became an enclosed cube of featureless plaster with no way to escape until she woke up. Last night, she had run to near exhaustion and tripped over her own feet, slamming back to consciousness before she'd hit the floor.

One hand slid off her face and dropped to her lap, jolting her from her thoughts. She propped her chin on the other, her eyes fixed on the darkened screen. *Stop being such a wuss*, she berated herself for the thousandth time.

Sure, in the beginning, he'd been cocky, somehow knowing just what buttons to push to get a rise out of her. But he could also be kind, and had been so giving, more concerned about her pleasure than his own. Until she'd gone and ruined it.

You don't know that for sure, a tiny voice piped up from the back of her head.

With a sigh, she reached out and picked up the phone again, the motion waking the screen and unlocking with a scan of her face. She didn't have a picture of him stored in her phone, but as she stared at the generic little silhouette above Ciaran's name, she saw his face, and its many varied expressions, anyway. The knowing smirk as he bent to release the hidden drawer on her table. The storms clouding over the hopefulness in his whisky-brown eyes when he rose from the table that first time at Amicetto, a moment before she walked out the door. The sight of him standing in the doorway to her apartment clutching that ridiculous trophy, his eyes going wide as she grabbed a fistful of his shirt and hauled his lips to hers.

Jal ran a hand through her hair to get it out of her face and gave a handful a yank. Anything to clear her head. Her eyes shifted to the chair to her right, its only occupant now a single unassuming throw pillow.

Heat coiled through her, settling deep down in her gut as she remembered the way he had held her on his lap, their hips pressed tight together as he tortured her with his mouth on her breasts. First nibbling, then slow licks to soothe, then sucking hard until she'd cried out. Her riding his hand until...

"Oh, for the love of—" her thumb reached for the call button, but just as it touched the screen, a notification came in and she selected that instead. The screen shifted to the text string with Elena and Lexi.

> Elena: Reservation at Reina for 8pm tonight.
> Plus ones optional.

Jal blew out her breath. *Talk about saved by the text.* she thought, even as she wrenched her brain away from dirty memories to whether she had been anywhere called *Reina* before. Then it came to her, a fancy midtown penthouse restaurant owned by a chef who had made it big on some cooking competition. It was trendy, and way too upscale for a certain ex-con ex-boyfriend.

Jal sent back a quick reply and flipped back to her contacts. She hesitated only for a moment, and then tapped the text button.

> Jal: Reina. 8pm Tonight

She hit send before she could lose her nerve. As she set the phone down, the memory of the notes that he'd left all around her apartment bubbled to the surface. She smirked and scooped the phone back up.

> Jal: Dress Elegantly.

Ciaran's feet were dragging as he emerged from yet another mind-numbing staff meeting, clutching an empty mug in one hand, his laptop tucked into the crook of his elbow, when his phone buzzed. He scrambled to free a hand, balancing the mug precariously on the laptop, and reached into his pocket. The mug started to slide, but Catherine reached over to rescue it before it could fall. Her sigh told him that she had also given him one of her famous eyerolls, but he was too focused on his phone to actually see it.

For a moment, he scowled at the message. Just a name and a time from an unknown caller. His brow furrowed as he wracked his brain for a reason why someone he didn't know would be texting a name and a time.

A shadow crossed the screen and he looked out of the corner of his eye to find Catherine leaning around his shoulder. "What is it with you and your phone lately?" she asked.

"Och, away wi' you," he waved her back with the hand holding the phone. She laughed and leaned away but didn't give him any more space. True, he had been a bit more glued to his phone than normal, but Jal had his number now, and she'd yet to use it.

Jal. Ciaran's brow knitted again as he reread the three words, and then again... The notes! That's why just a restaurant name and a time sounded familiar. A corner of his mouth turned up and his heart started beating a little faster. It was almost racing when the second text came in. He laughed.

"What's so funny?"

Ciaran glanced over at Catherine, whose chin was practically on his shoulder now. She arched a black brow at him from only a few inches away, a twinkle in the eye beneath it.

He glanced around, but for once, Cliff was nowhere to be seen. He turned the screen more in her direction, not that she hadn't been able to read it before.

She bent closer anyway, her hair tickling his ear. "Reina?" She glanced at him quizzically. "You mean that swanky place up the street with the killer views. Fancy, fancy!"

Ciaran fought to maintain a neutral expression. *What are you up to, lass?*

"Sounds like she wants you to meet her for a romantic, rooftop dinner."

Ciaran winced as she breezed by him into the aisle where their desks were. *Did she have to say that so loud?*

"What I don't get," Catherine continued. A sheet of

stick-straight black hair slid over one shoulder as she glanced back at him. "Is what's so funny about that text."

Ciaran dropped into his seat before he replied, "it's an inside joke of sorts."

Catherine perched on the edge of the stool at her drafting table, hands clasped between her knees, and studied his face. After a moment, her red lips parted in a knowing grin. "So… things are going well enough with this girl to have inside jokes," she said slowly, her hands now waving gently through the air in front of her as she worked out what she was going to say. "But *not* enough to have her number saved in your phone?"

Ciaran chuckled, and playfully tossed a binder clip at her. "Something like that."

She swatted at it, her college field hockey goalie reflexes sending the small black clip with its silver butterfly wings neatly into the trash can with a loud clang. Ciaran clapped appreciatively and Catherine bowed with an elaborate wave of one hand.

"Gray! Cheng! Are you here to work, or play games?" A voice roared from across the room. "I need that Gramercy Park proposal by end of day."

Ciaran looked up to see Old Man Dougherty glowering at them from the doorway leading to Cliff's office. "Sorry, sir!" he called, cheeks heating.

Catherine ducked her head, her shoulders shaking with laughter and Ciaran couldn't help himself joining in quietly as he turned to his computer. This day was looking up.

Eighteen

The elevator drew to a smooth stop and an old-fashioned bell dinged over the elaborately sculpted brass door that echoed the building's Art Deco décor. A breeze rushed in tinged with a tantalizing mix of saffron and garlic. Jal hesitated to let the others in the small space go first before smoothing her suddenly sweaty palms over her hips and following, her heels clicking on the marble floor.

She fought to keep her mouth closed as she took in the glittering chandeliers and gilded wallpaper. The wall of floor-to-ceiling windows at the far side of the restaurant were framed in black, giving the room the illusion that there was nothing between the dozens of tables and the dazzling skyline beyond.

The host's stand was fashioned like a golden pillar of rock with an angled top. Behind it, a man in a crisp white shirt and slicked black hair glanced up from his tablet and smiled. "Good evening!"

Jal thought of the far different greeting she'd received at Amicetto and smiled. "Reservation for eight o'clock. I think it's under Sandoval." As she spoke, movement brought her head up to see Elena turned around in her chair, waving at her from halfway across the room. "Ah, looks like they're already here."

The host turned to see the wave and turned back, sweeping his arm out in permission. "Do you want me to take your wrap?"

Expecting to go from door to taxi to door again, Jal had wrapped a thick, knitted scarf around her shoulders instead of a coat. She handed it over, taking the ticket he offered and tucking it in her clutch purse. "Enjoy your night, madam."

Jal straightened one shoulder of her dress as she circled around a couple of tables to the high-top Elena and Lexi now stood next to. Her friends were dressed in simply-cut, but striking, dresses. Elena wore blue, the color so deep it could almost be black, but it sparkled like a star-filled sky when she moved. Lexi was in green, a beautiful apple green that suited her creamy skin and golden blonde hair. Calligraphy strokes formed leaves that clustered on the bodice and flowed down the heavy material nearly to the floor.

Elena's brows rose as Jal stepped closer and she stopped a little distance away. "What?"

"*Ay nena,* where did you get that dress?"

Jal glanced down self-consciously, then looked around the room, eyes landing on sparkling dresses and neat suits, and inwardly sighed in relief that she wasn't over-dressed. The fabric that fit like a second skin was a mottled blend of fresh and patinaed copper that made her pale skin glow. It fell almost to the floor, just heavy enough to sway with each step. The neckline draped high across her chest, revealing little, but the same could not be said for the back, which consisted only of two thin straps crossing over her shoulder blades, leaving the smooth skin bare until just above her ass. Her hair cascaded down her back and over one shoulder in a fall of raven-black curls, held back from her face with a pair of glittering, beaded combs.

"The back of my closet," she replied with a chuckle. "Metaphorically speaking."

"You should go shopping in there more often, I think." Elena replied as she kissed Jal on the cheek.

Jal gave Lexi a hug. Her friend returned it warmly, and they took their seats. Lexi studied her for a moment and said, "I think I loaned that to you maybe three years ago," over the rim of her martini glass.

Jal's cheeks heated a little as she took her seat across from them. She glanced at the empty chair. "Are we expecting anyone else?"

Lexi gave her a knowing look. "Why? Are *you* expecting anyone else?"

"Me? Oh, no. No reason."

Her friends exchanged a look, and Jal was relieved when the server came and took her drink order. She picked up the single sheet of paper that served as a menu and studied it as if her choice of the half-dozen selections was a life-or-death decision. With her other hand, she slipped her phone out of the clutch in her lap. The screen lit, and she glanced down as discretely as she could. The clock said it was nearly quarter-past eight, yet there were no missed calls or texts.

Relief and concern warred inside her. He hadn't responded to her earlier texts. Maybe he hadn't seen them? Maybe he had and he ignored them? She hoped it was the former and she hadn't scared him off... She suddenly found herself without much of an appetite and set the menu aside. She took a sip of her wine and turned to Elena.

"How are things with that guy?" she asked. "What was his name? Eric?"

Elena just shrugged.

"That good, huh?" Lexi asked, her voice soft. She placed a hand on Elena's forearm. "What happened? You guys were pretty hot and heavy for a while there."

"We were," Elena's eyes lost some of their usual gleam as she patted Lexi's hand in thanks. "And then, we weren't. I'm honestly not sure what happened."

Lexi turned to Jal. "And what about you?" she asked. "Tell me what you and Elena talked about at Lima on Thursday, I'm dying to know."

Jal opened her mouth, but before she could speak, Elena jumped in, the mischief returning to her eyes now that the heat was off her. Jal made a mental note to ask her about it later. "Want the good news," she waggled her eyebrows, "or the bad?"

Lexi tilted her head and gave Jal a quizzical look. A slow smile spread from whatever she saw on Jal's face. "Oh, the good," she said, practically rubbing her hands together. "Definitely, the good."

Jal put her face in her hand and waved the other helplessly at Elena in permission.

"Well, let's just say that I don't have a favorite chair in Jal's apartment anymore."

Jal peeked cautiously between her fingers and caught the gleam in Lexi's blue eyes. "Did you and Ciaran break Elena's favorite chair?" she asked mock-scandalized, hand on heart.

Jal let her hand fall to the table with a thump and glared at her friend. "See what you started..."

Elena grinned.

"No, we didn't break the chair."

"But they did do lots of scandalous things on it," Elena declared, though she still had a devilish grin on her face.

Lexi's eyebrows disappeared under her bangs. "Oh, really?" she asked, drawing the word out, her voice rising in pitch.

Jal blushed, thankful that the music and the clamor of the crowd at the bar was just loud enough that their voices didn't carry very far. "We didn't go all the way or anything." Jal said, "but what we did get up to was pretty great, until..."

Her words were drowned out by Lexi's squeal. "I'm so happy for you! After all this time."

Elena raised her eyebrow at Jal as if asking whether she wanted to tell Lexi the rest. Lexi caught the look and her shoulders slumped. "What is it?"

Jal sipped her wine, her heart starting to race. "That's the bad news." she said. "There was a little moment when—" Her head snapped up at movement near the host's stand as a familiar figure with brown hair shrugged out of a familiar tan coat and handed it to the man behind the rocky pillar of a desk. The man pointed in their direction and Ciaran's whisky-colored eyes at once met hers.

Elena and Lexi stared at her for a split second before both turned in their seats to see what had captured her attention.

Seeing Ciaran heading their way, they whipped back in perfect synchronization to level Jal with almost twin expressions of surprise and suspicion.

"Subtle, guys." Jal muttered into the bowl of her wine glass, the tips of her ears burning. "Real subtle."

Ciaran stepped up to the table, his hands in the pockets of a tailored gray suit. His face was calm, and though there were clouds in his eyes, there was an echo of the heat that had filled them since they'd stood outside of Amicetto just before his lips had brushed across her cheek.

Jal's attention was fixed on him too, her hands twisting the napkin in her lap.

Someone cleared their throat, jerking both of their attention across the table to her friends, both of which were watching with knowing expressions.

Jal leveled them both with an expression that said, "behave."

Elena waved her off and held out a hand to him, "You must be Ciaran."

Jal suddenly remembered her manners. "I'm sorry, Ciaran Gray, this is Elena Sandoval and Alexia Wheaton."

"Call me Lexi," she said and offered her hand, fingers pointed downward as if offering her knuckles for a kiss. Ciaran, to his credit, took it and bowed his head a little. Lexi smiled.

"Please, join us."

Ciaran glanced at Jal, who nodded at the chair beside her. A corner of his mouth ticked up, and he took his hands from his pockets before squeezing between her chair and the one behind it. She swallowed the gasp before it could escape when his fingers skimmed along her bare back as he passed leaving a trail of heat on her skin. She couldn't suppress the reflexive tightening of her thighs, as they squeezed together. Jal's head turned, following his every move as he released the button of his suitcoat, revealing more of the matching vest beneath, buttoned high over a light blue shirt and a striped tie, and settled onto the remaining seat.

Elena, damn her, didn't miss a thing. "So, Ciaran, Jal has told us so much about you," she said. "And by that, I mean practically nothing."

Ciaran chuckled and flagged down a passing waiter, ordering a neat whisky and a refresh for the rest of their drinks. The waiter asked if they wanted to put in any food, and they scrambled for the menus and peppered him with selections.

Once the waiter left, Ciaran turned back to Jal. The clouds had cleared in his eyes, leaving behind the usual mischievous twinkle, the whisky-on-ice now had a flicker of something hotter when he looked at her. "Is that right?" He turned to Elena as the waiter set a double whisky in front of him with a small glass of ice and continued around the table distributing drinks. "Well, then. What would you like to know?"

Elena considered for a moment. "Well, going by that accent, I'd say you aren't from Jersey."

Ciaran chuckled and took a sip of his drink. He clicked his tongue and added a couple of ice cubes to his glass and swirled it idly. "You would be correct," he replied. His accent seemed thicker than Jal had ever heard it. She would have rolled her eyes if the deep timbre of his voice wasn't doing wicked things elsewhere. "Parkside, Glasgow, born and raised."

"And what do you do for work, Ciaran?" Lexi asked.

"I'm an architect," he replied, "my office is just up the street." He draped his arm along the low back of Jal's chair, his fingers sliding under the curtain of her hair to rest along her spine. Jal forced herself to drink her wine and not show what his touch was doing to her. Still, there was something in her friends' expressions that said they knew anyway.

"What types of things do you design?"

He continued to swirl his drink on the table, the glass spreading the ring of condensation around on the wood, while his fingers traced idle circles on her back. "Office buildings mostly, the odd country club. Nothing too exciting."

Elena considered a moment and then, something glinted in her eyes that Jal didn't like the looks of at all. "I hear that's not the only talents you have."

Ciaran inhaled the sip of whisky he had just taken and started to cough. Jal scrambled to set her wine aside to thump him on the back.

Elena's hand shot out to keep the glass from toppling.

Her glare softened slightly while she continued to tap between his shoulder blades until Ciaran waved her off and dragged in a deep breath, but still his voice was almost a croak. "What have you been telling them, lass?"

Jal scowled at her friend, who laughed and then turned back to him. "What's to tell?" she asked. "They know that you're the guy who broke into my apartment, and—"

"Oh my god, is that Maks Brody?"

The question had come from the table next to them. It hadn't been loud, but their ears all perked up at the name. Everyone but Ciaran looked over the to the table next to them in time for one college aged woman to elbow another and point, not at all subtly, toward the elevator and the small number of restaurant patrons who had surrounded a tall man with dark blond hair and a close-cropped reddish-blond beard who had just exited the elevator.

There was some color in Lexi's cheeks when she turned back to the table. "Did you know he was coming?" Jal asked.

Lexi waved her off. "He said he might try to come by after practice, but wasn't sure if he was going to make it or not." She turned around just as he arrived at the table, drawing most of the eyes around them as usual. Lexi slid off the chair and gave him a hug in greeting. He slid her chair in for her as she sat back down.

To add more chaos to Maks's arrival, the server chose that moment to arrive with their food. While Elena directed the food deliveries, Maks turned to the table of three women beside them, each at least a half-dozen years younger than him, but each with stars in their eyes.

The server murmured something about her plate as he set an order of paella down in front of her, but the food was the last thing on her mind. She was too engrossed in the scene, which looked like something out of a reality dating show, as Maks wrapped his hands around the seatback of the empty chair beside a busty brunette.

He flashed one of his million dollar smiles at them. "Good evening, ladies."

Jal could swear that one of them sighed dramatically, and she suppressed a snort of laughter. They all greeted him with breathless variations of "hello."

The brunette, already sporting a low-cut neckline, puffed out her chest at him and brushed a lock of hair behind her ear.

Did she just flutter her eyelashes?

"Do you mind if I take this?" he asked.

The brunette deflated a little, as did her friends, though one maintained enough composure to assure him that it was fine. Maks thanked them and spun the chair around toward their table. This time Jal couldn't contain her snigger, neither could Elena. From the corner of her eye, Jal saw Ciaran conceal an uncertain smile behind his whisky glass.

Before Maks could even sit down, he was intercepted by a passing businessman who shook his hand and clapped him on the shoulder before moving on. Maks took it in stride. After nearly a decade in the league, it had to be a common occurrence. He signed an autograph with a brilliant smile, but politely declined the request for a selfie before he was finally allowed to take his seat.

Lexi and Ciaran shifted their chairs to make room. Jal scooted her chair a little to the side and lifted her plate to take it with her. She yelped and dropped it with a clatter.

"What is it, lass?"

"I burned my hand," she hissed, blowing gently on her fingers, which had already started to turn red.

"The waiter warned you that the plate was hot," Lexi chided, lifting a piece of shrimp from her own dish to her mouth.

Ciaran gently placed his hand under Jal's and studied the marks. "That's none so bad," he murmured and added his cooling breath, though that only added heat elsewhere. The hair on her forearms rose.

Jal looked over at him and their eyes locked. After a long moment, she blinked and slid her hand from his.

"I'm going to go run my hand under some cold water." She informed the table and reluctantly slid off her chair and out of Ciaran's reach. She needed to run more than her hand under cold water, but her skin cooled quickly in the absence of his touch and his breath on her skin, so much so that she almost shivered as she made the long trek to the restroom, which was located all the way back by the elevators.

Jal ran her hand under the water until her fingertips stopped pulsing in time with her heartbeat, then wet a towel and wrapped it around her fingers as she emerged into the hallway and stopped.

Leaning against the wall across the hall, his hands in his pockets, one foot propped on the wall like a Scottish James Dean, was Ciaran.

Nineteen

She hadn't expected him to follow her, but had hoped that he might. She gave him a soft smile and looped her arm through his, dragging him off the wall as she passed.

"Aren't we going the wrong way?" He asked, as she led him away from the tables.

She just flashed him a smile, a corner of her lower lip curled between her teeth, as she started up the black treads of the floating staircase that led to the restaurant's rooftop lounge. Ciaran's fingers slid down her forearm and linked with hers as they climbed, him matching her step for step.

He pushed open the glass door at the top and was met with a cool breeze redolent with woodsmoke and green, growing things, a strange combination for being fifty stories up. It blew back her hair and pressed her skirt to her legs as it rushed down the stairs. Ciaran ushered her through ahead of him and followed close behind, the door swinging gently shut behind them.

Jal's steps faltered as she took in the space before them. There were pictures online, she'd found them when she'd researched the place, but those had been taken in the daytime, and still, they didn't do it justice. At night, the lounge was even more stunning. It easily took up more than half of the roof and resembled the garden of some Mediterranean Hacienda.

The copper-colored ceramic tiles covering the floor formed paths between small clusters of sofas and tables, each surrounding a wood-burning chiminea that cast out light and heat to combat the evening chill, still palpable despite the glass walls that blocked the bulk of the wind. Strands of small white lights twined with draping greenery overhead, winking in the breeze like the fireflies she used to chase as a child in Pennsylvania.

There was little shelter from unsettled weather, but, thankfully, the sky tonight was clear, or at least cloudless. Even when the sun had fully set, it only got so dark in mid-town Manhattan with all the light pollution. Here and there a few bright stars were visible above a skyline brilliant enough to take her breath away. Even after living in New York for a decade, it never really got old.

"I believe that this is yours," he said from her right. She looked down to find he held her clutch purse, left behind at the table when she'd fled in search of cold water.

Jal accepted it with a grateful smile. "How thoughtful," she murmured and had to fight to keep her jaw from dropping when she noticed what looked like a flush of pink high on his cheekbones. Must be a trick of the light. Ciaran Gray didn't blush.

Ciaran took a step closer and slid an arm around her.

She thought that he might draw her into the circle of his arms, but he only rested his hand on her lower back and exerted gentle pressure there to direct her across the roof to an empty seating area that faced east.

As they walked, the scalloped spire of the Chrysler Building came into view, glowing like burnished gold among a cluster of taller and far more modern buildings that cast a much harsher light.

They sat close together on a small, cushioned sofa set in the bubble of warmth created by a bronze-colored chiminea, the wood inside merrily crackling away. Though they barely touched, Jal could feel him along every inch of her skin.

"Is your hand all right?" Ciaran asked, his voice soft and a little rough. He gently unwrapped the towel and bent close to examine it in the dim lighting.

The redness had cleared some, though she knew the skin would be tender for a day or two. He ran his finger over the injury, his touch so feather-light she barely felt it, though he was close enough that his breath raised goosebumps on her arms.

Jal shrugged. "It'll be fine."

Ciaran nodded, and to her surprise, raised their joined hands so he could place a kiss to the middle of her palm. He brought their hands down to rest on his thigh, his cradling hers from underneath, and settled back into the cushions. He draped the other hand behind her shoulders, along the back of the sofa.

Jal found herself wanting to lean back so he had to touch her, needing that touch to ground her. But now that they were alone, her heart was racing and not in a good way, her mind spinning over what they had done, and what had to be going through his head.

Her chest was getting tight, too tight to get a good breath. She put a hand on her chest and curled around it.

Ciaran's hand closed around her shoulder. "Whoa, steady on there, lass. What's amiss?"

His melodic voice, smooth as the whisky his eyes reminded her of, was one thing she could hear. The strum of flamenco guitar was another. The distant honking of cars far below was a third.

Part of her wanted to dig in her purse for a pill that would help, but another part of her, one that had been dormant for a long time, recognized that it wasn't his touch that had set her off. In fact, the touch of his hand on her skin was like a tether, one she could use to pull her out of this downward spiral, if she only dared to take it.

She fought to draw in a deep breath, but it was choppy.

Try again, she ordered herself. In for five, hold for five, out for five. And again.

After she managed three breaths, she slowly raised her head and looked around, anywhere but at Ciaran. Not yet.

She took a deep breath. "Woodsmoke," she murmured under her breath, putting names to the things she could smell. "Evergreen."

"What else?"

Jal looked up at his face then, eyes wide.

He gave her a reassuring smile and nodded his head.

A trembling, tentative chuckle escaped her lips. "Your aftershave," she replied. "Vanilla and cedar."

He smiled. "And what can you feel?"

Her eyes locked with his. "The breeze," she replied as it lifted a lock of hair from her cheek, gentle as a caress. Her heart ratcheted down a notch toward a normal rhythm. Inside, a hand grasped that tether between them and made the first pull.

"Go on."

"These cushions are soft, but the fabric is surprisingly scratchy on my back."

He chuckled, his thumb stroking once over the point of her bare shoulder. Another pull, another notch.

"And?"

"The warmth of your touch on my skin."

His hand caressed slowly down her arm and back up, his eyes locked on hers. Down and up. The coiled spring in her chest released and her breathing finally eased. She continued counting her breaths, after the third, she realized that he was breathing with her, holding his breath when she did.

"How did you know?" she whispered.

"That you were grounding?" He asked, and one corner of his lips lifted. "My youngest sister Nicola started getting panic attacks in secondary school. She used something similar. Three things you can see, three things you can touch, three things you can smell, right?"

Jal nodded.

"Let me go get you some water."

His arm slid away from her shoulder, and he was halfway to the bar before she could tell him that she was fine. She braced her elbows on her knees and scrubbed her face with her hands, then linked her fingers under her chin.

She stared into the fire, studying the way the light flickered inside the chiminea, the flames dancing along the wood they slowly consumed. She kept breathing, hoping it would keep away the memories that had started the panic attack in the first place, but they floated back anyway. The oh so good, but also the bad.

Your truth is your own. Wasn't that what he'd murmured into her ear as she'd fallen asleep in his arms? Hadn't he also said that her truth was safe with him?

What he hadn't done was run. Just the opposite, he'd held her, and then put her to bed. And the first time that she'd reached out to him? He'd come.

Ciaran returned with a glass of water in each hand and held one out to her. "Here, this should help," he said. "It always helped Nic."

Jal drank half of it in a few long gulps and leaned back on the sofa, her eyes closed. "Tell me about her. Is she still in Scotland?"

"Aye, she is," Ciaran replied. "She's five years younger than me. Married, with seven-year-old twin boys. She's a teacher at the local primary school."

Jal opened her eyes and looked at him. "Twins?"

Ciaran nodded and patted his pockets for his phone and came up empty. "My phone is downstairs, but I have a picture of them as my background from when they were three. Back before they became the source of the gray hairs Nic likes to complain of."

Jal chuckled. Five years younger would make Ciaran's sister a year or two younger than Jal herself, but so far her black hair was gray-free. She sat up a little straighter. "Do you have any kids, then?"

Ciaran shook his head. "No," he replied. "And I've seen enough of your apartment to know that you don't either."

Jal smiled and nodded and finished the water before leaning back, this time finding Ciaran's arm there to rest her head on. She closed her eyes and just breathed in the fragrant air, dominated by Ciaran's aftershave and a woodsy undertone that was just him.

After a while, she felt a feather-soft touch brushing the hair back from one temple. She opened her eyes to find he had turned as much as he could to face her while leaving his forearm under her head. He gave her a patient, soft smile that nearly broke her heart with its sweetness. "Better?"

Her lips twitched, forming what she hoped was a smile. She sat up and turned toward him. "A little," she replied. "Listen, Ciaran—"

He started to speak at the same time. "Lass. I—"

They stopped speaking when their voices overlapped, both laughing. Jal's cheeks heated but she forced herself to not look away from him and the amusement dancing in his eyes.

She chuckled. "You go."

He shook his head. "No, you."

She sighed again. "Okay," she replied and took a deep breath before continuing. "I just wanted to say that I don't regret what happened, though I do feel like I need to apologize for how it ended." When she'd gotten lost inside her own head and done the unthinkable: mistaken Ciaran for Andy.

"What is there to apologize for?"

Jal looked around self-consciously, but there wasn't anyone within earshot, especially with the gentle strains of a guitar playing from somewhere. At first, she thought there might be speakers hidden in the greenery, but her eyes fell on a small stage beside the rooftop bar.

A young couple were perched there on folding chairs. The man, dressed in a white shirt and colorful vest, bent over a polished acoustic guitar as he tuned it. Satisfied, he brushed a lock of straight black hair behind one ear and his fingers began to dance along the strings, plucking out a Flamenco melody that was stirring and soothing at the same time.

The woman provided the percussion by clapping her hands in time with the music. Gentle at first, then steadily stronger as the music built and built. The music swelled in her as it reached a pinnacle, furious as lovemaking, and then descended the other side until it drew to a soft conclusion. Jal closed her eyes for a brief moment as the last note faded, then she opened them to find Ciaran studying her.

The expression on his face was curious, fascinated even. His lips were parted just slightly, though his mouth closed when he caught her looking his way.

She reached up and brushed away that lock of hair that always seemed to fall across his forehead. A tremor went through him, palpable even from that glancing touch, but he didn't otherwise move, just watched to see what she would do. "Maybe I don't *need* to apologize, but I want to. We did what we did, and then I—"

"If I pushed you, please tell me."

"No, no, you didn't push me to do anything I didn't want to do." She shook her head so hard in defiance that one of the combs started to come loose in her hair.

She reached up to fix it, but he gently brushed her hand aside and reseated it among her curls. Releasing it, his thumb trailed along the shell of her ear and down her cheek. She wrapped it up in both of her hands and held his hand in her lap. She studied his callused fingers, the scars across his knuckles, souvenirs of his rough upbringing, and marveled at how his hand seemed to almost dwarf both of hers.

Jal considered her next words carefully, and when she spoke, her voice was quiet enough that Ciaran leaned closer. "It was me who did things that I shouldn't have."

His hand twitched in hers. "Jal, you don't need to explain."

She shook her head. "I *do*, but I don't think I'm ready yet." She squared her shoulders and finally looked up at him. "There are *many* things about my past that I'm not quite ready to talk about. But what I will promise, is that when I am ready to share 'my truth' as you call it, I will."

He curled his fingers, tangling them with whatever parts of her hands they touched. "And I promise that when you do, I'll be there." He leaned even closer until he was almost breathing his words onto her lips. "Whatever you have to tell me, lass, it will not scare me away. And whatever you may need from me, you need only ask, and it is yours. If time is what you need, then that is what you shall have."

Jal slid a hand free and cupped his cheek. His eyes remained open and watchful as her thumb stroked his cheekbone, the stubble from a day's growth of beard rasped pleasantly against the skin of her palm. "Kiss me, then."

His lips curled. "As you wish," he replied and did just that.

TWENTY

His hand slid into her hair and cupped her head as his lips touched hers. Jal's mouth opened almost immediately, and he drank her in. Their tongues met, danced, the tension slipping away as she practically melted into his arms. Her arms wrapped around his neck, holding him to her while she kissed him.

And kissed him, she did. Ciaran smiled against her lips and changed the angle of the kiss, tasting the red wine she'd drunk, and something else that was just her.

A moment, or a year, later, she eased back and, as she had in her apartment, rested her forehead against his for a breath, and then two. The tenderness of the gesture, as if she wanted to extend the contact just a little longer, did funny things to his stomach. Ciaran slowly opened his eyes and found her watchful, gazing at him through her eyelashes.

When their eyes met and locked, the shy smile that stretched her lips punched him low in the gut.

He pressed a soft, closed-lipped kiss to her lips and got to his feet. "Come along," he said as he held a hand down to her. "You must be getting cold, much like our food, I'm sure."

As if on cue, his stomach growled. He clapped a hand over the spot, and grinned.

She shook her head ruefully, but she was smiling as she took his hand and let him pull her to her feet.

He tucked her in against his hip and put a hand around her, marveling at how soft and smooth her skin was, at how easily her body molded against him now that the air was a little clearer between them. Jasmine filled his nose as she brushed close in front of him to pass through the glass doors and back into the warmth of the building.

The image of her sitting across the table from him that first night she'd met him at Amicetto rose to his mind as she started down the stairs. She had been so full of indignation then, her lovely, but wickedly sharp, emerald eyes shooting daggers at him.

And she'd had such an effective way of persuading him.

"So, I have to ask. If your dress that night was meant to 'kick my ass' as you so charmingly put it. What is this dress meant to do?"

The devilish look she shot him as they descended the stairs went straight to his groin and his foot slid off the next step. He caught himself with a hand on the railing.

Her smoky curl of laughter echoed off the wall as she continued down, and if he wasn't mistaken, the sway of her hips was a little more exaggerated with each step. She stopped at the bottom and half-turned, her expression confirming she knew exactly what she was doing.

When he continued to stand frozen, mesmerized, she tilted her head inquisitively and held her hand up to him.

Ciaran cleared his throat and joined her.

Ciaran walked close behind her as they wove through the narrow space between the rows of tables. The softness of her skin still lingered on Ciaran's fingers, as he walked close behind her while they wove through the rows of tables. The scent of her hair was still the only thing he could smell, even with the fragrant steam rising from the meals they passed.

Her friends were seated where they had left them, with their male friend taking up half of what little walking space there was between the tables. The servers probably weren't too happy about it, though the stir his arrival had caused told him the man was probably important enough for him to get away with it.

He looked up as they approached, but Jal's friends had their backs to them and didn't turn. As they rounded the table and her friends' eyes fell on them, Ciaran began to feel a little like something squished under a microscope. He glanced at his watch as he pulled out Jal's chair and was shocked to find that they had only been gone for ten minutes.

The dark haired one—Elena, he remembered—looked at Jal thoughtfully for a moment, then caught her eye and ran a thumb along the edge of her bottom lip and lifted her eyebrow slightly.

An adorable flush rose to Jal's cheeks and she copied the gesture, straightening the slightly-smudged line of her lipstick.

Ciaran schooled his expression and fought the urge to puff out his chest, even a bit. The same couldn't be said to the heat rising to his own face.

"We had them take the food back to the kitchen to keep warm," Lexi said, her tone suggesting that she was trying to be helpful. Ciaran suspected that it was to keep Elena from asking just what they had been up to while they were gone.

He gave her a grateful smile at the same time as Jal turned to her and said, "Thanks, Lex. That was very thoughtful of you."

Their male friend looked over at Ciaran then and offered a hand. "Maksim Brody," he said by way of introduction. "Call me Maks."

Ciaran took it and introduced himself. "Quite the hubbub when you arrived," he remarked. "Are you a film star, or something? Broadway, maybe?"

Jal choked on her wine. The two women seated across from him had frozen, and stared at him with twin expressions of disbelief, though they couldn't have been any more different in appearance.

"Do you even have ice hockey in Scotland?" Elena asked him. The tone of her voice was amused, but not mocking.

Ciaran smiled crookedly. "Of course we do, somewhere."

"Ciaran's a soccer—" Jal patted his arm. "I mean, football fan."

"I went to my first game with Cliff a few weeks ago, I'll have you know." he replied, though most of the indignant tone in his voice was forced. "The Legion were playing New Jersey if I remember correctly."

Maks thought for a moment. "I had two assists in that game, I think." he said, and took a sip from his drink, something clear and bubbling.

"Oh, aye?"

Lexi sat up a little straighter in her seat and gestured to the man who sat between them. "Maks is starting left defensemen for the Legion."

Two servers arrived carrying plates and Ciaran continued speaking while Lexi directed where to place them. "Oh, aye? Quite the spectacle it was, with all the lights and the music and the food, not to mention what was happening down on the ice."

"Well, let me know when you want to catch a game, and I'll hook you up," Maks offered. He sipped his drink and, seeing that they were waiting, gestured at them to start. "Oh, I ate after practice. Please, go ahead."

The conversation died off as they dug in. He suppressed a groan when the first forkful of paella hit his tongue with an explosion of saffron and garlic in his mouth. The shrimp was tender, without any of the tell-tale rubberiness it normally took on when in the kitchen too long. He reached for the basket of flatbread in the middle of the table just as Jal did the same. Their hands brushed, sending tingles up his arm. She glanced at him, cheeks pink, as they each selected a piece and returned to their meals.

"I've been back in town since June and I've not seen Jal out with anyone," Maks remarked. "How long have you two been seeing each other?"

Jal reached for her wine. There was a flash of green as she glanced at him quickly and then away. A corner of her mouth twitched.

Ciaran cleared his throat and dabbed at his mouth with his napkin. "Not long. And you two?" He gestured between Maks and Lexi with his fork.

He was met with a ring of incredulous faces. Chagrined, Ciaran looked slowly around the table. He thought he saw a twinkle of amusement in Elena's eyes, but as his gaze settled on Lexi and Maks, he was met with almost twin looks of surprise. They exchanged a glance, eyes locking for a moment before both broke out laughing.

"No, man," Maks leaned back and hooked an elbow over the low back of his chair. He scratched his chin, the definition of nonchalance, but Ciaran also noted that he made a point of not looking in Lexi's direction. "We grew up together. We're just friends."

"My apologies." Ciaran schooled his expression and returned to his dinner, as did everyone else.

Soon, their plates were empty, and their drinks drained. The waiter deposited the bill on the corner of the table between Ciaran and Maks. Both men made a grab for it, but Maks was faster.

Must be those hockey reflexes, Ciaran thought as he pulled his wallet from a back pocket anyway and pulled out a credit card. The women, he noted, were also reaching into their purses for cash and cards.

"I got it," Maks said, waiving them off.

"Aye, no, don't be ridiculous, you had only a fizzy drink," he protested, ignoring the cards being pushed across the table or the cash coming from beside him and plucking the bill from Maks's hand. "I'll take it."

Ciaran was sure the man made more playing a single game than Ciaran did in half a year, but that didn't matter. Elena and Lexi retrieved their cards and put them away at the dismissive wave of his hand.

Jal took a bit more convincing before she took the bills he pressed back into her hands and returned them to her purse. He handed his card to the waiter to process through the handheld card machine he held.

The group rose from the table and threaded their way back toward the elevator. Ciaran and Maks waited while the host retrieved coats for Lexi and Elena, and a length of deep copper knitted cloth for Jal. Drawn in by the urge to touch her, Ciaran took the wrap before she could reach for it and shook it out. Stepping behind her, he draped it around her shoulders, allowing his fingers to trail along her collarbones.

She looked up at him in silent thanks, and their eyes locked. An echo of the expression that had lit her face in the moment before she'd hauled him into her apartment returned. As if drawn by a magnet, he leaned forward, closing the distance between their lips.

A shrill whistle separated them before he could reach his goal. They turned together towards the sound. A corner of Elena's mouth turned up as she pointed a thumb over her shoulder at the open elevator.

Jal put a hand to her mouth, that bottom lip curling between her teeth, color burning high on her cheeks. How was it possible for the look in her eyes to both admonish him and promise more?

Ciaran swallowed hard and put a hand on Jal's back as they followed her friend inside. After some jostling around with a few other patrons, Ciaran found himself standing in a corner with Jal in front of him. The door had almost closed when one last person slipped through the gap in the golden doors, causing a ripple effect as those inside scrambled back that ended with Jal and her perfect arse pressed tightly against him, not that he minded in the least. His hands came to rest on her hips and her scent filled his nose once more.

She stiffened at his touch for a moment so brief he wondered if he'd imagined it before she melted against him. His cock twitched and he forced himself to breathe and think of unpleasant things, like the incessant screech of his old auntie's endless complaining and the revolting smell of pickled herring on her breath while she did it, anything to keep from giving in to the urge to nuzzle her neck, or do any of the other more enjoyable things his mind was concocting that weren't appropriate to do in public.

The elevator descended rapidly enough for Ciaran's ears to pop every few floors, the numbers over the doors dropping so quickly they were almost a blur of red. Though he could see it coming, the car drew to a lurching stop at the lobby with enough force that he heard several gasps and the clatter of high heels.

Jal stumbled, her head bumped against his chest, barely missing his chin. Her arms flung out, reaching for the walls of the elevator on either side of his hips to catch her balance, the consequence of which was her arse pressing even tighter against his groin. He hissed a muffled "Christ" through his teeth.

There was a quiet snigger of laughter from directly in front of him, barely audible over the echoing din in the lobby.

Ciaran risked making a scene as everyone filed out when he ducked his head and nipped her earlobe. "Like that, is it?" He murmured low enough that only she could hear.

She shivered from his breath blowing on her ear. "I don't know what you're talking about," she replied coyly, or at least she tried, though her voice still wrapped around him like smoke.

He laughed softly. "Oh, I ken fine that you do."

She shivered again. He placed a hand on her lower back and followed close behind as they exited the elevator so he didn't lose her in the throng that nearly packed the lobby. He quickly lost sight of Jal's friends as the boarding passengers flowed around them like a parting sea of humanity. They passed between a queue of people waiting for the elevator, and another that led to a smoky glass doorway with a red velvet rope and two imposing guards granting or refusing entrance to the speakeasy night club in the basement. In the middle, lay a milling mass of people overflowing the bar area that took up about a quarter of the large open space.

When they reached the exit, Ciaran found himself stepping into the same wedge of the revolving door, and bent close to her ear. "All you need to do is say the word."

She looked up at him as they emerged onto the street and her eyes flared. The simmering embers burning there told him that she understood his meaning.

Her friends had formed a circle to one side of the entrance. Elena looked over at them. "We're going to head to *Darcy's* for a nightcap, you wanna join us?"

Jal shook her head. "No, I think I'm going to turn in."

She hadn't glanced his way, but he noticed that she had

drawn a corner of her lower lip between her teeth. Ciaran could tell that Elena had seen too, though she was doing an admirable job of not showing it. Much.

"I can take her home," Ciaran offered. "My car is just up the street."

A little sparkle came into Elena's eyes and a corner of her mouth turned up. She looked back and forth between them. "Works for me," she replied. "I'll call you tomorrow."

Lexi threw her goodbyes over her shoulder as Elena herded them up the street. They had only gone a few feet before they erupted in giggles, clutching at each other to stay on their high heels. Maks just shook his head and kept walking beside them, his hands casually in the pockets of a black pea coat.

"Those two are about as subtle as a hydrogen bomb."

Ciaran turned to find Jal standing at his shoulder staring after her friends. He smiled. "I think the bomb would be less noticeable."

Jal looked up at him and the broad smile on her face froze, then became something softer, as their gazes locked. Her lower lip disappeared behind her teeth again and the expression in her eyes, those lovely emerald eyes, seemed to darken as they shifted down to his mouth. The look punched him low in the gut. Lower.

Quick as a snake, she rose up on her tiptoes, threw her arms around his neck, and devoured him.

Unlike their kiss on the roof, which had been a gentle sealing of a bargain between them, this time their bodies and lips collided. The world fell away in an explosion of light behind his closed eyelids that had nothing to do with passing headlights or the glittering marquee across the street.

He dragged her flush against him, his hands sliding under her wrap to the bare silken expanse of her back. Their tongues battled, his advancing into her mouth then beating a hasty retreat, twisting and turning around each other as if wrestling for dominance, though if this night was heading where he hoped it was, neither would truly lose.

In true New York fashion, a hail of catcalls and whistles sounded from around them from the queue of people who hadn't yet made it inside. Unphased, Jal eased back only far enough so she could whisper, "where did you say your car was?"

Ciaran took her hand and spun around, heading in the opposite direction her friends had gone. Jal's free arm swung out to keep her balance then gripped his wrist as she scrambled to keep up with his longer-legged pace. He forced himself to slow and she caught up, one hand slipping through his elbow, as they rounded the corner.

His blue two-door coupe waited a half-block up. It wasn't anything fancy, or all that new, but it got him where he needed to go when public transportation didn't, or would take too long, and it was the perfect size to fit into tight city parking places.

Jal surveyed the clearance around the car where it was wedged between a massive SUV and a pickup truck. She put a hand to her mouth and giggled. "Looks like we're not going anywhere."

He leveled her with a look and opened the passenger door. "Oh, ye of little faith," he chided, helping her in. "I'll have you know that I once got my mate's Mini Cooper out of a spot much tighter than this." He closed the door and raced around to climb in behind the wheel.

Despite having parked between the same two vehicles before dinner, Ciaran sent up a quick prayer that he wouldn't embarrass himself before putting the car in reverse and executing the first of many zig zags, each one smooth and controlled, without making any contact with either of the expensive-looking vehicles. After one more small adjustment backward, he popped out into traffic, cutting in front of a taxi who rode his bumper and blared the horn, its driver making none too friendly gestures out the window.

Jal smothered a laugh with her hand and then patted his on the gearshift. "I should never have doubted you."

Twenty-One

Jal was going to come out of her skin if the car in front of them didn't get the hell out of their way. Under her fingers, Ciaran's hand clenched around the shifter tight enough to send a fine tremor coursing through him and into her. The air in the car nearly vibrated with it.

She didn't dare move a muscle, just sat with her back pressed into the soft leather and stared at the flashing red lights in front of them. Without moving her head, she risked a glance to her left.

Another flare of brake lights struck his angular features, throwing his deep-set eyes into shadow. The muscles of his neck and jaw stood out, his nose scrunching up and blowing air like a bull every time the car braked at a small gap between parked cars or whatever the heck they were doing that didn't involve getting out of their way.

As if the driver heard her thoughts, they stopped short and put their reverse lights on. Ciaran swore and jumped on the brake and clutch at the same time. Jal tensed, throwing a hand toward the dashboard, but the seatbelt caught and pulled her back.

"Sorry," he muttered. He waited for a moment to see if the driver would start backing up. When they just put their signal on, he muttered another curse and spun the wheel, accelerating around the car, narrowly missing their bumper as it chose that moment to swing their way. She had no idea what he said, but the tone was something along the lines of "the hell with this."

Jal chuckled and braced with her legs to keep from getting thrown into the door, swallowing a gasp when her thighs squeezed together, making her very aware of just how the energy in the car had affected her.

At least she thought she'd smothered it, until Ciaran glanced over at her with a heated gaze. The corner of his mouth twitched. "We're almost there."

The brightly lit arch in Washington Square Park came into view ahead of them, but he cranked the wheel a couple of blocks before it onto a narrow one-way street that cut between two rows of brownstone townhouses barely visible in the illumination cast by the streetlights they passed. Halfway down the block, he slid the car neatly into a parking space and cut the engine. The hand beneath hers disappeared as he threw the door open, and circled around to open her door before she could even reach the handle.

He offered down a hand and drew her to her feet, raising her arm up over his shoulder so her body collided with his, evidence that he was just as worked up as she was pressed against her belly. She tipped her chin up just in time for his lips to crash down on hers.

He wrapped his arms around her, and she giggled against his lips as they stumbled through a little dance, so he had room to close the door that ended with her pressed against the car with him standing between her knees.

The door handle dug into the back of her hip, but it was a price she was willing to pay to have his tongue exploring her mouth, and his body molded around hers, the hardness of him trapped between them.

A few moments later she broke the kiss and grabbed his hand. She made it a few steps up the street before she stopped. "Um, which way?"

Ciaran laughed and spun her in the opposite direction. Jal clutched the ends of her wrap together and scrambled to keep up. A few doors down, he mounted the stairs and led her through two sets of doors and up another flight of stairs. He stopped in front of the lone door and fumbled with his keys.

Jal bounced on her toes, a split second from pushing him against the door and dropping to her knees when he found the right key and opened the door.

He had barely managed to turn on the lights before she slid her hands up his chest and over his shoulders, sending both of his coats to the floor. Their eyes locked, both breathing hard, both waiting for the other to make the next move.

A low growl in his throat a moment later was the only warning she had before he pulled the wrap from her shoulders and stepped into her, his arms wrapping around her waist as his mouth claimed hers. He sent her stumbling back a step, then two, somehow managing to keep from rolling an ankle.

She broke the kiss and bent over in the circle of his arms

to slip her shoes off, sending them clattering to the floor. She straightened and reached up to remove his tie, tossing it behind him before starting in on his vest buttons.

He released her one arm at a time to let the garment drop as he continued to herd her backwards across what she assumed was his living room. There was warm light, and cream-colored walls, a scattering of decorations on the walls, but Jal's focus was on more important things than whether or not Ciaran was a good interior decorator.

She soon had his shirt unbuttoned. Ciaran released her to remove his cufflinks one by one and tossed his shirt aside. The cufflinks clattered onto a table as he stalked toward her, eyes locked on her breasts as they rose and fell with her breathing.

The toned muscles of his chest had just the slightest dusting of hair. The muscles of his abdomen, which were well defined but not starkly chiseled, were bare to his navel where a trail of hair disappeared into the waistband of his pants.

He gave her a moment to study him, a pleased look coming into his eyes when she couldn't help licking her lips in appreciation. Then, she let out a whoop of surprise as he wrapped his arms low around her waist and lifted her off her feet.

Jal tried to wrap her legs around him, but the long skirt got in the way. She kicked feebly to get free of it, but the material was trapped between them. She growled, then laughed as her feet swung helplessly in the air. "Let me down."

Ciaran laughed as he set her down. She took his hand and turned, finding the doorway to his bedroom only a few feet away. A frantic heartbeat later, he stepped up behind her, one hand splaying across her stomach, and matched her step for step through the doorway, all the while nuzzling at her neck.

He found the sensitive spot beneath her ear that made her moan just as they passed into the shadows of his room. He latched onto that spot, sucking gently, then licked away the delicious sting with his tongue until she was panting against him, knees trembling. It would likely leave a mark, and she found that she didn't care.

He slapped for the light switch, managing to find it on the third try. A lamp on the nightstand came to life, illuminating a room with pale blue walls, a scattering of dark wood furniture, and a large bed, neatly made with a dark gray duvet.

Ciaran's hands slid down over her hips and bunched up the fabric of her dress, dragging the hem up her legs handful by handful. It passed her knees, and then his hands were on the bare skin of her thighs, then her ass, and then it was gone, leaving Jal wearing only a lacy copper-colored thong. The cool air of the room hit the already heated skin of her breasts and belly, tightening her nipples and sending a shiver through her.

She turned slowly, and forced her hands to remain at her sides. Though he had already seen her breasts, there was something different this time, knowing where things were heading.

Ciaran swallowed. "You're the most beautiful thing I've ever seen." His voice was deep, almost a growl, as his hands slid up her sides and cupped her breasts, his thumbs brushing slow circles around the tight peaks.

Jal's head fell back, a moan escaping her lips as he pinched one nipple then bent to kiss away the hurt, using his tongue to torture her. He sucked at her nipple and her knees gave out. This time, when he scooped her off her feet, Jal wrapped her legs around his waist.

"Please," was all she could murmur as she buried her hands in his hair. He moved to the other breast as he walked to the bed, carrying her as if she weighed very little with one hand under her rear, the other buried in her hair.

Just when she thought he was going to lower her to the bed and climb on top, he turned and sat on the edge with her straddling his lap.

He released her nipple with a pop that made her laugh, the sound low and sultry. His eyes flared at the promise in it and kissed her again. There was nothing gentle about this kiss, and Jal found that gentle was the last thing she wanted, anyway. The night had been building to this since the moment he'd met her eyes as he crossed the restaurant. There would be time for gentle later.

For now, she wanted to feel all of him, every inch of skin she could touch. She broke the kiss and put two hands on his chest, and eased him slowly onto his back. She leaned over him just enough for her breasts to brush across his chest.

He tried to sit up to kiss her again, but she pushed him down, with a little more force this time, and sat up. "Stay put, please."

He crooked an eyebrow at her, but then just tucked an arm behind his head and waited to see what she had in mind. The muscle of his bicep flexed in a way that made her mouth water. In the dim pool of light from the room outside, shadows pooled in the valleys of his muscles and the angular planes of his face.

Jal slid her hands down the length of his abdomen, the bumps of muscle tensing under her touch. She got the impression that her touch had only done so much and like with his bicep, he was flexing a little for her. "Really?" She asked with mock disbelief.

"What's a man to do when he has a beautiful woman on top of him doing wicked things?"

Wicked, eh?

Her hands went to the buckle of his pants while she bent and pressed a kiss over his heart, then slowly worked her way down. She spent a moment teasing each nipple before moving across his abdomen, running her tongue across the grooves between muscles. The belt parted with a rattle of metal, and she went to work on the fastenings of his pants to spread them open.

He hissed as her hand brushed over the bulge now covered only by a thin layer of some soft fabric that was nearly as silky as the skin beneath it. Despite the state she'd been in that day in her apartment, she had full memory of how he had felt in her hand, and however briefly, in her mouth.

She stroked her hand over him again then met his eye almost as if asking for permission as she hooked her fingers over the waistband.

Ciaran just looked back at her with those half-lidded eyes. The muscles in his arms and stomach trembled with barely-leashed tension as if it took physical effort not to take command of the situation. Permission enough.

Jal pulled the waistband down and his erection sprang free to rest on his belly, reaching nearly to his navel. She wrapped her hand around him and stroked from root to tip. His eyes rolled back in his head and his chin kicked up. His hips rose with the next stroke. The third had him barking out,

"Oh, Christ, Jal."

She gave him another of her smoky laughs at that and crawled off his lap. He opened his eyes, giving her a look of disbelief. In response, she gripped his pants and yanked. He shifted down the bed with them eliciting an amused grunt of surprise.

"Strong wee thing, aren't you?" he remarked as he lifted his hips and pushed the material down over his ass. With a second yank, they slid free, his belt narrowly missing her face as the material flew past over her shoulder. There was a loud crash as the lamp toppled to the floor, plunging the room into darkness.

Jal ducked instinctively at the sound. A wave of cold banked the heat deep inside, and her muscles went rigid, bracing for Ciaran's reaction. "I'm sorry," she said, her voice wobbled.

There was a rustle of sheets, and her mind showed her an image of him standing over her, hand raised, fury creasing his beautiful face. She closed her eyes, refusing to believe what she was seeing, and shook her head.

Instead, he only touched her with a knuckle, gently stroking up and down her arm.

When she dared to open her eyes, she found Ciaran sitting on the edge of the bed watching her as he removed his socks of all things. She was absurdly relieved at the sight. There was nothing more ridiculous than a naked man still wearing socks.

His eyes still blazed with heat, but not from anger. "It's nay bother, lass." he replied. "Come here to me."

Jal reached up and removed the two fan-shaped combs from her hair and dropped them to the floor. The heavy curls cascaded down over her shoulders, brushing the sensitive peaks of her breasts with each step toward him, stopping when she stood between his knees.

He wrapped his arms around her hips and pressed a kiss to the hollow between her breasts. She arched her back, leaning into his touch and buried her hands in his hair as he blazed a trail of kisses to her nipple and wrapped his mouth around it.

Her breathing hitched when his tongue swirled around the tight tip while his thumbs slid under the lace covering her hips and slid the thong to the floor. She stepped out of the scrap of material and kicked it away.

There was a flash of delicious pain as he nipped at the flesh in his mouth, and he once again eased the hurt with his tongue. He looked up at her, his mouth still wrapped around the tip of her breast, and a steady throb between her thighs pulsed in time with her heartbeat. Fast, and not at all steady.

Craving the taste of him, she tore his head away from her breast and captured his mouth with hers. The first taste of him was enough to burn away the last scrap of fear that he could ever hurt her. The first stroke of his tongue sliding along the length of hers, made the world disappear in an inferno where only the two of them existed, where only he could keep her from being consumed entirely, or else burn with her.

There came a rumble from deep in his chest and his hands slid down to grip her ass. Then, without any warning, he scooped her feet out from under her and dropped to his back. She barely managed to catch herself before she crashed down with her full weight on his chest, but she still ended up sprawled across him, legs split around his hips, his hardness sliding through her core and rubbing against the bundle of nerves there. She locked gazes with him and rocked her hips once, feeling the tip of him slide past her entrance, but he did not slip inside.

Rational thought pushed through the haze in her mind, reminding her that, while she was on birth control, it was better to be safe than sorry. "Do you have a condom?"

He turned his head and swung one arm out in the direction of his nightstand. She chuckled at the helpless little grunting noises he made as each slap of his hand didn't bring him any closer and crawled up over him to dig inside the drawer. He took the opportunity to suckle her breast while it was in reach. After a moment spent moving around the items inside, she withdrew a small box and returned to his lap.

Ciaran plucked the box from her hand and removed one of the foil packets and tossed the box over his shoulder. He tore it open with his teeth and rolled the condom down his length. When he looked back up at her, the blaze in his eyes said much more than words.

She licked her lips and wrapped her hand around the tip of his erection and slid slowly to the base with a firm pressure that brought back that rumble in his throat. She held him in place as she rose up on her knees and pointed him at her entrance. They groaned in unison as the head of him slid inside, stretching her in a way she hadn't felt in a very long time, if ever.

She slowly lowered another inch, two, then withdrew before sliding down again, claiming a few more inches. To torture them both, she rose up until just the tip remained and then locked eyes as she slid slowly down his length, feeling every delicious stretch until he was buried to the hilt inside her.

She paused for a moment to adjust to the incredible sensation of fullness, as if he touched all of her from the inside and, when she started to move, it was with small circles of her hips. His head kicked back on a curse, and she swirled another circle, a satisfied smile curled her lips at the groan that followed.

His hands slid over her hips, and gripped firmly, urging her upwards. She went but clenched her muscles around his cock as she did, only to relax on the way down with enough force that her ass slapped against his thighs. She repeated the motion, soon falling into a rhythm with him lifting to meet each of her downward strokes. The air filled with the sound of flesh meeting, the gentle creak of the bed punctuating each movement.

Jal's hands roved her own body, sweeping over her breasts, and up into her hair, lifting the weight to cool the skin of her back and neck as she rode him. A throbbing started deep in her belly, growing in intensity with each squeeze of her walls around his cock, which seemed to stiffen and swell even more inside her, until it was almost too much to bear anymore without coming undone. It was exactly what she wanted, but still she needed more. More. More.

As if Ciaran could sense how close she was, his hands dug deeper into her skin, dragging her down harder with every upward thrust of his hips, driving him deeper. Deeper than she ever thought possible. For sure, he was going to leave marks on her skin, but she found she didn't care if it meant that he kept meeting her thrust for thrust. His pants soon turned to grunts, his head pressed hard against the bed but his eyes, though dark and hooded, never once left hers.

She gripped his forearms as the first tremors began, her hips losing some of their rhythm, as the wave built up, and up, and up. "Come with me," she panted, each word timed with a frantic thrust. Her lips parted, growing wider as she teetered closer and closer to the edge.

He arched his back and rolled his hips, pressing deep. Deeper. His cock seemed to swell even more, if that were possible. His voice was deep and strained from effort, but also triumphant. "As you wish."

She came apart on the next thrust, pressing down with all her weight as electricity spiraled across every inch of her skin, her muscles rhythmically clenching around him with a ferocity that made her cry out, her back arching, head thrown back.

Ciaran thrust into her once, twice more and then held her tightly to him as he kicked back his head and roared.

She shuddered over him, every slight movement, every spasm of his cock inside her, created an aftershock almost as powerful as the orgasm itself. Moments stretched into an eternity of sensation, until finally the waves receded and she stilled and gazed down at him.

He sprawled beneath her like a Celtic god who had crashed to earth, with her rising triumphantly above. The dim light from the living room cast harsh shadows on his angular features, and scattered silver into his tousled hair.

When she leaned forward to press a gentle kiss to his lips, he slid out, leaving behind an emptiness that made her whimper at the loss. He laughed softly against her lips, then wrapped an arm around her and rolled to the side, urging her mouth open at the same time, the strokes of his tongue now soft and soothing. A moment later, he broke the kiss and eased out of her arms.

"I'll be right back."

There was just enough light for her to admire the taught muscles of his legs and ass as he left the room. She heard the closing of a door and the flush of a toilet and then the sound of his footsteps as he moved through the apartment securing the front door, extinguishing the lights.

Her eyes had long since adjusted to the gloom, but she could only make him out as a darker shadow moving across the room when he returned. The bed dipped, and then, he was there, drawing her into his arms, her back to his front.

"Sleep, lass." he whispered in her ear. "There's no one but you and me tonight."

Twenty-Two

Something jarred him out of a deep, contented sleep and, at first, he wasn't sure why. The room was nearly pitch dark, only a faint light through the curtains illuminated Jal's silhouette, still secure within the circle of his arms, her back to his chest, his knees behind hers. That glorious arse of hers cradled in the hollow in between. But something was different.

He lay in the dark, waiting for a repeat of whatever had roused him from a very pleasant dream, in which he'd been relishing in the memory of her rising above him like a triumphant siren, arms raised and twisted around her head to hold her hair up off her neck. Her eyes were closed, head thrown back, face and chest flushed from exertion.

Her hair, now spread on the pillow between them, tickled his nose and he smoothed it away. The space between them filled with the scents of jasmine and woodsmoke still clinging to the strands.

As if sensing his touch, even in her sleep, she stirred, her body seeming to ripple slowly. Her breasts lifted, then her back arched, and finally her arse pressed back against him, sliding over his cock, which had stiffened again in his sleep.

Ciaran looked down between them, even though it was too dark to see anything. He could feel what was going on perfectly fine though. Her gentle movements against him were what had roused him from sleep in more than one way. His cock slipped between her thighs while she rubbed herself against him, sliding past her entrance without dipping inside.

"Are you dreaming, lass?" he murmured in her ear. His hand slid across her hip and up her stomach, coming to rest between her breasts. Her breaths were slow and even, as was her heartbeat under his fingers.

A sleepy moan escaped her lips and her body rippled again. "If I am, I don't ever want to wake up." she replied. Her voice, though thickened with sleep, was as languorous as her movements.

Laying still while she writhed against him was a new kind of torture. But lay still he did, until the heartbeat under his fingers started to pick up its pace, and her breathing changed. It was quicker, shallower, interspersed with soft gasps.

Ciaran slid his hand slowly down her stomach and over one hip to cup that soft place between her thighs that his cock strained toward but couldn't yet reach. He slid a finger into her slit and groaned at the slickness he found there. He stroked slowly from her entrance to that tight bundle of nerves at the top, brushing lightly before repeating the long, slow path that was as much a tease for her as it was for him.

She clenched her thighs, squeezing his cock between

them when he moved to stroke small circles around her clit. Her gasps became a more unsteady panting. Slowly, her arm lifted and wrapped around the back of his head, urging him closer.

He slid his arm out from under her neck and rose up on his elbow, brushing her hair back so he could press his lips to her jaw and down to that spot he'd found under her ear that she enjoyed so much, all the while keeping up his steady stroking of her center.

Her breathing hitched and her hand tightened in his hair as an orgasm rippled through her. Her clit pulsed gently under his fingertips.

For a few moments, she lay still in his arms, long enough that he thought she might have fallen back asleep. But then, she started to thrust back against him, this time more deliberate, more urgent.

"I need you inside me." she demanded, her voice far less sleepy.

Ciaran rolled onto his back, his cock reluctantly sliding out from between her thighs and searched the top of the nightstand until he found the box he'd tossed there earlier. He tore a packet open and rolled a condom over his cock before turning back onto his side. His hand splayed across her stomach and drew her arse tightly against his cock. One of her hands rose to cover his on her stomach, while the other reached back and grasped his hip, urging him closer, to get him where she wanted him.

"So demanding," he purred in her ear as he slid his hand along her inner thigh and lifted her leg up and over his to give him access to her core.

Jal shifted against him as he wrapped a hand around his straining cock and fitted the head to her entrance. He took her hip in his hand and pushed inside. She was warm, and tight, and more than ready for him and he slid to the hilt in one slow, torturous thrust. He withdrew part of the way and slid home, again. And again.

They soon found a gentle rhythm, their bodies rippling apart and coming back together like the advance and retreat of waves on the shore. Neither made a move to force the pace, each moment stretching out into an eternity that he never wanted to end. Each stroke felt to him like the swing of a hammer on iron, forging something between them that didn't yet have a shape, yet nevertheless connected them in a way he had never experienced with Annie, especially not in so short a time.

When he felt her turn her head toward him, demanding a kiss, he found her mouth unerringly in the dark as if he would always know where it was. This kiss was just as tender, just as sweet, their tongues sliding in time with each torturously slow thrust. He pressed in deep, pausing there, and made a small circle with his hips. She broke the kiss on a groan and threw her head back against his shoulder.

He retreated and then repeated the movement, and again, her inner muscles clenching harder and harder on his cock as she grew closer to her release. He tensed, his balls drawing up tight in response, a current of energy barreled down his spine.

Another stroke, two, and he thrust as deep into her as he could, buried his face in her hair, and went thoroughly to pieces. Dimly, he heard her make a sharp gasp and then a long, low groan as she toppled over the edge with him.

They lay curled together for a long moment as his cock slowly deflated and the rhythmic clenching of her sex eased. Reluctantly, he pulled out of her and left the bed, only long enough to dispose of the condom before gathering her in his arms once again.

She sighed contentedly at the return of his warm body against her back and soon her breathing slowed, evened out once again to the rhythm of sleep. Her body relaxed completely in his arms.

Ciaran remained awake a little longer, gently smoothing his hand over her hair, unable to keep from touching her. He listened to their mingled breathing, the only sound in the night. Her chest rose and fell under his hand, and he found himself wondering as he had so many times these past few weeks how it only took one look from her to have him craving her. And that laugh of hers? The one full of wicked promises? Well, that practically brought him to his knees. And now that he finally had her in his bed?

Heaven help them both.

He took a deep breath and settled his head more comfortably on the pillow. His hand slowly slid down low on her belly and came to rest just above the neatly trimmed curls that paved the way to her core. Beneath his fingertips was a thin line of roughened skin a couple of inches long. Ciaran frowned, his fingers tracing gently over it. Jal stirred in his arms, snuggling against him before subsiding back into the stillness of sleep.

Ciaran lay his hand flat on her stomach once more, closed his eyes, and forced himself not to dwell on thoughts that suddenly raced through his head. There was only one reason for a woman to have a scar in that particular spot.

Instead, he concentrated on his breathing, on matching the calm, steady rhythm of the woman in his arms. A woman who clearly had more secrets than he'd thought. Sooner than he could have expected, he was asleep.

Twenty-Three

When Ciaran woke the next morning, his arms were empty. He cracked his eyes open, squinting against the glare and found that she had retreated to her side of the bed. She was on her stomach, but her face was turned his way. Her eyes were closed. Her long, black eyelashes stark against her pale skin, though there was a touch of color in her cheeks. Her arms were wrapped around the pillow, her hair a midnight cloud around her. The covers pooled at her lower back leaving a smooth expanse of creamy pale skin that beckoned him to touch it. His hand, tingling as if in response to her siren's call, drifted across the duvet.

The cotton was cool under his fingers, since there had been other matters on his mind last night than turning up the heating. By comparison, her exposed skin was almost feverish, her body churning out a comforting heat that at once seeped into his skin and spread through him.

He skimmed his hand up and over her shoulder to her

neck and then down her spine as he drank in the way the light struck onyx sparks in her hair, the way her skin soaked it in so it almost shimmered.

Her limbs were long and lean, though the top of her head barely reached the level of his nose, even when she stood in heels. Her talented pickpocket's hands were hidden now under her pillow, but he couldn't forget the way they had felt on his skin, or buried in his hair. And those luscious breasts? They too were hidden, but his hands remembered how they filled his palms, each crowned with a nipple that he craved to worship with his mouth. Her glorious backside was a shapely curve beneath the sheets, but he remembered how it had fit into the curve of his hips, pinning his cock between them.

Jal stirred, roused by his touch, but did not wake fully. She lifted her head, but only to turn it the other way before settling in, and returning to the stillness of sleep.

His hand continued to stroke in slow circles as he inched his way across the space between them. The mattress dipped gently, and while it felt as wide as an ocean, it was really only a foot. He did not want to disturb her sleep, but like with his hand, something pulled at him, urging him to move closer, to take her in his arms and never let her go.

When only a few inches separated them, he slid his hand across and over her hip, exerting a slight upward pressure, a request that she roll toward him. After a moment, her arm slid from under the pillow and she rolled onto her side, the curve of her hip emerging from beneath the duvet.

His hand came across her stomach as he tucked his knees behind hers. He hissed at the friction over his cock, her small movements sending a rush of blood into it. He pressed a kiss to her shoulder and closed his eyes. Whatever it was inside him that craved the feel of her settled with a contented purr.

Ciaran had nearly fallen asleep, the jasmine of her hair filling his nose, when she murmured something and shifted against him. Half-asleep, his mind drifted back to the night before, when she had urged him into a second round with her arse rubbing against his cock. He adjusted his position, only to slide the arm pinned beneath him under her pillow, his other arm holding her gently but close against him.

The sound that came from her then was a whimper, but not one of pleasure.

It was the last thing he had expected, and he moved his hand across her belly in small circles. But where last night his touch had soothed, now it had the opposite effect. Her whimper became more pained, her movements more forceful, more frantic as she struggled to free herself from his arms.

Ciaran raised himself up on his elbow and looked down. Her face was no longer peaceful, her eyes were clenched tightly shut, deep furrows creasing the skin between them. He called her name, but she only shook her head, her hair tangling on the pillow. Her hands grasped handfuls of the duvet and pulled, not to cover herself, but to drag herself away. He put his hand on her shoulder and shook gently.

"Jal," Ciaran pleaded into her ear. "Jal, wake up."

She didn't open her eyes, too deeply ensnared in whatever nightmare made her shy away from his touch, and continued to fight, to claw her way to the edge of the bed until she crashed to the floor in a heap.

Ciaran cursed and scrambled across to peer over the edge of the bed, mind racing. *What the bloody hell is going on?*

Jal sat with her knees drawn up to her chin. Her eyes were open now, and showing entirely too much white around the brilliant green irises. Her gaze darted around as if looking for something, anything, familiar.

"Jal?" he prompted uncertainly.

Her gaze turned his way. A tremor went through him as she seemed to look *through* him.

A choked sob came out of her throat and she scooted back. "Keep away from me!"

He said her name again, his voice now desperate, almost pleading, but it had no effect. She had to still be dreaming, he told himself, but he didn't know how to wake her up. Pushing the covers aside, he slid to the ground beside her.

Jal scrambled away until she hit the wall, her wide, staring eyes never leaving the general direction of his face, but not truly seeing him.

"Jal, please, come back to me."

Her chest rose and fell far too quickly. "Don't come any closer!"

Ciaran reached out a hand and she lashed out with her foot, kicking it away. He turned the curse that wanted to come out into a grunt and pulled his hand back. A second kick connected with his shin. "Bloody hell!" he cried before he could stop himself.

"Get the fuck away from me, Andy!"

Ciaran froze, his hand hovering in the air between them. *So that's the bastard's name.* He didn't have time to dwell on that thought. She was still breathing much too fast, her face bone white.

"Jal, love, you have to wake up now." He reached for her

again, his hand visibly trembling. In this moment, he was just as scared as she.

She tried to retreat along the length of the wall, but fetched up against a bookcase, her legs tangled in a blanket that had fallen from the bed sometime in the night. As if the fight had gone out of her, she sat curled tightly into a ball, her knees pulled up under her chin, her arms wrapped around her head. It was as if by making herself small, he wouldn't be able to see her.

Or do any major damage to anything vital, he thought cynically. This Andy must have been one foul bastard.

Ciaran inched his way closer, making soft, soothing noises. Shifting slowly, inch by torturous inch until he was close enough to put a hand on her shoulder, but when his skin met hers, she jolted as if he had built up a static shock getting to her.

She didn't move for the longest time, and though he couldn't see her face, something had changed. The muscles under his hand were still tight, but no longer rigid as stone.

He spoke her name in a cautious whisper, and she lifted her head at the sound of his voice. Her eyes at once focused, really focused, on his face.

"Ciaran?" she whispered, still trembling. Then the realization of what had happened hit her, and she started to shake. "Oh God, not again."

He reached down and untangled her legs, then shook the blanket out and paused half-way to wrapping it around her. A corner of Jal's mouth lifted as she scooted a little away from the wall to make room, but didn't fully emerge from the balled-up position.

Ciaran wrapped the blanket around her and gently stroked his hands up and down her arms. The shiver that shook him then reminded him that he too was naked to the cool air of the room, but he didn't want to crowd her under the blanket, nor was he willing to leave her side just yet, even to put some clothes on. The endless rotation of council flats with dodgy heating in his early twenties had conditioned him to tolerate cold enough to ignore seeing his breath every time he'd breathed. This was nothing.

Slowly, too slowly for his liking, her muscles started to thaw, her knees came untucked from under her chin. He continued to rub up and down her arms, chafing whatever warmth he could into her. As her muscles relaxed, she listed to one side and Ciaran caught her, gathering her into his arms. After a moment, her hands slid around his waist and she melted against him, her shoulders shaking.

When she lifted her head from his shoulder a little while later, he was starting to shiver in earnest, a fine tremor wracking his whole body and threatening to make his teeth chatter. Her eyes, red and swollen from the tears that stained her cheeks, met his and her face colored even more with shame. "I'm sorry." she whispered, barely more than a breath.

He pressed a kiss to her forehead, by way of acceptance, though there was nothing for her to apologize for. "Give me one second," he told her as he eased her back, releasing her only when he was sure she wouldn't topple over again.

She nodded and wiped her face with a corner of the blanket.

He could feel her eyes on him as he moved around the room, pulling on a pair of sweatpants, digging a dressing gown out of his closet for her. He crouched beside her and traded the light blanket for a heavier cotton.

She wrapped it around herself and tied the belt, then allowed him to pull her to her feet.

Ciaran eyed the bed for a moment, taking in the rumpled covers, half of which had fallen to the floor. For the first time, the pillows on both sides of his bed had deep indents, rather than just his side, the other half untouched and cold. He wasn't prepared for the rush that came over him at the sight. His heart thumped hard, seeming to grow a little bigger with each beat, until it filled his chest and threatened to burst free.

"Are you okay?" she asked when they stood there a bit too long.

He looked down at her and smiled crookedly. "Shouldn't I be asking you that?"

Giving the bed a pass, he ushered her into the living room and tucked her into one of the chairs, walking away only long enough to make tea and carry it back. She accepted the mug without a word, but didn't drink it immediately, instead clutching it between her hands as if it were a lifeline.

Ciaran went to the wall by the door and adjusted the thermostat. There was a click, and, almost at once, the room filled with the hiss and creak of the city's ubiquitous steam system moving through the radiators between the windows. He stayed where he was and studied her for a long moment as she stared into the depths of the cup.

She was pale, her face drawn and distracted, her eyes still red, but the tremors had eased at least.

Ciaran called her name, his voice gentle. It took her a moment before she lifted her eyes to his. "Who's Andy?"

Jal blushed again and looked back down. "You're angry, aren't you?"

His heart clenched, that her default was to assume the worst. He crossed the room, approaching slowly with his hands loose and at his sides, then knelt at her feet, sitting back on his heels. "Not at you."

She looked down at him and took a deep breath as if to steady herself, blowing it out on a sigh. "Andy was my last boyfriend." She gripped the mug a little tighter. "We were together for a little over a year. Everything was great at first. He was sweet, and generous. He promised that he could help give me a life where I didn't need to steal anymore. I'd been living in a shoebox in Chinatown at the time, and his place in the Bronx seemed like a palace, even if it was in a rough neighborhood."

Words seemed to fail her, and she took a sip of tea. "I moved in with him after only dating for a few months." Her mouth twisted. "That was my first mistake."

He took a deep breath and blew it hard out his nose, swallowing against the lump in his throat.

"Things were fine at the beginning. But then, I started to see more of the things that he had managed to hide when we lived apart. He worked long hours, and then would go to a bar. He drank more than I thought he did, and it ended with him getting into fights. He got into debt with the wrong people and, for a while, I managed to ignore it all, because he kept it outside the house and the bills still got paid."

This wasn't going to end well.

Jal released a shuddering breath, and her voice started to tremble. "Then, he started to come home drunk, to demand my money to pay his debts to the loan sharks. To demand I sleep with him on command, and when I didn't, he would beat me, and... force himself on me." She trailed off and buried her face in her hand.

Ciaran took the cup from her and set it on the coffee table so he could take her hands in his. His heart cracked when she clamped down and held on for dear life just to stop the trembling in her fingers. He wanted to kill the man who took the beautiful and brave woman he knew she was inside and turned her into someone who almost couldn't bear to be touched.

"Two years ago, when I finally worked up the nerve to leave, he lost it and pushed me down a flight of stairs." Her voice cracked, the last words barely a whisper. "He almost killed me."

Ciaran swore under his breath, his earlier fears realized. His thoughts dissolved into a mass of confusion and anger. In his mind, any man who would dare lay a finger on a woman was worse than the lowest snake. Ciaran wondered where this Andy was now, and hoped that he was far, far away for Jal's sake.

Twenty-Four

Ciaran swore viciously under his breath, and it took everything she had not to flinch. She repeated over and over in her mind that, though her words were making him angry, he wasn't angry *with* her.

She hung on to his fingers like a warm anchor keeping her from getting swept away by the cold wave of Ciaran's emotions. Even so, her words were not so lucky and the silence stretched out between them, interrupted only by the grumbling radiators across the room.

She didn't blame him for not knowing how to respond, either. It wasn't every day the woman you barely knew just admitted to almost being beaten to death by her last boyfriend.

The silence was interrupted by the faint ring of a cell phone coming from somewhere. They looked at each other for a moment, both listening to the ringtone. "That has to be yours," she told him.

Ciaran cocked his head, listening, and then something

dawned on him. "Christ, what time is it?"

Jal shrugged and glanced around the room, but there were no visible clocks, at least not ones she could read from this distance. "No idea."

A corner of her mouth twitched up as he leapt to his feet and followed the sound, circling ever closer to the door and his discarded jackets where they had been unceremoniously dropped last night. He dug through the pile, his movements becoming more and more frantic. "Come on, come on," he urged himself on.

He let out a crow of triumph as he yanked the phone from a pocket and jabbed for the answer button, perching a hip on the armrest of the chair closest to him. "Hello? Catherine, hello?" He lifted the phone to check the screen and put it back to his ear, still calling the name.

Catherine?

"Oh Ciaran, thank god," came a relieved female voice through the phone. Ciaran moved it away from his ear, realizing he'd somehow hit the speakerphone button. He glanced at the screen again, and his eyes widened, his eyes shot to the windows, gauging the brightness outside in disbelief. "How is it already ten a.m.?"

"It comes after nine a.m. which is when you should have been here," she remarked. Her voice was distinctly American, so that ruled out family.

Ciaran ran a hand down his face and scratched the stubble on his chin. "I'm feeling a bit peely-wally," he replied, the twinkle in his eye, suggesting he'd chosen that particularly Scottish-sounding phrase on purpose. He coughed. Unconvincingly. "You'll tell Cliff, aye? Peely. Wally." he repeated slowly, smiling now.

The noise that came out of the phone was the auditory equivalent of an eye roll. Jal almost spit out the mouthful of tea she'd just sipped.

Ciaran cut her a glance and she gave him a mock-contrite grin.

"Yeah, yeah, fine." Catherine grumbled. "Only if you tell me where the plans for the Murphy academic building at New York College are. OMD is on the warpath and I can't find them on the server. He needs it by end of day, or, and I quote, 'it will be both your asses.'" Her voice descended into a deep baritone.

Jal snorted through her nose and clapped her hand over her nose and mouth. Ciaran directed an annoyed, but amused, look her way and started searching for his computer. "That's because I was working on it at home on Tuesday and forgot like an idiot to save it to the server." He disappeared into the bedroom at a half-run as he talked, appearing a moment later with a laptop under one arm. He went to the kitchen counter and turned it on. "Okay, give me a second and I'll upload it." He turned to Jal and mouthed, "sorry."

"Thanks Ciaran," she replied. "You owe me one."

"Aye, I do."

The phone beeped as Catherine hung up. Ciaran's fingers flew over the keyboard.

"OMD?"

"Huh?" he asked without looking up. The question sunk in a moment later and he shrugged but continued typing. "Oh! Short for Old Man Dougherty, my boss. Though he'd be my ex-boss, and Catherine's, if he ever heard us calling him that. Or OMD."

Jal chuckled. She set her cup down and rose to her feet, drawing the robe tighter. His scent rose from the cloth and she glanced over her shoulder at his hunched figure bent over the keyboard before raising the cuff to her nose.

It was a thoroughly female thing to do, to relish the feeling of wearing something of his, soaking in his scent that clung to the soft kiss of terrycloth against her bare skin, but Ciaran certainly wasn't paying attention. Jal took a moment to look around, finger combing the tangles from her hair as she did so.

His living room was larger than hers, decorated in browns and tans with a bank of large windows along one wall. Her bare feet sank into the thick cream carpet as she wandered her way over to an antique iron fireplace set into one wall. The narrow wooden mantle held a collection of photographs, but her eyes were drawn up to the stunningly life-like portrait hung above, presumably of some ancestor.

The woman sat in a wooden chair with upholstered arms and back. She gazed out of the frame with kind, but watchful, light-brown eyes. A red, white, and green tartan draped over the shoulders of a white blouse, pinned at her throat with a large golden stone that seemed to glow like the sun, reminding Jal of the glow of Ciaran's eyes.

Jal stepped closer, placing a hand on the mantle as she studied a ring made with the same stone, flanked by smaller diamonds that glittered on the woman's hand where it rested on the arm of the chair. Jal put her in her mid-sixties, noting that the artist had captured only a few wrinkles on her forehead and hands, the hair bound up in a neat but elegant style at the back of her neck was the soft white-gold a redhead took on as they aged. A strip of the same tartan was draped over the frame and pinned back like a curtain.

"That's my Gran."

Jal jumped, her hand flying to the neck of her robe.

Ciaran put a hand on her back as if he couldn't help himself.

Jal waited for the instinctive urge to pull away from his touch to come, but it didn't, and she found herself leaning into him instead. He made small, soothing circles on her back. She glanced up at him through her eyelashes to find him looking down at her.

Catching her gaze, he smiled.

Something deep inside released further. After what she had put him through, the fact that he could smile at her so easily was a tremendous relief. "Thank you for last night." she said. "For everything, really."

He pressed a kiss to her temple and for a moment, they just looked up at the painting.

"You look a little like her," Jal said, finally. "It's the eyes, I think. You both have the same whisky-colored eyes. Kind eyes."

"Kind eyes?" he asked and grinned down at her. "You think I have kind eyes?"

Jal couldn't help but blush as she nodded. "Among other things, some less than complimentary," she kept her voice serious by sheer force of will.

"Oh? Like what?"

"Well, you're great with a soccer ball for one, and you have one wicked tongue." He smirked, and somehow, she managed to keep her face neutral. She tapped a finger on her chin. "But you can be one cocky SOB."

"'One cocky SOB?'" There was a flash of white teeth in his smile.

Jal lost the battle with her smile and shook her head. "That sounds so wrong in your accent."

He flicked a finger down her nose. She playfully nipped at it, but missed, and he hooked it under her chin to bring her gaze to his. "Oh, aye? Well, let me show you what this wicked tongue can do."

He bent his head and fused his lips to hers. She opened for him and his tongue swept in, twisting with hers, tasting every corner of her mouth. The kiss was brief, but thorough, and her legs were shaky when he stepped back a moment later.

His eyes were dark, his breathing as ragged as hers. He cleared his throat as he sat on the arm of the chair behind him and drew her to stand between his knees. "Now, let me see what I can call you." His thumb stroked once across her lips. "When I first met you, you had yourself so tightly guarded by sarcasm and anger that I couldn't see the real you. But the closer we became, despite your efforts to the contrary, I might add, I began to see the real Jal Morrow."

"Oh?" she asked. "And who is the 'real' Jal Morrow?"

"You're smart," he replied, brushing a kiss over the inside of one wrist. "And talented." He kissed the other wrist. "I wouldn't even have attempted half of the picks that you pulled off so easily."

He brushed her robe back from one shoulder. "You're resourceful, canny, trustworthy, and beautiful." Each compliment was punctuated by a kiss, to her shoulder, her collarbone, her neck.

Her eyes widened and she put a hand on his cheek turning his gaze up to hers. "No one's ever called me beautiful, except you."

He brushed his lips across one cheekbone. She shivered at the brief contact. "The rest of the world be damned." he told her. "You *are* beautiful, but with one fiery temper. If you didn't have all of this," he buried his hands in her hair, tilting her head up. "I'd swear you were a ginger. A redhead," he clarified at her furrowed brow.

She laughed. She hooked a thumb over her shoulder. "My father's grandmother was a 'ginger'." She tried to pronounce it as he had, but failed miserably.

He rewarded her attempt with a kiss, speaking the next words a breath from her lips. "And you're so, so brave."

"I'm not brave."

"But you are," he insisted. "After everything you've been through, you've managed to rebuild your life, even as you have struggled through what Andy did to you. It's one of the reasons that I lo— "

Her entire body went cold. She closed her eyes and staggered back out of his reach, shaking her head furiously. "No, please don't say that you love me."

His hands remained hovering in the air, and it took every ounce of her to resist stepping right back into place. She craved the comfort of his touch, more than she'd ever thought possible, but there was no way he could love her. There was still so much he didn't know.

"Why not?"

"Because—" her words choked off as her throat grew thick with tears. She swallowed hard and tried again. "Because anyone who has ever said that they loved me, and really meant it, has died. That's why."

Twenty-Five

His heart landed somewhere near his toes.
Ciaran wanted to reach for her, but her eyes were filled with such anguish, and yes, panic, that he didn't dare. He let his arms drop into his lap. She stood only a few feet away, but it could have been miles. Her chest heaved like she had just sprinted to the finish line only to be met by the grim reaper himself.

Without another word, she turned and fled into the bedroom, locking the door behind her. Ciaran remained where he was, feeling as if a knife had been plunged into his stomach, one long enough to scrape his heart from the inside.

He could hear her moving through the room, presumably locating her belongings from where they had been hastily discarded the night before. When the door opened, she looked like Cinderella leaving the ball as the clock struck midnight. After having one wild night.

The sun struck sparks off the clutch and hair combs bundled in her arms. She hurried through the room, pausing only long enough to retrieve her shoes and wrap. In her haste, she fumbled with the locks, but then disappeared into the hallway without even a glance in his direction. Her feet thundered down the stairs at a near run.

The slamming of the door to the street finally jolted him free as if some invisible force had released its grasp, Ciaran dashed to his room, kicking the doorframe in his haste. He yelped and half-hopped across the floor to grab the first shirt, and pair of shoes he could find.

He shrugged into the sweatshirt he'd snared on the way out as he descended the stairs and narrowly avoided tripping on his untied shoelaces. Skidding to a halt on the street to tie them, he looked both ways, spotting her most of the way back to Fifth Avenue. Even barefoot, she was fast.

He took off after her, heart pounding more from the fear and confusion in her pained expression just before she had bolted than from the actual effort. He closed to within a half-block and called her name. It was hard to tell from this distance, with her hair spreading out like a cloud around her, but he thought she shook her head in response. She didn't slow as she crossed the street and headed in the direction of the park.

He poured on a bit more speed, calling her name. As she crossed into the shadow of the arch, he called again. "Jal, please stop!"

She drew to a sudden halt, her hands and cheek pressed to the cool marble. Ciaran skidded to a stop a few feet away and watched her carefully. The next move, whatever it was, would be hers.

Finally, she took a deep breath and the muscles in her shoulders bunched before she turned to face him. "Please Ciaran," she begged in a choked whisper so faint that he had to take a step closer to hear her. "If you do love me, turn around and go back home."

"Never," he told her. "You can keep running for the rest of your life, but I swear this to you, I will never stop following."

"Why?" she asked. A single tear slid down her cheek. "Why would you do that?"

He brushed it away with his thumb. "Because despite how hard you've tried, I see you for what you are." He waved her off when she opened her mouth to protest. "I see a woman who has always been independent, strong-willed, and capable. But you are also someone who does not know who she is."

"I'm a thief, Ciaran." she replied. "That's who I am."

"Aye, you are that." he agreed. "But you are also a woman, one who has seen too much of the horrors of the world, I think. You have never really had the life you deserve, full of warmth, safety, and yes, even love. It's about time that ended."

She started to turn away so that he couldn't see the tears his words brought to her eyes, but he took hold of her shoulder and pulled her back. Ciaran brought his hand up to brush away the tears that clung to her eyelashes. "You know that you don't want to be a thief for the rest of your life."

Her temper began to flash in her eyes. "I don't need charity, Ciaran."

"I'm not offering you charity."

"Then what are you offering?"

As if you didn't already know. He thought as he caressed her cheek. "Something that you have had almost since the first moment I met you." He brushed his thumb gently across her lips. They parted under his touch and released a trembling breath.

"What would that be?"

Ciaran leaned so close that their lips were only a breath apart. She watched him closely, but didn't pull back. "My heart." He brushed his lips across hers, barely a kiss, and breathed his next words between her parted lips. "You have it, whether you want it or not."

"Haven't you heard me, Ciaran?" She pulled her head back even as the rest of her body swayed against him. "I *can't* return your feelings."

"Can't or won't?"

That stung, he could tell, but there was no apology coming.

She took a step back and pushed his hand gently aside. "Won't." she said. "My heart won't survive another breaking. I'm cursed when it comes to love."

The words of reassurance in his mind had almost made it to his lips when Jal looked over his shoulder and her whole body went rigid, her eyes wider than he had ever seen them.

Ciaran turned slowly. The man who stood on the sidewalk a few feet away was equally frozen in surprise. His dark brown hair was long enough that it flopped over into sharp hazel eyes, which were currently fixed on Jal, but the look on his face was one of wonder or triumph. His shoulders stretched his flannel shirt wide over a white t-shirt, the muscles bulky enough to strain the collar almost to bursting. A colorful tattoo started just below one ear and emerged from under the rolled-up sleeves.

"Sam?" he asked, taking a step forward. "Samantha, is that you?"

Jal retreated, and Ciaran instinctively put himself between them. The man narrowed his eyes at him, then craned his neck to try to see around to the woman pressed tightly to his back. He smiled, and his eyes lit with excitement, even relief. It made Ciaran's blood run cold. "I know that's you."

"I think you must be mistaken." Ciaran told him.

The man's lip curled, his expression saying that he thought Ciaran was an idiot. "Oh no, I know my Sam."

Ciaran was just about to speak when he felt Jal's feather soft touch at his shoulder and her terrified whisper in his ear. "He's not wrong, Ciaran," she murmured. "That's Andy."

Twenty-Six

It was as if the last two years spent rebuilding her life and her confidence had never happened. He'd bulked so much more muscle that his t-shirt struggled to cover his shoulders and chest without tearing at the seams. His hair was a little shaggier, his hazel eyes a little wilder than she remembered, making him seem even less like the calm businessman she had first met and more like the man who had always lurked beneath the surface, the one who had beaten her to within an inch of her life.

"Sam?"

Jal closed her eyes and fought the storm of emotion his voice set off inside her.

She hadn't been Samantha in two years. No, that girl had died so Jal could live. "What do you want, Andy?" she asked, appalled at the tremor in her voice.

Many times, she had imagined what would happen if they ever saw each other again, though she had hoped that it would never happen. All the words she wanted to say with him standing not five feet away, vanished like vapor.

"I lost everything when I went to prison."

"Nearly beating me to death and then killing someone with your car will do that."

Anger flickered through his eyes at her tone, and when Ciaran stepped even closer to her, his upper lip curled back.

Almost as quickly as the looks appeared, they vanished leaving a calm, almost hopeful look on his face that made her blood run cold. "But now I'm a rehabilitated citizen. I've been looking for you for weeks. I was hoping that I could lay the first brick in rebuilding my life by getting you back."

Every cell in her body screamed bullshit. But Ciaran was able to voice the words in her head before she could say them. "Are you bloody delusional?"

Andy rounded on him. "And who the fuck are you?"

"At the moment, I'm the man standing between you and the woman you almost killed." There was so much ice in Ciaran's voice that she was shocked Andy didn't freeze solid and then shatter.

"Why the hell do you care?"

Ciaran took her hand. "Because I love her."

In Andy's present state, it was not the smartest thing that Ciaran could have said. Andy moved faster than someone with his amount of bulky muscle should have. "She's mine!" his voice thundered in the semi-enclosed space. He shouldered Ciaran aside.

Jal shrieked as his head collided with the marble and he started sliding to the ground. She scrambled for him, but Andy's hand wrapped around her upper arm and hauled her toward him. "She has always been mine!"

She went limp in his grasp, and dropped to the ground. Her belongings clattered to the pavement, scattering in the struggle. "Get your fucking hands off me, Andy!" Her voice echoed shrilly under the arch as he hauled her feet almost off the ground. His other hand wrapped around her waist, digging deep into the skin over her hip, deep enough to bruise. She pounded on his arms, scraped with her nails, but nothing worked to loosen his grasp.

And then, she was free. She stumbled and fell to all fours. Pain erupted in her hands and knees.

Andy staggered away, his back fetching against the other side of the arch. His tongue prodded his cheek as if checking that all his teeth were still in place.

Ciaran stalked forward, sending another roundhouse punch into the other side of his face.

Despite their differences in size, Andy's head cranked around, blood flying from a split lip.

Ciaran turned to her. "Go, Jal! Run!"

With a roar, Andy charged at him. For a moment, she couldn't move, hands pressed tightly to her mouth as the two men grappled, trading body blows. Andy threw Ciaran to the ground, holding him down with his forearm, his other arm cocked back readying for a crushing blow.

Jal scrambled to her feet, but instead of leaving, she took two running steps toward them and kicked Andy in the shoulder. With bare feet, it had about as much impact on Andy as kicking marble. Pain shot up her leg and she hopped back. Still, it made both men look in her direction.

The fury in Andy's face froze her like a deer in headlights, until he pushed off Ciaran and lunged at her.

Ciaran rolled off the ground and leapt onto Andy's back. "Run!"

Heart in her throat, Jal ran. She elbowed her way through the crowd that had gathered and dove into traffic to a blare of horns. A taxi slammed on its brakes as she dashed by, the sound of screeching tires quickly followed by a bang and crunch of metal. She didn't waste time looking back toward the accident, but took off up Fifth Avenue, her bare feet slapping on the pavement.

She reached Ciaran's street and turned the corner without thinking, sprinting to his front door. She jiggled the knob, unsurprised to find it locked. A gust of wind blew across her exposed skin, and she shivered, twisting the knob again with renewed desperation, driving her shoulder into the door for good measure. When it didn't budge, she slid into a heap on the top step, clutching her bruised shoulder and pressing herself as tightly against the door as she could.

Breathe, Jal. Breathe. She repeated over and over, while tapping the back of her head against the door in an attempt to clear her thoughts so she could figure out her next move without her purse, or her shoes, or her knitted wrap. Especially her wrap. It didn't provide much warmth, but anything was better than a dress that left her arms and her back completely bare.

A car rolled slowly down the street in search of a parking spot, locking eyes with the female driver as she spotted Jal and bent low to give her a curious look as she passed.

Feeling much too exposed, Jal climbed to her feet using the door for support, her legs screaming with exhaustion, and descended the stairs to the sidewalk. She looked up and down the street, looking for a good place to hide out of sight. She leaned over the railing to her right and spotted a pool of shadows under the stairs.

The gate was icy under her fingertips as she pushed it open and tucked herself into the doorway of the basement apartment and danced from foot to foot, arms wrapped around her body. Chafing her arms in search of any spark of warmth, she settled in to wait.

Shuffling footsteps approached from the street. Jal pressed her back deeper into the shadows, shivering.

"Jal, are you there?"

The sound of his voice would have made her knees give out if they weren't locked and knocking together. She forced frozen muscles into motion, and put one quivering, aching foot in front of the other, one hand braced against the stone stairway.

Ciaran stood at the foot of the stairs. His sweatpants were dirty and torn at one knee, his lip split. She whispered his name, too cold and relieved to shout, and flew across the sidewalk to him.

He caught her and held her tight. "Are you all right, lass?"

She nodded into his shoulder.

He eased her back and the weight of her wrap settled around her shoulders. Jal burrowed into its warmth, and studied him again, finally noticing that he was holding her clutch, her heels dangling from his hand. She held out her hands and he handed them over.

"Well, maybe I should— "

"Let's go back inside."

Her eyes widened. "But I ran away and left you."

Ciaran's brow furrowed. "I distinctly remember telling you to run."

Jal shook her head. "No, you don't understand," she pleaded, hands wringing together. "I *ran*."

He studied her for a moment, then held out a hand. "Come inside." When she stared at it but didn't move, he blinked and said gently, "please, lass. It's very cold."

She ducked her head, her hair falling in a curtain to cover her face. The color in her cheeks had nothing to do with the cold, as she took his hand.

"Christ, your fingers are like ice!" he exclaimed and wrapped an arm around her shoulders. He rushed her up the stairs and unlocked the door using a keypad hidden in the trim. There was a faint buzz and the door opened with a gentle bump of his shoulder.

Jal clutched her wrap and purse to her chest as Ciaran led the way up the stairs to where his door still stood half-open. He pushed it the rest of the way open, gesturing for her to walk inside first. She stopped halfway into the living room, unsure what to do next. If her hands hadn't been full, she'd be wringing them.

The door closed with a quiet snick behind her and she turned to see Ciaran standing against it, watching her. "Are you okay?" she asked.

"I'll do for now," he replied, voice tight.

"And Andy?"

"The cops showed up and they took him." he replied. "There were enough people watching to convince them that I was rescuing you from an attempted kidnapping."

Jal sighed and put a hand to her heart. "Is there anything I can do for you? Get some ice for your jaw, maybe?" She took a few steps toward his kitchen.

He stopped her with a hand on her wrist. She stopped and looked down, remembering the first time he had taken her wrist, his fingers wrapped just as gently, only enough to make her stop, and how different her reaction had been.

"Some answers will do fine," he replied.

She nodded, and he led the way to the sofa. Jal dropped her belongings on the floor and perched on the edge, her hands clenched together in her lap. Ciaran slowly lowered himself on the other side with a hand on his ribs and leaned back against the cushions, eyes closed.

"Are you sure you don't need to go get checked out?"

Ciaran cracked one eye. "Andy called you 'Samantha'?"

Guess not, she thought, and took a deep breath. *Here we go...*

"My birth name is Samantha Colleran," she replied. After all this time, it felt like she was talking about someone else. "After Andy... did what he did, I needed a new start. So, I went back to my hometown in Pennsylvania and changed my name so the records would be harder to find if, and when, he got out of prison and went looking for me."

"How did you choose Jal Morrow?"

Despite the quiver of her lips, they curled up at the corners. "My mom's name was Angelica and I wanted to honor her, but it was Elena who suggested shortening it to 'Jal.'" she explained, "Morrow came from my father's grandmother. And there you have it."

He sat up with a groan and poked at the split in his lip with the tip of his tongue before dabbing at it with the cuff of his sweatshirt. "Can you tell me about what happened two years ago?"

She looked down at her hands, seeing the ghost of the bitten down nails and scabbed cuticles, the product of never knowing which Andy would walk through the door. "He had been out celebrating something, I can't remember now what it was, but he came home drunk and ready to party... with me." She clenched her hands together, pressing them to her stomach. "He walked into the living room to find me waiting, a suitcase packed at my feet."

"You were leaving him."

She nodded. "Elena was on her way, but he got home before I got outside. We fought, and I tried to grab my things and run, but he followed and pushed me down the stairs. I woke up in the hospital and was told that Andy left me lying there, got into his car and ended up in an accident. The other driver didn't make it."

He cursed and moved a little closer to her on the sofa.

"I was covered in bruises, a sprained neck, a broken leg, and torn ligaments in my shoulder and considered myself lucky. That is, until the doctor came in and told me that—"

"That you were pregnant."

Her jaw dropped. "How did you know that?"

He shrugged. "I felt the scar last night and figured that it had to have come from a cesarean."

She nodded. "The other injuries I could recover from, but

that alone almost killed me. I was on bed rest for five months, Ciaran. It would have been so easy for me to lose the baby, and I thought about that so, so many times, but I just couldn't. No matter how horrible the father had been to me, it wasn't the baby's fault. The moment they placed her in my arms, I knew that I couldn't keep her, that I couldn't give her the life she deserved. So, I put her up for adoption."

Ciaran watched her curiously, then his eyes darted to her lap and back to her face. Jal looked down. While she had been talking, her arms had come up as if holding an infant. She dropped them to her lap again.

Ciaran scooted a bit closer and took her hand. Jal wrapped both of hers around his and held it like a lifeline.

"What did you name her?"

"Everly." She swallowed against the knot in her throat. She hadn't spoken her daughter's name aloud in over a year. "Everly Anne Colleran."

"Where is she now?"

"I don't know." Her heart constricted around the hollow place in her heart that had existed since the nurse had taken Everly from her arms for the last time. "It's been fifteen months. I don't even know where to start."

"Have you ever thought of trying to get her back?"

"Every day," she murmured, unable to meet his eyes. "But I've seen too many stories on the news about birth mothers tearing their children away from the only homes and parents they knew to be with a total stranger. I couldn't do that to her. She's better off wherever she is."

"But are you?"

Jal looked up into Ciaran's face. "I'm really sorry, Ciaran."

A lone tear slid down one cheek.

He brushed it away, his hand lingering to cup her cheek. "I knew that whatever it was that made you fear my touch had to have been bad." He said, and gently tucked her hair behind her ear. "But I told you whatever your truth was— "

"That it was safe with you."

He smiled. "Aye, and I meant it. Whether your name is Samantha, or Jal, or even Angelica."

She scrunched up her nose.

"Okay, then," he replied with a chuckle. "It doesn't much matter to me. I love *you*. And want to be with you, to help you, in any way I can. If you will let me."

She ducked her head then, unable to bear the emotions swelling up in her.

He put a finger under her chin and brought her gaze back up, a soft smile on his lips. "All I ask is that from now on, if you ever feel the need to run again, that you run *to* me. Here, in my arms, I swear you will always be safe."

She went into his arms and went thoroughly to pieces.

He wrapped his arms around her then and held her while she cried, releasing all of the pent up grief, and fear, and pain. He brushed her hair away from his face and rested his chin on the top of her head. She snuggled into him as close as she dared, and breathed in his scent, tinged now with sweat and blood, but calming, nonetheless.

"I promise."

Twenty-Seven

She couldn't run any more.

Her hands landed on her knees as she staggered to a stop and tried to draw air into lungs that felt like they were being crushed. The intersection where she stood was the same as dozens of others in this bright, colorless, featureless maze.

What's the point? she thought, eyes prickling with tears, as she slid to her knees in hopes it would ease the shaking in her legs. There was no way out, just one endless hallway after another. She should just lay down here on the floor and stop.

A small part of her wanted to keep going. Knowing something, or someone good, was waiting at the end to make all of this endless searching through a soundless, beige nothingness worth it. But that part was so small. Under her knees, the floor was invitingly warm, as if the stone, or concrete, or whatever, was heated from underneath. It would be so easy to just curl up. So easy, that her hands reached for the floor and she started to list to one side.

A sound from her right froze her in place, a loud electric click of a light being doused. She caught herself on one elbow and turned her head and sure enough, the shadowy darkness at the end of the corridor seemed to be growing as if someone was turning off the lights one by one.

It started off slowly, another click as the light farthest away went out. Then a few heartbeats later, the next. And then the next, the darkness gaining speed, the clicking rising in volume as it grew nearer, until it seemed to be cascading toward her in a wave of darkness.

She didn't know what would happen if it caught up with her. So, she scrambled to her feet and staggered off in the opposite direction. Almost immediately, her skin began to tingle as if she'd run through an electrified spider web. It clung to her skin, growing in intensity as she ran.

There was nowhere else to go. The darkness nipped at her heels. She whimpered as her heart pounded in her throat, choking off her breath. On and on she ran, her skin burning with crackling energy. Her feet skidded out from under her, sending her hard into the wall. She shrieked, the wall searing her skin like a hot iron. She stumbled away, clutching the injured side, trying to keep ahead of the sweeping darkness.

On and on she ran, half-staggering. Looking behind, more than she did forward.

She was looking back when the hallway made another abrupt turn and she collided with the wall. She fell to the floor in a heap, every inch of her skin searing with pain... and the darkness swept in.

Jal struggled up out of the dream, pushing against the blackness that was reluctant to release its grip. She swam to the surface and realized that the pounding in her ears was not her heart, but pounding on the door. She kicked at the covers, which had become tangled around her legs in her sleep. She was back in her own bed, and alone.

Ciaran had offered to drive her home, thinking that she would want her own space after all of the emotions of the day. He'd been right, of course. A shower and a good night's sleep should have done the trick. But their encounter with Andy had shaken memories loose. No wonder she'd had a nightmare, the details of which were quickly fading as they always did, but the emotions lingered, despair, exhaustion, and then pure panic.

She finally managed to free her legs from the twisted mass of sheets and blankets as the pounding at the door grew louder. Grabbing a hoodie from the hook on the back of her door, she shrugged it on as she padded across the living room.

"Couldn't help yourself, could you?" she called through the door, smiling as she worked the locks.

"Miss Morrow?"

Jal froze, hand on the knob. Definitely not Ciaran. "Yes?" she called cautiously.

"Open up please, it's the police."

She squeezed her eyes shut and tried to take a deep breath. "Can you hold your badge up to the door?"

"Of course."

She pressed her eye to the scope in the door to see a gold shield with all the right engravings and emblems. The officer turned the leather holder to show an ID and though the words were blurry through the scratched glass, the face of the man holding the ID matched the photograph. A second officer in a deep navy coat stood behind him, a radio raised to her mouth.

Jal gave the room a once over, and opened the door, putting it mostly between her and them. "Can I help you officers?" she asked, pleased that, though her voice was a little higher than it should be, at least it was steady.

"Are you Jal Morrow?" The woman asked from over her companion's shoulder in a no-nonsense kind of way that made Jal dislike her immediately.

"Yes."

"Can we come in, miss?" the man, who couldn't be more than three or four years older than her, asked. He had short black hair, brown almond-shaped eyes and a mouth that seemed to always try to smile even when he was being as serious as possible, as he was now.

"Uh, sure," she replied, tugging the zipper up to her chin. The two officers came in once she opened the door wide enough and Jal watched nervously as they stood in her living room and looked around. The apartment was as neat and tidy as it had ever been, not a book or piece of furniture out of place. As for the places she'd rather stay hidden? She just had to hope that the cops didn't find them.

"Can I get you anything, officers?" she asked, drifting toward the kitchen, not only for refreshments, but to where her phone was plugged in charging on the counter. "I can put on some coffee, or tea, maybe?"

"Thank you, coffee would be nice." he said, the woman looked at him with a raised eyebrow, but ultimately shook her head. Her dark eyes were searching the room as if she could see through the walls and floor directly to where her stashes were, and was just chomping at the bit to be set loose.

"My name is Detective Derek Takeda. This is my partner Detective Breanne Ward."

"Nice to meet you," Jal said, keeping her voice as polite as possible while she reached into the cabinet and pulled down coffee and a filter with one hand while unlocking her phone with the other. "I was wondering what it is that I can do for you?"

> Jal: Cops are here.

Ciaran's response was almost immediate.

> Ciaran: I'm on my way!

> Ciaran: I'm so sorry. I had to give them your information for the report.

Jal's heart lifted as she locked the phone again and went to the sink to fill the pot, even knowing that it would take a while for Ciaran to get uptown.

"We have some questions about an altercation that happened at Washington Square Park yesterday," Detective Ward said in her brusque Brooklyn accent. She reached into the inside pocket of her jacket and pulled out a tri-folded piece of paper. "We also have a warrant to search these premises." She said solemnly, though there was an undertone that belied her eagerness. "We received an anonymous tip that there is a large amount of stolen goods hidden in this apartment."

Jal took the paper and studied the few lines of stark black lettering authorizing a search that could end in her being led away in handcuffs. The flourish with which the judge had signed the order turned her blood to ice. She sent up a prayer that Ciaran arrived sooner, rather than later.

She nodded in agreement and Detective Ward spoke into her radio, then got to work. A uniformed officer appeared at the door a moment later and stood just inside to observe, and to guard the door. Against her trying to run away, she supposed.

Ward started with the kitchen, searching drawers and cabinets, opening anything she couldn't immediately see inside. Jal was surprised that she put things back in more or less the same place, though she seemed to relish in the racket she made pushing items around on the shelves.

Detective Takeda gave her an apologetic look and gestured to the sofa. "We can sit in the living room while my partner works."

Jal nodded and sat down, her hands twisted in her lap, watching the detective search her kitchen and waited for her world to come crashing down, to feel the cold bite of handcuffs around her wrists.

"Miss Morrow?" Detective Takeda called her name as if he had called it several times already.

Jal looked his way. "Hmm? Oh, I'm sorry." She replied, realizing she'd zoned out watching the other officer. "What was the question?"

Takeda gave her a kind, patient smile. "I was asking if you could tell me, in your own words, what happened at Washington Square Park yesterday?"

Jal swallowed and nodded. She told him about her relationship with Andy and how it had ended without mentioning that she had changed her name after it did. That she had found out recently that he was out of prison and was looking for her. She released a shuddering breath that was not at all fake. "We had just gotten to the park when Andy showed up out of nowhere. And then he grabbed me, tried to drag me away, tried to say I still belonged to him." She wrapped her arms around her stomach. "Ciaran punched him to get him off of me. They started fighting and Ciaran told me to run, so I did."

"Ciaran?" The detective studied his notes. "Ah yes. And what is your relationship with Mr. Gray?"

There was a commotion by the door before she could answer. She looked up to see the uniformed officer standing with his arm braced across the door. Ciaran called her name from behind him.

Jal called across the room. "It's okay, let him in." She looked at the detective. "He's my boyfriend."

Detective Takeda gestured to the officer, who removed his arm. "Come over here, please, Mr. Gray."

Ciaran glanced at the detective who had moved on from the kitchen to the desk under the window in the dining room, and then came and sat next to her. Jal studied the bruise that had bloomed along his jaw beside the scabbed-over split lip. Another brush-burn like bruise colored the opposite cheek, but he otherwise seemed okay. Jal cupped the injury gently and Ciaran gave her a small smile and kissed her palm before taking her hand and lacing his fingers with hers and holding it on his knee.

"I was just telling the detective here about what happened in the park," she said. "How you came to my rescue."

"Oh, aye," Ciaran responded, and gave her hand a squeeze. He pointed to his face. "As you can see, Detective, the lout—"

"Mr. Paolinelli?"

"Aye, Mr. Paolinelli." Ciaran pronounced the name carefully, sounding like he was grinding every syllable between his teeth. "Jal didn't do anything other than just be there. He declared that she was his, grabbed her, and started trying to drag her away."

"Yes, we have your statement, Mr. Gray." Detective Takeda replied. "And the statements of several bystanders on the scene. Ms. Morrow just corroborated it. Though I do see that one of the witnesses said that Mr. Paolinelli was saying that your name was 'Sam'?"

Jal nodded. "I declined the protection that was offered after he was convicted, but I did legally change my name to make myself harder to find when he got out."

"What was your old name?"

Jal told him, though her mouth had trouble forming the words. Sam Colleran was the person who had almost died by Andy's hand. Jal Morrow was the one who had lived. The detective made a note.

"Takeda."

They all looked over at the dining area to find Detective Ward standing beside the table, holding up a few small bundles of dollar bills in her gloved hand. By where she was standing, she must have found the hidden drawer.

Ciaran gripped Jal's hand as the detective crossed the room to his partner, motioning for them to remain on the sofa.

Detective Takeda studied the bills and rifled through the drawer's few remaining contents with his pen. In her mind, Jal saw a handful of coins, a necklace that actually belonged to her own grandmother, and a single ladies wallet wiped clean of any fingerprints and containing only cash. "Looks to be maybe a thousand or so," he murmured to his partner, though it was clearly audible across the room. "This is a lot of cash Ms. Morrow."

"I know," she replied, keeping her voice casual even though her heart was racing. "I've never really done much with banks. I grew up in rural Pennsylvania with a grandmother who lived in a trailer in the middle of nowhere. The nearest bank was thirty minutes away when the car was actually running. We used cash for everything, and I just never made the switch."

"What do you do for work?" Detective Ward demanded.

"I work at a friend's restaurant mostly, and pick up odd jobs here and there. The building is rent controlled, so I don't have a lot of expenses." she explained. "I still have a little of the inheritance from my parents when they died when I was a kid, but it's not much. A couple thousand. I can show you where it's hidden."

Detective Ward placed the money on the table and was none too gentle as she pushed the drawer shut. Jal cringed at the sound the table made skidding across the floor as she got to her feet. She led the way into her bedroom and dragged the chair by the door over to the bathroom doorway. She gestured to the detective and then sat on the end of her bed. "That grate above the door lifts down, you'll find an envelope inside."

The detective eyed her warily for a moment as if wondering what else Jal might be hiding in there, but she glanced at her partner who had moved to the doorway, Ciaran's pale face visible over his shoulder, and climbed onto the chair. She staggered as her heeled boots sunk into the cushion, but she managed to retrieve the envelope and stepped down to the floor, dropping the grate with a clang at her feet. She removed the rubber band and opened the envelope. It was worn, the gold color faded nearly to white. The logo under Detective Ward's thumb was nearly illegible but had come from one of the banks back in her home town. No lie there, at least.

"My parents didn't have much, but I was their only child, and my grandmother made sure most of it was saved." Jal told her, the lies rolling easily off her tongue now. "But it's been almost twenty years. I think there's about eight or ten thousand there. That's all that's left."

Ward thumbed through the contents of the envelope, near bursting with bills, and tipped her head to study what was left of the logo.

Takeda stepped inside and took it from his partner and looked inside. "Do you have any records for the inheritance?"

Jal shook her head. "I left home at seventeen right out of high school. I didn't think to take something like that with me. Just took the cash and moved to the city to try to make a better life for myself." That part at least was true.

Takeda considered that for a moment. The envelope crinkled in his grip when he glanced at his partner. The eager glint in Ward's eyes sent a chill down Jal's spine.

Ciaran's eyes burned into the back of her neck, but resisted the urge to turn, certain that if she did, there was no way she could conceal what she was thinking from showing plainly on her face. As long as he was behind her, Jal could keep her thief's stony façade in place.

Before her partner could speak. Ward took the envelope from his hand with an expression that said she thought Takeda was crazy for having any kind of restraint, and pointed toward the bedroom door. "If you could go back out in the living room, we'll finish the search in here."

Her tone was polite, but there was no mistaking that she was enjoying this. Jal went, her calm mask cracking as she had expected as soon as she saw Ciaran's face. She went straight into his arms and hid her expression in the folds of his coat.

Ciaran wrapped his arms around her and put his mouth close to her ear. "They have a search warrant? For what?"

"What do you think?" She murmured back. Though having her home searched felt like yet another violation, her heart slowed just from having him nearby. "It's Andy, I'm sure of it."

Ciaran turned backed into the living room but still kept his voice to the barest breath of a whisper. "Bet you're glad I cleared out all those hidey holes when I did now, aren't you?"

Jal huffed a nervous laugh and led the way to the sofa. From the bedroom came the sounds of drawers being opened and slammed shut, of the mattress being tossed around. She winced and Ciaran gripped her hand.

She burrowed into his shoulder when he put an arm around her, breathing in his scent of musky soap and sandalwood, and tried to remember if there was anything hidden in her room that Ciaran hadn't already found.

Ciaran pressed a kiss to her temple and held her close until Takeda emerged from her bedroom. From behind him came the sound of clattering bottles, Ward must have turned her sights on the bathroom.

A memory flashed through her mind, and she clamped down on Ciaran's hand. He glanced down at her, but couldn't ask what was wrong before Takeda was standing before them.

The detective perched on the edge of the coffee table. "I think we're just about finished here."

"Is Andy going back to prison?"

"That remains to be seen, Ms. Morrow."

Ciaran scowled. "What does that mean?"

"It's up to the courts."

"He just spent two years in prison. Within weeks of release, he tried to kidnap me and assaulted my boyfriend, and 'it remains to be seen'?" Jal demanded, her voice rising.

It was Ciaran's turn to squeeze her hand in warning. She took a steadying breath and looked down at their linked hands, trying to draw some of Ciaran's steadiness into her. "You won't disclose my address to him, will you?" Jal asked, her voice was soft, but much more even.

"No ma'am."

She brought up her head and locked her gaze on Takeda. "I'll file a restraining order if I need to," she continued, running a hand through her hair to clear her vision. "I need you to please do whatever it takes to keep him away from me."

"Of course," Takeda agreed.

"Takeda."

All three of them snapped their attention to the bedroom door, where Detective Ward stood with a trio of bracelets hanging from the shaft of a ballpoint pen, two tennis bracelets sparkling with diamonds and a half dozen shades of amethyst, and a gold charm-style chain with a single heart hanging from the clasp.

"Are these part of your inheritance as well, Ms. Morrow?" Ward asked, the triumph that now filled her eyes turned Jal's stomach. In her other hand was a blue glass jar and a yellow lid which had held the bracelets instead of the menthol cream the label advertised.

When the silence stretched a little too long, Takeda sighed and got to his feet. "Miss Morrow, I think you're going to have to come with us."

Twenty-Eight

The heating in the small holding room was cranked so high it gave a new definition to making suspects 'sweat it out.' Moisture beaded at her temples and trickled down between her shoulder blades. Beside her, Ciaran shifted in his chair. It had been hours since the officers had led them to the unmarked car parked out front and ushered them into the back seat.

Thankfully, the detectives had allowed Jal to change out of her pajamas and hadn't put her in handcuffs. But still the ride from her apartment to the precinct couldn't have felt any worse had she actually been under arrest. And because she wasn't, they had allowed Ciaran to go with her. His presence had been a steady calming influence that had kept her from completely spiraling out.

But they had been cooped up in this room for hours and Ciaran swore they had been slowly ratcheting up the heating the whole time. He had already loosened his tie and the collar of his shirt, and rolled his sleeves up his forearms, and his patience was starting to wear thin if the hand reflexively opening and closing was any indication. The action made the corded muscles of his forearm bunch and release in a way that had her mouth watering.

No, you will not ogle him in a police station, she told herself and forced her gaze to the closed door, flanked on either side by large windows, covered now with dusty black blinds. Yet, that's what she had been doing, even as her worst nightmare was coming true. Her skin was flushed with heat from more than just the temperature, as if she could still feel his strong hands on her body, ghosting over her skin. Stop it!

She welcomed the cool air that blew in when the door opened, even when it *was* opening to admit the two detectives. But all too quickly, the door closed again, and the stifling heat returned to the room.

"Sorry to keep you waiting."

Takeda took a seat in one of the two chairs across from them and placed two clear evidence bags, one holding the envelope of money, the other holding the bracelets and the jar, and a leather portfolio on the table. The diamonds sparkled merrily in the light over the table, oblivious to all the trouble they were causing.

Detective Ward lingered by the door a moment longer, studying them with her piercing dark eyes, then took the chair beside her partner and placed her phone on the table, its screen open to a recording app, and made a show of tapping the red button at the bottom of the screen. The timer started ticking.

Takeda opened his portfolio and flicked through the short stack of papers. "Miss Morrow," he began. "Or is it Colleran?"

Jal's hand stilled where it had been toying with the end of her thick braid. "It's Morrow," she replied. "As I told you, I legally changed it two years ago."

"Of course," Takeda replied. He made a note. "And where was that again?"

Jal cleared her throat. "Um, it was Clearfield County. Pennsylvania." She added the state as an afterthought.

Takeda made more notes, then slid one of the evidence bags into the spotlight in the middle of the table. "I'd like to start today with this first bag. The contents of which are: two tennis bracelets, one diamond, the other diamond and amethyst; one gold charm bracelet with a gold heart; and one jar made from blue glass with a yellow plastic lid."

Detective Ward poked at the bag with a pen, shifting the bracelets around so they continued to glitter in the light. "Now, Miss Morrow, can you corroborate where these items were located?"

Jal looked at her and tried not to get too riled from her tone and the haughty superiority that radiated out of her pores. Innocent until proven guilty, my ass. "Of course. You—Detective Ward, I mean—found the jar in a box of random toiletries in the back of my bathroom linen closet that I have not touched since I moved in a year and a half ago."

"Yet the jar says menthol cream." Ward countered, "Not diamonds."

"I don't know about you Detective, but I grew up in a household where the margarine container in the fridge rarely actually contained margarine." Jal said, pleased that only a fraction of the snark she wanted to use came through in her voice. "Have you never reused a single-use container for another purpose?"

"We're not talking about me, Miss Morrow. And what was the purpose for this reuse?"

Jal looked down at the evidence bag and inwardly sighed in relief that at least this interview wasn't going to start off with lies. That would come later. "The bracelets were gifts from Andy, from early in our relationship. When I first met him, Andy worked in finance, and he made good money, before he started gambling all of it away, that is. I was naïve, detectives. I never had anything fancy growing up, and he wooed me pretty easily with sparkly things."

Ciaran took her hand and gave it a reassuring squeeze.

Jal gave him a thankful half-smile. "That didn't last long, and when things ended between us, and he went to prison, I didn't want to see *any* reminders of him, even a couple of bracelets in my jewelry box. So, I put them in the jar when I was packing up my old place, and put them in a box that ended up in the back of a closet. I knew they were real, and I held on to them in case I ever needed the money. Is there a crime in that?"

Ciaran took her hand and gave it a warning squeeze. She glanced down and then up at his face, to the soft understanding in his eyes and only then noticed the vibrating tension in her muscles, the heat that burned in her cheeks.

She closed her eyes for a moment and took a deep, steadying breath. "I'm sorry. The last few days have been dredging up a lot of memories of a time that wasn't exactly pleasant."

Takeda glanced up from his notes. "I understand."

"Do you have any documentation for the bracelets?" Ward asked, the look on her face saying that she already knew the answer and was just itching to pounce. What gives?

Jal shook her head and just barely kept from rolling her eyes. "Of course not," she replied sharply. "They were gifts."

"Jal—" Ciaran warned under his breath.

"Again, my apologies," Jal replied slowly so she could make sure her voice was even. "I'm just not sure why I'm being grilled over a couple of bracelets when I've done nothing wrong."

Takeda held up a hand. "No one is grilling anyone," he said, giving his partner a meaningful look. Ward didn't even look his way, but the sparkle in her eye said she was enjoying whatever game she was playing.

"Why don't we move on?" Ward grabbed the other evidence bag and tossed it on top of the first with an audible slap. She leaned back in her chair, pen poised over the paper, and looked ready for the main event. "Can you tell me in your own words where this money came from?"

Takeda consulted his notes. "For the record, we are referring to the envelope hidden in the ductwork above Miss Morrow's bathroom door. There is a total of $11,465.00 in cash, primarily in twenties and hundreds. An additional $965 was found in a hidden compartment in the dining room table."

Ciaran's thumb paused in drawing circles on the back of her hand, but only for a moment. The money he had returned to her had been less than a quarter of that. She couldn't help the bloom of pride that lasted for only a moment before she remembered that the "work" she'd done to get that money was the reason they were sitting in this room. Right. *Focus, Jal.*

"For the record, can you explain to us again Miss Morrow, how you came into possession of such an amount and why it was hidden in your apartment."

Jal swallowed, the sides of her throat rubbing together like sandpaper and began, telling the detectives about her upbringing, such as it was. The car crash that had killed her parents, the grandmother who had given her shelter, if little else. She gave them the story she'd rehearsed in her head on the drive over, building on the inheritance story that she had blurted out in her apartment.

"I never really knew how deep my ex's connections went. So, under my new name, I did my best to keep my head down and my footprint small. I didn't open any bank accounts or credit cards. I rented my apartment from a relative of a good friend and have used cash for everything. As I told you, my needs are few and I do some work on the side to help preserve my savings."

While she spoke, Takeda took notes, despite the recording. Jal suppressed the urge to fidget while he finished. Ciaran squeezed her hand gently to get her attention, and the glow of pride she saw in his eyes would have had her blushing at any other time.

Takeda opened his mouth to speak, but Ward jumped in before he could. "And again, for the record," she began, and her scornful tone put Jal's teeth on edge. Ciaran's eyes flared wide once in warning before too much of her irritation showed on her face. "You stated that you do not have any paperwork for the inheritance money your parents left you upon their deaths twenty years ago?"

Jal tore her gaze away from Ciaran. "That is correct," she replied. "They were only in their late 20s, so they never thought to make a will. From what I understand—because

I *was* only seven—they rented their apartment. My dad was self-employed and did construction and handyman jobs that paid mostly in cash. My mom didn't work."

Her throat closed, choking off her words. The memories of her parents were fuzzy after all these years, but she remembered clearly how her mother had always been there. Remembered her gentle touch while cleaning a skinned knee, the gentle circle of her arms holding her when she woke up from a nightmare. Until suddenly, she was gone.

Talking about them, even though some things were made up, brought back some of that pain and confusion of a seven-year-old child being told that her parents were gone. And they were only the first of many to leave her behind, each one taking a part of her with them when they did.

"Miss Morrow?" Takeda prompted.

Jal shook off the memories. "Ah, I'm sorry detective, it's just been so long since I've talked about them."

Unlike his partner, who looked like she had already made up her mind, and not in Jal's favor, Takeda's eyes were kind and patient. "Of course, can I get you anything? Coffee? Water?"

Jal shook her head, but Takeda still turned to his partner. "Do you mind getting some water?" he asked, running a finger under his collar. "It is pretty stuffy in here."

Detective Ward's eyes widened. Clearly not used to being dismissed, she rose stiffly to her feet and left the room. Takeda tapped his pen on his notepad and gave her a reassuring smile. "Now, you were saying?"

The room was somehow cooler without his partner scowling at them and Jal felt like she could finally take a deep breath. "After my parents died, my grandmother got everything, and she, thankfully, set some of it aside for me, and used the rest for my upkeep. She died two years after I moved to New York–so a little more than eight years ago–and I went back to sell the trailer and the little bit of property that she had. I've lived on the proceeds ever since."

Takeda continued to write a moment longer and then paused to reread it. *Please say something*, she thought as the silence stretched a little too long with him studying his notes. Another interminable moment later, he raised his head, and gripped the pen between the fingers of both hands.

"I think the last thing I need to ask is why someone would want to make an allegation that you had stolen goods in your apartment." His words were careful, as if he were still working out what he wanted to say as he asked it. "The judge wouldn't have granted a search warrant just based on a random allegation."

Jal's heartbeat ratcheted up a little. "As I said, Detective, I never knew how deep my ex's contacts went. Two years ago, when I told him I was leaving, he nearly killed me by pushing me down a flight of stairs, then drove off and got into an accident and killed someone."

Takeda's eyebrows rose, but he kept making notes.

Jal sighed, but only so she wouldn't scream. "Andy got two years for reckless driving resulting in physical injury. Not vehicular homicide, not attempted murder, but reckless driving." She pounded her fist on the armrest for emphasis. "He should have gone away for far longer than two years, but he had some fancy high-powered lawyer to get him out of it."

Ciaran squeezed her hand, and only then did she notice how much she was trembling. She gave him a grateful look and turned back to Takeda. "Ciaran told me the police arrested Andy yesterday after the fight in the park. I guarantee that this was all just a retaliation. Andy has made it very clear that if I won't be his, then no one can have me." She shuddered. "Maybe he wanted to terrorize me by having my home searched, my privacy violated. Maybe he thought that he'd get some kind of leverage out of it, I don't know."

Takeda took more notes and then nodded. "Well, I think that's all we need for today." He reached into the center of the table and the plastic crinkled as he piled the bags on top of his portfolio. "I'm afraid that we need to keep these for now, but I'll make sure you have the paperwork to take home so you can claim it at the appropriate time." His hand moved again, this time to turn off the recording, and then stood.

Jal climbed laboriously to her feet as if the weight of memory and no small amount of guilt had settled between her shoulders like a boulder. Her eyes locked on the envelope on the table, which held nearly all of her money. Ciaran stepped close and tucked her against his side and pressed a kiss to the top of her head.

Takeda extended a hand, shaking each of theirs in turn. "Thank you for coming in," he said. "We'll look into everything and get back to you soon. You're not under arrest at this time, but I will ask that you don't leave Manhattan, and make sure we have up-to-date contact information."

"You have that already," Ciaran said. "For both of us."

"Then you're good to go."

"Thank you, Detective." Jal forced a smile.

Takeda gestured to the door, and they circled around the table just as it opened. Ward froze with her hand on the knob, her other arm laden with bottles of water. "Derek?" she asked, her eyes shooting to her partner.

"We're done here," Takeda replied.

Her eyes narrowed, but she stepped aside to allow them to pass.

"Which way?" Ciaran asked.

Ward pointed to their right. "See that exit sign down there? Follow it."

Jal thanked her, though it rubbed something raw to do so. Anything to get the hell out of here as soon as possible.

"Stop at the desk warden before you leave to get your receipt." Takeda said, joining his partner in the doorway.

"Thank you, detective." She repeated, though it was much easier the second time.

Ciaran put a hand on her lower back and led the way. From behind them, Jal heard the sound of the door closing again and then a raised female voice. They picked up their pace, before Ward could convince her partner of whatever grudge she had and they came running after her.

They waited at the counter just before the door to the small reception area while a kind woman with dark skin and the widest bun of tiny braids that Jal had ever seen atop her head, printed out the receipt for her property. She took a couple of steps backwards and hovered her hand over where the paper would come out of the printer ready to catch it, but instead of paper came a grinding noise and her smile became a scowl.

"That's the fifth time today," she groused and pulled open an access door. "I'm sorry folks, it will be just a minute."

"No problem," Jal replied, the fingers tapping away on the

counter belying her casual tone.

"We'll be out of here soon, lass," Ciaran told her, his hand rubbing slow circles on her lower back. She gave in to the urge to lean against him, needing to be closer to him. Like skin-to-skin closer.

"Thank you," she said, looking up to meet his gaze. "I didn't get a chance to say it earlier, but thank you for coming so quickly. I didn't pull you out of anything important, did I?"

"It doesn't matter. This was more important." His tone was casual, as he leaned in and placed a quick kiss on her lips, but she got the impression that he wasn't being completely honest. Before she could say anything, there was an electronic buzz and the large metal door to their right slid open, hitting the end of its track with a metallic clang that boomed through the space.

The officer continued digging in the bowels of the printer. She probably heard it dozens of times a day, but Jal's head snapped over, the sound vibrating through the desk and up her arm.

A middle-aged man in a gray suit and combed back hair appeared first, a coat slung over his arm with a briefcase clutched in the same hand. He looked vaguely familiar, but Jal couldn't place him until he said something over his shoulder and the response turned her blood to ice.

"Yeah, yeah, Vic. I heard ya," Andy grumbled as he emerged from the doorway and straightened to his full height. He didn't immediately spot them, his attention was fixed on his lawyer, Victor Troiani, the same one who had represented him two years ago and almost got Andy off without penalty.

Pond scum, she thought, *the both of them.*

A bit of satisfaction filled her chest as she studied him. One of Andy's eyes was blackened, a cut over his other eye was crisscrossed with white strips to hold it closed. His clothes were dirty, though he now wore a sweatshirt that didn't quite hide the blood spots on his t-shirt.

Jal tilted her head in Ciaran's direction and whispered out of the corner of her mouth, "nice work."

It might have been the movement, or the sound of her voice, however faint, that did it, but Andy's head snapped in her direction. Jal would have cursed if she wasn't using all her focus to keep her back straight and her chin high.

The smile that spread across Andy's face at the sight of her was pleased, like a jackal who had just spotted its next meal. Her skin already felt like it was coated with something slimy, like Vic's hair gel or the trail they left on the floor as they approached. "There you are!"

He spotted Ciaran behind her as he approached and his eyes narrowed for a moment before his lips shifted, his smile becoming much more feline. He held out his hand as if he were expecting her to take it. "Nice of you to bring her here, man," he said to Ciaran, like he was just the chauffeur. "Ready to go, Sam?"

She looked down at his hand, at the calluses and rough skin that showed just how far from the polished businessman he had come. She stepped back out of Andy's reach and collided with Ciaran's chest.

"Go?" If there was a limit to how much incredulity someone could put into two little letters, she shattered it with a sledgehammer. "Go? Are you fucking kidding me? And for the last time, Sam doesn't exist anymore. You killed her, along with any right to anything to do with me, when you threw me down the stairs."

Andy gritted his teeth, and a red flush creeped up what little neck he had above his massive shoulders. He reached for her hand again and Jal wrenched it away so hard she whacked her knuckles on the desk behind her. She fought to keep her face blank, but the pain did help clear her head.

"Do we have a problem here?" the desk officer barked from over Jal's shoulder.

Jal spared a quick glance to find her standing with her arms braced on the counter, glowering at Andy.

To their right, the two detectives appeared from the interview room, drawn by the raised voices. For the first time, Takeda's eyes were dark chips of flint, his lips drawn in a thin line. Both detectives had their hands poised instinctively over their weapons.

Jal returned her gaze to Andy and raised her eyebrow. She didn't know where the confidence came from, whether it was the man behind her, the fact that they were in the middle of a police station, or maybe just that she had changed. Whatever it was, there was nothing that Andy could do other than back down and leave.

His lawyer broke the silence when he put a hand under his elbow. "Let's go."

The look Andy leveled on him was nothing short of murderous, but he knew that he didn't have many choices that didn't end with him right back in a cell and a one-way trip back to Rikers. He didn't resist when Vic towed him away until he stopped at the door and leveled a look at the desk officer who had to buzz the door.

She ground her teeth as if debating the merits of letting such an "upstanding citizen" back out onto the streets. "Is there a problem, officer?" Vic asked.

She sized up Andy for a moment and then clicked her tongue and pushed the button.

Andy wrenched the handle and pulled the buzzing door open, ushering his lawyer through first. The smile on his face was tight, but his eyes sparkled with promise when he met her gaze.

"I'll see you soon, Samantha."

TWENTY-NINE

The strength left Jal's legs as soon as the door to the waiting area closed, but Ciaran was there to catch her before she sank very far. Jal turned and buried her face in his chest for a moment and just breathed in his scent.

"Are you all right, Miss Morrow?" Takeda's voice came from nearby.

Jal turned her head to find him standing a few feet away, while his partner remained where she had been. Though his eyes had softened, Jal found that it just made her more upset. "Am I alright?" she demanded.

At the same time, Ciaran snapped, "You told us that you would keep him away from her."

Takeda grimaced and rubbed the back of his neck. Good, he should feel bad. "My apologies," he replied. "We should have escorted you out."

Jal didn't bother to respond and turned her attention to the desk officer. "We'll take that receipt, please."

The woman handed it over. "Here you go."

Jal folded the paper neatly and tucked it into her pocket.

"Is there anything else that I can get you?" the woman asked, leveling Takeda a meaningful look that had him retreating to his partner's side.

Jal glanced up at Ciaran, who reached over and laced his fingers with hers, and she could swear her legs felt stronger as if some of his strength passed into her at the contact. She turned back to the officer. "Yes, you can give me the paperwork for an order of protection."

The woman glanced at the door where Andy and his snail-trail of a lawyer had disappeared and then over to where Takeda still lingered. The look she gave him was one that made Jal hope that Takeda was religious and that he had made peace with his god.

Her gaze softened when she turned back to Jal. "Honey, I'll even help you rush it through."

The five-floor walk-up had never felt longer than it did now, though her exhaustion was far more mental than physical. Jal mounted the last step and stopped. At the other end of the hallway outside her door, stood Elena and Lexi.

She whirled on Ciaran, her eyes wide, and prickling. That the tears she had so far warded off weren't going to be held back much longer. "How?"

"I texted them while we were in the taxi."

Jal smiled. "How do you have their numbers?"

Ciaran shrugged. "They conned me into it when we were

at Darcy's a couple of weeks ago."

"And where was I?"

"Washroom? Jukebox? Does it really matter?"

Guess not. She rose up on her toes to kiss him, then went to meet her friends who were already heading toward them. She met them halfway, the three of them embracing in a tangle of arms. They surrounded her, their voices overlapping as they expressed relief, and peppered her with questions, none of which registered. Jal just soaked up as much of their support as she could.

How had she made it through the last two years while pushing these two women away?

From behind her, Ciaran cleared his throat. Jal turned, her head resting on Elena's shoulder. "I have to get back to work," he said reluctantly.

Jal detached herself from her friends and crossed to him. Without hesitation, or concern for their audience, she wrapped her arms around his neck and pulled him down for a kiss. One she had been meaning to give him since they left the station.

He wrapped his arms around her waist and hauled her against him, her feet dangling a few inches from the floor. She gasped in surprise against his lips and he took advantage, his tongue swept in, claiming her mouth. It could have been seconds, or minutes, or days, that he kissed her, but she knew that no matter how long it was, it wasn't long enough. It would never be long enough.

A decade later, Ciaran broke the kiss, but didn't let her go.

"Get a room, you two."

Jal tapped his shoulder and Ciaran sighed, and loosened

his grip just enough so she stayed pressed tightly against him as she slid to her feet, an obvious hardness trapped against her belly. She turned and Ciaran's arms fell away, leaving her feeling like a balloon whose string had been cut.

There was a rustle of material from behind her as if Ciaran was adjusting his coat. "You two happen to be blocking the way." He groused, though his voice was laced with amusement.

Jal chuckled and swatted him playfully on his chest. "Go, I'll be fine." She told him, and gave him a quick kiss in dismissal. "Dinner later?"

"Try and stop me, lass." he replied and left her to her friends.

Thirty

After letting her out of their sight long enough to shower and change, her friends sat her on one end of the sofa with a mug of tea in her hands, clustered together on the other end, and demanded every detail since she and Ciaran had left Reina together the night before last.

Jal still couldn't believe that it had been less than forty-eight hours. So much had happened in such a short amount of time, and there hadn't been time to digest it yet, but telling her friends helped. She couldn't help but laugh, and then blush spectacularly, when Elena pumped a fist in the air and crowed, "about damned time, nena!" when Jal told them about the night of, and the early morning after, the penthouse dinner.

Face flaming, Jal had thrown a pillow at her, then told them the rest, including that Ciaran now knew her biggest secrets: Andy, her real name. Her daughter. And what had he done?

The last thing she would have expected. The opposite of what any sane man in his position would do when she confessed to such a checkered past and far, far too many secrets. He hadn't said that it was all too much after only a few short months and walked out the door. Or, since they'd been at his place, kicked her out.

Instead, he had held her, comforted her, and said those three very big words.

Lexi squealed and bounced in her seat at the news and wrapped her in a hug. Elena sprang to the rescue and deposited her mug on the coffee table before she could spill lukewarm matcha over them both.

Over Lexi's shoulder, Jal caught Elena's eye and her friend gave her a look that said she understood. But still, Jal eased back and brushed her hair, and maybe a little wetness out of her eyes. "And then I ran."

Elena tilted her head. "And he followed," she countered.

"Only to get into a fistfight with my ex-boyfriend!"

"Stop," Elena demanded. She got up and gently elbowed Lexi back so she could sit between them and wrap an arm around Jal's shoulders. "We're not going to go there, and do you know why?"

Jal shook her head. This time when her hair fell in her eyes, she left it there. If she couldn't see her friend, her friend couldn't see the shame that colored her cheeks. "Why?"

Elena gently brushed the curls behind her ear. "Because after everything you've been through, you deserve a guy like Ciaran," she replied. She glanced at Lexi and jerked her head. Their friend got the message and rose to her feet, squeezing in on Jal's other side. "You deserve to be happy."

"He fought Andy off so you could be safe," Lexi added, cupping her hand around Jal's shoulder and ducking so she could look Jal in the eye. "And he came when you needed him and stayed with you all the way to a police station for chrissakes. Why are you fighting us on this? And against your feelings for him?"

Why indeed?

Jal blurted out the first thing that came to mind. "It's all just happening so quickly." She grimaced at how whiny her own voice sounded.

"Sometimes love just happens that way," Lexi replied, then shot Elena a look. "Not that we would know."

Elena laughed. "Speak for yourself, Lex. I happen to fall in, and out, of love all the time."

Lexi snorted and Jal couldn't help joining in and soon they were clutching at each other, their laughter egging the others on until Jal felt like she couldn't breathe.

"I love you guys," she said, pulling them even closer. They threw their arms around her so Lexi's chin rested on her shoulder, and Elena's at the top of her head.

"Isn't there someone else you should be saying that to?" Elena countered from above.

Jal scoffed and swam through their arms to snatch up the remote control from the coffee table and aim it at the TV, jabbing meaningfully at the power button. Elena snatched it out of her hand and started scrolling through movie options.

"Fine, if you want to be evasive, I'm picking the movie." She waved the remote in the air out of Jal's reach. "You can just sit there and deal."

"It's my TV!"

Elena pivoted to put her head in Jal's lap, her feet draped over the back of the sofa. "And?" she asked, looking up through her eyelashes.

Jal playfully bared her teeth at her just as a familiar country tune started to play. It was soon joined by the rumbles of an approaching thunderstorm as two kids appeared running down a beach. Jal recognized it at once. If it was an option, Elena was going to watch it, there was never any negotiation.

Jal groaned loudly and collapsed back against Lexi, who patted her arm in mock-pity. She batted her hand away, but she was grinning and Lexi just put it right back on her shoulder again. This time, Jal hung on to her fingers like they were a lifeline, and in a way, they were. Her friends had no way of knowing just how much she had needed them after everything that had happened over the last few days. Or maybe they did.

Her phone buzzed and Jal dug it from the pocket of her hoodie to find a text from Ciaran.

> Ciaran: I'm going to be here for a while yet.

> Ciaran: Hopefully, your friends can keep you company a little longer.

> Ciaran: I'll be there by eight.

Lexi, unabashedly reading over her shoulder, squeezed her fingers in confirmation, or sympathy that she was stuck with them, and Jal shook her head ruefully while she typed a quick response and stowed her phone away. To cover her disappointment, Jal reached for her tea, but it was out of her reach, and her hand just swatted empty air.

Elena huffed dramatically and handed it over. The movie

moved on to show that the thunderstorm had been a dream. "She stays with the ridiculously attractive estranged husband, who looks a little like Maks," Jal told her even as she cast a meaningful look over her shoulder at Lexi. Her friend rolled her eyes, which made Jal's grin a little bigger. It wasn't like she was spoiling an ending they didn't all know by heart, and, despite herself, had come to love. Not that she would ever admit that to Elena. "You know that right?"

"Hush now," Elena chided, wriggling her head and shoulders to find a more comfortable position, when all she really did was dig the clip holding her hair in a twist into Jal's thigh. She plucked it from Elena's head and tossed it to the end of the sofa. Elena rolled her eyes up and shot her a grin. "And watch the damned movie."

For the rest of the afternoon, they did just that, only taking breaks long enough to replenish drinks and snacks, or to use the restroom. While the credits rolled on a sappy rom-com about a dad making his young daughter guess which of three ex-girlfriends was her mother, Jal headed for the bathroom and her attention was drawn to the metal grate over the bathroom door, concealing an emptiness that she could almost feel in her bones.

If she thought too long about how most of her life savings was sitting in a police evidence bag, she'd... no, she was not going to worry about that today.

When Jal returned to the living room, she snatched the remote out of Elena's hand.

"Hey!"

Jal stuck her tongue out at her as she plopped into the oversized armchair, ignoring the knowing grin Elena's indignation turned into when she did. Jal scrolled until she found the movie she was looking for and relished in the groans that erupted when the first notes of the score to a sci-fi masterpiece where a campy tv series became real life for the show's actors trumpeted through the speakers. Like the movies they'd already watched, she had discovered this one thanks to the wonders of streaming, and knew the lines by heart, badly dubbed swear words and all.

"My turn."

Just as the engineer turned out to be the bad guy with a shapeshifting device, an alarm blared from Lexi's pocket and her friend leapt to her feet. Jal glanced out the window and noted for the first time how dark it had gotten.

They watched with amusement as Lexi raced around, gathering her purse, coat, and shoes. "Got a hot date, *nena*?"

Lexi swept a curtain of blond waves back as she wobbled on one heel, struggling to secure the ankle strap of the other. "Nah," she replied, "I just have a game to get to."

Elena caught Jal's eye and raised an eyebrow as Lexi circled the room to hand out goodbye hugs. "I thought I saw some country band was playing the Garden tonight."

Jal's first thought had also been hockey. Lexi paused for a split second with her hands in mid-air before settling the strap of her purse diagonally across her chest. "Are you sure?" she asked as she pulled the door open. "Later, girls."

The door swung shut leaving Jal and Elena staring at each other, neither paying any attention to the intrepid crew winning the day.

"That was weird," Elena finally said. She bent to look out the window, even though it was too dark, and they were on the wrong side of the building, for her to see Lexi leave.

She flopped back on the sofa and dug out her phone, her thumbs flying across the screen. "Ha! They're on the west coast this week." She didn't need to say who 'they' were.

Jal glanced at the door as if Lexi would realize the same and come back any second, then turned back to Elena when she didn't. She shrugged and burrowed back into the chair. The overstuffed cushions almost seemed to embrace her, which absolutely did not bring to mind other arms that had held her, and done other things to her, in the same chair.

Reminded of Ciaran, Jal dug her phone out again and glanced at the time. It was past eight, and she had another missed text from Ciaran apologizing that he would be a little longer.

Elena raised an eyebrow at her from where she once again reclined across the sofa cushions with one arm draped over her head like she was one of those French girls rather than Latina.

"One more?"

By the time Ciaran arrived, it was nearly ten, but the pizza boxes he carried were a good first step in making up for it. The zesty scents of pepperoni and oregano wafted out as he planted a quick kiss on her lips and breezed by to drop the boxes on the kitchen counter.

Jal's stomach growled loud enough for Ciaran to shoot her an amused look as he shrugged out of his coat and draped it over a kitchen chair.

"Hey, Ciaran!" Elena's hand popped up over the furniture

between them from her prone position on the sofa. Ciaran chuckled and returned the greeting with the same half-bored cheerfulness.

Jal studied him as she crossed the room. Though there were shadows under his eyes, the whisky gold depths were bright as they took her in. He held open his arms, and Jal stepped into them, wrapping her arms around his waist, and buried her face in his shirt, breathing in clean laundry and musky soap.

"Where's Lexi?" he asked, his chest vibrating under her cheek.

Jal eased back enough to look up at him. "She said she had a game to go to."

Ciaran lifted an eyebrow as he reached to brush a curl out of her face. His fingers skimmed over her cheekbone and left a trail of warmth there.

Jal shrugged, and warmth gathered elsewhere the longer he held her gaze. A few moments later, Elena sighed dramatically from the sofa and climbed to her feet.

"Okay, okay, I get the hint," she said, though neither of them had said anything about her leaving.

Jal lifted the lid on the top box to find pepperoni and cheese with just the right amount of crust. "Please, take some pizza with you."

"There's a veg one underneath." Ciaran added helpfully.

"A what?"

Jal rolled her eyes at the devilish glint in her friend's dark eyes. "Vegetable," she responded, enunciating each syllable carefully.

"Oh right," Elena replied, in a tone that was all innocence.

She reached around her to tear off a length of paper towels and held it out for Jal to hand over a slice. "*Gracias, nena.*" She looked over at Ciaran. "She's all yours."

Elena strode to where she'd kicked her shoes off by the door and slid her feet into them, then left without another word. Jal watched as Ciaran went to the door and locked it behind her. He crossed the kitchen and took down two plates from the cupboard.

He lifted the lid a little further and reached in for a slice. "Are you hungry?" he asked, and froze with the pizza in his hand at the look she cast his way.

Jal put her hand on the lid and pushed it closed, forcing Ciaran to drop the slice inside. Her hand went to the zipper pull on her hoodie and drew it down. His eyes darkened as she bared one shoulder and then the other. "I sure am."

Thirty-One

For the next few days, Ciaran and her friends wouldn't let her out of their sight. She wasn't about to complain about him taking the night shift, but she wasn't sure what was worse during the day, being cooped up inside, or being cooped up inside with one or both of her friends playing babysitter.

"I can take care of myself, you know." she muttered for the dozenth time as Lexi handed her a sandwich, then retreated with her own to the table where her work laptop sat beside a scattering of papers and files.

"I know you can," she said, already tapping away on the keys as she chewed. "But why be alone when I can work from anywhere?"

Jal bit into the soft French loaf piled high with turkey and cheese, and the herbed oil and vinegar dressing was a delightful explosion on her tongue. "Well, somehow you managed it for the last two years." she replied, mouth full.

Lexi froze, and Jal felt a flash of guilt. She brushed the

crumbs off her hands and deliberately finished chewing before she spoke. "I'm not going to apologize for just following your lead," she said, her back ramrod straight at the table, not quite able to completely mask the hurt in her voice. "Besides, Andy was securely behind bars the whole time, and you needed space to heal. Do I wish you had included us more in that? Of course I do. But this is totally different."

Jal set her plate aside, her appetite gone. The sunlight streaming in through the window suddenly felt like a spotlight on how much of a jerk she was being. She drew her knees up under her chin and wrapped her arms tightly around them. "I'm sorry, Lex." she said, her voice small. "I'm just going crazy in here."

There was a scrape of the chair and then Lexi was there, crouching down so she could get into Jal's line of sight. Her blue eyes were soft, which only made Jal feel worse. "It's like when someone says don't think about white elephants, and that's all you can think of." Lexi said. The absurdity of it made Jal laugh. And think of white elephants.

"Being cooped up inside when it's your choice is easy. Being cooped up inside when you have no other choice, is torture. I *do* get it, believe me. But let's give it a little more time. Hopefully Andy will give up soon and life will return to normal."

Jal nodded though her stomach was now twisted in knots and the sandwich had lost all its appeal. How 'normal' could things get when the police had all her money? And now that she was on their radar as a suspected thief, how could she go back to picking pockets when she had a reason to look over her shoulder all the time? Two reasons, if you counted Andy, which she definitely did.

As stir-crazy as it made her, Jal understood that Andy could be anywhere, just waiting to pounce. Manhattan was a very big place, but if he'd found her once, he'd find her again even if she never went back to her usual places. Besides, the police had her address. Could it be just a matter of time before Andy's contacts got a hold of it?

So far, thank God, that hadn't happened. But it could and there wasn't a damned thing she could do about it. His intentions, as far as she was concerned, were pretty fucking clear. She belonged to him. Though to what end, she didn't know.

"You okay?"

Jal blinked, to find Lexi's worried features still a foot away. She shook off the thoughts and took another bite of her sandwich, smiling around it to try to reassure her friend enough to go back to her own lunch, and work.

Lexi gave her a dubious look, but patted her knee and got to her feet. She sat back down behind her laptop, but Jal could still feel her eyes on her as she finished her sandwich, and picked up a book, the same one she'd been trying to finish for weeks. And today was not going to be that day. Jal just opened the book and stared at lines of type that could have been in a foreign language with the circles her mind had been spinning in all day.

Dimly, she heard Lexi's phone ring but didn't pay any attention until her voice rose in pitch and volume. "Whoa, whoa, wait Elena," she was saying. "Slow down!"

The book slipped out of Jal's hand and clattered to the floor. Her head snapped to Lexi, who was sitting stiffly with her hand around her throat, eyes large as she listened. "What's going on?" she demanded.

Lexi put the phone down on the table and hit a button. The sound of pounding feet and heavy breathing filled the air. Jal rushed across the room and skidded to a halt beside her friend.

"He's behind me!" Elena's voice came out of the speaker.

"Who's behind you?" Jal asked, though there could only be one person. At the same time, Lexi shrieked, "where are you?"

"I'm on Ninth, about a block from Lima." There was a thud and a shout of outrage. "Sorry!"

Jal looked down at the clock on Lexi's phone, and cursed. There was still a half hour before the restaurant opened for lunch. The front door would be locked and the dining room would be empty. "Go down the alley."

"I don't have my keys!"

Jal ran back to her phone and dialed a number from memory. "Just do it," she yelled as the phone rang.

"Lima y Sazón," the familiar voice of Elena's cousin Marilena, the restaurant's bar manager, said cheerfully. "How can I—"

"Mari, it's Jal. I don't have time to explain but I need you to go to the back door right now and get it open, as quickly as you can."

"What?"

"Back door, now! Get it open!"

There was the sound of a glass crashing to the floor and a lot of frantic breathing, but the boom of the kitchen door and a sudden burst of cooking sounds and Merengue told Jal that she was doing as she was told. Next, came the bang of a metal hotel pan hitting the floor, followed by a stream of Spanish curses, and a grunt as Mari slammed into the back door, too frantic to stop in time.

Jal's head whipped to Lexi, who was listening to Elena's updates. She caught something about a car turning into the narrow alley in Elena's wake, while closer in her ear came a frantic rattle of the kitchen door locks and the screech and groan as Marilena shoved the door open with her hip.

"Look out!" Elena's voice came from both phones. An engine roared to a deafening level, followed by the screech of tires, a loud metallic crash, and the call on Lexi's phone went dead.

"Elena!"

Lexi abandoned her phone and ran to Jal's side. "Elena, answer us!"

For a moment, Jal couldn't hear anything over the roar of her blood in her ears, but then Elena's voice broke through and it was the best thing she had ever heard. "I'm okay," she replied through Marilena's phone.

Lexi clutched at her in relief and Jal let her drag them both down onto the sofa. "Oh, thank God," Lexi gasped, her blue eyes brimming with tears of relief. "What happened?"

Elena let loose a string of Spanish curses.

Jal understood only half of it, but there were several creative things that Elena wished Andy would do with himself.

"Asshole almost ran me down in the alley. Mari got the

door open just in time," she finally said over the din of half the kitchen staff demanding answers. Elena barked an order for them to get back to work and the sound ebbed away.

"I'm sure you'll be devastated by this, *nena* but it looks like we're going to need a new door."

"Did you see what he was driving?" Jal asked.

"Yeah, a beat-up maroon Toyota, now even more worse for wear on the driver's side. I didn't catch the plate, other than it was yellow and I think it started with a K." Elena cursed. "*Cabrón* also owes me a new phone."

Despite the adrenaline running through her, Jal laughed at that. "Stay there," Jal told her. "I'm calling Takeda."

"I'll be here," Elena replied and hung up.

Jal went to the fridge where she had pinned up the detective's information and dialed. He picked up on the second ring and Jal told him everything that she knew. After asking whether Elena was okay, he said he would head for the restaurant and Jal promised to meet him there.

"I'll call for a car," Lexi rushed to the table and started gathering all the files and papers into a haphazard pile, stuffing them and her laptop back in her bag.

Jal bolted for her bedroom to change into something more presentable and, in less than five minutes, they burst out onto the sidewalk just as a black town car was pulling up to the curb. They piled into the cedar and leather scented interior, and the car whisked them across town as fast as it could in New York City traffic.

Ciaran needed to know where they were going, so she dialed his number, but her stomach dropped when it went straight to voicemail. She listened to the message, hoping that even the recorded sound of his voice would help soothe her frayed nerves, but it wasn't like the real thing. With a sigh, she hung up and sent him a text with all the details.

She put her head back on the seat, and watched the tops of the buildings crawl by. It was funny how much had changed, that now, when anything happened, her first thought was that she wanted -no, needed- Ciaran to know everything. Especially when it came to Andy. Coming after her was one thing, but using her friends to do it? How long until he moved on to Lexi, or Ciaran?

This was turning into a nightmare.

"You, okay?"

Jal turned her head and met Lexi's worried blue eyes. There were tears caught in her eyelashes and Jal reached over to give her hand a reassuring squeeze. "Yeah, I'm good."

They stayed that way until the car pulled up to the curb. Jal threw the door open the second they stopped and rushed inside with Lexi on her heels. Elena was perched on a bar stool with a towel filled with ice pressed to her face.

Her father and cousin hovered nearby, the elder Sandoval's face as livid a red as the stack of cloth napkins at his elbow. His arms waved in the air as he demanded explanations in Spanish as they rushed to Elena's side. He didn't stop when they surrounded her, but a moment later, he froze, eyes fixed on the door.

Her heart skipped a beat, thinking that Andy might have come back, but as she smoothed away the curls of Elena's hair that obscured her vision, she caught sight of Takeda's much more slender build. His partner was right on his heels, removing her sunglasses so her too-alert eyes could scan the much dimmer room. Her eyes settled on Jal, leveling an icy look that said she still wasn't in the mood to play nice. Wonderful.

Takeda was tucking his own glasses into a jacket pocket as he crossed the room. "Good to see you, Miss Morrow."

"Wish I could say the same, Detective." she replied, eyes narrowed. "How many times does Andy Paolinelli need to attack someone before you keep him behind bars?"

Takeda's mouth tightened, but he didn't respond and instead turned his attention to Elena, who sat up a little straighter under his gaze and lowered the compress to her knee. Jal craned her head around to see the beginnings of a bruise across one high cheekbone. "Are you all right Miss..."

"Sandoval," she replied. "Elena Sandoval. This is my father Roberto and my cousin Marilena. And yes, I'm fine, couple scrapes, a little bump on the head."

"Can you tell me what happened?"

Elena cleared her throat. "I was a couple blocks away, getting a coffee like I usually do most mornings between prep and lunch service." She glanced up at Jal, who couldn't help but wince. Of course, Andy would remember her friends' routines as much as hers. There was no condemnation in her eyes, but Jal felt the stab of guilt anyway.

"I came out of the café and there he was, waiting for me, wanting to know where Sam—I mean, Jal—was. I ignored him at first, but he followed me, and when he got impatient, he went to grab me, but I shoved him away and ran. He ran back to his car and followed me, honking and yelling out the window."

"What was he driving?" Detective Ward asked coolly. Like her partner, she had a pen in her hand poised over a notepad.

"It was a maroon Toyota, maybe ten or so years old, looked like it had been in an accident or two." Elena continued, her voice still shaky. "One of the front fenders was new and hadn't been painted yet, almost like it was in the middle of being repaired."

"It's going to need more repairs now," Lexi snorted.

"Along with my door!" Elena's father exclaimed. "What about that?"

Takeda cocked his head. "Door?"

Elena nodded, "I went down the alley to the kitchen door, and he followed." Her breathing hitched and Jal could feel a fine tremor going through her. "I think he tried to run me down. My cousin got the door open just in time. He missed me, but he crashed into the door, and drove off."

"Can you show me?" Ward asked.

Elena's father nodded and motioned for her to follow him into the kitchen. Lexi followed and Jal stayed where she was. She settled into the stool beside her friend and Elena reached for her hand and held on tight.

"How did you know to open the door?" Takeda asked, turning his attention to Mari.

"Elena called Lexi, and Jal called me," Mari explained. "I rushed into the kitchen and got that cranky old door open just in time for Elena to leap through. She got the bump on her cheek hitting my elbow. But the door was wide open, and the car pretty much took it off its hinges."

Takeda made some notes. "Do you have cameras?"

Elena shook her head. "Not in the alley," she replied. "I'm not sure if anyone else on the block does."

Takeda nodded and made another note. "And being inside

the restaurant, you wouldn't have seen which way he went."

The statement had been rhetorical, but Elena shook her head anyway.

"We used to live in the Bronx before he went away," Jal offered. "I think that he's living somewhere in that area. You should have his address on file though, since he's on parole. For now."

Elena nodded her head in agreement. "He came in here once looking for Jal right after he got out of prison and said he was working in Hunt's Point. He left a phone number, but I burned it as soon as he left."

A corner of Takeda's mouth twitched, but he didn't look up from his notebook. "We'll look into it."

"You do that."

Takeda opened his mouth to say something else, but his partner returned through the kitchen door, followed closely by Lexi and Roberto.

"I can call my brother to come and cover it until the insurance inspector can get here." Roberto was saying, but his posture was still tense.

"Very well," Ward replied and handed him a business card from a slot in her notepad. "Give the station a call in the morning and they'll give you the report number for the claim."

"Thank you, detective."

Ward turned to her partner, but not before her eyes swept Jal from head to toe. "Are we done here?"

"Yeah, I think we have everything we need." He tucked his notebook back into a pocket. "Miss Morrow, please let me know if you need anything else."

"I already told you what I need, Detective," Jal replied,

shaking the hand that he held out to her. "But thank you for coming so quickly."

"Of course," He gestured to his partner. "Let's go."

Jal watched them leave and then scanned the room, where only a few tables were occupied waiting for their orders. No one was looking their way, but there was no way they hadn't listened in. Her attention fixed on Roberto last. "I'm so sorry for all of this," she said to him.

His eyes softened as they met hers. "*No te preocupes, mija,*" he replied, and held open his arms.

Jal untangled herself from Elena and went to him. She held on tightly, breathing in the citrus and spice scent that always clung to him from the kitchen. It calmed her like nothing else had since her phone rang.

Roberto had called her 'daughter' for years, and Elena often joked that he loved her more than his own daughter most of the time. It mattered more than he knew that he didn't hold all of this against her.

He gently set her back and looked down at her with a gentle smile. "Doors can be fixed, *mija*" he told her, giving her shoulders a squeeze. "But as long as you are all okay. The police will find him."

Jal nodded, her throat too thick with emotion to speak.

"Well, if we're good here," Elena said abruptly.

Jal turned to see her get to her feet and hand the icepack to Marilena who dumped the ice with a clatter into the sink behind the bar.

"I'm going to get to work."

"Are you sure?" Lexi asked. "No one would say anything if you wanted to take the day." She shot a meaningful look at

Roberto.

Roberto held up his hands. "Of course not. Go home, nena, get some rest."

Elena shook her head. "We're already shorthanded today, *papá*," she protested. "Really, I'm fine. Thank you both for coming." Without another word, she gave Lexi a quick hug and disappeared into the kitchen.

Lexi exchanged a look with Jal, who shrugged. Better to give Elena her space, if that was what she wanted.

"You girls should go back to your day," Roberto told them. His eyes trained on the door and worry deepened the lines on his face. They hadn't had the best relationship over the last few years, not since she had given up working in the restaurant for a dance career that was very off, *off* Broadway. But she was still his daughter. "I'll make sure she's alright."

Reluctantly, Jal nodded and gave him another brief hug. Lexi gathered up her stuff and started heading for the door. Jal stopped her with a whistle. "You know what? Before we go, I have to see that cranky old door one last time."

Thirty-Two

Ciaran stepped out onto the street in front of DJ&R and took a deep breath of the crisp air. Darkness had fallen, but not all that long ago going by the faint orange glow deep in the canyon of skyscrapers to the west.

Spring was well on its way. He glanced at his watch and winced, feeling both the hour of the day and the strain on his back after sitting for most of it at the drafting table, hunched over a blueprint that OMD had insisted be drawn by hand. It was his penance for the "family emergency" right before the New York College presentation, he was sure of it.

It wasn't that big of a deal, since Catherine had been planning on running the presentation anyway, but it *was* his design, and he should have been there. So, all of the feedback from the demo had to be updated on the computer and then drawn out.

Ciaran didn't mind the manual labor, just the time it took to do it. A few months ago, he would have looked forward to going home to a hot shower, a dram of something warm and peaty, and a relaxing, early night.

Now, he wondered what Jal was up to. Spending the evening and night wrapped up in her was exactly what both of them had needed lately.

Come to think of it, his phone *had* been uncommonly quiet all day. He retrieved it from his backpack and frowned when he raised it up and the screen stayed dark. Oh right, he'd turned it off going into that status meeting just before lunch. Resisting the urge to clap a hand to his face, he pressed the power button and the screen came to life, soon followed by a chorus of notifications.

"Oh, fuck me," he muttered as he read through them, his eyes growing wider with each message. He had texts from Jal, that she and Lexi were heading to Elena's family restaurant because... Andy had tried to run Elena down? He bit out the most vicious curse in Gaelic that he knew. A passing pedestrian gave him an odd look and a wide berth as he passed by.

Not only had Jal left him a string of texts, but so had Elena, asking him to come by the restaurant before he went home. Intrigued, he shot her a response and didn't have to wait long before his phone was ringing.

"Hey, Ciaran," she said over the clatter of pans and shouts of a busy kitchen.

"'Hey, Ciaran'?" he parroted back to her. "Tell me what the bloody hell is going on?"

Elena sighed. "Short story is that Andy chased me down the alley behind the restaurant and nearly ran me over."

"Christ, are you alright?"

"Yeah, I'm good." She replied, and barked an order in

Spanish that he caught only a few words of. Someone was doing something they shouldn't do with chicken. That was all he could catch.

"I have something I want to talk to you about, though. Can you come by Lima tonight?"

He scratched his eyebrow. "Sure, I can swing by Jal's and we can be there by eight."

"No, just you."

Just as he opened his mouth to question her, a loud rumbling of a revving engine pierced through the background hum of the city. Thanks to the decent lightning on this part of Fifth Avenue, it wasn't hard for him to zero in on a dark red car parked across the street. The driver's side window was up but the shadowy figure inside was almost too big for the small sedan, a sedan with substantial damage to the front fender.

"Em, Elena. Was he driving a maroon sedan?"

"Yeah, why?"

"Because there is one with a completely rearranged fender parked outside my office."

Her gasp came clearly though the phone. "Can you go back inside? How far is your car? Want me to call the cops?"

"My car is just at the next block in the car park." He was already moving, his dress shoes slapping on the pavement. The headlights on the car flared to life before he'd made it five feet.

Ciaran picked up the pace. The car pulled out of the parking spot and rolled slowly to keep in line with him. Ciaran thought about turning around and going back inside but he'd be damned if he was going to let this piece of shit intimidate him.

As he approached the corner, the light on Fifth went red,

and Ciaran dashed across the side street before the traffic could move. From his right came the roar of an engine and the screech of tires.

Headlights filled his peripheral vision as he dove for the far curb, making it just in time to avoid the crunch and groan of tortured metal as the maroon car caught the corner of the car parked closest to him before righting itself and peeling away, horn blaring.

Ciaran watched him drive out of sight and put his hands on his knees, only to find that one hand still clutched his cell phone, and Elena was shrieking his name out of it. He ignored the pedestrians around him, who were trying to figure out what happened and marched into the parking garage.

"I'm here."

"Oh my god, what happened?"

"The bastard tried to run me down, too." he replied, unlocking his car. "I'll be right there."

He left the parking garage and eased into the usual traffic. At the next light, he turned left, then right, working his way west until he had passed out of Chelsea and into the Kitchen. He searched the brightly lit signage over blocks of restaurants, bodegas, and shops until he located the restaurant and managed to find a parking spot only a block away.

He held the door open for a couple coming out and then stepped inside, his nose filling with the spices of Dominican cuisine. The man who greeted him at the door had a stack of menus tucked under one arm and looked to be in his late fifties or early sixties, with a bald head, and a goatee that was more salt than pepper. There was something in his eyes that reminded Ciaran of Elena.

"Good evening, *señor*," he said. "Picking up takeout?"

Ciaran shook his head. "I'm actually here to speak with Elena for a minute if I could. I'm a friend of Jal's."

The man studied his face for a moment. The bruises on his face had started to fade and Ciaran hoped that they weren't all that visible in the atmospheric lighting over the tables. The man's eyes seemed to fix on the split in his lip, forcing Ciaran to suppress the urge to prod it with his tongue.

After an interminable moment, he nodded and led the way to the back of the restaurant where a bar spanned much of the space. He jabbed a finger at an empty stool, and Ciaran sat faster than he would have had the command been yelled in his face.

Elena's father went to the door to the kitchen and yelled something in Spanish inside. Ciaran's knowledge of the language was rusty, but he remembered enough to recognize that the man said the word for daughter.

Elena came out of the kitchen a moment later, wiping her hands on a towel. She was wearing a black chef's coat with the restaurant logo on the breast pocket, her long hair bundled up under a cloth cap similar to what a nurse or a surgeon would wear. Her face was flushed, the stormy expression in her eyes, one of which had a new, and painful looking, bruise under it, told him it wasn't just from the heat of the kitchen. "*Ay papá, como esperas que lo hag—*" The rapid-fire Spanish cut off when she saw him at the bar. "Oh, Ciaran! That was quick!"

"Well, I had that wee bit of motivation."

Elena nodded, her expression an odd mix of concern and amusement as if she wasn't sure which one she should be feeling more. She pushed open the door to the kitchen.

Ciaran slid off the stool and followed, only to be greeted by a wall of fragrant heat and steam that made his mouth water and his stomach growl. Elena led him back to a small office, barely big enough for a desk, a chair, and a few filing cabinets. He took the extra chair, and Elena perched her hip on the desk, her arms crossed. Though her back was stiff, there was something in her eyes that told him those arms were trying to hold her together.

"That looks bad," he said, pointing to her cheek.

"I'm not going to lie and say it doesn't throb like a bitch." She dabbed at her face gingerly and hissed when she hit a particularly tender spot.

"Please tell me what happened," Ciaran asked, and was surprised at the tremor and desperation in his voice.

Elena's eyes went hard, and then, she launched into the story, and she didn't hold back. From Andy waiting for her outside the coffee shop to her last-ditch leap through Lima's back door before he could run her down, presumably for keeping Jal from him. His whole body vibrated with anger by the time she finished. Or maybe that was just his hands, which were shaking hard enough, he had to clutch the arms of the chair to stop them. So, maybe it wasn't just anger.

He had to unclench his teeth to speak. "And then, he must have made his way over to midtown and parked outside my office." He surmised. "How could he possibly know where we would all be?"

"Well, I'm a creature of habit," Elena said dropping into the desk chair. It creaked and threatened to tip over, but she slapped a hand on the desk and righted herself with a self-deprecating roll of her eyes. "But you? I have a feeling that it's the same reason why he got let back out on the streets in the first place rather than having his parole revoked. That *pendejo* always seemed to have the right connections."

"What kind of connections?"

"Could be mafia, could be someone through his business connections, I don't know." Elena shrugged. "They couldn't prevent him from going to prison completely, but the *cabrón* got off easy for what he did, that's for sure."

Ciaran ground his teeth. Why was it always those that most deserved it that got off easy? He cut that thought off before he could ponder the close calls in his own life. Elena's tapping foot kept him in the present.

"Jal is at home right now, if you're wondering, and so far, it seems like he hasn't managed to find out where that is." At the cock of his head, she added, "Lexi is with her."

"Oh good, that's probably the safest place for her. Andy doesn't know where she lives now."

Elena heaved a sigh and crossed her legs, propping her chin on one hand. "Running into him at Washington Square was part prediction, part bad luck. It's always been one of her favorite places to pick pockets, and he just 'happened by' at the right moment." She waved two fingers of each hand in a helpless gesture at what was ultimately manufactured coincidence.

Ciaran rubbed his thumb across the split in his lip, his eyes unfocused as the memories of grappling with a man who reminded him of the human equivalent of the rock monster in Jal's favorite movie. "Doesn't feel lucky." He said, with a wry chuckle. The fist that had split his lip certainly hadn't felt that way. A thought crossed his mind and he looked up at her. "So,

Elena, I have to ask, why didn't you want me to bring Jal with me?"

Elena met his eyes without hesitation. "I lied to the police earlier when they took the report."

That startled a laugh out of him. "Well, that's no' exactly what I expected you to say. What did you lie about?"

"I told them that I didn't know where he lived." She ran a hand through her hair. "Well, that part is true. He came in here a few weeks ago and mentioned that he was living near the place he and Jal had shared in the Bronx, but he didn't give an address."

"So?"

"What I didn't tell the cops was that he also said that he's working at an auto body shop in Hunts Point, DiBattista Motors, I think he said."

"But why not tell Jal?" he asked, though he had a pretty good idea why. It didn't sit right keeping anything from her, especially something like this, but the man had put her through enough already.

"I think you already know why." Elena responded. "I've known that girl since she was seventeen, way before she met Andy. After all that he did..." She shook her head. "The depression, the nightmares, all of that is because of him."

Ciaran's knee started to bounce. "Jal said he had been working for an investment firm before—"

Elena nodded, following his train of thought when his voice failed. "He did, before he got in too deep with the wrong people and went over to the dark side. He got desperate and Jal paid for it."

Unable to stay seated any longer, Ciaran leapt to his feet

and muttered a thanks as he lurched for the door.

Elena sprang from the chair to stop him with a hand wrapped around his arm. "What are you going to do?"

"I just want to talk," Ciaran said, though he couldn't help one hand curling into a fist. "See if I can find a way to keep him away from Jal."

Elena didn't miss a thing as she looked him up and down, likely sizing him up against the man who easily had the advantage of fifty pounds of solid prison muscle. She, ultimately, just nodded her head and smiled. "Well, let me know if you need backup. I owe him a few punches myself."

Ciaran chuckled, expecting nothing less, and some of the frustration he felt melted away. He would have been disappointed if she *hadn't* offered to help pummel the bastard. "Will do."

He opened the office door and a humid wave of spice, and garlic, and citrus flooded in. His stomach growled again.

"Here, I'll let you out this way," she offered and headed for the back door. Make that no door at all. He took a step into the alley where a metal door that looked like it had seen better days, even before it had been hit by a car, was propped.

He glanced back at Elena, who shook her head with a sad smile. "It's kind of like losing an old friend."

Ciaran gave her a reassuring smile. "You know what, I think I'll order some dinner before I go."

Thirty-Three

It took almost everything he had to take the food and drive to Jal's place instead of heading for the RFK Bridge and combing every street in Hunt's Point until he found what he was looking for, even if he hadn't really known what that was. What little restraint he had left, he used to have a pleasant night with Jal and not ruin it with pesky things like plans to have a good heart-to-heart with someone who had nearly ruined her.

He'd nearly told her a half dozen times. During dinner, while watching a movie. But after all the excitement of the day they'd fallen asleep on the sofa and had only woken up long enough to get into bed and tuck her into his arms. Before he knew it, the sun was up and he had to leave for work. He'd tell her everything, but only after it was done. No sense in her worrying about him.

The thought of keeping her in the dark left him with a queasy feeling in his stomach that he couldn't shake, even hours later as he stared at a single red pin on a map of one of the roughest neighborhoods in the city.

The auto body shop hadn't shown up on any of the usual maps or search engines, not that Ciaran had been at all surprised. It had taken quite a lot of poking around on some less than legitimate websites to find it, and given Andy's record, he probably fit right in.

He zoomed in on the map until he could switch to the street view. The place wasn't much to look at, just a box of corrugated steel with rolling doors at both ends and little to no signage. There were places just like it back home. Small, unmarked garages, usually tucked into odd places like under elevated roadways, or deep in dodgy industrial parks. The junkyard or repair business existed only as cover for more illegal activities in the back.

"Earth to Scotty."

Ciaran jumped. He closed the browser and looked up to see Cliff standing on the other side of his monitor with a smirk and an empty coffee cup. He heard a hint of a snicker and shot Catherine a look. She put her hand up to block her face from his view and went back to her sketchpad.

"Traitor," he groused and then greeted his friend slash boss. "Thanks again for the support yesterday."

Cliff perched a hip on the edge of the desk even though Ciaran hadn't invited him to come closer. "No problem," he replied. "But tell me, what was this 'family emergency' you just had to rush off to? I thought all of your family was still across the pond."

Ciaran resisted the urge to remind him that his brother lived in San Francisco. "It was Jal," he admitted, and gestured to his face. "Or rather, her abusive ex that got out of jail and tried to stir up a little trouble."

"What kind of trouble?"

"The kind that's not really my place to talk about, if that's all right." It came out a little sharper than he had intended.

Cliff put up his hands in mock-surrender. "All righty, then." he replied, managing a surprisingly good imitation of the movie quote, ferocious head shake included. He stood from the desk and leaned toward Ciaran. "I get the message, but you owe me one."

"Understood."

Cliff turned and headed for the breakroom.

"Not a word," he warned Catherine.

She shook her head. "Wasn't going to say anything." She didn't look up from her work, but the eye that was visible was crinkled at the corner. "Other than to remind you that you owe me one too."

Ciaran mock-scowled at the curtain of black hair that obscured everything but that eye. "Add it to my tab."

It was shoddier than he had expected. From behind the wheel, Ciaran studied the building that the dark side of the internet said was DiBattista Motors. The steel walls and roof had seen better days and were spotted with rust, the glass door to the tiny waiting room sported a spiderweb from a well-placed boot that had been patched with a board or piece of cardboard from the inside.

The pair of roll up doors looked like they had gotten into a fight with the Greek restaurant across the street, one door was closed, the other only half-open, both with numerous scuffs and dents. The wheels of a car dangled down like the teeth that hadn't been knocked out, while a pair of mechanics worked from underneath, sparks cascading down around them.

Ciaran shifted in his seat. He'd been in the same spot long enough that his back and his bladder were starting to take bets on which could be more of a nuisance. With a sigh, he rolled his shoulders, and his neck popped loud as a gunshot. As he put the shifter in gear, he muttered a prayer to whoever might be listening that he didn't end up on the wrong end of one of those blow torches by the end of this and parked just outside the open door.

As he climbed out, the door rumbled up, revealing a man with a thick black goatee and eyes nearly as dark beneath a bandana tied around his brow. Oil-stained coveralls protected his clothes. The man took a step outside the shop, squinting into the setting sun, and wiped his hands on a rag that was more oil than its original orange. "Can I help you?"

There were at least three unspoken expletives in that short question. Ciaran flipped his keys around the ring to smack into his palm as he swung the car door shut. "My clutch just started to make this horrible grinding noise. I was hoping that I could get it checked out."

"Sorry, this is a private garage," the guy replied, his voice heavy with an Italian New Yorker accent. "Referral only, so I think you need to get back in your car and go back to wherever you came from."

Ciaran flipped his keys again. "Oh, well then. It just so happens that I have a pal who works here."

He scratched his head for a moment as he worked out what Ciaran had said. Once he did, the rag twisted around one meaty fist. "And who's your 'pal'?"

"Name's Paolinelli. Andy Paolinelli."

The guy glanced over his shoulder and back to Ciaran. "He didn't mention anyone coming by."

Ciaran just flipped the keys again, landing in his palm with a musical clink. "We talked about it being in the next few days, and I found myself out of work a little early today."

The meathead twisted the rag a little tighter as he considered. This could go one of two ways. The guy could knock him out with one punch or—

"Yo, Pauli!"

A muffled response came from deeper in the shop.

"Some fancy man here to get his car looked at!"

There was a ringing of metal on concrete and the roll of wheels. Andy emerged a moment later from the bowels of the shop and came to stand next to his friend. Dressed similarly, with a streak of grease across one of Andy's cheeks, the men looked like twins. Or ex-cellmates.

Ciaran took satisfaction in the greenish purple bruise beneath one eye which narrowed the second Andy recognized him. A flush of red rose up from his collar, but he didn't speak.

"You know this dandy?"

Ciaran glanced down at his own clothes and then gave the guy a mock-offended smirk. He'd come from work and was dressed only in a simple gray suit and vest over a white dress shirt. *Guess a waistcoat makes me a dandy.*

He flicked a speck of lint off the sleeve and flipped his keys again. "We go back."

Andy's eyes narrowed further until only a slit of black remained. "Yeah, we do."

His buddy just shrugged and clapped him on the shoulder. "All yours then, Pauli."

Jal's ex waited until his friend was out of earshot before he took a step in Ciaran's direction. "Is Sam with you?" He ducked down and looked inside the car, straightening with a scowl when he saw that it was empty.

"No, *Jal* is not with me."

"Then what the fuck are you doing here?"

Ciaran folded his arms and leaned a hip on the fender. "I thought we could talk."

"Unless it's to tell me where *Samantha* is," Spit flew from his mouth as he said her name, enunciating each syllable as if Ciaran was an idiot. "We don't have anything to talk about."

"Oh, I don't know about that." Ciaran crooned. "You mentioned at the park that prison cost you everything. There must be something that you could want more than a woman you haven't seen in two years, who doesn't want to see you."

The flush spread up Andy's thick neck again. "She'll come around," he replied as if there wasn't any alternative. Ciaran was sure that if he got his hands on Jal, she'd never see daylight without him again, and that was not something that Ciaran was willing to even contemplate.

He forced his calm and cocky mask to remain in place when inside he wasn't sure which sounded more enticing, to roll his eyes or bury a fist in the prick's face. "Let's agree to disagree on that one, pal, all right?" Ciaran said. "Come on, there has to be something."

"What could I possibly want from a scrawny suit like

you?"

"Eh, there's more to me than all that. Before I came to America, I was much like Jal, doing what I could to make ends meet, stealing what I needed to when more legitimate work fell short, which it usually did." He flipped his keys and this time Andy's eyes narrowed. He kept the satisfied smile inside. "That's how we met actually, we picked each other's pockets. It was quite romantic."

He probably shouldn't be riling Andy up this much, especially since there were plenty of reinforcements inside, but the words came out of his mouth without much effort or conscious thought. If he wasn't leaning against the car, he'd have his hands in his pockets, rocking back on his heels in a way that made many a man see red.

Andy ground his teeth. "You? You were a thief?"

"Don't look so surprised." Ciaran replied, one side of his mouth tipping up.

The cogs were already turning in Andy's brain, he could see it in his eyes, the cock of his head. "What kinds of jobs?"

"Pockets, cars, businesses, couple of houses." Ciaran ticked them off on his fingers. "Oh, and I did a museum once." Though, he wasn't going to tell Andy how *that* one had ended.

"Any banks?"

Ciaran shook his head. "And contrary to what you and your mate might be thinking, I'm not flush with cash. But if it's money you're after, maybe we can work together to steal something that you could turn into cash. Maybe even a lot of cash."

One of his feet was going numb from the position he'd been holding against the car, but Ciaran resisted the urge to stand up. "Surely, there's something you've had your eye on?"

Andy stood there thinking for so long that Ciaran wondered if he was just going to tell him to go to hell and walk back inside. He kept up a steady rhythm of flipping his keys into his palm and waited. A moment later, a light came into Andy's eyes and Ciaran knew that he had him.

"I think I know of something," he replied. "There's a guy, just bought a mansion up in Fieldston, been driving back and forth across the Bronx with one flashy antique car after another. A rare Mustang, a '62 Corvette, some real James Bond looking shit with the steering wheel on the wrong side of the fucking car. If you can get me in, I'll find something that will work."

Ciaran had only heard of the affluent neighborhood on the northern side of the borough, because someone he knew had bought a house there. *Surely, it can't be...*

"I'll be wanting something in return."

"Yeah, and what's that?"

There was only one thing that he could possibly want. "I help you with this job, and that's you when it comes to Jal." He pushed off the car and put his keys in his pocket. "You leave her be. No stirring up trouble with the police, no more searching for her. No more trying to run everyone close to her down with a car. She's free."

The flush rose up Andy's collar again, the muscles standing out so much that Ciaran was surprised that the fabric didn't split down the back. "We'll see."

Ciaran shook his head. "Not good enough," he replied, finally shedding the nonchalant mantle to show the steely determination underneath. "We do this, and that's it."

Andy ground his teeth. For a long moment, there was no sound except the sparking of a welder from inside the shop, and the rush of cars on the street at his back. "Yeah, all right."

Ciaran let just a sliver of the satisfaction that was practically singing through him show in his smile. He held out a hand.

Andy hesitated for only a moment longer before his meaty hand engulfed it.

"Then we have a deal."

Thirty-Four

Ciaran climbed back into his car and just sat there gripping the wheel to steady his trembling hands. He didn't dare show any reaction on his face, not while Andy stood next to the open door, hand poised over the controls.

They locked eyes as he put the car in gear and then Ciaran looked away to back into the road. The garage door was already starting to close by the time he glanced over while shifting gears.

Jal's ex was still watching him, and Ciaran found himself staring back until the door obscured his face. A car behind him laid on the horn and he cursed, hitting the accelerator hard enough that the car bucked and threatened to stall.

He didn't make it far. After a few blocks, he found an empty spot to pull into and shut off the car. Crossing his arms over the steering wheel, he put his head down and took a shuddering breath. "Christ."

From his pocket, his cell phone chimed. Ciaran dug it out

and stared at the screen.

> Jal: How's your day been?

Ciaran blew out a breath, and his chest felt so much lighter. Instead of responding to the message, he called her. She answered before the first ring had even finished.

"Well, hello there." She purred into his ear. There was a murmur of people around her.

He leaned back and closed his eyes. "It's good to hear your voice," he replied. "Corny as that may sound."

Her soft laughter tickled his ear. "Not corny, at all."

"Where are you? It doesn't sound like you're at home."

"I'm at Darcy's with the girls, but I was thinking of heading home soon."

"Hi, Ciaran!" A chorus of female voices sounded through the phone. Jal's amused rebuke was followed by peals of laughter.

He couldn't help smiling. "I'm on my way home now. Why don't I swing by and pick you up? Give me about twenty, thirty minutes."

Her confusion was clear. "Where are you coming from?"

"I'll tell you when I see you."

He knew her well enough to know that she wanted to push, but wouldn't in front of her friends. "All right," she said, instead.

"I'll let you know when I'm close. See you soon." He hung up the phone and sat for a minute longer, gathering his thoughts before easing back out of the parking space and heading back to Manhattan.

Jal dashed out to the car as soon as he pulled up. It had started to sprinkle as he crossed into Manhattan, but had turned to a full-on downpour since.

Ciaran reached over and released her door so she could climb in. Over her head, he caught sight of Elena and Lexi standing under the overhang in front of the entrance having kept her company while she waited. He appreciated that they were being so careful, even though Andy was a borough away.

Jal smiled at him as she closed the door.

Ciaran couldn't help himself and slid a hand behind her neck and drew her in for a kiss. Jal stiffened slightly in surprise, but quickly, mercifully, returned it. She tasted like tequila and salt.

Many moments later, he reluctantly eased back and merged with traffic. Jal waved to her friends and then turned back to him. "What was that for?"

"Can't a man just kiss his girlfriend hello?" It still felt odd to use that term, but it gave him a little thrill. Besides, she'd started it. You couldn't get more official than declaring him to be her boyfriend to the police.

"Of course you can," she replied. "And I'm not complaining." She placed her hand over his on the gearshift and it just felt right for it to be there.

They fell into silence while he drove and, since much of the adrenaline had worn off, the queasy feeling in his stomach was back. Darcy's was in the Bowery, so it didn't take long before he was turning onto his street. It almost took longer for them to find a parking spot than it had to drive there. On their third circle of the block, a car pulled out a few doors down from his flat and he slid neatly into the space.

Once inside his apartment, Jal shrugged out of her jacket and hung it by the door. She watched him expectantly while he hung his coat beside hers, and then went to the kitchen to put the kettle on.

It might be a very Scottish thing of him to do, but after the day he'd had, the only thing he wanted was a hot cup of tea. If a good dollop of whisky also found its way inside, then all the better. He took down the fixings from the cabinet, then braced himself for her reaction as he leaned against the counter.

"I went to see Andy." Her eyes grew wide, and he held up his hands to show they sported no new marks. "Just to talk."

He tried to ignore her arms curling reflexively in front of her, her hands twisting together. Somehow it made her look smaller, standing there in the middle of the room. He pushed off the counter and wrapped her in his arms and she held on just as tightly, clutching the back of his shirt with her forehead pressed hard against his breastbone.

"What did you talk about?" She asked into the fabric of his shirt.

There was a fine tremor going through her, so for a moment, he just held her. It helped him too, easing the tension through his neck and shoulders that had been there since he'd decided to drive to Hunt's Point.

After a while, her hands released their death grip and slid down to his lower back. He eased her back so he could look her in the eyes while he told her everything, about their deal that would bring Ciaran out of retirement for one more job, and if successful, which it had to be, they would be free of him.

Her laugh was bitter. "I should have known that's all it would take." She sighed, and her eyes grew distant, but they focused again almost as quickly. "So many of our... arguments, were over money."

He brushed a stray curl behind her ear and pressed a kiss to her temple. "Can't say that I'm at all surprised myself."

"Do you have any idea who the mark is?" Jal asked.

Behind him, the electric kettle began to bubble aggressively and clicked off. Ciaran reluctantly returned to the kitchen and busied himself with making tea. "I think I have an idea."

Her back went a little straighter. "Who is it?"

He pushed a steaming mug of green tea and honey into her hands and she let him lead her to one of the living room chairs. She perched on the edge of the seat, the mug on her knee, her back still stiff.

"Let me see what I can suss out." He set his mug aside and opened a text string on his phone he hadn't used since the day he'd broken into Jal's apartment and typed out a quick message. He put a hand on her forearm. "As soon as I know anything, you will."

She nodded, though her hands kneaded the sides of the cup where it sat on her knee. "I trust you, Ciaran." She lifted the cup and blew on the surface. "Just please be careful. He's not someone you want to trust, or cross."

"Aye, especially since he's already tried to run me down with a car."

Her jaw dropped. "I'm sorry, what?"

Thirty-Five

A few hours later, Ciaran was awoken by the sound of his phone rattling its way across the nightstand.

Beside him, Jal stirred. "What is it?" she murmured sleepily.

He pressed a kiss to her temple and threw back the covers, grabbing his phone as he stood. "Go back to sleep, lass."

Jal burrowed deeper on her side, chasing what was left of their warm cocoon.

Ciaran stepped out into the living room and pulled the door closed behind him with a quiet click as he looked at the caller ID. It said only Luna.

"Thanks for getting back to me so quickly." Ciaran said by way of greeting. "Though you could have waited until the sun was up."

There was a snort of amusement through the phone. "Considering the last time you reached out to me, you needed a couple grand worth of jewelry fenced in twenty-four hours,

I figured better sooner than later."

"Aye, fair point," Ciaran conceded, running a hand through his hair, disheveled first from Jal's hands, then from sleep. "This ask is different."

"Out with it, Gray."

"Right, best not to waste time on the pleasantries."

"Fuck you," Luna quipped, but there was amusement in his deep growl.

Ciaran huffed a laugh through his nose. "I have a job that needs doing, one that I can't refuse, and I need your help."

There was a creak of leather as if Luna was getting comfortable. "I love a good story time," he responded in that smooth and deep way of his.

They hadn't ever met face-to-face, but the voice conjured an image in Ciaran's head of a tall man who wouldn't look out of place on an American Football field, with a chest big enough to produce that voice.

"Go on."

Ciaran mentally flipped him off, but leaned against the kitchen counter and gave him the abbreviated version.

Luna cut him off when Ciaran got to the part where they ran into Andy in Washington Square Park. "Wait, is this the same girl whose apartment you robbed?"

Ciaran winced. "Robbed isn't exactly the word I would use, but yes." he replied. "And to be honest, it ended up being for the good in the end."

"Oh?"

"After the cops took the bastard away, he must have tipped them off, because they showed up and searched her apartment. Her hidey holes turned up empty—"

"Thanks to you." Luna interjected cheerfully.

Ciaran chuckled. "Aye, and she was able to convince them that the wad of cash hidden in an air vent was an inheritance from her parents stashed away, because of a rural upbringing and an aversion to bank accounts."

Even Luna's impressed whistle was an octave lower than a normal person. "Girl's quick on her feet. I'll give her that."

Ciaran made a noise of assent and finished the story. "I thought the collection Andy described might be yours since you'd bought that house on the hill in Fieldston. Parading your flash cars about sounds just like you."

He chuckled. "Sounds like, doesn't it?" Luna replied. "What do you plan to do?"

Ciaran blew out a breath. "I've been trying to work that out since I agreed to the job. So, whatever we do, has to look legitimate. If Andy smells a rat, it's all for naught."

"So let me make sure I have this straight. You want to get onto my property, break into my garage, give a felon the pick of my cars... *and* you want to make sure he gets caught somewhere in the process and not get caught yourself."

It all sounded ridiculous when someone else said it. "Aye, that's the gist of it."

"Fuck that."

Ciaran glanced over at the closed door. "What will it take to convince you?"

Luna was silent for long enough that Ciaran thought the call might have dropped. He took the phone away from his ear, but sure enough, the call timer was still ticking up. He hastily put the phone back to his ear when the other man spoke.

"Hey, Gray, question for you?"

Ciaran put a hand to his forehead and made an inquiring grunt.

Luna snorted in response. "What gives? I mean, you made it very clear when you came to New York that you were done. And now, for the second time, you're getting pulled back in." There was no mistaking the incredulity in his voice. "And there seems to be a certain common denominator."

"I'll do whatever I can to protect her."

"She must be some woman."

Ciaran nodded, though Luna couldn't see it. "She is."

Luna was silent for another long moment, then came a long, loud exhale. "All right," Luna said, and there was another creak of leather, then the clink of glass on glass and the glug of liquid. "This is what I'll do, let me reach out to my contacts at PD and see what they have on your friend and on this body shop. If it's as... what was the word you used?"

"I think it was 'dodgy.'"

"Yes, right. If the body shop is as *dodgy* as you say, then I'll reach out and we can time it all up. Give our boys in blue a chance to practice their SWAT raid techniques, and then, have them waiting for this Andy when he returns with my vehicle. Two birds and all that. But, please, for the love of God, keep him away from the Aston."

"I'll do my best. And thank you, Luna. Truly," Ciaran replied. "I owe you."

Luna made a dismissive noise, "More than you already do? Someday, something will come along that will balance the ledger."

Ciaran didn't want to think too hard about what that might be. It didn't matter, as long as Jal was safe. "Understood."

"Good," Luna replied. "Then I'll let you go back to bed. Oh, and Gray?"

"Aye?"

"Scratch the paint on any of my cars and I'll let the cops take you too."

Ciaran closed the door to the bedroom as quietly as he could and padded across the thick carpet to the bed, his way lit only by a dim glow seeping between the slats of the blinds despite being tightly shut.

There was enough light for him to see that Jal had sprawled out in her sleep and was now laying on her stomach. Her breathing was slow and even, punctuated by the softest of snores. The inky black of her hair drifted around her like a dark corona.

He lifted the covers and slid into the narrow space she'd left him with, drawing the duvet up to cover them both. Unable to help himself, he reached over and moved the curls away from her face.

She let out a soft hum and nuzzled into his hand until he was cupping her cheek. Her eyes, nearly black in the dim light, slowly opened. "Everything okay?"

He smiled, though with the light behind him, she likely couldn't see it. "Aye, lass." He leaned forward and pressed a kiss to her forehead. "I'll tell you about it in the morning."

She made a sleepy sound that was somewhere between agreement and a yawn and rolled onto her side. Ciaran slid closer and put an arm around her. She snuggled in against his chest, her hand over his heart and fell back asleep.

He stayed awake a little longer, watching her, feeling her soft breath against his skin, and thought again that it didn't matter what favor he may owe Luna later. It was a small price to pay to have the woman he loved safe in his arms, and he never wanted to let her go.

Thirty-Six

When Jal awoke the next morning, the bed beside her was empty. She sat up a little too quickly, the sheet clasped to her chest, only to collapse right back onto the pillows. She lay still with her arm draped over her eyes until the room returned to its normal stationary position and her temples finished their game of ping pong with her brain.

The blue walls that greeted her when she finally managed to peel her head from the pillow confirmed she was in Ciaran's bedroom, as if the musky citrus coming from the buttery soft sheets hadn't been enough. The door leading out to the living room was closed, but the sun shone through the heavy curtains over the windows and around the door.

When she strained her ears, there was only the faint, but now familiar hum of the heating system. Her brow furrowed. Swinging her feet to the floor, she reached for her discarded clothes and dressed quickly, running her fingers through her hair as best she could on the way to the door.

The sunlight slapped her back a step. "Damn you, Elena, and your tequila shots," she grumbled, rubbing her eyes. After a moment, the pain in her head eased and she looked around the empty room.

"Ciaran?"

She checked the bathroom, which was also empty. Frowning, she looked for her coat and found it draped over the back of a chair where she'd tossed it the night before. She dug her phone out of the pocket and noted the time before she saw the texts from Ciaran.

> Ciaran: Good morning beautiful.

> Ciaran: I had to get to work and you looked so peaceful sleeping in my bed that I didn't dare wake you. I left you a muffin on the counter and you know where the tea is.

> Ciaran: I promise I'll explain everything tonight. I love you.

Jal spotted the small white bag sitting next to the electric kettle. She opened the bag and breathed in the tangy scent of a lemon poppyseed muffin. Her heart swelled at his thoughtfulness as she flicked the switch on the kettle.

She nibbled on the muffin as the water boiled and made herself a cup of matcha from the tin he now kept in the cabinet beside his Scottish loose-leaf black tea. He'd told her once that his Gran, ever watchful from her portrait across the room, would roll over in her grave if he dared to use bagged tea.

Jal carried her breakfast to the sofa and saluted the portrait before taking the first sip. For a while, she scrolled through her social media, watching meaningless funny animal videos and cooking tutorials until her phone dinged with an incoming message. She pressed play on the video and realized that what she'd thought was just Elena having a shutterbug moment last night had been a little bit more.

Her temples pounded as she watched herself take a tequila shot and bite into a lime wedge. The Jal on the video made a face at the bitterness and Elena laughed, making a joke about building her tolerance back up after all this time. Then Elena flipped the camera and moved her arm so all three were in the frame.

"*Sonrisas*, bitches," Elena cried, while Jal and Lexi huddled in closer.

Jal paused the video, her mouth dropping open. From the screen, they all beamed at the camera, cheeks flushed from alcohol and dancing, but what caught her attention was her own expression. Her fingers trembled as she swiped back to the home screen to the photo strip that was on her dresser mirror at home. She studied her expression and then flipped back to the video.

Gone was the shadow of pain in her eyes, the smile that didn't quite reach them. Instead, the woman wearing her face beamed at the camera with a smile that lit her up like a candle.

There was an ease to the way she looped her arm around Elena's waist, the way she accepted Lexi's arm around her shoulders without any hint of reservation or tension to keep from showing how much pain lurked just beneath the surface.

Tears prickled in her eyes as a smile slowly spread, until it resembled the one she wore in the video. Slowly, her hand lifted, and she traced her lips, the muscles in her cheeks quivering from long disuse.

A tear slipped free and slid down her cheek. She laughed in wonder as she brushed it away. Her phone dinged again.

> Elena: Welcome back, *nena*.

Thirty-Seven

"Come on man, hurry up! You said you'd done this before."

Ciaran rolled his eyes and removed the pen light from between clenched teeth. "For the tenth time, I *have* done this before." His voice slightly muffled by the motorcycle cowl covering the bottom half of his face. "I would rather not trip off any alarms. If that's all right with you?"

Andy's beady hazel eyes shot daggers through the gap in his own mask, but he closed his mouth. From where he leaned against the thick white granite of the perimeter fence, he wouldn't be seen from the house. Unlike Ciaran, who had to stand partially exposed to work the keypad embedded in the wall.

Who knew what cameras Luna had on this behemoth property, and which, if any, were still functioning. For all he knew, *all* of them were on for "insurance" should something go wrong, or he hoped—he really, *really* hoped—that turning the cameras off was part of the arrangement.

Luna had taken it to heart when Ciaran had said that he needed to make the job look convincing. He hadn't shared any of the security codes, only the brands and models of the equipment.

Ciaran had been equal parts relieved and very concerned since much if it was state of the art. Still, it was completely doable as long as he had enough time, and he didn't lock anything up with too many attempts. And Andy didn't goad him into doing anything idiotic, like smash his face into the keypad, if he didn't stop asking stupid questions.

A film of dirt coated the keys, telling Ciaran that this particular keypad wasn't used very often. It made sense given most of the system had to run on remote control, but delivery drivers and the cleaning crew still needed a way onto the property, he supposed. Some keys showed more wear than there would be if Luna had installed them only recently, though he seriously doubted the current code still used any of those digits.

Ciaran had brought what tools he had, and what he'd been able to borrow on short notice, but he still felt rushed. That was all Andy's fault. It had been less than forty-eight hours since they had made their deal. He'd been Upstate touring the country club site when his phone had pinged with a series of rapid-fire texts, an address, a time, and details of when the house would be empty. Where he got that information, Ciaran didn't want to begin to guess.

Andy had insisted that Ciaran meet him no later than six p.m. at the train station across from Manhattan College—an ironic name given they were in the Bronx—or their deal was off. It was a short walk from there, arriving right around dusk.

As soon as the walkthrough had ended, Ciaran had jumped in his car and raced back into the city only to load up the same trusty, slightly frayed messenger bag that had seen him through many a job back in Scotland with everything he had that could possibly be useful, and high-tailed it for the train.

There were many things that Ciaran had envisioned waiting for him at the station, top of the list being a group of Andy's overly muscular coworkers ready to beat him to a pulp to extract Jal's whereabouts before they dumped him in the East River. Even finding no one at all had ranked higher than actually finding Jal's ex standing at the top of the stairs dressed in black, carrying a small bag that emitted a rhythmic metal on metal clink as he walked.

Speaking of walks… The one from the station to Luna's house had been the longest 12 minutes of Ciaran's life, what with Andy alternating at random between rapid fire questions and oppressive brooding.

That was until they got to the house, a sprawling four-story Tudor perched on a rise so it could rule over the surrounding mansions in the upscale neighborhood. The gates were surrounded by trees, which mostly hid them from nosy neighbors while Ciaran worked. Now, the bastard's impatience seemed to rachet up a notch with each passing minute, though Ciaran expected that he would probably be the one to snap first.

"Should I start pressing buttons?"

Ciaran tapped at the screen of his tablet with a little more force than was necessary. It was connected wirelessly to a device attached to the side of the keypad with a magnet. "I would appreciate it if you didn't," he grumbled through clenched teeth, jabbing a few more buttons.

The device made a soft ding modeled by some programmer to sound like an old kitchen timer, and the red "processing" message changed to display a code. He made a satisfied sound, but still held his breath as he keyed the six digits into the keypad, only two of which matched the worn keys.

The red light in the corner turned green and there was a rattle as the gates started to move. Ciaran blew out his breath and stashed the equipment away.

He checked that his mask was still fully in place and slipped between the gates, ducking behind the first of several clusters of evergreen trees that lined the driveway. The tarmac stretched out at least a hundred feet before circling around to the V-shaped rear of the house and its array of garage doors.

Andy followed close behind, crouching when Ciaran crouched, sprinting when he sprinted, until they were only a dozen feet from the garage doors. This time, there were no visible keypads.

Ciaran scratched his temple. This would be so much easier if he didn't have to also get inside the house itself. The system Luna had running to guard his art and antiques needed much more prep time than Andy had given him. Their only saving grace was that a part for the upgraded system for the garage was still on back order. Lucky us.

After making sure there was no direct door access to the garage that wasn't big enough to fit a car, he withdrew his tablet again along with a small wireless transmitter. He keyed in the make and model for the garage door opener Luna had given him and pointed the transmitter toward the house.

Unlike with the keypad, a garage door opener didn't lock out or set off an alarm after even a dozen or a hundred pings. No, the alarm was what came next.

After what felt like ten minutes, but was probably only two, the door farthest to the left, which of course was the furthest from where they were hiding, slowly began to lift. A rhythmic two note beeping began to chime from inside.

Ciaran hurried across the driveway and ducked under the door before it had risen too high. Andy shuffled behind him, freezing just inside with an audible gasp.

There wasn't time for Ciaran to stop. They had maybe thirty seconds before the alarm went off. He reached the keypad on the wall, its blue lights flashing in time with the chimes which, if he wasn't mistaken, were speeding up.

He lifted the cover over the keypad and grinned, the fabric of the mask stretching tight over his mouth. He punched in a four-digit code, one that should work on all the units of this brand.

The beeping continued, and if anything, sped up even more. The grin faded. He tried the code from the main gates, but it only made the beeping faster. A counter on the screen hit single digits.

"Come on, man." Had his mouth not been covered, Andy would have been breathing on his neck.

The timer ticked down to five, then four and Ciaran threw caution to the wind and punched in the only other code he could think of.

Three.

Two.

The warning message on the screen changed to "not ready" and the beeping stopped. Ciaran blew out a breath and braced a gloved hand against the wall, his legs suddenly shaky.

Andy whooped, the sound echoing through the surprisingly cavernous space, which had to extend at least fifty feet under the back lawn. At the front was an open space that was set up as a maintenance area, with cabinets and tool carts lining the walls. Further on, at least a dozen cars were parked on each side facing a central aisle. Some were raised on lifts, particularly those at the rear of the garage.

Jal's ex stood in the middle, his eyes bright, his slack jaw revealing incongruously white teeth, the only remaining glimpse of the polished man Jal said he used to be. His hands rubbed together as he studied the millions of dollars' worth of vehicles.

Ciaran didn't know much about American cars, but there were a few he recognized. Closer to home, an early '60s Jaguar and an Aston Martin of an only slightly newer vintage sat side-by-side about halfway down. To his dismay, Andy was making a beeline toward the latter.

He cursed as Andy peered under the open hood for a long moment and let out a low whistle. "What a honey," he murmured as he bent down to look inside the passenger area.

"It's a right-hand drive," Ciaran informed him, hoping that would dissuade him.

Andy threw a look over his shoulder. "So?"

"And a manual."

Andy snorted as if shifting gears with his left hand wasn't a problem and reached for the handle.

"And probably the only one like it on the whole East

Coast. It would be quite the trick to fence that without drawing much notice. And it's far too beautiful to chop up."

The door only opened a few inches before Ciaran's words sunk in. Andy pushed the door closed with more force than was necessary, the sound echoing off the concrete. "Whatever, man."

What did Jal ever see in this guy? Ciaran blew a silent breath of relief and followed as Andy moved down the row. He passed half of the collection by, including a black convertible with a large "SS" in the grill, and an almost new yellow Corvette with a thick black racing stripe, before pausing at a creamy white two-door car with a blue racing stripe deliberately applied off-center.

Just like me for getting talked into this. Ciaran thought to himself as Andy ran a hand along the hood, which had a pair of large air scoops and pins to hold it down.

"Now, this is more like it."

Ciaran stopped in front of the vehicle as Andy pulled the door open and slid inside. He searched the cabin, flipping down the visors, checking in the glove box. Finally, he stuck his head out the window and said, "Yo, where are the keys?"

"Hell, if I know." Ciaran replied, looking around the room. There were so many places that Luna could keep the keys for the vehicles and for a moment, his blood went cold, thinking they'd need to search the whole house to find them. Then he spotted a white cabinet attached to the wall over one of the red mechanic's cabinets near the door to the main house and almost punched a fist in the air.

Ciaran jogged over to it, his bag bouncing against his hip as he went. It was the kind of cabinet that a valet might have on the side of a stand. And just like a valet stand... he tried the bar-shaped handle, and wasn't at all surprised when it didn't budge. He ripped open the zipper on the flap of his messenger bag and withdrew a small black pouch.

His fingers tingled as he withdrew a pair of picks and got to work. There was a time when he could have had this lock open before he could count to fifty. It was a simple tumbler lock, but his tools kept slipping off of the pins inside. It took far longer than he would have liked, but finally, cheeks blazing, the last tumbler flipped, and the handle turned freely.

Inside, nearly every hook had keys dangling from a different keychain, most with a fob in the shape of an emblem or symbol related to the vehicles they went to. Ciaran ran a finger through them, turning some to the light, but nothing jumped out at him to represent the white and blue vehicle Andy had chosen.

He swallowed his pride. "What does that car's emblem look like?" He called.

"The fuck? Have you never seen a Mustang before?" Andy called back.

"Aye, I've seen Mustangs before," Ciaran muttered under his breath as looked them over again. After a moment of fruitless searching, he sighed. "I don't see any horses that don't clearly scream Porsche."

"For fuck's sake..." There was a creak of a door opening and an echoing slam, then footsteps thundered across the garage floor. A meaty arm snaked over his shoulder and plucked a set of keys off a hook.

Ciaran followed. "That's a snake."

Andy sighed like Ciaran was an idiot and walked away.

"A cobra." He yanked the door open a second time. "This is a 1967 Shelby Cobra GT500. They only made a couple hundred of these and a honey like this one, with so few miles, could easily fetch half a mil."

Ciaran seriously doubted that this car would be any easier to dispose of than the Aston, but then he reminded himself that if everything went as planned, he wasn't going to get to do anything with this car anyway.

Andy cranked the key, only to get clicks in response. He pounded his hand on the steering wheel with a loud curse.

Before he could climb out of the car, Ciaran yanked the cotter pins free from the bonnet—Andy would call it a hood—and lifted it up. He glanced around and spotted the problem. After connecting the battery cables, he dropped and resecured the pins. "Now, give it a go."

Andy tried again and the car roared to life. The sound filled the air as Andy revved the engine once, twice and it settled into a purr any tiger would be envious of.

Ciaran went to the passenger side, but the button on the door just sank in. He jammed his thumb on the button a few more times, yanking on the door each time, but still the door wouldn't open. It shouldn't have been a surprise when he bent down, just in time for Andy to put the car in gear and flip him off, before the car started rolling forward.

Yet, somehow it did.

He jogged alongside, his hand still wrapped around the handle, as if there was actually a chance that the bastard would change his mind and unlock the door. Once on the apron just inside the doors, Andy stopped.

Ciaran tapped on the window, and pointed at the stem of

the door lock, but Andy just flipped him off again and revved the engine. "Looks like we're out of time," he yelled over the rumble.

Ciaran's head snapped around, in time to see the flashing red and white lights illuminating the trees. A moment later, the first police car passed through the gate in the distance, its siren barely audible over the din inside.

"Let me in!" Ciaran ordered, yanking on the handle.

"I don't think so." With another gun of the engine, this time deliberately spinning the tires until the garage filled with black smoke and the foul smell of burning rubber, Andy took off.

Pain erupted in Ciaran's hand as it was yanked free from the door handle, the force of it sending him spinning away to sprawl across the hood of a Mercedes. He groaned, clutching his hand to his stomach, as the Cobra sped down the driveway toward the advancing police car, gaining speed.

"Turn away," he muttered through clenched teeth. "Turn away!"

At the last second, the police car slammed on its brakes and Andy swerved, cutting deep furrows in the grass and roared away through the gates.

Thirty-Eight

"Elena, wait up!"

Jal staggered after her friend, her heels seeming to find every crack in the sidewalk. She tried to keep her eyes on Elena's caramel-colored leather jacket, but the crowd just seemed to wrap around her as she passed, obscuring her from view. She had never understood how Elena could move so quickly in the sky-high heeled boots she was wearing.

Jal sighed and swept her hair out of her face with one hand and reached behind her for Lexi with the other. Her friend grabbed on while they slid between a man in a dark puffy jacket and long, thick braids and an older woman in a felted dress coat who smelled strongly of some musky perfume. Jal wrinkled her nose as the scent tickled her sinuses and threatened to make her sneeze.

They flanked Elena where she stood right at the yellow line of police tape and followed her gaze across the street to a dilapidated repair shop that stood with its doors open. Light spilled out across the cracked concrete driveway, illuminating at least a half-dozen police officers milling around.

They'd arrived just in time for a pair of officers to emerge through one of the open bay doors, escorting a burly man with a black goatee from the building with his hands cuffed behind his back. They each held an arm as they led him to a marked patrol car and stuffed him inside.

"Why don't they have any lights on?" Lexi asked as the car drove off.

Jal looked up and down the street. "You're right, I don't see any more marked cars." She looked accusingly at Elena.

It had been a good night so far. After dinner at a restaurant Elena liked in the Heights, they went to a salsa club until Jal thought her feet would fall off. Elena had spun from one partner to another, showing off that rhythm that coursed through her blood. Then, she had gotten a text and said they had to leave, though she'd refused to say who it was from.

Halfway home on a crowded downtown train, she'd grabbed their hands and practically dragged them through the open door and across the station to the cross-town 2 Train heading for the Bronx, the last place Jal wanted to be. There were far too many memories best left behind here.

"What are we doing in Hunt's Point, Elena? What is this place?"

"It's where Andy has been working since he got out of jail." Elena replied cheerfully. "And from the looks of it, he fit right in."

Lexi chuckled. "Please tell me they took him, too."

A corner of Elena's mouth turned up and she turned enough for Jal to see the twinkle in her eye. "Not yet."

Jal's eyebrows drew together. "What do you mean 'not yet'?" she asked. "The police have already raided the place, and I assume, taken away everyone that was inside. If Andy had been inside, he'd be in a squad car. Unless he wasn't working... Are you telling me that he made a run for it?"

Elena put a hand on her shoulder and gave her the look that told her to take a deep breath before she went off the deep end. Jal scowled and filled her lungs with air that reeked of car exhaust and musky perfume. She coughed.

Elena smirked. "All I know is that Ciaran texted me and said to get here as soon as we could. He has a surprise for—" She made an indignant, sputtering noise at the sudden face full of curls.

Jal spun around, searching the crowd for the familiar sharp features she had woken up to this morning, for the whisky-colored eyes she could stare into for hours and still not be able to figure out their true color. Brown or gold. Amber or citrine. All fell woefully short to describe them.

A flurry of radio chatter jolted Jal back around and she tried to stamp down her disappointment at not spotting Ciaran. All of the visible officers scattered like the world's biggest game of hide and seek had just started.

Within moments, the street was empty except for the milling crowd, mostly hidden in the space between streetlights, murmuring quietly to themselves.

For a few moments, nothing happened. No other cars passed on the street, not unsurprising at this late hour, though Jal couldn't rule out that there was some out of sight police barricade. The murmuring of the crowd slowly died as a palpable tension grew in the air.

Just then, a rumble began in the distance and a row of headlights pierced the darkness to their right. A sleek muscle car rolled forward, stopping in the street just short of the garage's driveway, the white paint job reflecting the light spilling out through the doors like a beacon.

Jal leaned forward, straining her eyes to get a good look at the driver, but she couldn't make out more than a burly outline that clearly wasn't Ciaran's. The driver rolled forward a little, his eyes fixed on the garage.

"He smells a rat," Elena muttered. "Come on, come on, just a little more."

"Who does?"

The car protested sitting in one place and started to sputter. The driver revved the engine, shattering the silence with a deep, throaty growl that, at any other time, would have been music to her ears.

A second growl followed before the car settled into a contented purr, rolling slowly forward until one front wheel kissed the concrete. The driver paused there and honked the horn once.

A loud crash sounded from inside the shop, as if someone had knocked over a parts tray, and the ringing of metal on concrete seemed to almost echo through the night.

Jal winced, but her attention was fixed on the driver, who sat bolt upright with a barked curse audible even from where they were standing, and frantically shoved at the gear stick.

The car emitted a sickening grind as it lurched forward, screeching to a stop a second later as a marked patrol car, who had been hiding at the side of the building, threw on its lights, and shot into the street.

The lights were enough to illuminate the interior of the car, painting Andy's olive complexion sickly white and cherry red. The whites in his eyes were briefly all Jal could see before they narrowed into squinty-eyed rage. He threw the car into reverse, the tires spinning as he tried to escape back the way he'd come.

He only made it a few feet before he stomped the brakes again to avoid another patrol car roaring up behind him.

An officer emerged from the front car and pulled his weapon from the holster at his waist, holding it low as he advanced. "Turn off the vehicle and drop the keys out of the window!"

Other officers converged on the car like so many ants, some with their weapons pointed at the car, most of them shouting similar orders. Jal silently prayed that he wouldn't do anything stupid and damage such a beautiful car trying to escape.

Andy hesitated only a few heartbeats. His eyes closed, the muscles in his throat working as he swallowed hard. Slowly, the rage leeched out of his face, leaving behind a calmness that Jal knew was even more dangerous.

He revved the engine one more time, but only to kick it down to idle before he twisted the keys and the rumbling ceased. They hit the street with a clatter. The streetlight struck sparks off the enameled cobra, coiled to strike.

The officer took a step closer. "Place both of your hands through the window and open the door from the outside."

Andy complied, and slowly unfolded his large frame from the driver's seat, stepping to the side so the officer could cross the last few feet and push the door shut. He holstered his gun so he could take one of Andy's meaty arms and spun him to face the vehicle. It was an impressive feat given her ex was at least four inches taller and forty pounds heavier.

The flashing lights struck sparks of gold from the shield around the neck of a detective as he approached, brandishing a pair of handcuffs. Jal recognized Takeda by his almond-shaped eyes and dark black hair.

Hunt's Point was at least a half dozen precincts outside his jurisdiction, though she was glad to see him being the one to see this through. Despite his partner's eagerness to arrest her, Takeda had been nothing but kind and sympathetic.

Takeda handed the cuffs to the officer, and with each click, something inside her released, at least until Takeda spoke. "Andrew Paolinelli, you are under arrest for conspiracy, grand theft auto, and assault."

"Assault?" Her heart kicked hard in her chest. Lexi put an arm around her shoulders, rubbing soothing circles on her upper arm. Where the hell is Ciaran?

As Takeda took one of Andy's elbows, Elena muttered under her breath, "please resist arrest, maybe one of them will shoot him."

Still, Jal heard and whacked her friend on the arm. "Elena!"

Elena rubbed the spot. "What? We're all thinking it."

"He's not—" Her retort died in her throat when the officers led Andy toward the front patrol car and her ex's eyes locked with hers.

His footsteps slowed, then stopped, and the feline smile that spread across his lips made her glad for the handcuffs, the officer's firm grip, and that she was on this side of the police tape.

At first, her instinct was to wither under the furious fire that gleamed in his dark eyes, but then her friends each took one of her hands. Though their support flowed through the contact, she found that, for once, she had plenty of her own.

Jal straightened up to her full height, lifted her chin high, and let a different fire, one of triumph, flare to life in her own expression.

"I should have known you'd be behind this, Samantha."

Elena started to speak, but Jal squeezed her hand, and she closed her mouth.

"It's Jal," she replied. "And I hope they put you away for good this time."

A growl ripped from his throat as Andy took a step in her direction. Jal held her ground while the officers hauled him away. In the corner of her eye, Elena lifted a hand and fluttered her fingers in a wave that had always made Andy see red.

It had the intended effect. He made a second attempt to wrench free of the officers' grasp, but Takeda slammed Andy into the police car, his torso and face plastered across the hood with a forearm across the back of his neck.

"I could add resisting arrest to the charges," Takeda warned loud enough for them to hear.

Andy grunted in response and his body seemed to deflate. He didn't resist as Takeda stood him up and led him to the door the patrolman held open, stuffing him inside.

Takeda glanced at Jal as he swung the door shut and gave her a raised eyebrow. Jal ducked her head, but she was smiling. *So much for not leaving Manhattan.* She thought, hoping that Takeda would let it slide.

As if he heard her thoughts, a corner of his mouth lifted and he nodded his head once in a formal way that in decades past would have involved tipping a hat. The two officers got into the patrol car and drove off, lights flashing and sirens blaring.

The adrenaline left her in a rush, and Jal's knees started to shake. Her friends sprang into action, wrapping their arms around her, trapping Jal between them so she didn't fall.

She sighed with relief and dropped her head to Lexi's shoulder and her friend pressed her cheek to the top of her head. "It's over."

"Damn right it is!" Elena crowed.

Lexi nodded, the motion rubbing across Jal's hair. "I hope we never see that bastard again."

Jal's eyes drifted shut, sending a tear of relief that had been clinging to her lashes down her cheek. She wanted to be excited, she really did, but she was still worried about Ciaran, and about whether Andy was really, truly out of her life.

Elena smiled softly and brushed the tear away with her thumb. "Come on, let's go to Lima to celebrate," Elena urged them. "Papá had that *pollo guisado* you like so much on the specials board today. I'm sure there's some left."

Jal shook her head. "Much as I would love that, I need to find Ciaran," she pulled out her phone. "Something must have happened to him, or else he would have been here."

Elena took it from her hand and held up a hand when Jal protested. "Don't worry about him," she replied and started heading in the direction they had come. "He said earlier that he had something to take care of and he'll meet us there."

"Why didn't you say that earlier?"

Elena swung her arm out dramatically at the garage, the white Mustang parked in the middle of the street, and the swarm of police officers. "Hello!"

Jal grabbed her arm and linked theirs together. "Okay, fine. But you're making me a margarita."

"As many as you want, nena." She replied. "As many as you want."

Thirty-Nine

The rhythmic percussion and plucked guitar of Bachata thundered from the sound system Elena's father had only recently installed. Coupled with the bank of colored lights projecting from the top of the bar, and the Sandoval family's restaurant had become a night club.

Jal and Lexi sat at one of the few tables that hadn't been pushed aside to create a space large enough for dancing, a space that was now near to bursting. Half of the Kitchen seemed to have shown up.

The table between them groaned under the weight of platters and bowls heaped with roasted meats, a few token vegetables, and plantains. So many plantains.

A cloud of fragrant steam seemed to hover in the air over the spread. Normally, there wasn't one thing to come out of that kitchen that didn't make her mouth water, but Jal found herself pushing a spoon through a bowl of stewed chicken, corn, carrots, and potatoes without much interest in actually eating it.

Instead, her attention was fixed on her phone, which Elena had eventually returned, and the string of text messages only on her side of the conversation. She kept one eye on the door, which periodically opened to let in a burst of cool air followed by more people ready to party.

She looked up when it opened again, admitting a trio of giggling women, wholly underdressed for the weather, but slightly overdressed for a night out clubbing. They joined a group mingling on the perimeter of the dance floor, greeting others with a hug or a kiss on the cheek.

Beyond them, Elena held court in the middle, as always, joy seeming to burst out of her as she moved through the rhythmic steps of the dance, her long hair fanning out as she pivoted and spun, never spending more than a few minutes with the same partner.

Elena had tried several times to drag her into the throng, but like with her food, Jal had little interest in dancing, because the one person she wanted to be celebrating with still wasn't there.

Lexi reached across the table and covered Jal's hand with hers. "He said he'd be here, so he'll be here."

Jal tried to give her a smile, but her lips didn't cooperate. She knew Lexi was right, but it didn't make her worry any less. Where was he? Why wasn't he answering his texts? How was he connected to what went down in the Bronx tonight? And where had Andy stolen that car from, anyway?

Before her mind could spiral any further, the door opened, admitting a burst of chilly, evening air. Jal dropped her spoon, ignoring the splatter of soup and clattering silverware as she nearly flew across the room toward the figure dressed all in black who had just entered.

Ciaran caught her with a grunt as her momentum drove them into the wall beside the door. She didn't give him much of a chance to recover before she buried her hands in his hair and crushed his mouth with hers.

He was here! And he was safe!

Jal pressed herself closer, needing more reassurance that Andy hadn't harmed him.

Ciaran broke the kiss and let out a hiss of pain. She drew back and, only then, noticed the bandages on his right hand.

She gently scooped her hand under his and raised it into the light. Two of his fingers were splinted, the other two taped together. A white compression wrap started at the second knuckle and disappeared up his sleeve.

"Oh my god, Ciaran, what happened?"

He cradled her cheek with the uninjured hand and she leaned into his touch. He gave her a soft smile, and then, looked up, surveying the room, the swaying crowd, the music that promised to give them all hearing loss. He eased her back a step and took her hand, wading through the fringe of the crowd toward the kitchen door.

Jal looked over her shoulder as she passed through the swinging door to see Elena watching her, though her feet didn't miss a beat. She gave an encouraging wave of her hand and turned her attention back to the person she was dancing with. Her father.

The door closed behind them with a soft thwap. The kitchen was still stiflingly hot, but mostly quiet, the few remaining staff milled around stacking clean dishes and wiping down prep areas. Ciaran led her through the maze of cabinets, tables, and stoves to the corner office as if he had been there before. Which he must have been, when he and Elena had hatched their plan, or whatever it was.

Ciaran put a hand on her back and propelled her into the small room ahead of him and shut them inside. Before she could take another breath, his mouth was on hers, his fingers on her chin, drawing her lips apart so he could deepen the kiss.

It was a desperate kiss, one of reassurance, of confirmation that they were safe, and whole, and alive. When they came up for air, a few moments, or an hour later, Ciaran pressed his forehead to hers, breathing hard.

Jal gripped the back of his neck and tried to kiss him again, but Ciaran turned his mouth just far enough out of reach.

"I just need to hold you for a moment," he murmured, his breath tickling her ear, sending a blast of heat down her spine. "Are ye alright, lass?"

Jal lifted her head, and an eyebrow. "Am *I* alright?" Her laugh was more than a little incredulous. "What about you? Where were you? And what in God's name happened to your hand?"

Ciaran sighed and dropped into the desk chair as if it had taken all of his energy to remain standing as long as he had.

Jal ignored the rickety steel folding chair she had always hated and leaned against the desk instead. For a moment, he just studied her, his eyes heating as he took in the dress that, while modest in terms of the neckline and tight full sleeves, hugged her curves and came to an abrupt stop mid-thigh.

A flush rose up her neck under his scrutiny. She smoothed

imaginary wrinkles from the burgundy stretch velvet over her hips. He followed her every movement and she resisted the urge to allow the look in his eyes to distract her by, say, climbing into his lap, and making sure the rest of him was still in working order.

She cleared her throat, and his eyes slowly rose back up her body. "Elena," she muttered by way of explanation for her wardrobe and then raised her eyebrow meaningfully. "Your hand?"

Ciaran jerked his head and looked down at his bandaged hand as if it was the first time he was seeing it too. Then, some of the daze left his eyes and he flashed her what she knew was supposed to be a reassuring smile. "It'll aye be well soon enough," he replied. "Doctor said it's just a couple of simple fractures. I'll be good as new in a month or two."

"Simple fractures... Right. Yeah, no big deal." She echoed in what she was sure was a terrible approximation of his accent. He snorted a laugh. "For fuck's sake, Ciaran. How?"

"It's a long story, lass," he responded. A corner of his mouth quirked up and he ran a finger down one exposed thigh. "And I'll tell you, as long as you stop looking at me like that."

"Then stop calling me 'lass'." she retorted. "Though it seems that you're the one who can't seem to keep his hands to himself."

He chuckled and shifted in his seat, but didn't remove his hand.

Jal deliberately kept her eyes on his face, no sense confirming that he was as worked up as she was in the small, enclosed space. The whisky-gold of his eyes, reduced to a thin sliver around pupils blown wide despite the light in the room, were proof enough.

"Fair point," he replied. "So, I was leaving work when my phone rings, and it's Andy saying that tonight was the night to make good on our deal. So, I rushed home, got my gear and off we went to this extremely posh house, where I proceeded to break into the perimeter gate, and the garage, then disable a security system so your ex could steal a car and ride off into the bloody sunset and out of our lives for good."

"In a 1967 Shelby Cobra?"

One eyebrow raised, and he nodded with a smile. "Apparently, of all the vehicles in that garage, it was what he chose." he replied. "So, I take it that Elena got you girls over to Hunt's Point in time for the festivities, then?"

"Sure did." A wide smile stretched across Jal's mouth. "Seeing Andy get led away in handcuffs will never get old. Doesn't explain how you hurt your hand, though."

"Well, the police were coming up the drive and I was the numpty who had my hand wrapped around the door handle when Andy made a break for it."

Jal hissed in sympathy. "I bet he thought that he was leaving you to the cops," she replied, then tilted her head. "Speaking of, how are you not in jail yourself right now? Not that I'm not ecstatic that you aren't."

Ciaran's good hand found her thigh again and began moving slowly up and down her leg, each time reaching a little higher up before retreating almost to her knee. "Andy had no way of knowing that the owner of the gate, the house, the garage, and the car was in on the whole thing," he replied. His eyes were focused on what his hand was doing.

Jal swallowed, the delicious friction of his hand fraying

her restraint. "Who was it?"

"Someone I knew in another life," Ciaran replied. "He's helped me out in the past and was all too willing to help put Andy back where he belonged. But Andy had to believe that it was real, and so it became real, for both of us. And Christ, I forgot what it felt like."

His fingers skimmed the hem of her dress, mere inches from his goal, and where she wanted him to be. "The satisfaction? The rush of adrenaline?"

He nodded, his eyes hooded as his fingers dipped beneath the fabric. "Aye, all of that."

She knew that euphoria well. It wasn't so different to what his touch did to her, was doing to her, as his fingers delved even further.

Andy had always been willing to help scratch the itch when she came home worked up after a successful steal, but he had never been the source of the feeling itself.

But Ciaran was. Being with him was as heady as any job she had ever pulled off.

Whatever he saw in her eyes brought him to his feet, maneuvering so he stood between her knees and hauled her hips against him. Her legs wrapped around his waist as he captured her lips and ravaged them.

His good hand wove into her hair and tipped her head back further so he could latch onto the spot below her ear that had her knees clenching tighter around his hips.

She palmed his cheek and brought his lips back to battle with hers. Her other hand slid down his chest and lower, to cup him through his pants. He broke the kiss with a groan and put a little space between them, breathing hard.

"We should go back to the party." he murmured against her lips. "I don't think Elena's father would appreciate us doing what I want to do to you in here."

She nipped at his bottom lip. "Then take me home. There's plenty of room there."

Forty

The door to the bedroom creaked open as Jal added a few fresh strips of bacon to the pan. The meat sizzled and popped as she went to the fridge for eggs. She glanced over to see Ciaran tugging his arms into a sweatshirt as he crossed the living room.

His hair was damp from a shower and tousled like he had scrubbed his head with a towel. His eyes squinted against the light pouring in through the windows. She smiled and went to turn the bacon.

An arm came around her waist and drew her back against him as the other brushed her hair aside so he could access her neck. She sighed and placed her hand on top of his on her stomach. "Good morning," she murmured, her body humming to life at his touch.

"I don't know what is better to wake up to, you or the smell of a good fry up." His breath tickled her ear.

She swatted his hand, and he released her with a hiss

of pain. She gasped, realizing what she had done, spinning around to see him standing there clutching his injured hand. "Oh, I'm so sorry!"

"It's no bother, lass," he said, though the look on his face said otherwise.

She reached into the cabinet over the sink and brought down a bottle of Ibuprofen and filled a glass with water. "Here."

He took the glass with a grateful expression on his face and held out the other hand for her to shake a couple of pills into. His Adam's apple bobbed as he swallowed them down.

"Do you want some ice?"

"I'll do, thanks." he replied with a shake of his head and took the fork from her to tend to the bacon, holding it awkwardly in his non-dominant hand.

Jal stood beside him and cracked eggs into a bowl, added a splash of milk and some pepper and scrambled them with quick flicks of her wrist. After a few moments, she plucked the fork away and added the bacon to the paper towel-lined plate. She adjusted the burner and added the eggs to the pan. "Do you want to make some toast?"

He went to the cabinet she used as a pantry, and took down the loaf of bread, adding a couple of slices to the toaster. For a few minutes, they circled around each other like it was a dance they had performed for years to finish everything and plate up. There was an easy domesticity to it that made her heart do a little flutter, and warmth rise in her cheeks.

"Go and sit," she told him as she picked up the plates and carried them to the table, then circled back for their drinks. Black coffee for him, matcha for her.

With her hands on the handles, she paused and looked over at him and watched him take a bite of eggs. Her heart fluttered again. Had it only been a few months since he'd barged into this apartment, and into her life?

Yet, here he was, sitting at her grandmother's table, the only piece of furniture that she had from back home, and eating breakfast as if he had been doing it for years. It struck her then that she wouldn't mind every morning being like this.

He glanced up and caught her looking. His mouth curved up, his eyes light as amber. "What is it?"

Her first impulse was usually to brush away that kind of question, but this time it didn't come. Instead, she picked up the cups. The food smelled incredible, and her stomach growled in anticipation, but her mind was focused on something else. "I was just thinking that it feels like more than just a few months since you came into my life. I hated you for breaking into my home and stealing from me—"

"I've apologized for that, numerous times," Ciaran replied, his expression wary, though there was a hint of mischief in his eyes.

"Yes, you have," she replied, her heart broke into a gallop as she crossed the room slowly, carefully, so she didn't spill hot liquid on her hands.

Once the mugs were safely on the table, she pulled out a chair and sat on the very edge. "And I've realized that there is something else that you've managed to steal, something I didn't think I could ever live without."

Ciaran set his fork down. "And what is that?"

Jal reached out her hand, but just as Ciaran reached for it, her phone began to ring from where it was plugged in on the other side of the table. "Ignore it," she said when Ciaran leaned toward it.

He picked it up and unplugged the cable. "It's Takeda."

Jal's eyes widened. "What does he want?" she wondered as she took the phone and put the call on speaker. "Hello, Detective. What can I do for you?"

"Miss Morrow, I'm just calling to let you know that we've revoked Andy Paolinelli's parole, and with the new charges, he is likely facing a very long additional sentence."

Jal looked up at Ciaran as tears filled her eyes and spilled over. Ciaran swallowed hard, his own eyes red. It was his turn to reach for her hand, and when she took it, he squeezed it and beamed at her.

"Miss Morrow?"

She opened her mouth to reply, but she couldn't get any words past the thickness in her throat.

Ciaran squeezed her hand again. "That's wonderful news, Detective."

Takeda made a startled noise. "Oh, Mr. Gray, you're there as well." he replied. "Good, then, that news should come as a relief to the both of you."

"It does, sir, thank you." Ciaran replied. When Takeda didn't immediately speak, he gave Jal an inquisitive glance.

She swiped at the tears on her cheeks with the heel of her hand and cleared her throat. "Was there anything else?"

"We've decided to close the case we had opened on you as well. You were right that Mr. Paolinelli had made the allegation out of spite."

The news should have had her jumping out of her chair with excitement, but there was something in Takeda's voice that made her stomach twist.

Ciaran was also looking at the phone suspiciously as if he heard it, too.

"But?"

"I'm afraid, we can't return the items recovered from your apartment unless you can prove the provenance." Takeda sighed. "If you were able to produce documentation, then we would be happy to return them to you. But without any proof, I'm afraid there isn't anything that we can do."

What little excitement she'd felt collapsed under a crushing avalanche of ice. The smell of bacon in the air was suddenly cloying and her empty stomach churned with nausea.

"So, he's cost me everything, after all."

"I'm very sorry, Miss Morrow." Takeda responded, and he truly did sound sincere. "If there is anything more that I can do for you, please reach out."

"Thank you, Detective," Ciaran responded, though his tone implied that thanking him was the last thing he wanted to do. He punched the button to end the call.

Jal couldn't move. She stared at the now-black screen of her phone, tears rolling unheeded down her face.

There was a creak of wood as Ciaran got out of his chair, and then his bandaged fingers were on her cheek, gently turning her head. His eyes were now at her level where he knelt in front of her. He cupped her cheek, her tears soaking into the bandage, but he didn't even seem to notice.

"What am I going to do now?" she asked, her voice barely a whisper. She didn't have to tell him what that money meant. It wasn't all of her savings, but what little remained wouldn't last long.

He gave her a reassuring smile. "*We* will figure that out." He replied, his thumb skimming over her cheekbone. "We have each had a time in our life where we have started over. Now, we have the opportunity to do that again. Together."

She wiped at her cheeks and drew in a shaky breath. "You're right."

His eyes flashed and one corner of his mouth lifted.

She snorted. "Don't let that go to your head, Ciaran Gray," she warned, though her voice was light. "I gave myself a new name, but never really created a life around it, out of fear. But now?" She leaned her cheek into his hand. "Now, I can. With you."

Ciaran leaned forward and kissed her gently on the lips. He was silent for a moment, then his head cocked slightly to the side. "Before Takeda called, you were about to tell me about something I stole from you."

She felt her cheeks warm. "Now, there's something else that I was wrong about," she replied. "I see now that it isn't actually something you've stolen from me, but something that I gave to you, that I give to you, freely."

"And what's that?" he asked, though the expression in his eyes said that he already knew.

She placed her hand on her chest, over the thing that now belonged to him. "My heart."

He'd said something similar, right before they'd run into Andy. The flare of his eyes told her that he realized it, too. "Jal—"

She moved her hand, placing her fingers over his mouth. "Please, just let me say it."

Ciaran's lips twitched against her fingers.

Jal took her hand away and gripped her hands together in her lap. "For the last two years, I've been solely focused on survival. My friends did their best, knowing what I had gone through, but there was only so much they could do when I didn't really want to help myself."

She looked down when her eyes threatened to fill and pulled her sleeves down over her hands and fiddled with one cuff.

"But you came along and pulled me out of it, without even trying." She lifted her head and looked him in the eyes. "So many men would have run from me as fast as they could... and I wouldn't have blamed them. But not you." A lone tear slid down her cheek and she brushed it away with a self-deprecating laugh.

Ciaran swallowed, a hint of redness returning to his eyes.

Her own throat grew tight in response, and she had to force herself to remain still when her body sought an outlet for her nervous energy by fidgeting or pacing. She dropped her eyes to her lap again. "I'm doing this all wrong."

He brushed her hair back out of her face. "I think you're doing just fine, lass." He took both of her sweatshirt-shrouded hands in his. "And you don't have to say the words for me to know how you feel."

She squeezed his good hand. "But I *need* to say it," she insisted, shifting forward in her seat. "Ciaran, you saved me just by being there. Your patience, your generosity, they *saved* me. You promised me once that your arms would always be a place of safety, and there is nowhere else that I want to be."

Ciaran's eyes shone, and when he spoke, his voice was hoarse. "Will you just say it already?"

Jal laughed and cupped his face in her hands. "I love you, Ciaran."

And though her vision was blurred by tears, she felt his answering smile under her fingers. "I love you, too."

Epilogue

"Oh, come on..."

Her voice dissipated into the deafening silence as the corridor ended at yet another intersection. To the left and right were more corridors, endless stretches of lifeless beige. Her legs trembled with exhaustion, and she braced her hands on her knees to try to catch her breath.

It felt like she had been wandering forever, and while she hadn't faced any major obstacles, the air itself had dragged at her feet like the knee-high snow she'd trudged through from her grandmother's trailer to the street to get to the mailbox or the school bus.

Yet, the energy in the air was different. It kindled a sense of anticipation that was starting to feel like the worst kind of torture. It also spurred her on, like a whispered promise that there was something waiting just around the next bend that would make this all worth it.

Yet, each intersection had just been more of the same.

She looked to the left and right, took a slogging handful of steps in one direction, and then lurched back the other way. At so many other intersections, she had relied on that telltale electric charge on her skin to decide her path, but this time, there was nothing to guide her.

She finally gave in and let her trembling knees give out, landing in a heap on the floor. It was smooth and cool as marble under her hands and, for a moment, she was tempted to stretch out and let that cold seep into her. Her hair fell like a curtain around her as she released a shuddering breath, closed her eyes, and listened.

For so long, the uninterrupted silence, including the sounds of her own footsteps, had been its own kind of torture, and it still was. Now, the only sound that she heard came from inside, the whoosh of air moving through her lungs, the beat of her heart as it slowly steadied.

Breathe in for a count of four, hold for four, out for four, hold for four. Repeat.

Repeat.

Repeat.

She fell into something of a trance, just breathing. Then, way in the distance to her left, a noise finally broke through the silence.

It was faint, so faint that she wasn't sure at first that she had actually heard it. But then, it repeated, so far off, and so, so faint. Her head snapped up, her eyes trained on the shadows where the sound originated. It came again, clearly a voice, but too indistinct to identify.

She dragged herself to her feet, swaying as her legs threatened to buckle. The call sounded again, and she took a step towards it. And another. And another, using the wall for support.

Slowly, it grew louder, still a one syllable call, the voice neither male nor female. Slowly, each step became a little easier, as if the invisible snow was now only ankle deep. And if her mind wasn't playing tricks on her, the lighting overhead was different, warmer, with a slightly greenish tint.

On and on she went, and slowly, the endless distance didn't seem quite so endless. Then, a dot of a darker greenish light appeared in the black far ahead, and it continued to grow.

The unbroken beige of the walls and floors became gray. Lines formed, like invisible paint brushes were moving with her, at first as faint as a pencil, then darker until the walls resembled cinder blocks. Soon, the floor was no longer smooth, but gritty like dirt or stone.

The greenish light started to cast rippling shadows on the walls and floor, as if it was filtering though leafy branches swaying in a breeze. On and on she went, squinting as the light grew brighter, until only a dozen feet separated her from what was now clearly the curved mouth of a tunnel. The call continued to beckon her forward, and her footsteps became easier as it grew louder, and clearer, in her ears.

She paused just before the end of the tunnel, her heartbeat throbbing in her ears and let her eyes adjust. Ahead, the floor became a path through a wooded area that seemed vaguely familiar. Cautiously, she eased a toe onto the gravel path and, when nothing held her back, she took a full step, then another, following the call that now thrummed in her blood.

The trees parted at a wider road and beyond, in an open

field, two figures were waiting, an adult who held the hand of a young child. She sloughed off the last of the weight from her shoulders and took quick, deliberate steps towards them.

The man smiled, the expression lighting up eyes the color of sunlight through whisky. His lips moved and the call came one more time. Clearly male, and entirely familiar. It beckoned her across the grass to where they waited. The one syllable word...

Her name.

Jal's eyes came open slowly, adjusting quickly to the sunlight streaming in through the window beside the bed. For a moment, it obscured Ciaran's sleeping form with light, but then she was able to focus on his face, only a foot away from hers. It was all that she could see, and if it was the only thing that she ever saw again, that was okay.

Their legs were tangled together, his injured hand draped over her hip. She tried not to move, but after a moment, his breathing changed, and she knew he was awake. One eye cracked open and the visible corner of his mouth rose. "I don't know whether you staring at me while I sleep is endearing or obsessive."

Jal laughed and reached over to brush a lock of hair out of his face. She leaned in and kissed the sharp blade of his nose. "Whichever works."

Both eyes opened and studied her for a moment, and his hand slid from her hip to gently cup the back of her head so he could claim a longer kiss, though truth be told, she didn't need much encouragement.

A few moments later, he eased back and Jal settled her head back on her pillow. As she looked into his eyes, her mind replayed the dream, for that's what it had become. No longer a nightmare, but a dream.

It was starting to fray a little at the edges now that she was awake, but she knew she would never truly forget the sight just before she'd woken up of Ciaran standing in the park, holding the hand of a toddler, waiting for her.

"What's going on in that head of yours, Jal?" he asked, his hand cupping her shoulder. "I can see the wheels turning from here."

She smiled, but it was tentative. The moment he'd spoken her name, something clicked into place with a certainty that shook her more than the admission she'd made the night before.

"I want to find my daughter."

Ciaran's eyes widened and he sat up. The covers pooled at his waist, his chest with its scattering of short hair bare to the cool air of the room.

Jal followed, holding the sheets to her chin even though she had a tank top on. She leaned against the headboard, her heart beating in her throat and watched him as the meaning of that statement sunk in.

"You talked yesterday about starting over, and while I have no idea what that means for me, for us, I just know what it starts with her."

When he didn't speak after a long moment, she couldn't help fidgeting, fingers twisting over each other where they gripped the sheet in her lap.

The smile he gave her a moment later was cautious and slow to spread across his face. Her heart sank. "I think that's a great idea," he replied.

She sagged with relief, her eyes burned as tears threatened.

He sighed. "I just want you to manage expectations. She may have a new family who cares deeply for her."

"I just need to know, Ciaran," she replied, and it was the truest thing she had ever said. "I just need to make sure she is safe, and well cared for, and loved."

He watched as one tear slid down her cheek and brushed it away with his thumb, then wrapped her in his arms as he leaned back against the headboard. She nestled into his chest, and she felt his chin rest on the top of her head.

"Then find her, we will."

Thanks for Reading!
Want to know what comes next?
Scan the QR code or go to the website below to join my mailing list and receive a sneak peek at Lexi and Maks's story in:

TO SETTLE THE SCORE

Coming in 2026!

https://mollykerr-author.eo.page/wd7vm

Acknowledgements

Thank you to my small, but mighty, editing team: Sharon Kerr and Sandy Kerwin. Your insight, suggestions, and fresh eyes were invaluable.

Thank you to Aisling at Pretty Indie Designs for the amazing cover art. It was great working with you and I can't wait to collaborate on future projects.

And lastly, thank you to all of you, dear readers, for picking up this book. I hope you enjoyed it as much as I did writing it. Your support means more to me than you can ever know.

About the Author

Molly Kerr grew up with a pen in her hand. It started with sneaking to the back of Miss Campbell's second grade classroom for extra sheets of lined newsprint to practice her lettering while telling the story of a kingdom inhabited by butterflies. For many years, writing became purely academic or as part of her full-time job without any room for writing for fun. Now, many years later, she is writing for enjoyment again and sharing her stories with the world. Her debut novel, *Hunted,* was released in 2024. A native of Tonawanda, New York, she currently lives in Lowell, Massachusetts with her beloved Black Lab, Remy.

Use the QR Code or visit
mollykerrauthor.com
to join my newsletter!

www.ingramcontent.com/pod-product-compliance
Lightning Source LLC
LaVergne TN
LVHW091617070526
838199LV00044B/824